*Praise for Glyn Iliffe*

'*King of Ithaca* is a great read which embodies the finest elements of war, friendship and betrayal that can be found in Homer's great works ... This is a must read for those who enjoy good old epic battles, chilling death scenes and the extravagance of ancient Greece' *Lifestyle Magazine*

'The world of this novel appears as many scholars see that of Homer: a rich melange of different eras ... It has suspense, treachery and bone-crunching action ... It will leave fans of the genre eagerly awaiting the rest of the series'
Harry Sidebottom,
author of the bestselling Warrior of Rome series

'This daring debut is a stirring retelling of classic Greek mythology complete with all its adventure, passion, battles and, of course, the characters who have remained fascinating over thousands of years. *King of Ithaca* proves to be a voyage of discovery – both for Odysseus and the readers. It's an epic tale told with an academic's eye for history and a born storyteller's feel for credible dialogue and the power of suspense' *Lancashire Evening Post*

'The reader does not need to be a classicist by any means to enjoy this epic and stirring tale. It makes a great novel and would be an even better film' *Historical Novels Review*

# THE GATES OF TROY

Glyn Iliffe studied English and Classics at Reading University where he developed a passion for the ancient stories of Greek history and mythology. Well-travelled, Glyn has visited nearly forty countries, trekked in the Himalayas, spent six weeks hitchhiking across North America and had his collarbone broken by a bull in Pamplona.

Also by Glyn Iliffe

*King of Ithaca*
*The Armour of Achilles*

GLYN ILIFFE

# THE GATES OF TROY

PAN BOOKS

First published 2009 by Macmillan

First published in paperback 2010 by Pan Books
an imprint of Pan Macmillan, a division of Macmillan Publishers Limited
Pan Macmillan, 20 New Wharf Road, London N1 9RR
Basingstoke and Oxford
Associated companies throughout the world
www.panmacmillan.com

ISBN 978-0-330-45252-6

1 3 5 7 9 8 6 4 2

A CIP catalogue record for this book is available from
the British Library.

Typeset by SetSystems Ltd, Saffron Walden, Essex
Printed in the UK by CPI Mackays, Chatham ME5 8TD

Visit *www.panmacmillan.com* to read more about all our books
and to buy them. You will also find features, author interviews and
news of any author events, and you can sign up for e-newsletters
so that you're always first to hear about our new releases.

FOR ROBIN ILIFFE

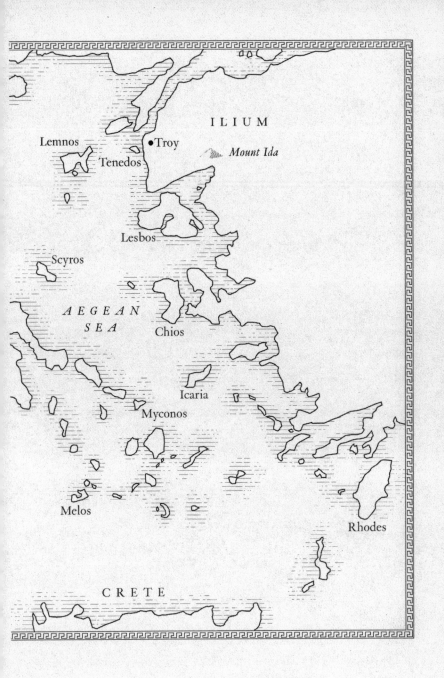

# Glossary

## A

| | |
|---|---|
| Achilles | — Myrmidon prince |
| Actoris | — Penelope's body slave |
| Aeneas | — Dardanian prince, the son of Anchises |
| Agamemnon | — king of Mycenae |
| Ajax (greater) | — king of Salamis |
| Ajax (lesser) | — prince of Locris |
| Andromache | — daughter of King Eëtion of the Cilicians, allies of Troy |
| Antenor | — Trojan elder |
| Antinous | — Ithacan lad, bullying son of Eupeithes |
| Antiphus | — Ithacan guardsman |
| Apheidas | — Trojan commander |
| Aphrodite | — goddess of love |
| Apollo | — archer god, associated with music, song and healing |
| Arceisius | — squire to Eperitus |
| Ares | — god of war |
| Artemis | — virgin moon-goddess associated with childbirth, noted for her vengefulness |
| Athena | — goddess of wisdom and warfare |
| Aulis | — sheltered bay in the Euboean Straits |

## C

| | |
|---|---|
| Calchas | — Trojan priest of Apollo |
| Chelonion | — flower native to Ithaca |
| Clytaemnestra | — queen of Mycenae and wife of Agamemnon |
| Ctessipus | — Ithacan lad, friend of Antinous and son of Polytherses |

## D

| | |
|---|---|
| Deiphobus | — younger brother of Hector and Paris |
| Demeter | — goddess of agriculture |
| Diomedes | — king of Argos and ally of Agamemnon |
| Dulichium | — Ionian island, forming northernmost part of Odysseus's kingdom |

## E

| | |
|---|---|
| Eleusis | — port town on the Saronic Sea |
| Eperitus | — captain of Odysseus's guard |
| Eteoneus | — herald of Menelaus |
| Euboea | — large island off the east coast of mainland Greece |
| Eupeithes | — Ithacan noble and former traitor |
| Eurotas | — Spartan river |
| Euryalus | — companion of Diomedes |
| Eurybates | — Odysseus's squire |
| Eurylochus | — Ithacan soldier, cousin of Odysseus |
| Exadios | — Trojan soldier |

## G

| | |
|---|---|
| Galatea | — a priestess of Artemis |

# H

| | |
|---|---|
| Hades | – god of the Underworld |
| Halitherses | – former captain of Ithacan royal guard |
| Hecabe | – Trojan queen, wife of King Priam |
| Hector | – Trojan prince, oldest son of King Priam |
| Helen | – queen of Sparta, wife of King Menelaus |
| Hephaistos | – god of fire; blacksmith to the Olympians |
| Hera | – goddess married to Zeus |
| Hermes | – messenger of the gods; his duties also include shepherding the souls of the dead to the Underworld |
| Hesione | – sister of King Priam, abducted by Telamon |
| Hestia | – goddess of the hearth and protectress of the household |

# I

| | |
|---|---|
| Ida (Mount) | – principal mountain in Ilium |
| Idaeus | – herald to King Priam |
| Idomeneus | – king of Crete |
| Ilium | – the region of which Troy was the capital |
| Ionian Sea | – sea to the west of the Greek mainland |
| Iphigenia | – eldest daughter of Agamemnon |
| Ithaca | – island in the Ionian Sea |

# K

| | |
|---|---|
| Kerosia | – Ithacan council meeting |

# L

| | |
|---|---|
| Lacedaemon | – Sparta |
| Laertes | – Odysseus's father |
| Leothoë | – daughter of King Altes of the Leleges, allies of Troy |

| | |
|---|---|
| Lemnos | – island in the Aegean Sea |
| Lycomedes | – king of Scyros |

## M

| | |
|---|---|
| Medon | – Malian commander |
| Melanthius | – Ithacan lad, brother of Melantho |
| Melantho | – Ithacan girl, sister of Melanthius |
| Menelaus | – king of Sparta and younger brother of Agamemnon |
| Menestheus | – king of Athens |
| Mentor | – close friend of Odysseus |
| Mnemon | – servant of Achilles, employed to remind him not to fight any of Apollo's sons |
| Mycenae | – most powerful city in Greece, situated in north-eastern Peloponnese |
| Myrine | – Helen's old nursemaid |
| Myrmidons | – the followers of Achilles |

## N

| | |
|---|---|
| Neaera | – Helen's body slave |
| Neoptolemus | – son of Achilles and Deidameia |
| Nestor | – king of Pylos |

## O

| | |
|---|---|
| Odysseus | – king of Ithaca |
| Omeros | – Ithacan boy |
| Orestes | – son of Agamemnon |

# P

| | |
|---|---|
| Palamedes | — Nauplian prince |
| Paris | — Trojan prince, second eldest son of King Priam |
| Parnassus (Mount) | — mountain in central Greece and home of the Pythian oracle |
| Patroclus | — cousin of Achilles and captain of the Myrmidons |
| Peisandros | — Myrmidon spearman |
| Peloponnese | — southernmost landmass of Greek mainland |
| Penelope | — queen of Ithaca and wife of Odysseus |
| Pergamos | — the citadel of Troy |
| Perithous | — Mycenaean gate guard |
| Persephone | — goddess of the Underworld, wife of Hades |
| Philoctetes | — Malian archer who lit the pyre of Heracles, for which he was awarded the hero's bow and arrows |
| Phronius | — Ithacan elder |
| Pleisthenes | — youngest son of Menelaus and Helen |
| Podarces | — Thessalian leader, brother of Protesilaus |
| Polites | — Thessalian warrior |
| Polymele | — Clytaemnestra's body slave |
| Poseidon | — god of the sea |
| Priam | — king of Troy |
| Protesilaus | — Thessalian leader, brother of Podarces |
| Pyrrha | — daughter of Lycomedes |
| Pythoness | — high priestess of the Pythian oracle |

# S

| | |
|---|---|
| Samos | — neighbouring island to Ithaca, also under the rule of Odysseus |
| Saronic Sea | — body of water between Attica and the Peloponnese |
| Scamander | — river on the Trojan plain |

| | |
|---|---|
| Scyros | – island east of Euboea |
| Simöeis | – river on the Trojan plain |
| Sparta | – city in the south-eastern Peloponnese |
| Sthenelaus | – companion of Diomedes |

## T

| | |
|---|---|
| Talthybius | – squire to Agamemnon |
| Taphians | – pirate race from Taphos |
| Tecton | – friend of Iphigenia |
| Telamon | – former king of Salamis, father of the greater Ajax |
| Tenedos | – island off the coast of Ilium |
| Tenes | – king of Tenedos |
| Teucer | – famed archer, half-brother and companion to the greater Ajax |
| Thersites | – Aetolian hunchback |
| Thessaly | – region of northern Greece |
| Thoosa | – friend of Iphigenia |
| Troy | – chief city of Ilium, on the eastern seaboard of the Aegean |

## X

| | |
|---|---|
| *xenia* | – the custom of friendship towards strangers |

## Z

| | |
|---|---|
| Zacynthos | – southernmost of the Ionian islands under Laertes's rule |
| Zeus | – the king of the gods |

book
ONE

*Chapter One*

# UNWELCOME VISITORS

Odysseus, king of Ithaca, lay on his stomach amongst a clump of fern. Leaves and twigs were tangled in his thick, red-brown beard, and his face and hands were smeared with earth so that only the whites of his eyes were visible in the undergrowth. He remained perfectly still and silent as he looked down the slope towards a clearing in the dense woodland, where two dozen men sat around a large fire and ate stew from wooden bowls. Their features were grey and blurred in the twilight, but it was clear from their armaments and the sound of their heavily accented voices that they were not Ithacans.

'That's them, Eperitus,' Odysseus whispered, nodding decisively. 'They're not a hunting party or a group of woodsmen – they're the bandits we're looking for. Can you hear what they're saying?'

Eperitus, captain of Odysseus's guard, lay shoulder to shoulder with the king. 'Most of it,' he replied, turning an ear towards the circle of men. Despite the distance, his acute hearing – which, like the rest of his god-gifted senses, was unnaturally sharp – could easily pick out the words of their conversation. 'Something about a troop of dancing girls and . . . well, you can probably guess the rest.' A roar of harsh laughter broke out below them. 'They met the girls in Pylos, but from their accents it sounds like they're Thessalians.'

'Then they've a long journey back home,' Odysseus said,

watching the men thoughtfully and tapping at his teeth with a nail-bitten forefinger.

Eperitus scratched at his closely cropped black beard. 'The problem is that we were told there were six of them, not four times that amount. And we've only brought twenty men with us.'

Odysseus leaned his large, muscular torso to one side and looked at his old friend, a glimmer of playful mockery in his green eyes. 'When we landed on Samos yesterday morning you told me you were itching for a fight. In fact, hardly a month's gone by in the past ten years when you haven't reminisced about the old days or longed for a proper battle to come along. Now the opportunity's arrived, all you can do is complain.'

Eperitus screwed his lips to one side and fixed his eyes on the camp below. Even though he knew Odysseus was poking fun at him, the king's words still stung. No other man on Ithaca – not even Odysseus himself – desired glory in battle as much as he did. The islanders were simple folk whose happiness was found in their homes and families, but Eperitus was an exile from a distant city who had never lost the unsettling need to prove himself. It drove everything he did, and though he had long since earned his place amongst the Ithacans he struggled to share their contentment. The handful of skirmishes he had fought in the past few years had left him hungry for a real chance of glory, and it was not until the news that a large group of bandits were terrorizing Samos – the neighbouring island to Ithaca – that he had realized how deep that hunger had eaten into him.

'I'm not complaining,' he replied. 'I'm a warrior, and a warrior wants nothing more than to kill his enemies. It's just that you're the king, Odysseus, and I'm sworn to protect you. Zeus's beard, if we take these lads on as we are there's a good chance they'll win and you'll be killed. And just look at them: I thought brigands were supposed to be armed with daggers and rusty swords, not breastplates, shields and spears!'

He pointed to the weapons piled against the mouth of a cave

at the back of the clearing, and then at the armour worn by each man and the long swords hanging from their belts. Both he and Odysseus knew that the men who had been robbing the people of Samos were not a band of disorganized thugs, stealing at need and fleeing back into the woods; they were soldiers, turned to common robbery for survival in a country where peace had reigned for a decade. They had arrived from the Peloponnese by ship several days before, and if they were allowed to establish themselves on Samos they would not only continue to threaten the welfare of the islanders, they would soon pose a challenge to Odysseus's own power and authority.

'Well, we need to deal with them,' the king said, resolutely. 'And I can't wait for more of the guard to be fetched from Ithaca – we have to defeat them here and now, with the men we've got.'

'What about Penelope?' Eperitus responded, noticing the look in Odysseus's eye at the mention of his beloved wife. 'She's three weeks away from giving birth to your first child, the child you've been trying for ever since you were married. This isn't the time to go risking your life.'

'I love my wife,' Odysseus said, simply but seriously. 'And no pack of outlaws is going to prevent me from returning home to her. But a king who isn't prepared to risk his life for his people isn't worthy of the title, and for the sake of my unborn son I have to live up to who I am.'

Eperitus looked at his friend and knew he had spoken truly. 'Well, evening's not far away,' he sighed, glancing up at the azure sky through the canopy of budding branches overhead. 'And there'll only be a faint moon tonight. We could bring the rest of the guard up here after dark and . . .'

'And kill them in cold blood? We won't need to resort to that.'

'Why not? You slit the throats of a dozen sleeping Taphians once, so what's the difference?'

'I had to do that,' Odysseus answered. 'They were invaders, whereas these poor swine,' he pointed a thumb towards the men below, 'are just soldiers fallen on hard times – warriors, like you and me. I won't kill them without giving them the chance to leave peacefully first.'

Eperitus shook his head resignedly. It was not that Odysseus was too proud to accept advice, it was just that he always thought he knew better. And he invariably did: if anyone could think of a way to defeat the bandits, it was Odysseus, the most clever, devious and resourceful man Eperitus knew.

'I assume you've got a plan,' he said.

'Of course I have,' the king replied with a grin. 'Now, let's get back to the others and tell them what we've seen.'

He raised himself on all fours and backed away from the screen of ferns, followed by Eperitus. Once they were sure they would not be spotted by any of the men around the campfire, they stood and quietly made their way back through the wood, picking a route between the silvery-grey trunks in the darkness. Soon they found the path they were looking for – a rutted cart track that crossed from one side of the forest to the other – and began the trek east towards their own camp.

'I dreamed about her again last night,' Odysseus said after a while. He was looking up at the early evening stars, which could be seen pricking the sky through the fissure in the canopy over-head.

'Athena?' Eperitus asked, pausing to look at the king, who avoided his eye and carried on walking. Eperitus ran to catch up with him. 'What did she say? Was it about Penelope again?'

He knew Odysseus had long enjoyed the blessing of the god-dess. As a child he had often seen her in his waking dreams, sitting on his bed at night and comforting him when he was lonely. She had once saved him from a wild boar, and when he became a man he had repaid her by making her his patron goddess. Ten years ago she had appeared before him and Eperitus on Mount Parnassus – where they had gone to seek the advice of the oracle – and then at Messene. A few months later she had brought Eperitus back to life after he had died saving Odysseus from the knife of an assassin.

But since then the king had seen or heard nothing of her – until she had come to him in a dream two nights ago, telling him Penelope would shortly give him a son.

'She didn't speak this time,' Odysseus said. 'We were standing on a plain under the moonlight, with the sound of the sea behind me and the smell of brine in my nostrils. Before me was a great city built on a hill. Its walls and towers were gleaming like silver, and it was both beautiful and terrible at the same time. Even though Athena was beside me the sight of that city struck me with fear and sadness, as if it were a symbol of the end of my happiness. Of all happiness.'

'What does it mean?'

'I don't know. Perhaps nothing, but I don't think so – it left me with a feeling that doom is approaching. You remember the words of the oracle, of course: I will be king over my people for ten years, and then I will have to choose between my home and Troy. This is the tenth year of my reign, Eperitus.'

Eperitus recalled the meeting in the caverns beneath Mount Parnassus, where the priestess had spoken the prophecy that had haunted the king for so long. It was there, also, that she had told Eperitus his fate was bound up with Odysseus's, for good or bad.

'I haven't forgotten the words of the Pythoness,' Eperitus replied. 'Yet I can't see what will happen to force such a choice on you, or, if it comes, why you can't just remain on Ithaca.'

But Odysseus did not reply. Before long they saw the orange light of a fire through the trees. As they approached, a man stepped out from the shadows and levelled his spear at them.

'Not a step closer,' he ordered, brandishing the weapon threateningly in an attempt to disguise his own nervousness. 'Who are you and what do you want here?'

'Apollo and Ares, come to bring death and destruction to all who stand in our way,' Eperitus replied, pushing the point of the spear away from his chest.

The man was similar in height to Eperitus, but had short, hairy legs and a large stomach that hung down over his belt. He squinted at Eperitus through his small, pig-like eyes, then with a half-sneer of recognition raised his weapon and stepped back.

'Oh, it's you,' he said with badly disguised contempt. Then, turning to Odysseus, he gave a quick bow before offering his hand. 'Welcome back, cousin. I'm sorry I didn't recognize you in this darkness.'

Odysseus gripped the other man's wrist and smiled. 'Who let you stand guard, Eurylochus? Everyone knows you've got the eyesight of a mole.'

Without waiting for an answer, the king clapped his cousin on the shoulder and strode off towards the welcoming light of the campfire with Eperitus at his side. They could see the figures of several men eating and drinking around the vivid orange flames, and the rich aroma of roasted meat made their mouths water in anticipation.

'I don't know what you've got in mind for dealing with those bandits,' Eperitus said, 'but I pray to the gods you'll leave Eurylochus here. He should never have been allowed to come with us, Odysseus – he's a clumsy, self-important idiot with no idea about fighting. If we're not careful he'll put us all in danger.'

'Laertes insisted he come,' Odysseus replied with an indifferent shrug, 'and I wasn't going to argue with my own father about the matter. Besides, if you're lucky Eurylochus'll get his head chopped off and you'll never have to put up with him again.'

Eperitus ignored the comment. Eurylochus had shown him nothing but disdain since he had been made captain of the royal guard ten years ago, a position that Eurylochus, as Odysseus's cousin and a lesser member of the royal family, felt should have been given to him by right. The fact he had skulked out of the greatest battle in Ithaca's history – against a rebellion supported by a Taphian invasion force – did not stop him from despising Eperitus's good fortune. Nevertheless, Eperitus did not want to see the fat fool slain needlessly.

'And how do you intend to defeat two-dozen heavily armed warriors, assuming they refuse your invitation to return peacefully to the mainland?' he asked as they paused at the edge of the broad clearing.

'That's easy,' Odysseus answered blithely. 'You've been itching for a chance of glory, Eperitus, so I'm going to send *you* to fight them.'

*Chapter Two*

# THE QUEEN OF SPARTA

A lone wolf stood on the empty road and sniffed the cold air. The sable heavens were filled with stars, whilst a thin crescent of moon was rising over the dark peaks of the Taygetus Mountains in the west. Its light shivered on the surface of the fast-flowing river that ran alongside the road, the noise of which almost drowned out the gentle bleating of sheep that had drawn the hungry wolf down from the hills.

Seeing the low wall of a sheep pen not far from the road, she knew from experience that a man would be sleeping across the single entrance, his crook close to hand. But the animal had not eaten in two days and was desperate. She trotted across the field towards the enclosure, drawn by the sound and the smell of the fat sheep within, instinctively readying herself to jump the sleeping shepherd and snatch a lamb. Saliva was already dripping from her pink gums as she anticipated the taste of warm flesh running with blood, when another sound stopped her in her tracks.

Turning her head to the south, where the smell of the sea was carried strongly on the night breeze, the wolf saw a line of torches moving up the road, carried by tall men in armour that glinted in the moonlight. Skulking low to the ground, her grey fur indistinguishable amongst the rocks and scrub, she watched the procession coming closer and closer until it was no longer safe for her to remain. She raised herself and was about to run back towards the hills when a low whistle stopped her. Looking back at the men, she saw one of them hand his armaments to a comrade and leave the road. He strolled directly across the field towards the waiting animal.

Curiously, the wolf realized she did not feel afraid. She watched the man pull something out of a bag that hung from his shoulder, dangle it from his fingertips and give another low whistle. The smell of dried meat caught the wolf's nostrils. Against her instincts, which seemed unable to function naturally in the man's presence, she began to edge closer towards the strip of flesh that hung from his hand. Then, her caution forgotten, she lifted herself to her full height and trotted straight up to the proffered meat.

'I knew you were hungry,' the man said, feeding the length of beef into the animal's jaws and stroking her mane of coarse hair. 'And you don't want to go risking those sheep. You leave them alone and go find yourself a rabbit or two instead.'

He stood and pointed to the hills. The wolf looked up at him, her yellow eyes shining, then turned and ran off into the darkness. Paris watched her go with a smile on his lips, before returning to the road where his men awaited him.

There were a dozen of them, all grinning with pleasure at their leader's mastery of the wild animal. A handsome young warrior stepped forward and handed Paris his spear and tall, rectangular shield.

'Let's hope you can have Menelaus feeding out of your hand, too,' he said.

'The king of Sparta's no animal, Aeneas,' Paris replied, slinging the wooden-framed shield over his shoulder; it had clearly seen many battles, the layers of ox-hide slashed and pierced by numerous weapons. 'And I'm only a simple warrior, not a diplomat.'

'Nonsense,' declared a tall warrior stepping out of the file of soldiers to join them. At fifty years he was the oldest in the party by more than a decade, though his hardened face retained the good looks of his youth and his black hair and beard were untouched by grey. Beneath his dusty cloak he wore a cuirass of bronze scales. 'You're one of the best negotiators Troy has, Paris. Don't forget, I was there when you persuaded the northern tribes to swear an oath of fealty to your father. Can you imagine it, Aeneas – this "simple warrior" turning King Priam's bitterest enemies into his newest allies? And yet,' he added, turning back to Paris with a serious look in his eyes, 'I don't think even you'll succeed this time. These Greeks aren't savage tribesmen, and in their pride they think themselves second only to the gods.'

'But we have to try, Apheidas,' the prince answered, scratching the tip of a pink scar on his right temple. It ran across the bridge of his flat nose to the left corner of his mouth, where it ended in a narrow salient through his thick beard. 'We *have* to. First with Menelaus here in Sparta, then north to Mycenae to speak with his brother. If anyone has the power to return Hesione to us, it'll be Agamemnon.'

Hesione was King Priam's sister, who had been brought to Greece by Telamon thirty years before, after he and Heracles had sacked Troy and taken their choice of the spoils. Priam, though, still regarded her abduction as a stain on his country's pride and longed to bring his sister home. All previous envoys had failed, with some nearly being killed, but now he was sending his second-oldest son to negotiate for Hesione's return. And Paris was determined not to disappoint his father's trust in him.

Apheidas spat on the road. 'It doesn't matter who you speak to, they'll never give her back,' he said, his dark eyes glistening angrily in the moonlight. 'Don't forget I was brought up in northern Greece, though my father was a Trojan. I lived among these people for most of my life until they exiled me, and I know them better than anyone in Ilium does. No matter what old Priam says – may the gods protect him – I tell you the best way to deal with the Greeks is to kill the bastards. Every last man, woman and child of them.'

'Well,' Paris said, frowning, 'if the mission fails, you might just get your wish.'

He thought of Hector's parting words before the voyage to

Sparta. His older brother had always trusted in Paris's ability as a warrior and posted him to the northern borders of their father's kingdom, to fight the small wars that were constantly flaring up or to defend Troy's vassal cities against raiders. But Paris's recent victories and the peace treaties he had engineered had made the borders safer than they had been for years, leaving him free to serve Hector's other machinations.

'Spy them out,' Hector had commanded in his strained, gravelly voice, his large bulk dominating the small antechamber as he had paced up and down with his hands behind his back. 'Father's sending you to negotiate for the return of his sister, but I'm telling you to keep your eyes open while you're there: check the capabilities of their armies; see if their city walls are in good repair; find out whether their leaders are still at each other's throats. We might as well get something worthwhile out of this.'

'Then you don't think Hesione is worthwhile?' Paris had asked.

'Hesione's been gone decades, little brother – she'll be one of *them* by now. If they want to give her back to us, fine. At least father'll be pleased. But they won't, and that's even better. It'll be a good justification for war.'

Paris had known for a long time that Hector's mind was quietly set on war with Greece. Frictions between the two cultures had been growing for years, but not because of Hesione. The Trojans were an insular, authoritarian people, loyal to their king and concerned with the protection and controlled expansion of their borders. The Greeks, however, were outward-looking, competitive and greedy. Their merchants were ubiquitous, and even Hector's decision to demand tribute from their ships crossing the Aegean Sea had not curtailed them. Instead, as Paris had known it would, it had only served to anger the Greeks and turn the eyes of their kings evermore eastward. Knowing that one side must eventually gain dominance, and determined it should not be Greece, Hector had already started marshalling his forces and calling on the allies of Troy. A giant fleet was being assembled that could take an army to Greece and crush its upstart kingdoms, and by this time next year the forces would be ready. Hector just needed an excuse to attack.

Paris looked across the dark plain towards the city on a hill to the north, where numerous lights burned and the high buildings within its walls glowed like bronze. As he watched, a trickle of smaller lights flowed out of the city gates and down the road towards the river.

'Look,' he said, pointing towards the distant procession. 'What do you make of that?'

'A welcoming committee?' Aeneas suggested.

'Doubtful,' Apheidas snorted. 'Someone must have warned them we were here.'

Paris's rugged face was emotionless.

'We've no choice but to sit and wait for them. If they turn out to be unfriendly, then it's a quicker retreat to our ship from here than if we were to meet them halfway. But I don't think it'll come to that, unless the Greek sense of honour is worse than we expected.'

Nevertheless, he ordered his men to form a double line across the road and to have their shields and spears ready as they waited. Some of the soldiers discussed what would happen when the Spartans reached them, whilst others gnawed at their meagre provisions or stood in silence, watching the stars make their slow progress through the night sky and wondering what level of hospitality they would receive. The people they had met in the port where their ship was now docked had been suspicious and unfriendly, confirming the Trojans' low opinion of Greeks. But they were yet to meet noblemen or warriors. It was from these classes, rather than fishermen and farmers, that they were likely to receive the proper welcome that *xenia* required. This was the age-old custom where strangers exchanged gifts and oaths of friendship. It ensured protection for visitors and led to networks of alliances that were enforced through a sense of honour. Without it, trade between nations and states would cease and be replaced by endless war; there would be no prosperity or peace, no progress or communication. And yet, despite Apheidas's assurances that *xenia* was observed in Greece, in a crude fashion, the Trojans doubted the Greek sense of honour and did not trust their foreign ways.

Before long the Spartans were no longer specks of light, but were becoming visible as an armed force of at least three score men. Their bronze helmets and the points of their spears gleamed in the light of their torches as they came ever nearer along the road that ran parallel to the River Eurotas. The unnatural tramping of their sandalled feet seemed unstoppable, making some of the Trojans feel they would march straight over them. Then, when they were within bowshot, they came to a sudden, clanging halt.

At Paris's signal the Trojans locked shields and lowered their spear-points. A man approached from the Spartan ranks and stopped a few paces in front of them. His armour, though mostly concealed by his dark blue cloak, was expensive and indicated his rank.

'I am Eteoneus, herald of Menelaus, King of Sparta,' he began, his accent thick and difficult for Paris to comprehend. 'My lord has sent me to escort you safely to his palace, where a feast has been prepared in your honour. Rooms have also been set aside for you and your men – no doubt you're tired after your voyage from Troy.'

So they knew they were Trojans, Paris thought. That could be guessed by their armaments and clothing, of course, but he also had the feeling that invisible eyes had been watching their every step from the harbour and reporting their progress to King Menelaus. He only hoped they had not observed his own careful observation of the geography and infrastructure of Sparta: as per Hector's instructions, he had already considered the size of the harbour for accommodating an invasion fleet and the condition of the roads for passage of an army. He had noted the width and flatness of the plain between the mountain ranges on either side, as well as the breadth of the river and the number and quality of the crossing points. Even as the two groups of men faced each other, he was assessing the quality of their weaponry and armour. And it was dismayingly good.

'I am Paris, son of King Priam of Troy,' he announced, speaking in precise but broadly accented Greek. 'My men and I will be pleased to accept Menelaus's hospitality, if you'll lead the way.'

Without another word, Eteoneus turned sharply and cleared a passage through the ranks of the escort, which waited for Paris to form his men into a column and pass through before closing up again and following in their wake. They marched in silence for some time, the Trojans feeling slightly menaced by the sound of the heavily armed Spartans behind them, but before long the escort began to flag. Despite the magnificence of their armaments, Paris was surprised to note they were already losing their order and formation. The unified tramping of feet that had announced their arrival earlier was now ragged and the footfalls had lost their force. Some men were falling behind the march, despite its slow pace, and most of the soldiers repeatedly switched their spears from one shoulder to the other, a clear sign they were struggling with the weight. This pleased Paris, who had been ordered by Hector to watch for the quality of the soldiers they might face in the event of war. From what he could see, the Greeks – who had developed a reputation for toughness during their long years of civil war – were now atrophying with the peace that had existed between them for the past ten years. The Trojan armies, on the other hand, were constantly rotated on their northern and eastern borders, keeping them fit and battle-ready. If the rest of the Greek soldiery was comparable to the men surrounding him, Paris was confident that any meeting between equal forces of Greeks and Trojans would result in a Trojan victory. Hector would be delighted at the news.

Before long they were passing a series of tall mounds on either side of the road, which Eteoneus informed them were the tombs of Sparta's former kings. He named each one in turn as they passed the ancient, grass-covered mausoleums, recounting their glorious feats and often tragic ends. Then, as they reached the final two mounds – facing each other across the highway – he gave a curt bow and whispered a prayer.

'These are the graves of Tyndareus and Icarius,' he explained. 'Brothers and co-rulers of Sparta. Tyndareus was the father of our queen, Helen, though some say it was Zeus himself that sired her. If you're fortunate enough to see her, you'll realize why many think she has divine blood in her veins.'

'Rumours of her beauty have reached Ilium,' Paris said.

'Hearsay,' Aeneas sneered. 'I doubt she can match the looks of even the simplest Trojan girl.'

There was a sudden, angry murmur from the ranks of Spartans, who quickly forgot their tiredness and gripped their weapons tighter. Eteoneus immediately raised his hand to silence the threats that were being uttered.

'Peace,' he commanded, smiling confidently. 'Our young friend will soon realize his ignorance. When it comes to beauty, I think our queen can defend herself.'

The Spartan soldiers, who moments before had been ready to kill the young Trojan, now looked at him and laughed. Their laughter continued all the way through the ramshackle peasant buildings that surrounded Sparta, compounding Aeneas's hatred of Greeks, until they reached the high city walls. Here, helmeted heads stared down at the party as Eteoneus led them over a hump-backed bridge beside an orchard and on to the arched gates of the city. The large wooden portals were already open in anticipation of their arrival. More warriors stood by the gate, gawping at the strange-looking foreigners with their long beards and their outlandish armour. Several spat in the dust at their feet, but a stern glance from Paris warned his men against the temptation to retaliate and they carried on marching, their eyes fixed firmly forward until the last man was inside the city walls.

The wooden gates closed with a boom behind them and the Trojans felt their hearts sink. They were trapped inside a foreign city, surrounded by hostile soldiers, with nothing but the diplomatic skills of their leader or the spears in their hands to get them out again. Paris looked back at the gates, but not with the sense of claustrophobic fear that his countrymen felt. Instead, he was taking note of Sparta's defensive capabilities. The walls were in good repair and the guards were numerous, meaning the city could only be taken by surprise, stealth or a prolonged siege. But much of the defence of a city relied on the abilities of its king, and Paris wondered what sort of man Menelaus was. Was he soft and weak like Priam, or politically astute with the courage of a lion and the ferocity of a wild boar, like Hector? Was Menelaus a worthy king in his own right, or was he propped up by his more powerful brother? The coming feast, though ostensibly an act of welcome and friendship, would reveal much to both sides.

The sloping streets that led up to the palace were empty and every door shut, but Paris knew he and his men were being watched from the many darkened windows and alleys they passed. They must have looked strange to Greek eyes, he thought, and he wondered whether they were being regarded with fear, curiosity or loathing. A party of Greeks visiting Troy would have been treated with no less suspicion.

As he followed Eteoneus, he let his eyes roam across the simplistic, functional design of Menelaus's city. Its buildings were strong and well made, but lacked the opulence of their Trojan counterparts. Every public structure in Paris's home city was constructed to impress the wealth and importance of Troy on its citizens and visitors, and even the homes of the nobles and merchants boasted ornate architectural features and walls that were rich in murals. They were far superior to the plain and sturdy buildings of the Spartans, just as Troy surpassed Sparta in both size and beauty. But Paris's simple taste and his harsh life on the northern borders gave him a grudging appreciation of the modest strength of Greek architecture. The slabs beneath his feet were firm and well fitted, whereas the ornate cobbles of Troy were forever tripping him up; similarly, the tall, well-laid Spartan walls were easy on his eyes in the moonlight, while the walls at home were too busy, a constant distraction. It would be a pity, he thought, if Sparta ever chose to defy the invading armies of Troy and its neat, powerful buildings were put to the torch.

Eventually the steep, circuitous road reached the top of the hill, where the gateway to Menelaus's palace stood closed against them. Its high doors were covered in beaten silver that shone blue in the weak moonlight, framing the squad of six heavily armoured soldiers that stood guard before them. Paris suspected that he and his men were receiving a demonstration of Sparta's military power, from the escort led by Eteoneus to the well-manned walls and the guard that protected the high portals of the palace.

The Spartan herald did not slow down at the sight of the closed gate, and as he approached the doors swung smoothly back into a vast and empty courtyard. He waved the Trojans inside with one hand and dismissed their Spartan escort with the other, before ordering the half-dozen palace guards to close the gates behind them. The Trojans swept their eyes around the courtyard: there were long rows of stables along the western flank, with barracks along the southern and the eastern walls; on the northern side was the three-storeyed bulk of the palace, gleaming in the moonlight before them. As they took in their plain but powerful surroundings, three men emerged from a small door beside the main entrance behind them and approached Eteoneus.

'Are they familiar with the rules?' the first of them asked, giving a disdainful nod towards the foreigners. He was a short, balding man with muscular arms and a large stomach encased in leather armour.

'You're the guard,' Eteoneus replied. 'Why don't you enlighten them?'

'Gladly,' the man sneered, turning to face Paris. 'No weapons in the palace. You give 'em to me and my lads now, or you turn about and find yourself an inn in the town. You hear?'

His accent, like the accents of all the Spartans they had met so far, was broad and difficult to understand, but the intention was clear.

'No Greek's getting my spear,' Apheidas said firmly, talking to Paris in their own tongue. 'Unless it's in his gut.'

'Shut up, Apheidas,' Paris ordered. He turned to the rest of his men and looked at them sternly. 'Hand over your weapons, all of you. We're guests here, not invaders, so get on with it.'

As the Trojans parted with their weapons and shields, which the Spartans handled roughly and derided as inferior or ineffectual, they felt as if they were being stripped naked. All of them except Paris shifted uneasily and instinctively moved closer together, aware of the heavily armed soldiers watching them from beside the gates.

'Come with me,' Eteoneus said curtly, striding off towards the large square doors that opened into the palace.

The Trojans followed, looking about at the many darkened windows, where they sensed numerous eyes watching them.

'I don't like this, Paris,' Apheidas whispered as they were ushered into the palace. A long corridor stretched ahead of them, inadequately lit with sputtering torches every dozen paces. 'You're being too trusting. Don't forget the Greeks are treacherous.'

'So you keep reminding me. But what choice do I have? I've been given a mission and I'm going to carry it out, come what may.'

He followed Eteoneus down the corridor and into the heart of the palace, his men pressing close behind. They passed several darkened rooms, both small and large judging by the echoes of their footsteps as they hurried by, and many staircases leading to the upper levels, or down to the cellars and storage rooms. It was not long before the corridor opened into a large antechamber with a high ceiling, where more torches fought uselessly against the shadows. Here the walls were decorated with images of the war between the centaurs and the lapiths, the clarity of the struggling figures blurred by the murk and the different hues of the paintwork lost in the orange firelight. A pair of large, ornately carved doors dominated the far wall of the antechamber, from behind which they could hear several voices talking loudly. There was music, too, and at the sound of the feast the Trojans remembered they had not eaten a proper meal since that morning.

'This way,' Eteoneus sniffed, and without giving the Trojans a moment to compose themselves walked up to the doors and beat the flat of his hand against the wood.

The voices on the other side fell silent. Paris turned briefly to his men and gave them a reassuring look, then the doors swung open to reveal two guards in full armour. They glanced at Eteoneus and the knot of foreigners behind him, before stepping back to reveal the great hall of Sparta's palace. It was so long and wide that the heavily muralled walls were lost in deep shadow and the torches that hung from them struggled to force back the suffocating gloom. Four central pillars rose like mighty trees and disappeared into the darkness of the ceiling; between them a large, circular hearth burned fiercely with yellow flames, which for a moment were pulled towards the fresh air pouring in from the open doors. A gust of heat washed over the Trojans, drawing them instinctively into the large room, and as the last man entered the guards closed the doors behind them with a thud.

On either side of the hearth and the painted pillars were two parallel rows of heavy wooden tables. These were overflowing with food and drink – great haunches of roasted meats on broad wooden platters, baskets of barley cakes and different fruits, kraters of wine – which would have been a welcoming sight for the hungry Trojans, were it not for the hundred or so men seated at the tables and staring at them with harsh curiosity. Rows of male and female slaves stood behind them, their eyes glinting in the shadows as they, too, looked at the strangers from Troy. Then, as if aware of the hostility of the hall, a voice from the far side of the hearth called out to them.

'Welcome, friends. Come closer and warm yourselves by the fire – spring may be here, but the nights haven't forgotten the winter yet.'

Through the quivering heat haze above the hearth they saw another table on a raised dais. A man rose to his feet behind it and clapped his hands.

'Bring a table and stools,' he shouted to the slaves. 'Bring meat and wine, too. Let's make our guests welcome.'

As if released from a spell, the lines of seated men returned to their feasting, though their constant glances revealed the topic of their conversation. In a flurry of activity a dozen slaves brought a table and chairs from the shadows and placed them down before the Trojan warriors. Moments later, more slaves were crowding it with piles of food and kraters of wine, already mixed with water to dilute its strength. The newcomers could not stop themselves from glancing over their shoulders as platters of spit-roasted goats' meat, mutton and pork – all glistening with fat – were set down and punctuated with baskets of bread, barley cakes and fruit. But they were forced to resist their hunger for a little longer, as their host stepped down from the dais and walked around the hearth towards them.

In the firelight they could see he was still a young man, a little over thirty years old, of medium height with large muscles in his chest and arms. He wore a simple, green woollen tunic that stopped halfway down his broad thighs, contrasting with the knee-length tunics worn by the Trojans. His hair was auburn, though thinning on top and heavily streaked with grey, and his beard was black and wiry. His face was crossed by a smile that was both kind and friendly, but his leathery skin was lined and careworn beyond his years.

'Welcome again, friends,' he greeted them. 'I am Menelaus, son of Atreus and, by the grace of Zeus, king of Sparta. Forgive the simple hospitality of my hall tonight – if you'd sent news of your arrival earlier we'd have been able to show you some *real* Spartan warmth. But if you're not in any hurry to leave we can give you a proper welcome tomorrow night, and for as many nights as you're here.'

'I am Paris, son of Priam, king of Troy,' Paris replied, pulling himself to his full height and offering his hand.

Menelaus's eyebrows arched slightly as he gripped Paris firmly by the wrist. 'A Trojan prince, eh? Then this is no idle visit, and now I feel even more ashamed of this meagre excuse for a banquet.'

'Don't be,' Paris replied, relaxing slightly as he sensed the genuine warmth in Menelaus's welcome. 'Simplicity suits me. The constant feasting at home is tiresome – I'd much rather be round a barrack-room fire on our northern border, drinking wine and swapping stories with my men.'

'You're a true soldier then,' Menelaus grinned, finally releasing Paris's hand. 'We've had peace here for a decade, but sometimes I long for the old days. There's nothing like living on marching rations for a week and fighting a battle at the end of it! All this heavy food and sitting on uncomfortable thrones isn't good for a man,' he added wryly, patting his rounded stomach.

Paris found himself warming to the Greek. Despite the purpose of his mission and the broad gulf between their different cultures, he felt Menelaus was a man he could relate to.

'My father sent me to . . .' he began, but Menelaus held up a hand and shook his head.

'Unless your business here is urgent, let's leave talk of it for another night, eh? You and your men are welcome to stay for as long as you like, so relax and fill your stomachs – I know you haven't eaten anything hot since you set out from the harbour this morning. There will be a time for formal words, Paris, but it isn't now.'

Paris nodded and smiled for the first time since passing through the gates of Sparta. Then, as he was about to excuse himself and return to his men, he looked through the flames and saw the figure of a woman standing on the other side of the hearth. Though the heat haze was fierce, the light of the fire revealed her clearly. Her eyes captured his with an expression as intense as the flames that seemed to imprison her and Paris knew in an instant that this was

the renowned Helen, whose beauty surpassed any rumour or reputation. At the same time, he sensed Menelaus turn his head to look
across the raging fire at his wife, just as she turned her face away
and moved back towards the shadows. Heedless of Menelaus, Paris
watched the tall, slim figure of Helen recede into the darkness,
his mind reeling. The desires and emotions that had been tightly
locked away in his soldier's heart for many years were suddenly
breaking free in a confusing rush, escaping through the cracks that
a single look from Helen had prised open, coursing through his
whole body and threatening the discipline and restraint that had
given his life equilibrium for so long.

And as she reached the edge of the circle of light from the
hearth, just as the shadows were swallowing her, she turned back
and looked at him again, her eyes blazing briefly in the darkness
before disappearing. Paris felt a heavy weight shifting within him,
as something old died and something new was born.

## Chapter Three

# POLITES

The pale yellow light of morning filtered through the trees, waking the bright green ferns that carpeted the woodland floor and touching on the small white flowers that grew amid the roots of the pines. Birds were singing in the treetops, greeting the arrival of dawn, and there was a strong smell of new vegetation and damp earth in the air. Eperitus sat astride a donkey – his breastplate and sword concealed beneath his cloak – and scoured the trees discreetly for signs of movement. Heedless of any danger, his ride stumped its way along the wide path that cut through the wood, its head down and its tall ears twitching and flicking as a constant stream of flies irritated them. The bell about its neck clanged with every footfall, sending dull, monotonous chimes ringing through the trees.

A young man of around twenty years followed on foot. He had shoulder-length, brown hair that he was constantly brushing from his eyes, and boyish good looks that were partially hidden by a light growth of beard. His only armaments were the dagger in his belt and the long stick in his left hand, with which he would occasionally strike the bony hindquarters of the donkey.

'I wish you'd stop doing that, Arceisius,' Eperitus snapped as the stick smacked down again just behind him. 'The animal's moving along just fine as it is; there's no need to keep hitting the poor thing.'

'Sorry, sir,' Arceisius replied, his already ruddy complexion reddening slightly. 'It's just habit.'

'And a touch of nerves?' Eperitus suggested. He took a deep breath to calm his own anxiety before offering his squire a reassuring smile. 'Don't worry. Odysseus won't let us down. He never has yet.'

He turned back to look at the path stretching out ahead of them. Not much further along the trees thickened and the trail narrowed – a good place for concealment, but lacking the width and space required for an ambush – then shortly afterwards it swept around a spur of the hill and disappeared from sight. According to the locals, the bandits had already struck twice at the point just beyond the spur, and that was where Eperitus expected them to be waiting now. His unnaturally sharp eyesight had already spied figures moving furtively through the trees on the upper slopes – drawn by the sound of the bell about the donkey's neck – and from there they must have noticed the large leather bags hanging from the animal's flanks. An unprotected merchant and his young assistant would be too tempting a target to ignore.

They passed through the narrow stretch of path without incident, but as the trees thinned again and the trail turned around the spur of the hill, Eperitus noticed straight away that the birds were no longer singing and an unusual stillness had descended about them. At the same time, his keen senses picked out glimpses of sun-tanned skin amongst the clumps of foliage sprouting in unnatural places, the barely visible outlines of helmets nudging above the tops of boulders, and the thick, controlled breathing of several nervous men behind the trees and rocks. Eperitus absorbed all these things in a moment, telling him that at least twenty bandits were concealed on the slope above him. The trap was about to be sprung and suddenly, even though no enemies had yet revealed themselves, he felt his old battle instinct take hold of him, pouring new energy into his limbs and tensing his body like a bowstring.

Then a man stepped out from behind a large boulder a few

paces ahead of them. 'Stop where you are,' he ordered in a nasal voice, holding up his hands, 'and get down from the donkey.'

Eperitus leaned forward and looked at the short, unimpressive bandit before him, but made no move to dismount. The man's comrades were emerging from their hiding places to his left – some of them armed with bows and aiming their arrows directly at him and Arceisius – and it was obvious that the slightest wrong move-ment would bring swift death. Nonetheless, he had to fight the instinct to throw aside his cloak and draw his sword. Everything, he knew, depended on him holding his nerve.

'I can't do that, I'm afraid,' he replied in a calm voice. 'I'm on an important mission for the king, and time is of the essence.'

The bandit's eyes narrowed for a moment, then he placed his hands on his hips and leaned back, raising his eyebrows quizzically.

'A mission for the king?' he said with mock awe. 'Really? Well, I'm sorry to inconvenience his lordship, but we have need of the royal donkey and all the possessions of his servants.'

His comment was followed by a ripple of laughter from the men on the slope above.

'Normally I'd be glad to help the starving and impoverished,' Eperitus responded, throwing a casual glance back across the file of Thessalians, 'but I'm already on an errand of mercy. You see, the king's been told that his subjects on Samos are being beaten and robbed by a band of outlaws, and he's sent me to find them.'

'Well, it seems to me, my friend, that you *have* found them.'

Eperitus smiled. 'I don't think so. You see, the men I'm looking for were reported to be fearsome cut-throats – brutal, heavily armed men of violence, worthy of my skills as a bandit-hunter. Perhaps you can tell me where they are?'

'By Ares's sword, you've got a nerve,' the man hissed, clenching his fists and scowling. 'We're the only damned cut-throats you'll find on this pathetic rock, and if you've come looking for us then you'd better state your purpose – or else get off that cursed animal and start stripping, before you find an arrow in your throat.'

Eperitus remained where he was. He could sense Arceisius's nervous fidgeting at his side and placed a calming hand on his squire's shoulder.

'I can't say I'm not disappointed,' he sighed, 'but if you're the men I've been sent to find, then you'd better listen to me. King Odysseus of Ithaca, son of Laertes, offers you free passage back to the Peloponnese. If you go now, you'll not be harmed and you'll even be allowed to keep your armour and weapons.'

Some of the men on the slopes laughed incredulously, while others shouted angrily at the audacity of the man before them.

'And if we refuse?' asked the short bandit, his voice even more nasal as his temper edged higher.

Eperitus jumped down from the donkey and threw his cloak over his shoulder, revealing his leather breastplate and the sword hanging from his belt. 'If you refuse, then I challenge any man amongst you to fight me to the death. If I win, then the rest of you must leave Odysseus's kingdom and never return; but if your champion kills me, then Odysseus will cede the island of Samos and all its towns, villages, people, livestock and crops to you. What do you say?'

The bandit gave a derisive snort. 'The king's offer is generous, but there's another alternative. If I want, I can have you and your lad shot where you stand. Then my comrades and I can continue to take what we please from the people of this fat little island.'

'You could shoot us down if you wished, but then Odysseus would come to Samos himself, bringing his army with him. They'd hunt you down to the last man and leave your unburied bodies as carrion for the crows. At least if one of you has the stomach to fight me, you have a small chance of winning.'

'King Odysseus must have a lot of faith in your skill as a warrior, if he's prepared to stake part of his kingdom on you,' the bandit replied. He looked up at his comrades and there was the glimmer of a smile on his lips. 'It's an interesting choice: leave Samos without a fight; accept your challenge; or just kill you and take our chances with the king and his army. My head tells me to shoot you down and be done with it, but my heart wants to accept your challenge. And that is what we will do.'

There was a questioning murmur from the men on the slope, but the short bandit silenced his comrades with a wave of his hand. 'If you kill our champion we give you our oaths before all the gods that we will leave peacefully, never to return. But there are to be no rules in this match, and I insist on one condition: the fight must be decided without weapons.'

'Even better,' Eperitus answered, already sliding his sword from its scabbard and passing it back to Arceisius. 'I wouldn't want it to be over too quickly.'

'Of course not,' the bandit grinned, before signalling to the men on the slope. 'Send Polites down here! Now.'

'I don't trust them, sir,' Arceisius said, undoing the buckles on Eperitus's breastplate and prising the shaped leather away from his broad chest. He was looking up the slope to where the bandits were moving aside, their faces suddenly full of eager anticipation.

'Don't worry,' Eperitus said in a low voice, removing his cloak and throwing it over the back of the donkey. 'I only need to keep them distracted and buy us some time. Besides, there isn't a man amongst this lot who could match me in a fight.'

'I wouldn't be so sure of that,' Arceisius replied, his eyes widening as he watched Eperitus's opponent striding down the slope behind him, throwing off his armour and weapons as he came.

Eperitus turned and felt a sudden rush of doubt at the sight of the man he was to face. Polites was a full head and shoulders taller than he was, and his muscles bulged like boulders under his taut skin. His square face was dominated by his thick black beard and his dark, cruel eyes. He reached the path and pulled off his cloak and tunic, then stood naked with his arms hanging at his side and his huge hands flexing repeatedly, already anticipating crushing the life out of his opponent.

Eperitus glanced higher up the slope and further along the path, at the same time straining his ears for sounds of discreet movement through the trees and bushes. He could hear nothing. Taking a deep breath to calm the sudden flurry of nerves, he unbuckled his belt and pulled off his tunic – clothes would only allow Polites to get an easy grip – and stepped forward.

Without waiting, Polites lunged at him with arms wide and fingers splayed. Eperitus ducked aside at the last moment, just as the long, heavily-muscled arms closed on the place where he had been standing. Turning on his heel, he punched Polites in the kidneys with all his force, only to cry out in pain as his fist impacted on the hard muscle. Before he could move away, Polites swung his right elbow back into his face, sending him reeling into the hindquarters of the donkey. The animal kicked out, narrowly missing Eperitus's head, and broke through the circle of cheering Thessalians who had surrounded the fight.

Arceisius went to follow the donkey, but was pulled back by the short bandit. 'You're staying here, lad,' he snarled, his lip curling to reveal yellow teeth.

Eperitus wiped the blood from his nose and staggered to his feet, still dazed from the blow to his face. Polites grinned confidently and walked towards him, certain his victory would be swift as he threw his arms wide and lunged again. The ring of onlookers closed towards Eperitus so that, this time, there could be no dodging the wide span of their champion's immensely strong limbs. Realizing Polites had only one tactic – to crush the life out of him – Eperitus used his quicker reflexes to duck beneath his long reach and thrust his shoulder into the giant's stomach.

The force of the blow would have knocked any other man from his feet and sent him toppling into the dust, but to Eperitus's amazement Polites's legs held. Then, in desperation, Eperitus thrust upwards, taking Polites's full weight across his back and lifting him bodily from the ground. Then with a huge effort he stood and threw Polites into the dirt behind him.

There was a groan of dismay from the bandits, who shuffled back from the sprawling giant. Eperitus spun round, but Polites was already on his hands and knees and preparing to stand. Leaping forward, he swung his foot with as much speed and strength as he could muster into Polites's exposed genitals. The soft flesh flattened beneath the top of his foot and a moment later a deafening bellow of pain erupted from his opponent's lungs as he fell forward into the dirt, writhing in agony.

Eperitus was on him in an instant, thrusting his knee into his spine and hooking his right arm under his chin. He pulled back with all his strength, trying to snap the man's neck. Whether the other Thessalians would honour their oath if he won, he did not know; he only knew that, unless he killed Polites now, the man would tear him apart. He pulled harder, sensing his opponent weakening as the shouts of the crowd receded into a shocked silence.

Then Polites placed the palms of his hands down on the earth and, slowly and irresistibly, began to push himself up. Eperitus tightened his grip about his neck and concentrated the weight of his body down through his knee in a desperate effort to keep him pinned to the floor, but the Thessalian's strength seemed without measure. With a rage-filled roar, Polites thrust himself up and on to his side, pulling Eperitus's arms away from his neck. The next moment he twisted free and leapt to his feet.

His supporters exploded back into life. Eperitus, now flat on his back, saw the terrible anger in Polites's eyes as he reached down and picked him up, lifting him above his head as if he were no more than a child. With a huge grunt, he hurled the Ithacan across the circle of men to land in a heap at the feet of Arceisius.

For a moment Eperitus's vision was filled with flashes of light, beyond which the world seemed to be spinning about him in a whirl of faces and trees set against a cloudy sky. His whole body was awash with pain, a thousand spear-points of agony stabbing at him relentlessly, and his ears were filled with the deafening sound of his own heartbeat. Then he saw Arceisius's face bending close, his lips moving urgently.

'Sir, he's coming again!' he said, his voice distant and muffled by the blood pumping through Eperitus's ears.

Suddenly, with a rush and a loud pop, his senses returned to him. Seeing the looming figure of Polites approaching from the corner of his vision, he thrust aside his pain and rolled onto his hands and knees, springing away just as the giant leapt towards him. With his brain beating hard against the inside of his skull and every muscle in his body protesting at the movement that was forced upon them, Eperitus sprinted to the opposite side of the human arena and, gasping, twisted about to face Polites, who had turned and was coming at him again, his massive body covered in sweat, dust and blood.

Then Eperitus's fighting instinct came back to him. New strength filled his limbs and his senses sharpened to a fine point once more. His eyes searched the arena for anything that would give him an advantage, acutely aware that Polites was closing on him. Beyond the circle of Thessalians, he heard the faint rustle of undergrowth trodden under careful feet, and the small sounds of armour and weapons knocking against each other. Odysseus was coming.

'This time I will kill you,' Polites announced in a deep, slow voice, staring at Eperitus with a mixture of frustration and hatred.

Sensing the brigands close once more behind him, Eperitus knelt swiftly and picked up the rock he had spotted a moment before. It was smooth, round and large and he had to splay his fingers to fit it in his hand. Raising it above his head, he watched with satisfaction as the look on Polites's face turned to fear and doubt. Then he took aim and threw the rock, hitting the giant square on the forehead. Polites looked at him blankly for a moment, his eyes blinking, before toppling backwards with all the slowness and rigidity of a felled tree.

There was a moment of silence, followed by uproar. The short bandit pushed Arceisius aside and leapt forward, pulling his sword from its scabbard as he rushed across to where Eperitus was now being held by the others, his arms pinned behind his back.

'HALT!' boomed a voice from the slopes above.

Eperitus turned to see Odysseus standing in the trees, his short legs planted firmly apart in the undergrowth and his arms crossed over his broad, muscular chest. Two spears were stuck in the ground beside him and his leather shield was hung across his back. A score of Ithacan soldiers were spread out across the slope, many of them aiming arrows at the bandits.

At the sound of the king's voice, the Thessalians stopped and looked up. The men holding Eperitus pushed him into the centre of the circle and drew their swords. The rest followed suit, and as the short bandit moved forward to the safety of his comrades Arceisius ran across to join his captain, bringing him his cloak. Eperitus threw the garment about himself, then knelt and pulled his squire down with him, wanting to keep as low a profile as possible if the arrows began to fly.

'I am King Odysseus of Ithaca, son of Laertes,' Odysseus announced, his eyes travelling along the raised faces of the bandits. Their shields and spears had been piled in the undergrowth at the foot of the slope – left there as they had formed a circle about Eperitus and Polites – and now no man dared to retrieve them for fear of being shot down by the Ithacan archers. 'You are in my kingdom without my leave. If you want to live, throw down your swords now.'

'Don't be fools,' the short bandit shouted, looking around at his comrades. 'If we throw down our weapons they'll massacre us all. Keep your swords, lads; there are more of us than them – we can still make a fight of it.'

'Think about what you're doing,' Odysseus warned, glaring sternly at them. 'You are trespassers here, and by right I could have had you shot down where you stand moments ago. Don't forget, this is my kingdom – I have an army at my command. The trees all around you are filled with concealed archers; all I have to do is give the word and you will all perish. Antiphus!'

A scruffy archer with a large nose and hollow cheeks stepped forward. He held a tall bow in his right hand, the fore and middle fingers of which had been cut off – a punishment for poaching in his youth. Undeterred, he had simply taught himself to draw the bowstring with his left hand instead, and now stared straight down the shaft of the arrow at the bandit leader. The Thessalian shifted uncomfortably but retained his hold on his sword, whilst his comrades looked nervously at the trees around them, wondering how many more archers were hidden in the undergrowth.

'But I have no intention of murdering you,' Odysseus continued, breaking his harsh stare with a smile. 'I know you're not common brigands, and by the looks of you, you were soldiers once. Thessalians, too – a proud and fearsome people.' There was a murmur of approval from the men on the road. 'If you throw down your arms and take a solemn oath before all the gods not to return to my kingdom, I will allow you safe passage back to the mainland. I'll even give you provisions for a week. What do you say?'

The Thessalians looked at each other, talking and nodding in low voices, then one by one began to throw down their weapons.

'Cowards!' the short bandit shouted at them. 'Idiots! Can't you see he's lying?'

Suddenly the twang of a bowstring sang out from the trees. The bandit staggered backwards, the long shaft of an arrow sticking out from his chest. He clutched at it briefly, trying to pull it free, then the strength drained from his fingers and he fell lifeless to the ground.

Shocked, Eperitus looked up the slope. Instantly his eyes fell on the plump figure of Eurylochus, Odysseus's cousin, his hand still hanging in the air by his ear but the string of his bow empty. There was an arrogant, self-satisfied sneer on his face as he peered down at the man he had shot.

In the moment of shocked silence that followed, Eperitus quickly turned and saw a sword lying in the grass not far from him, where its owner had thrown it down in surrender. Now, though, surrender was the last thing in any of the Thessalians' minds and suddenly they were reaching for the weapons they had cast away. Eperitus sprang forward and swung his fist into the face of a bandit as he stretched a hand towards the sword. The man fell backwards and Eperitus snatched up the weapon, hacking off the outstretched arm of another of the Thessalians as he plucked his own blade from the dust. Arrows were flying all around and men were crying out as they fell. Eperitus grabbed the discarded sword of the warrior whose arm he had severed and tossed it towards Arceisius.

'Here, lad, use this,' he shouted, 'and stick close to me.'

Up on the slope, the Ithacan guardsmen had formed a line of spears either side of Odysseus and were charging down at the lightly armed bandits, howling like Furies as they came. Eperitus smiled grimly to see the men he had trained go into battle – many for the first time – wishing he were with them. Then he sensed movement behind him and turned to see that three of the surviving Thessalians were running directly at him, brandishing their swords. Now, more than ever, Eperitus longed for the comforting weight of his grandfather's leather shield on his arm and rued the fact that, due to his disguise, it had been left leaning idly against a tree at their camp. The first attacker reached him ahead of his comrades and swung his sword down at his head. Eperitus met the blow with his own blade, then threw the Thessalian's arm back and arced his weapon down across his face, slicing through his left eye and the bridge of his nose. The man staggered backwards and fell down the slope on the opposite side of the road.

Arceisius rushed to Eperitus's side, just as the other two bandits joined the attack. Eperitus's opponent quickly proved himself an experienced swordsman, forcing the Ithacan backwards under a ferocious but accurate torrent of blows. The onslaught was met with all the speed and skill that Eperitus's sharp instincts gave him, but his concern for Arceisius kept him distracted and prevented him from pressing his own attack. His worries were unfounded, though: he had spent four years training his squire for combat, teaching him every manoeuvre and trick with sword, shield and spear that he knew; and Arceisius had always proved a quick learner with no mean instinct for fighting. Now the endless drills were showing their worth as Arceisius fended off the Thessalian's probing thrusts with ease. There was no time for the young man to think about what he was doing, only to react intuitively. Within a few moments, he had turned from defence to attack, pushing his opponent back towards the steep slope on the other side of the path.

Eperitus recognized something of his younger self in Arceisius and smiled as he watched the fledgling warrior. Putting his concerns aside, he now turned his full attention on the man before him. He was young and bearded, with a single, angry eyebrow forming a black V across his forehead. His attacks were energetic and accompanied by grunts of exertion, but they were predictable and easy to parry. As Arceisius plunged his sword into his opponent's chest, Eperitus beat aside another attack and began to stab and hack at the Thessalian, forcing him to think and react quicker and quicker as each new thrust came at him. Eventually, Eperitus's skilful onslaught prised his enemy's guard wide open and he pushed the point of his sword into the man's liver. As the Thessalian fell to his knees, Eperitus withdrew his reddened blade from the man's gut and swept his head from his shoulders.

He turned and saw that the battle behind them was already over. Stepping across the corpse, he clapped Arceisius on the shoulder.

'Well done, lad,' he said. 'You showed real skill with that sword.'

'Thanks,' Arceisius replied uncertainly, looking down at the man he had slain. There was a shadow of distaste in his expression – a hint of doubt – but as he sensed his captain's eyes upon him he looked up and forced a smile to his lips. 'Thanks, sir.'

None of the bandits remained standing and at a quick count Eperitus could see that all the Ithacans had survived, which did not surprise him given the fact they had enjoyed the advantage of spears and shields against the swords of the Thessalians. Odysseus stood in the middle of the carnage, the gore running in rivulets down the shaft of his spear. He ignored the pleas of the wounded men around him; they had been given their chance to surrender and now the only mercy they would be shown was a dagger across the throat to quicken their passing.

'You were late,' Eperitus called to him. 'That giant nearly killed me.'

Odysseus smiled cockily. 'I was exactly on time. The fact you're still alive proves it.'

At that moment, Eurylochus came striding across the path to the point where the short bandit's body lay. He seized hold of his arrow, tugged it free from the dead man's chest and proceeded to wipe it clean on the corner of his cloak, but as he slid it back into the leather quiver that hung at his waist, Eperitus grabbed him by the chest and spun him around.

'What do *you* want?' Eurylochus asked indignantly.

'This!'

Eperitus drew back his fist and slammed it into Eurylochus's smug, round face. Blood exploded from his nostrils as the force of the blow sent him staggering backwards. He caught his heel on the corpse of the short bandit and fell in a heap, one hand clutching at his broken nose.

'What in Hades did you do *that* for?' he screamed in a thick voice, trying to stem the blood flow. The other Ithacans, who had been pilfering from the bodies of the Thessalians, stopped what they were doing and looked over.

'Because you deserved it, you oaf,' Eperitus answered angrily. 'What did you think you were doing when you fired that arrow? These men were about to give up, and if you'd held your damned nerve they'd still be alive now.'

There was a murmur of agreement from the others.

'Odysseus!' Eurylochus whined, stretching a pleading hand towards the king. 'You saw what he did. I *demand* you . . .'

'Just shut up, Eurylochus,' Antiphus hissed.

Odysseus held up a hand and an immediate silence fell. 'Step back, Eperitus,' he said. 'You've made your feelings known – now let him be. As for you, cousin, you can count yourself fortunate no

Ithacans died here. If they had I'd have held you responsible. Now, get back to the camp and tell Eurybates we'll be returning as soon as we've buried these men.'

Eurylochus struggled to his feet, still holding his nose.

'You'll pay for this, Eperitus,' he said, spitting blood on the ground at his feet, before turning on his heel and stumbling down the path.

'I know what you're going to say,' Odysseus said, holding his hands up to Eperitus. The authority he had shown a moment before was gone and they were just friends again. 'You warned me he'd put us in danger. I know.'

Eperitus shook his head in mock disapproval, then broke into a smile. 'Well, at least we're unharmed.'

As he spoke, one of the corpses sat up. The Ithacans stepped back in shock and stared at the massive, naked figure of Polites, rubbing the large bruise on his forehead and looking about in confusion. As soon as his eyes fell on Eperitus, though, his expression changed to sudden fury and he struggled to his knees. In a quick movement, Antiphus slipped the bow from his shoulder and fitted an arrow, aiming it straight at the broad chest of the Thessalian.

'Don't shoot!' Odysseus ordered, stepping between them and holding up his hands. He turned to Polites and met his angry stare. 'Look about you. The battle's over and your comrades are dead. I offered them their lives, but the stubborn fools chose to fight.'

Polites stared at the bodies of the other bandits, then at the armed men standing all around him. His puzzlement was clear, but eventually he understood what had happened. He stared up at Odysseus, his eyes dark and bitter.

'Perhaps you intend to kill me too,' he said in his deep, slow voice.

'I shall neither kill you nor banish you,' the king announced. 'You were a soldier once, but now you've fallen on hard times and have turned to less honourable means to feed yourself. Am I right?'

Polites lowered his proud eyes to the ground. 'Yes,' he answered, simply.

'Then I will give you a chance to restore your dignity and take up your former profession again. We could do with another experienced warrior – especially one of your size and power. If you'll take an oath of fealty, you can join my guard under Eperitus's captaincy.'

Odysseus indicated the man who, a short while before, Polites had tried to kill with his bare hands. Polites looked at Eperitus, who met his stare and nodded amicably. After all, he thought, Odysseus was right: what captain would not want a warrior of Polites's massive build and brute strength under his command?

'That would be an honour,' Polites said.

Then the king stepped forward and offered him his hand. After a moment's pause, the Thessalian took it.

## Chapter Four

# APHEIDAS'S REVENGE

'Shush now,' Paris said gently, stroking the broad neck of the excited mare. She pressed her nostrils against his shoulder and blew warm, horse-smelling breath over his skin. 'Be still. You'll get your breakfast and exercise soon enough.'

He withdrew from the affectionate rubbing of the animal's lips and gestured for the youngest of the three grooms, who were watching him with fascination, to join him.

'Even in Troy it's said Spartans are the best horse-breeders in Greece,' he announced, making the boy grin with pride. 'But this girl's special, even by your country's standards. What's her name, lad?'

'Lipse, my lord. After the wind goddess.'

'A good name,' Paris nodded. 'But if you want her to live up to it, you need to feed her better. Put more corn in her food and give her plenty of treats – my own horse likes grapes. Most importantly, you need to exercise her on the plains, not here in the palace courtyard. She needs her freedom, even if it's only for a short while every day. Give her that and you'll soon see the sort of horse she can really become.'

He gave the groom's shoulder a squeeze, before leaning over and offering the palm of his hand to the pure-black mare. She nudged it gently with her soft nose.

'Sir?' said one of the other grooms tentatively. 'Sir, how do you make the animals love you so much?'

'Make them?' Paris replied, arching his eyebrows slightly and shaking his head. 'No man can *make* a creature love him – he must earn its love through kindness and trust.'

'But you've only been here a few moments, sir, and already the horses act as if they've known you all their lives.'

Paris lowered himself onto his haunches and beckoned the boys to come closer. 'I can see there's no fooling you three,' he conceded, looking into their eyes as they sat before him. 'Well, I'll tell you my secret, but you're not to share it with anyone, do you understand?'

They nodded eagerly, and with a conspiratorial glance over his shoulder, Paris began the strange tale of his childhood. On the day he was born, he told them, a prophecy decreed that he would bring about the ruin of Troy. Though loath to kill his own child, King Priam was eventually persuaded to give the task to his chief herdsman. But Agelaus did not have the heart to run the baby through or drown him, so he abandoned him to his fate on the foothills of Mount Ida. When, five days later, he found the baby still alive and being suckled by a she-bear, Agelaus decided to bring him up as his own. Whether it was something in the beast's milk, or simply a gift of the gods, Paris grew up with the ability to gain the trust of any creature. The sheep in his flocks loved him dearly and followed him everywhere, and no wolf, lion or other wild beast would ever attack them so long as Paris was nearby. This same skill gave him the ability to train fighting bulls, for which he became famous throughout Ilium. When Priam himself ordered Paris to bring his best bull to sacrifice at Troy, the boy's nobility was impossible to disguise and Agelaus was forced to confess that Paris was the king's son. Having been wracked by guilt ever since ordering the infant's death, Priam ignored the old prophecy and welcomed Paris back into his family. He was made a prince, second only to Hector, the king's eldest son.

'But I've never lost the power to win the love of wild creatures,' Paris concluded, standing and smiling at the enthralled grooms. 'Be they horses, wolves, or even the birds of the air. I must go now, but I promise you I'll come again. And don't forget what I said about Lipse.'

He turned and walked further along the lines of restless horses. Every animal in Menelaus's stable was alert to his presence, each one pressing up against the wooden bars of the pens as he walked by. The rich odour of straw and dung filled his senses and reminded him of Troy, but his ever-present longing for his homeland was tempered by an unexpected reluctance to leave Sparta. It was now the third day since his arrival, and though he had no love for the austere city and its hostile people, their queen had cast a spell over him that had thrown his thoughts and emotions into turmoil. One flash of Helen's blue eyes had filled him with a madness that had cut into his very soul, disturbing his once peaceful conscience and threatening to rob him of his self-control. He had lain awake all night after the feast – during which he had eaten very little – thinking of Helen, seeing her face in the corners of his mind and recalling the look she had given him as she had left the great hall, a look that seemed filled with a longing to match his own. Was it possible that such a godlike woman could set her heart upon a hardened warrior like himself? The thought chased away all prospect of sleep and he had risen before dawn to roam the palace corridors in the hope of encountering her.

But he saw neither Helen nor Menelaus for the whole of that day, and to his disappointment only the king was present at the feast that evening. Menelaus apologized for his lack of hospitality during the day, as he was busy preparing for a visit to his grandfather in Crete; but he assured the Trojans he would be able to discuss the purpose of their mission within a few days. Until then he cordially offered them the freedom of his palace, although at this point the king's gaze rested briefly on Paris, as if he knew the malady that had struck his guest and the thoughts that were in his mind. Indeed, Paris did not see Helen the following day or night either, and the worry he might never set eyes on her again deprived him of yet more sleep and drove away all but the most rudimentary appetite. Before arriving in Sparta his life had been simple: he was a Trojan warrior, honour-bound to serve his king and country without question, earning glory where possible or death if required. Helen, though, had purged him of these trivialities and left him with nothing but a yearning to be with her – a hunger that could only be satisfied by stealing her from Menelaus and making her his own.

It was a shameful thought for a man of honour, but one which he could not free himself from despite all the arguments against it. The consequences of such an act were unguessable. Certainly his mission would fail and Hesione would never be returned to Troy. And even if he succeeded in taking Helen with him, Menelaus would surely do everything in his power to bring her back. These were the least of Paris's concerns, though. His noble blood and tough upbringing had given him the courage to take whatever he wanted, but to kidnap Helen from under her husband's nose meant going against his sense of duty to his father and his country. Ironically, such an act would also make him worse than Telamon, who when he took Hesione from Troy had at least been able to claim her as a spoil of war. But the greatest obstacle would be Helen herself. When he had looked into her eyes he had seen a trapped animal, longing to be free of its gilded cage. He could sense her pain, the pain of a free spirit slowly being crushed to death, and he had wanted to be the one to release her from that. But unless she wanted him in return then he could not force her to leave – not without the fear that he had removed her from one cage, only to earn her contempt by placing her into another.

This internal struggle between conscience and desire had dominated his thoughts when he should have been thinking of his mission. After the third night of feasting, when Helen was absent and her husband had again avoided all talk of the Trojans' purpose in Greece, he fought against his growing tiredness and rose early again to wander the palace corridors in contemplation of the Spartan queen. But as the dawn brought a day of difficult decisions and far-ranging choices, he found his old self returning in strength. The honour-bound soldier, the loyal Trojan and the dutiful son fought back with renewed vigour against the obsession with Helen. She could never be his, he told himself: she was married, and a foreigner whose background and customs were not his own, while he had a responsibility to his mission, his father and to his country that would not be denied. Even if Helen was willing to leave Sparta with him, her wild beauty would change his ordered life beyond recognition. The honour and pride that were the pillars of his existence would be pulled down for the sake of a woman he had only seen once, and as he thought of what it would mean to follow his heart and surrender everything for her he felt suddenly afraid. In a moment everything became clear: he must leave for Mycenae tonight, or risk stepping into an abyss, changing everything for ever.

He passed from the stables out into the broad palace courtyard. The quiet, moonlit space of the first night he had arrived was now filled with activity. A dozen slaves with wooden rakes were smoothing out the hoof-prints and wheel ruts of the previous day, only to see the neatly furrowed dirt trampled again by scores of servants hurrying about their early morning duties. Sleepy soldiers stumbled from their barracks, adjusting their armour as they went yawning to their posts, while over by the gates a group of light horsemen were discussing the morning's patrol, their mounts snorting and stamping with impatience. The sky above was flushed pink with the first light of dawn, and from the roofs and treetops of Sparta an army of birds were greeting the morning in song.

Paris did not share their enthusiasm. Feeling frustrated and moody, he lowered his head and walked across the newly levelled soil to the palace. Inside, the cool, gloomy interior was thick with bustling slaves, few of whom had time to take notice of the foreign prince. Weaving his way between them, he came to a flight of stairs and leapt up them two at a time, hoping to find somewhere to be alone with his troubled thoughts. Fortunately, the upper level was deserted except for a young slave girl sweeping the corridor. She stared at Paris with indignation – making him suspect he had entered the women's quarters – but he ignored her and continued up the narrow, white-walled passageway. Unlike the lower level, which was an organized collection of large, functional rooms feeding off from a central hallway, the floor above was a maze of corridors and small rooms where he soon became lost.

His dark looks as he moved through the upper level of the palace caused several slaves to avoid his eye or move aside. When he stopped one of them and demanded to know where the Trojans had been billeted, the old man could do little more than point and give hurried directions in a shaking voice. Paris strode on. He intended to discuss his plans with Apheidas and Aeneas, see his men fed, and then demand an audience with Menelaus regarding Hesione. The fact the Spartan king had witnessed the look that had passed between Paris and Helen on that first night would almost guarantee his agreement – he would want the foreigners away from Sparta and his wife as quickly as possible.

It was as these thoughts raced through his mind that Paris heard a sudden burst of laughter coming from one of the windows ahead of him. Despite his grim mood, he stopped at the window and looked out onto a small, rectangular garden below. It was enclosed by a high wall and bordered by spring flowers, whose rich scents reached as high as the upper window. In the middle of the garden was a circular pond covered with lily pads, through which Paris could see the flitting shapes of large, golden fish. Around the pond was a lawn where four children – three boys and a little girl – were chasing each other and laughing merrily. But Paris's gaze was immediately drawn to the slim, black-haired woman seated on a stone bench beside the pond. She was dressed in a dark blue robe that covered her shoulders against the morning chill, but fell open slightly to reveal the white chiton beneath.

Initially her hair shielded her face from his eyes, but with a sudden rush of nervousness he knew it was Helen. A moment later she lifted her face to the sky and with an easy movement of her slender fingers tucked the long strands of hair behind her ears. Paris stepped back from the window, where he could watch her from the cover of the shadows. When he had first seen her she had enthralled him with her untamed beauty, but now he looked on her with astonishment as her purity and perfection were revealed to him by the daylight. She lowered her face again to look at the children – her children – and as Paris saw the loving smile she gave them his heart yearned for her to smile at him in the same way. Then he remembered that he had resolved to leave Sparta before nightfall and a great swell of sadness and anger washed through him.

The smallest of the boys ran to his mother, who folded him into her arms and covered him with kisses. The child's face – like those of his siblings – showed a clear physical resemblance to both Helen and Menelaus, proving Helen's faithfulness to her marriage bed. And despite the withered hand that the boy held tucked into his chest, Paris envied him.

'Magnificent, isn't she?' whispered a voice over Paris's shoulder.

The prince turned with a start and saw Apheidas in the shadows. 'What are you doing here?' he said impatiently.

'Looking for you. Nobody's seen you since the feast.'

'I've been minding my own business, Apheidas. There are times when I wish you'd do the same.'

'Now, now,' the older man tutted with an amused smile. 'Besides, isn't it the business of both of us to seek the return of Hesione? That *is* why we're here, isn't it?'

'Keep your voice down,' Paris hissed as Helen's head turned in the direction of the window. 'Of course that's why we're here. What else do you think's kept me awake all night?'

'I'm glad to hear you're focused, Paris,' Apheidas replied tartly. 'Hector told me to give you my full support, and I want to see the mission succeed just as much as you do. It just irks me that, whatever we say, the Greeks are still going to send us back to Troy with nothing more than bellies full of their tough food and bitter wine. After all, if we're made to look like fools then Priam and the whole of Ilium will look like fools with us.'

'We won't go back empty-handed or looking like fools, Apheidas,' Paris snapped, wishing the man would leave him alone.

'Besides, I imagine you're more worried about your own pride than my father's.'

'A man's pride is his motivation, but unlike you, *my* motivation has been thinking of ways to achieve our mission.' Apheidas waited for Paris to react, but the prince merely narrowed his eyes and remained silent. 'Anyway, the Greeks hurt my pride ten years ago when they drove me out, and I don't intend to pass up this chance to have my revenge.'

'We're not here to satisfy your stung pride, so just forget whatever it is you're dreaming up and concentrate on what *I* tell you to do.'

'Our success will be all the revenge I need, Paris. Nothing else. And if you really want to see Hesione returned and Troy's honour restored, then you'd better listen to what I've got to say.'

Paris felt his anger rising again. 'You're forgetting yourself, Apheidas,' he warned. 'Hesione's *my* father's sister and I want her back home as much as anyone, but it won't be as simple as you seem to think. Has it occurred to you she might not *want* to return to Troy with us, whether she's given leave to by the Greeks or not? Why would she give up her home and family to return to a place she hasn't seen for years?'

'Who cares *what* the stupid woman wants?' Apheidas retorted. 'We've been given a mission to take her home to Troy, and it's your duty to carry it out. And if you haven't got the guts, then I'll do it myself.'

There was a long, tense moment as the men stared at each other, punctuated by the laughing of the children below and the smooth voice of their mother. Apheidas had directly challenged Paris's authority, an act that no commander could tolerate if he expected to maintain his position. But Apheidas was always standing up to those above him, and most had learned to tolerate this fault with magnanimity because it was outweighed by his excellence in battle. And perhaps Paris was in the wrong. He had assumed too much of Hector's attitude – that they would never bring Hesione back and the best they could do was to spy on the

Greeks and come back with a reason to make war on them in the future; however, it was Priam's wish that his sister be returned to Troy and the city's pride be restored along with her. And Priam was still the king.

'All right, tell me what you're thinking.'

Apheidas smiled. 'Simple. The Greeks took one of ours; I say we take one of theirs in return.'

He indicated the garden with his thumb.

'Only a fool would suggest something as ridiculous as that,' Paris snapped, shaking his head.

'Think about it, Paris,' Apheidas countered. 'Having her will give us the upper hand when it comes to bargaining for Hesione's return. And if the Greeks aren't interested then Troy will at least have its pride back – and you can have Helen for your own.'

He leaned back against the wall and gave the prince a knowing glance. Paris looked away, doubt furrowing his brow. Having just convinced himself that he must leave Sparta at once for the sake of his mission and his honour, his second-in-command was offering him a way to resolve all his dilemmas with one fell deed. Was it madness to consider such a possibility? he asked himself. But as he considered Apheidas's words, he realized that it was not. To kidnap Helen would be to *fulfil* his mission, not *abandon* it. Troy's pride would be reinstated and Priam would be able to offer Helen in exchange for Hesione. The Greeks would never agree, of course, and Hector would get his war. More importantly, Paris would have Helen for himself without betraying his mission, his father or his homeland. It was as if the gods had spoken to him, and yet his excitement was checked by uncertainty. He looked back down at the garden, his eyes dark as he stared at the oblivious Helen.

'I won't deny the gods have blinded me with Helen's beauty, Apheidas – a fact you seem fully aware of – or that I have already thought of taking her back to Troy with us. But Menelaus is our host and I like him, even if he is a Greek. What's more, to take Helen would be a dishonourable act, an offence to the gods.'

'Sometimes we must swallow our pride if we are to have our heart's desire,' Apheidas said earnestly. 'And as for offending the gods, don't you realize that our very presence here is their doing? It's by their will that we – *you* – are fated to take Helen back to Troy. In your pride, don't forget your mortality and the fact you are a pawn of the immortals.'

'You know it will mean war.'

'War's been brewing for years,' Apheidas said dismissively. 'The Greeks are growing all the time, and we Trojans are looking westward for a bit of elbow-room ourselves. It won't be long before one side goes too far, and then it'll be a war to the death – our culture against theirs. And the sooner we get the chance to wipe them out the better!'

Paris nodded, resigning himself to Apheidas's argument and, with it, the unknown future he had feared and rejected not long before. 'And how do you suggest we smuggle the queen of Sparta out of her own palace?'

'Menelaus departs for Crete in five days. It's a journey he can't postpone, but after that look Helen gave you the other night – oh yes, I saw it – he'll want to send us on our way before he leaves. We have to convince him to let us stay.'

'How?'

'Demand to speak with him today. Tell him the reason your father sent you here and ask him to send messages to Agamemnon and Telamon, requesting an audience on neutral ground in Mycenae. That'll give us a reason to wait in Sparta until we receive their response, by which time Menelaus will have sailed for Crete. He won't trust us, of course, but if you can make him swear an oath of friendship the customs of *xenia* will oblige him to let you stay here. And once he's gone, we'll steal his wife and head home.'

'And what if Helen doesn't want to leave – have you thought of that?'

Apheidas gave another of his self-assured smiles and looked down at the garden. 'She will. Her eyes may have been on you the other night, but I could see what was burning inside them. It's obvious she doesn't love Menelaus. She's like a trapped animal, desperate to escape.'

'There's no escape with a face like hers,' Paris replied. 'Men will follow her to the ends of the world. But even if you're right in everything you say, you're forgetting her children. We'll be hard pushed to take them with us, so your whole plan relies on her giving them up.'

'That will depend on how much she wants her freedom,' Apheidas said. 'But if she won't leave them behind, then we'll just take her without them.'

'No,' Paris said, firmly. 'I will gladly endanger my life trying to get her out of Sparta; I will even surrender my honour for her sake; but I will not force her to leave against her wishes, with or without her children. To do that would be to make Troy her new prison, and myself a new Menelaus!'

'Then you must find a way to speak with her, my lord,' Apheidas insisted. 'If you want her consent, then you must get it as soon as you can. In the meantime, I'll find Eteoneus and demand an audience.'

Apheidas rushed off and Paris returned to the window, only to find the garden below quiet and empty. His spirits plunged, but only for a moment as the thought of taking Helen with him to Troy quickly revived his mood. Apheidas's foolhardy plan would require suicidal courage and recklessness, but the risk had to be taken. It was the will of the gods, and what was more, Paris had finally accepted he would never find peace again without Helen at his side.

Helen sat by the pond and watched her children playing, aware that the Trojan prince was looking down at her from one of the upper windows. Her youngest son, Pleisthenes, ran to her and she wrapped her arms about him, enjoying the warmth of his small body against hers. She kissed his hair and sent him off to play again with his brothers and sister, telling him not to overexert himself because of his weak chest.

As he joined their game with enthusiastic energy, heedless of his mother's warning, she thought back to the feast three nights ago when she had first seen Paris. As soon as news reached Sparta that a delegation from Troy was approaching, she had left her quarters and joined her husband in the great hall, keen to see for herself these visitors from distant shores. Not that she had any interest in political embassies and the machinations of power, despite being a queen and the daughter of a king; rather she wanted to see their foreign garb and hear their rough, barbarian tongue being spoken; to look on their faces and imagine for herself their distant country and how different it would be to Sparta.

But Menelaus had demanded she return to her room, angrily insisting that it was the king's place to entertain such visitors and he did not want them distracted by her beauty, as so many before had been. He was only the king by marriage to her, she reminded him with equal venom, and she was still Sparta's queen; after all, he could not keep her out of the sight of every man who visited Troy! Menelaus had opened his mouth to answer her back, but at that moment the Trojan delegation arrived, ushered into the great hall by Eteoneus. Menelaus quickly composed himself, but as Helen's curiosity drew her into the circle of light thrown out by the circular hearth, she could not hide the frustrated rage still burning within her. Then her eyes met those of the Trojan prince and she felt something slipping within her, as if the props that held up her unhappy world were all collapsing at once. Was it because of her snap argument with Menelaus? Or was it because she had felt stifled by his jealous love for ten years and suddenly yearned for release? Was it because she had *always* wanted to escape Sparta, her prison since childhood, but marriage and motherhood had made her forget that? Or was it simply because there was something in the eyes of the scarred warrior on the other side of the flames that had reached into her heart and promised to set her free?

She did not know. All she did know was that she wanted this

strange foreign prince like she had never wanted any man before, and that he wanted her too. Not only had she read it in his eyes, but since that evening the maids who took the Trojans their food and fresh clothing every day had told her how he would question them about her. Though his interest seemed innocent at first – polite enquiries about the wife of the king – they quickly sensed the urgency of a man in love, too clumsy to hide his feelings. And now, though Menelaus had done everything in his power to keep her out of the Trojan's sight, he had found his way into the women's quarters and was watching her in her private garden. She felt the nervousness rising in her stomach at his sudden closeness, but knew at once what she had to do.

❦

Hurriedly retracing his way to a flight of stairs he had passed a little earlier, Paris bounded down the stone steps three at a time and turned immediately right in the direction of the great hall.

'What's your hurry, Trojan?' said a voice from the shadows of a side passage, startling him.

Paris turned and saw Helen.

She stepped into the diffused half-light of the main corridor and leaned back against the wall, pressing the flats of her hands against the smooth plaster and arching her back so that her robe fell open across her breasts. The thin material of the chiton beneath revealed every detail of her flawless body, which she wantonly displayed to Paris's gaze. Then her wilful eyes met his and did not turn away.

'I saw you watching me in the garden,' she continued, tipping her head to one side and raising her eyebrows slightly. 'What is it you want from me, Paris, son of Priam?'

He was tempted to say 'everything', but his warrior instinct warned him to take care. To rush in, to reveal his feelings and plans to her, would be to lose her respect. She was playing a game with him – probing his strengths, just as so many enemy captains had done on Troy's northern borders. But he had defeated them all and made many his captives, and he would do the same with Helen, even though every muscle and nerve in his body was crying out to take her in his arms and reveal his feelings for her with a kiss.

'I need to talk with you, my lady,' he replied.

'Then talk. There's no one else here but you and me.' She stood and drew the folds of her robe loosely across her chiton, before stepping forward so that her body was almost touching his. 'What is it you want to say, my prince?'

Paris sensed she was challenging him to touch her or step away, knowing that he wanted her but that at any moment someone could turn a corner and see them. But beneath her display of boldness – beneath her confidence in her own sexuality – he detected a flutter of uncertainty caused by his own nearness, as if she was afraid she might fail the challenge herself.

'Not now,' he said, holding her gaze. 'Not here. I must speak with you in private, where there is no risk of being overheard.'

'You are asking much, Paris. Menelaus is a kind and loving husband, but his jealousy is ferocious. That is why you have not seen me since the first night you arrived here. The fact you have met me this morning is only by the slightest chance.'

'Or the work of the gods,' Paris added.

Helen smiled. 'Perhaps. But one can't always count on their intervention, so I sent my maid to your room last night.'

Paris's heart jumped.

'But I wasn't there; I couldn't sleep.'

'So she told me. She had a message for you.'

'What message?'

Helen reached up and ran her finger down the length of the scar that dissected his face.

'It seems we both want the same thing, Paris. It asked for you to meet me in the temple of Aphrodite at sunset tomorrow.'

Paris was suddenly overpowered by the need to kiss her, but as his hands closed about her waist she seemed to melt from his fingers and return to the shadows.

'Where is this temple?' he called after her as she ran down the passage.

'You'll find it,' she called back, laughing.

And then she was gone.

## Chapter Five

# STORM WARNING

The Thessalians were buried in a small clearing not far from the track where they had been killed. Even with Polites's immense and tireless strength, it still took the Ithacans until noon to dig a grave wide and deep enough to lay the bodies in, with their shields and weapons beside them. Normally, any captured armament would have been taken back to stock the palace armoury, but as an act of respect and conciliation to Polites, Odysseus had allowed the men to be buried with full honour. Finally, they built a mound of large rocks to mark the grave and, leaving Polites to say farewell to his comrades, returned to the track. A great cry erupted from the clearing behind them – halfway between despair and triumph – as if Polites was calling on the gods themselves to come and claim the fallen.

Later, as the Ithacans made their way back to their camp at the edge of the wood, Eperitus watched the hulking figure of the Thessalian ahead of him, walking beside Arceisius. The young squire was chatting merrily, telling the giant warrior all about Ithaca, its people and their customs, whilst Polites walked in silence, with only an occasional grunt in response to show he was listening at all.

'Today has been a good day,' Odysseus said as he walked beside Eperitus at the back of the file of men. 'The bandits are all dead with no Ithacans hurt, and we've gained two new soldiers into the bargain.'

'Two?' asked Antiphus, who was strolling along at Odysseus's other shoulder, his bow strapped across his back.

'Polites and Arceisius. The lad fought well today, don't you think, Eperitus?'

'He's got the natural instincts of a fighter,' Eperitus confirmed, smiling with paternal pride. Arceisius's father had been killed during the Taphian occupation of Ithaca ten years before, and since then Eperitus had looked after him as if he were his own son. 'It won't be long now before he can become a full member of the guard.'

'What's stopping him?' Antiphus asked. 'You're not going to make him wait until he gets rid of those feathers round his chin and grows a proper beard are you?'

Odysseus and Antiphus laughed loudly, making Arceisius throw a questioning glance over his shoulder.

'Of course not,' Eperitus replied, shooting his companions an admonishing glance. 'I just think he needs a little longer, that's all.'

Eperitus thought of the look in Arceisius's eye after he had killed his man – a glimmer of doubt or regret – and wondered whether he truly desired to be a warrior. Time would tell, he assured himself.

'Well, there's no hurry – it's not as if we're at war,' Odysseus said, still grinning. 'But what do you think of the Thessalian? Will he be true to the oath he swore?'

'I think you took a risk with him, my lord,' Antiphus answered. 'But your instincts have always proved good, and I trust them now. You were the one who had to fight him though, Eperitus. What do you say?'

Eperitus remembered the awful power in Polites's arms and the iron-like strength of his grasping fingers, and gave a shudder. 'He's slow and he can't think on his feet,' he announced. 'He relies entirely on his strength, and that's a weakness. But, in the name of Ares, he's got enough muscle for three men and he's aggressive with it – he'll kill most men with ease, and enjoy it. As for his oath, Odysseus, I think he's got just enough intelligence to understand honour, but not enough for treachery. He should serve us well.'

'A good assessment,' said a voice from the side of the road.

All three men turned sharply to their left and drew their swords. At the same time, Arceisius whirled about and pulled a dagger from his belt, whilst Polites squinted stupidly into the shadows beneath the trees. There, sitting on a large boulder, was an ancient-looking man with a long beard and a shabby brown cloak, which was pulled about his knees. Despite his deeply lined, leathery skin and his silver hair, his large, round eyes were full of vigour and observed them keenly.

'Good morning to you, father,' Odysseus greeted him, sliding his sword back into its scabbard. 'You caught us by surprise just then. Is there anything we can do for you?'

The old man stared at the king, a faint smile just visible beneath the wispy strands of his moustache, but did not reply. Eperitus called to the rest of the file to halt then, replacing his sword, stepped forward and looked at the curious figure seated before them.

'Answer your king when he addresses you,' he ordered, trying to keep the anger from his voice.

'Forgive my friend,' Odysseus apologized. 'He doesn't realize you're not from these islands. You aren't an Ithacan, are you, or I'm sure I'd know your face?'

'I'm a visitor here,' the old man admitted, 'though I know these islands well. And I know you, too, King Odysseus.'

'Then tell us who *you* are, greybeard,' Eperitus insisted. His subtle senses detected something strange about the old man that set his instincts on edge.

The old man chuckled to himself. 'The years haven't calmed your impetuosity I see, Eperitus,' he said, shaking his head slowly.

Eperitus shot a glance at Odysseus, who returned his shocked expression with a shrug of his shoulders. Behind them, the assembled soldiers who had come to see why the march back to camp had been halted murmured to each other in confusion. Then the old man leapt lightly down from the boulder and swept his hand in an arc before them. At once, everyone except Odysseus and Eperitus fell unconscious to the floor.

The two men sprang back and pulled out their swords again, staring about at their sleeping comrades and then at the figure before them. He was as tall and straight as an ash spear, and his eyes burned intensely as he stared at them. Though his brown cloak was still held tightly about his body, it glowed as if a brilliant light was fighting to escape from beneath it.

'Don't be afraid,' he said, but as he spoke his voice was strangely changed – deeper and yet unmistakably female.

Odysseus threw down his weapon and fell to his knees, covering his face against the fingers of white light that were escaping from the folds of the cloak. Eperitus – confused and half-blinded – clutched the handle of his sword tighter and squinted against the light, readying himself for an attack. The figure of the old man was now almost completely lost in the blaze of light that was coming from his body. The features of his face were no longer discernible, and even as Eperitus tried to look at him he seemed to grow in height. Then a strong wind swept through the trees, shaking the branches and flattening the young ferns, tearing open the man's cloak so that it disintegrated into a hundred fragments and was blown away in an explosion of intense light. Eperitus staggered backwards, his vision an impenetrable wall of searing white, and fell over the sleeping body of Antiphus.

He lay on his back, his eyelids closed but his retinas still filled with the light. Then, as suddenly as it had come, the brightness faded and the comparatively dull radiance of day returned. Eperitus opened his eyes and saw branches overhead, creeping like black veins into the corners of his vision. Still fearful of an attack, and feeling dreadfully exposed with his senses stunned and reeling, he strained his ears against the diminishing wind. Twigs crunched nearby under a heavy weight, then a hand seized his ankle.

'Eperitus! Eperitus, wake up!' Odysseus said, shaking his leg.

'I'm awake,' Eperitus replied, sitting up and blinking at the king, who was on his hands and knees before him.

'Stop lying around like a pair of drunkards and start showing some respect!' said a voice. The tone was clear, commanding and familiar to both men.

They turned and squinted at the towering, marble-skinned woman standing where the old man had been moments before. She wore a pure white chiton that shimmered with an internal brilliance, filling the wood with light and making it difficult for either man to look at her for longer than a few moments at a time. Draped across her shoulders and left arm was a leather shawl edged with golden tassels, from the centre of which leered the hideous face of a gorgon, its eyes firmly shut but its fanged mouth frozen in a snarl. In her right hand she held a gigantic spear, as tall as two men, and on top of her plaited, golden hair was a bronze helmet, pushed back to reveal a face that was both beautiful and terrifying to behold. Her large grey eyes looked at them with stern expectancy.

Odysseus recognized the goddess at once. 'Mistress Athena,' he whispered, letting go of Eperitus's leg and pressing his forehead and the palms of his hands to the ground.

Eperitus quickly followed his example.

'King Odysseus of Ithaca, son of Laertes,' she boomed; then, in a much gentler manner, 'stand up and let me look at you. How long's it been since I last saw you?'

'Ten years, my lady,' Odysseus replied, getting slowly to his feet and daring to look up at the goddess. 'In the temple where you brought Eperitus back from the dead.'

'That long?' she asked, smiling broadly. 'To me it seems like only yesterday – we immortals don't count the years as you do. And yet,' she added, turning to Eperitus, '*you* seem hardly to have aged at all – despite the beard. Doubtless that'll be the effect of my healing you. Are your senses still as sharp, Eperitus?'

'Yes, my lady, although I've become more used to them now.'

'He has the instincts of a boarhound,' Odysseus put in.

'Does he now?' Athena asked, narrowing her eyes at Eperitus. 'A boarhound's first instinct is unswerving loyalty to its master – to stay at his side and serve his will before its own. Is that true of you, Eperitus?'

Eperitus looked into the goddess's eyes and saw his most secret desires reflected back at him. His friendship with Odysseus and his strict sense of honour had kept him at the king's side for ten years, but the peaceful boredom of Ithaca was no place for a warrior. Odysseus had his beloved kingdom and people to care for, and soon his precious Penelope would bear him a child – a son to carry on his memory long after Hermes had conducted his soul down to the realm of Hades. But Eperitus had no kingdom or family; his desire had always been to win eternal glory on the battlefield, a legacy to be measured by the bodies of his foes. On clear days, he would often climb to the lookout post on Mount Neriton and cast his gaze over the world, wondering what adventures were calling to him from beyond the hazy horizons. And always his eyes would turn eventually to the north – to Alybas, where his father had killed the king and set himself upon the throne. The shame of his father's treachery still stung ten years later, and Eperitus's thoughts had turned more and more to righting the wrong that had been done – to seeking out his father and wiping away the stain of dishonour that remained on his family's name.

But that would mean leaving Ithaca and breaking his oath to Odysseus, an oath that he had taken before Athena herself. As Eperitus looked at the goddess, he was certain she knew about the desires that had been eating away at him. He lowered his gaze.

'I am not a dog, mistress,' he muttered. 'But I have sworn to serve the king, and I remain a man of honour.'

'Good,' Athena said. 'For Odysseus will need you soon, more than he has ever done. A storm is approaching that will shake the world of men to its roots and plunge the whole of Greece into darkness.'

Odysseus, who had been looking inquisitively at Eperitus, now turned to the goddess. 'Ithaca too?' he asked.

'Yes, my dear Odysseus, even your happy little kingdom. A war is brewing that will wreak death and destruction beyond the imaginings of gods and men. And when it comes, even your scheming brain and quick wits won't be able to save you or your people from its effects.'

'War?' Odysseus repeated, as if the word were new to him. 'Then is this why you've come to me again, after all this time? To warn me?'

Athena stepped towards him and ran her fingers through his long, auburn hair. 'I've never been apart from you, Odysseus, even if you haven't seen me. But, yes, I have come to warn you. I'm forbidden to say exactly what my father Zeus has in mind, but you will realize soon enough. Remember what the Pythoness told you in the caves below Mount Parnassus: "As father of your people you will count the harvests on your fingers. But if ever you seek Priam's city, the wide waters will swallow you. For the time it takes a baby to become a man, you will know no home. Then, when friends and fortune have departed from you, you will rise again from the dead."'

Odysseus lowered his face and frowned, his eyes moving as the thoughts raced through his brain, piecing together the fragments of information that had been scattered before him. Then, after a few moments silence, he looked up at the goddess. 'A war against Troy – the city in my dream,' he said. 'Agamemnon wanted it ten years ago, and no doubt he still does. But if he couldn't unite the Greeks then, how will he do it now? And how can any war last for the time it takes a baby to become a man? What could keep a man from his home and family for twenty years?'

'The same things that men have always fought over,' Athena commented sardonically. 'But you should not try to foresee the future, Odysseus – prophecy is not one of your gifts. And remember, the words of the oracle are always enigmatic.'

'But the Pythoness only said these things would happen *if* Odysseus goes to Troy,' Eperitus added. 'That means he still has a choice.'

'Choice is an illusion that brings misery,' Athena replied. 'You mortals are always regretting your choices, after all. But you're right, Eperitus – a choice of sorts remains.'

'Then I will not go,' Odysseus said, firmly. 'I *can't* go! I'm king of these islands, and if there are dark times ahead then my duty is to protect my kingdom and its people.'

'Nobly spoken, Odysseus,' Athena smiled, though her grey eyes looked sadly at the man over whom they had watched all his short life. 'But there are things more compelling than kingdoms – sacred duties and binding oaths . . .'

'*No!*' Odysseus shouted, turning away and staring into the trees. After a time spent in silence, he turned back to face the goddess. 'No, my lady. I have a wife who I love more than all the things this sweet life can offer – a woman for whom I gambled everything, and who will soon be the mother of the son I have hoped for for so long. My place is with my family, and nothing Agamemnon can offer or threaten will draw me to war with Troy.'

'And you, Eperitus?' the goddess asked, turning her unyielding gaze on the captain of the guard. 'How will you react if the call to war comes? There will be more glory to be had in Ilium than even your courageous heart can long for – will you follow your yearning for battle?'

She did not move, but Eperitus felt the strength of Athena's will upon him, tempting him with his desire to seek fame against the armies of Troy and using it to test his loyalty to his friend.

'My place is at the king's side,' he insisted, looking from the stern eyes of the goddess to the impassive face of Odysseus. 'If war is coming, I will wait for it on Ithaca with Odysseus.'

'A friend's loyalty can be tried in many ways,' Athena persevered. 'Have you forgotten the words the priestess spoke to you under Mount Parnassus?'

Eperitus thought of the oracle's bitter-sweet promise, of glory mixed with the threat of his own treachery for love's sake. 'No, my lady. Her warning has never been far from my mind, and I've always been cautious of women because of it.'

'Even a cautious man can be caught off his guard,' Athena said. 'A time is coming when a female will tempt you from the path of your true destiny, but that cannot be avoided now. When a man called Calchas finds you, listen to what he says. His words will point you to your greatest desire, and warn of your greatest fear.'

She turned to Odysseus and looked at him with undisguised affection. 'Now I must return to Olympus, but before I do I have some parting words for you, Odysseus.'

'Yes, my lady?'

'I know you were thinking of staying on Samos for a few days and hunting boar,' the goddess began, glancing across at Polites and Arceisius who were already stirring, 'but you must forget your plans and return home as quickly as you can. Penelope is already in labour.'

And with her final words ringing in their ears, the goddess was gone.

## Chapter Six
# NEW BEGINNINGS

'What happened?' Arceisius asked, rubbing his head as he sat amongst a knot of ferns. 'I feel like I've been asleep for a week.'

'Get up,' snapped Odysseus, pulling him roughly to his feet. 'We're going back to Ithaca, straight away.'

The others were stirring and looking about themselves in confusion. Antiphus took Eperitus's hand and, with an exaggerated groan, rose to his feet. He patted the dead leaves from his cloak and looked his captain in the eye.

'What's going on, Eperitus? Why did we just fall asleep like that? And where's that old man?'

Eperitus glanced across at Odysseus, who was helping Polites out of a clump of thick fern. The king caught his eye and, after a moment's pause, walked over and placed an arm about Antiphus's shoulder.

'He wasn't just an old man,' the king said in a low voice. 'He – I mean *she* – was Athena.'

'Athena!' Arceisius exclaimed loudly, catching the king's words. 'The *goddess* Athena?'

'Of course the goddess,' said Eperitus irritably, gesturing for his squire to keep his voice down. 'She appeared to Odysseus and me after she'd put you lot to sleep.'

'But why would an immortal appear to you?' asked Polites in his deep, ponderous voice. 'The gods haven't spoken with men since before our grandfathers were born.'

'You've a lot to learn if that's what you think,' Antiphus sniffed, looking at the Thessalian with something between dislike and distrust. 'Athena has shown herself to Odysseus many times before now. The king is her favourite.'

'That's enough, Antiphus,' Odysseus ordered. He had told his close friends some years before that the goddess had appeared to him and Eperitus on Mount Parnassus and at her temple in Messene, and the news had quickly become common knowledge throughout Ithaca; but the king still felt uncomfortable whenever people mentioned it. 'The fact is, she came to tell me that Penelope is in labour and that I should return home as soon as possible.'

'Zeus's beard!' Antiphus shouted, causing the rest of the men to look over. 'But Actoris said the child wouldn't come for at least three weeks.'

Odysseus adjusted the shield on his back and picked up his spears. 'Actoris is only a nursemaid,' he said. 'Artemis is the goddess of childbirth and it's she who decides when and how a child comes into the world. So, with your permission, Antiphus, I'd like to set off for Ithaca at once.'

'Of course, my lord,' Antiphus said quietly, ashamed that he had kept the king waiting with his questions.

Odysseus smiled and patted him on the shoulder, then set off at a fast run along the woodland track.

Eurylochus was asleep with his back against the bole of a sycamore tree when Argus, Odysseus's boarhound, woke him with a bark. He opened his eyes to see the puppy standing by his feet, his ears erect and an expectant look in his eyes.

'Get lost, you stupid beast,' Eurylochus frowned. 'Can't you see I'm sleeping?'

He closed his eyes and turned his head away, but Argus placed his front paws on his lap and gave another bark, more urgent and much louder this time. Eurylochus's eyes snapped open and with an angry grunt he shoved the dog into the cold ruin of the campfire, where he gave a yelp and kicked up a cloud of ashes as he scrambled free.

'Damn you, dog!' Eurylochus shouted, wafting away the fine particles that filled the air and choking as he breathed them down into his lungs. He leapt to his feet and ran towards the puppy, bent on giving the animal a hard kick. Argus was too quick for him, though, and ran off through the trees, where the echoes of his barking could still be heard for some time.

Eurylochus patted the ash from his clothes and, feeling almost as annoyed as he had after his confrontation with Eperitus earlier that morning, looked around for something to wet his throat. A skin of wine was hanging from a branch at the edge of the camp, so he strolled over and took a mouthful of the cool, refreshing liquid. The camp was on the edge of the wood, overlooking a sloping pasture that led down to the narrow channel between Samos and Ithaca, and after another swallow of wine Eurylochus leaned his shoulder against a tree and looked out at the view. The bright, early spring sunshine was reflecting back from the choppy waters below and illuminating the white gulls as they wheeled and cried over the waves. Behind them, the rocky bulk of Ithaca loomed up like a black sea-monster basking in the morning's warmth. To the south of the island, the dark waters of the Ionian Sea spread out towards the mainland of the Peloponnese, a low, grey profile on the horizon.

Then Eurylochus heard Argus's bark returning through the woods, accompanied by the sound of crashing undergrowth and the shouts of several men. Fearing danger, Eurylochus ran to grab his shield and spear from the tree where he had leaned them then turned to face whoever was approaching the camp at such speed.

'Who's there?' he called, the terror clear in his voice.

Suddenly, Odysseus's heavy, triangular bulk could be seen weaving its way through the trees at a fast run, with Argus barking at his heels. 'Lower your spear and get the camp packed up,' he shouted. 'We need to return to Ithaca at once.'

'But why?' Eurylochus asked, leaning his spear back against

the tree. 'I thought we were going to stay on Samos for a few days' hunting.'

Odysseus leapt over the screen of ferns that edged the camp and came to a halt by the scattered remains of the fire. He rested his hands on his knees and breathed deeply, his face red with the exertion of running. The others, led by Eperitus and Arceisius, were now visible sprinting through the trees towards the camp.

'We received a message,' Odysseus gasped, 'that Penelope is in labour. So we're going back. Where's that squire of mine?'

'I sent Eurybates down to the ship to prepare food for the midday meal.'

'Well, if we eat at all, it'll be back at the palace. I'll head down to the galley – pack up this stuff and follow on as quickly as you can.'

'Wait for me,' Eperitus said, almost collapsing with exhaustion as he broke through the screen of ferns and stood wheezing next to Odysseus. 'Arceisius, gather up my gear and bring it down to the ship. I'll go with the king.'

'Yes, sir,' the squire replied, his usually ruddy face now an even brighter red and shining with sweat.

Eurylochus gave Eperitus a frosty glare, then turned his back on him and began angrily stuffing bowls and cooking gear into a large sack. The others had all reached the camp by now and were already rolling up their bedding and throwing their belongings into leather bags. Odysseus placed a hand on Eperitus's shoulder and pulled himself straight.

'Come on then, Eperitus,' he sighed. 'This is no time to take a rest.'

They jogged through the last of the trees and down the slope towards the water's edge. Argus bounded ahead of them, barking happily in the bright sunshine. Below them was a small cove edged by a thin crescent of sand, where their galley drifted gently at its anchor. Beyond it was the narrow sleeve of dark water that separated Samos from Ithaca, and as they ran they stared at the familiar outline of the smaller island. The southern half – where the majority of its population made their living as fishermen, or from farming the little fertile land that existed – was low, wide and sheer-sided. A tooth-like peak guarded the narrow isthmus that led to the northern half, where the near-vertical walls of Mount Neriton rose up to dominate the island. Beyond the mountain's mass was the principal town of Ithaca, and at its centre the palace of Odysseus, where Penelope was in the throes of labour. Eperitus caught sight of Odysseus's face as he looked towards his home, and could see the anxiety in his eyes.

With the help of Eurybates, a short, round-shouldered man with dark skin and curly hair, they fitted the spar to the mast before the others had reached the ship. Then, once every man was aboard and the oars had been fed out into the calm waters of the bay, they pulled up the anchor stone and unfurled the dolphin-motifed sail.

Eperitus and Antiphus sat next to each other at the back of the galley, with Arceisius and Polites on the adjacent bench; the rest of the men were spread evenly along the length of the ship, each pair gripping one of the long-handled oars. Odysseus stood in the stern accompanied by Argus, and at his command the crew lowered their oars and began to row, gradually easing the galley over the calm waters of the cove towards the rapid current of the channel beyond. But before they could feel the sweat prickle in their armpits, the wind caught the sail with a ferocious snap and sucked them out into the choppy sea. Each man pulled in his oar and, after helping Antiphus make a correction to the angle of the sail, Eperitus went back to join Odysseus.

'Penelope'll be fine,' he assured him, trying to disguise his own anxiety with a smile. 'She's a strong woman and the gods have always been with her.'

Odysseus nodded, his eyes focused on the open sea as he pulled at the twin rudders. 'I'm sure she will – and my son, too.'

'Actoris says it's a girl for sure.'

'Actoris also said the baby wasn't due for at least three weeks!' Odysseus scoffed. 'And now that we've seen Athena again, I know my dream of the other night was from her. It'll be a boy, whatever any old maid thinks.'

They fell silent for a while, their thoughts turning from the birth of Odysseus's child to the appearance of the goddess. Eventually, as the galley fell under the shadow of the steep flanks of Mount Neriton, Eperitus could hold his silence no longer. 'What do you make of it all, Odysseus – Athena's words, I mean, about war with Troy? And why on earth would you want to spend twenty years away from home?'

'I wouldn't,' Odysseus replied, simply. 'And I won't – not with a family to care for and a kingdom to rule. Ithaca's king owes no allegiance to Mycenae, and if Agamemnon still wants war against Priam then he'll have to do without me. I don't care for battle and glory – not like you do, Eperitus; my heart is here, in these islands with my family and friends. If the call to war does come, then I'll find a way out of it. It's you I'm worried about.'

Eperitus stared at him. 'What do you mean?' he asked, at the same time feeling like a thief caught in a man's home.

'I'm not a fool,' Odysseus said with a short laugh. 'You're a warrior, Eperitus, and these islands that I love with all my heart must be like a prison for you. I know that you often climb to the top of Mount Neriton and look out at the mainland, no doubt yearning to go and find adventure on some foreign battlefield. And I saw the way Athena questioned you – she knows where your heart is, too. It's only your vow to serve me that's kept you here for so long, and your friendship. And if you weren't the best friend I have, I would consider releasing you from your oath.'

Eperitus looked across the bow of the ship to the rapidly approaching harbour, where several fishing vessels were drawn up on the sand and two galleys lay at anchor on the smooth waters. 'I wouldn't want to be released,' he said quietly. 'As I told the goddess, if war is coming then I'll face it at your side.'

'Let's see what the Fates hold for us,' Odysseus replied. 'Now, get back to the benches and tell Antiphus to lower the sail – we'll row the rest of the way into harbour.'

But Antiphus had already given orders for the sail to be furled and for the oars to be readied. Eperitus took his place beside him, sliding the pine oar between its pegs and fastening the handle with a leather strap. He felt the strain in his arms and shoulders as the blade bit the water, then picked up the rhythm of the rest of the crew as they rowed the galley into the small inlet that nestled at the northern foot of Mount Neriton. The calm waters of the sheltered bay offered little resistance, and soon the splash of the anchor stone was followed by the shouts of men as they lowered a small boat over the side.

Odysseus told Antiphus and Arceisius to wait for him and Eperitus in the boat, then turned to Polites.

'Come with us, friend. You've not seen my home yet, and as you're now one of the palace guard I want your first experience to be a happy one.'

Polites bowed his head but said nothing. Leaving their weapons and equipment in the ship, they climbed down into the waiting boat – which dipped alarmingly as Polites stepped onto it – and rowed to shore. They left Arceisius to take the boat back to the galley, then ran up a narrow road that led to the town above. A group of women, filling clay jars from a spring at the side of the road, looked on in silence as they passed. Eperitus wondered whether they had any news about Penelope, but had no time to ask as the king led them on towards the town. Soon they were passing the first houses, and shortly afterwards had reached the open terrace before the palace walls.

Large numbers of people were standing around in the midday sun. Most were peasants or slave women, many with baskets of clothes under their arms, jars of water on their shoulders or babies on their hips. Here and there old men conversed with each other in animated tones, their grey beards wagging and their crooked fingers poking emphatically at each other's chests. Groups of children ran in and out between the knots of adults, shouting and screaming as they chased and caught one another. It annoyed Eperitus to see them gathered there, clamouring like vultures as they awaited news of the royal birth; they seemed not to care that their queen's fate was in the hands of Artemis, who from time to time saw fit to take the life of a mother or baby.

Odysseus had stopped and was staring at the open gate in the outer wall of the palace. At the sight of their king, the din of voices gradually grew quiet and soon all eyes were upon him.

'What is it, Odysseus?' Eperitus said in a low voice, standing next to him and holding his elbow. 'Do you want me to go in and ask?'

'No,' Odysseus said, shaking his head as if waking from a dream. 'No, of course not. I just felt a moment of uncertainty. As if . . .'

'Don't say it,' Eperitus said, squeezing his elbow. 'It's natural to be afraid, but she's in good hands. Promise Artemis the sacrifice of a goat if she'll see Penelope and the child safe, and then let's go in.'

'A goat?' Odysseus said, looking his friend in the eye. 'If everything goes well, she'll have my best bull before night-time – the thigh bones and fat, which all the gods love. And we'll feast on everything else, eh? Come on, Eperitus, let's find out whether I'm a father yet.'

They walked through to the courtyard, followed by Antiphus and Polites (the sight of whom caused a great stir in the crowd). The scene inside the walls was no less busy than on the terrace outside, with slaves and soldiers scurrying to carry out their duties. Since taking over from his father, Odysseus had transformed Ithaca from a poor, unsophisticated kingdom into a prosperous and bustling state. His palace had also grown in size and richness: in Laertes's day, it had been a tired and neglected place with no more than two dozen slaves and a guard of thirty men; now it was completely rebuilt, boasting hundreds of slaves and a standing army of three hundred soldiers.

It was an achievement that Odysseus could be justifiably proud of, though many of his decisions had proved unpopular to start with. The first of these concerned Eupeithes, the affluent merchant who had initiated the rebellion against his father. Laertes's last act as king had been to banish the traitor to Dulichium, but after a year on the throne Odysseus had brought him back and appointed him his chief adviser on trade. In a single stroke, he had gained the benefit of his former enemy's commercial acumen and guaranteed his loyalty and support (if causing Laertes a certain amount of anger and embarrassment). Odysseus also made peace with the Taphians, who had supported Eupeithes's rebellion, and now counted their chieftain, Mentes, as one of his closest friends. Eventually, the whole of Ithaca came to appreciate their king's wisdom and learned to trust his judgement.

Eperitus had always believed in Odysseus's cleverness, but it was for his hard-working nature that he respected him most. As they walked across the busy courtyard, he looked about at the many improvements his friend had made. Their visit to Sparta years ago had impressed on Odysseus that a king's home reflected his position and authority, and he had quickly set about redesigning the palace and helping in its reconstruction. The ash planks of the threshold to the great hall, which they were now approaching, had been cut to length and fitted by the king himself; even the cypress pillars that supported the roof had been tapered and rubbed smooth by his hands. His mark was in every aspect of the kingdom, and soon it would be made complete. The child that he and Penelope had wanted for ten years would continue his bloodline and, more importantly, preserve the memory of his deeds so that when death claimed his body it would not claim his renown also.

As Eperitus pondered these things, the doors of the great hall swung open to reveal a tall woman standing in the shadows. She was dressed in a white chiton with a bright-red cloak draped over her shoulders. Her tangled brown hair was tucked behind her ears, revealing a pale face with dark, tired eyes that blinked against the bright sunlight. Penelope's calm beauty reminded Eperitus of the first time he and Odysseus had seen her, at a feast in Sparta ten years before. Then she had worn a full-length, green dress and her hair had been tied in a ponytail that danced cheerfully with each movement of her head. Odysseus had fallen in love with her that night, and with a combination of persistence and wiliness he had won her heart and made her his queen.

She turned and received a small white bundle from her body slave, Actoris, who stood in the deeper shadows behind her. Then she stepped forward into the sunlight and, with a smile, held the silent baby at arm's length towards her husband.

'It's a boy,' she said, as Odysseus mounted the threshold and took the child in his arms.

The king looked down at his son and there were tears in his eyes. The people who had been criss-crossing the courtyard now stopped and stared at their king and queen, while at the gates the crowd pressed so close that many were forced over the porch. The hubbub of voices from beyond the palace walls fell silent, and in that moment of blissful peace Odysseus pulled Penelope to him and kissed her with a fierce passion. Then he stepped forward and, raising his son above his head, showed him to all who could see.

'A son!' he boomed proudly, the tears now flowing down his cheeks into his beard.

A great cheer erupted from the crowd of onlookers, and as the noise swept back through the town Odysseus took the sleeping child back into his arms and whispered something in Penelope's ear. Then he turned and beckoned Eperitus to join them.

Despite the continued cheering and his father's handling of him, the baby was still asleep as Eperitus looked down at him. He had a red face with little features that were screwed up as if with concentration; his tiny fists were pulled up to his cheeks, and his head was covered in shiny black hair that curled in every direction.

'What will you call him?' he asked, looking at Odysseus and Penelope. The king was still staring down at the child, studying the miniature details of his son, but Penelope met Eperitus's eyes and smiled.

'It's the father's duty to name his son,' she said.

'Telemachus. His name is Telemachus,' Odysseus answered.

He gave Eperitus a wide grin. 'And when he's old enough to walk, you can teach him to use a sword and throw a spear.'

'And I'll teach him how to use a bow,' Antiphus added, stepping onto the raised threshold. He was followed by Polites, whose brutal face was softened with wonder as he stared down at the baby. Then Actoris appeared and reminded Penelope that the child should not be exposed too long to the sun.

Eperitus slipped into the crowd that had formed before the threshold. As he made for the gate, an old woman stopped him.

'Is it true what they're saying, sir?' she asked eagerly. 'A son?'

'Yes, a healthy looking lad,' he replied, forcing a smile.

'Praise Zeus and Artemis and all the gods!' she exulted, holding both hands in the air and spinning round with glee.

But Eperitus was already starting to run, wanting to be as far away from the cheering crowds as his legs could take him. He forced his way through the press of bodies until he was beyond the town and climbing the twisting path that led up the flanks of Mount Neriton. When he reached the top he relieved the lookout of his duties and sat down beneath the thatched awning that provided the only shelter from sun, rain or wind, and looked out at the blue mass of the Peloponnese. He watched the merchant ships drift gently up and down the coast until the setting of the sun forced them to find ports or inlets for the night. The eastern sky was beginning to pale and the rocks all around him had turned a gentle shade of pink, reflecting the crimson fire in the sky behind Eperitus as the sun sank below the western edge of the world. Then he heard the sound of loosened gravel and saw Arceisius approach from the direction of the town.

'I saw Thestor wandering around the palace,' he said as he approached the awning, 'when I knew he should have been up here, so I guessed this was where I might find you.'

'Did you bring any wine?' Eperitus replied. 'I'm as thirsty as a hunted deer.'

'I've some water,' Arceisius said, slipping a leather bag from his shoulder and tossing it towards his master. 'You were missed down there. Odysseus was asking everyone if they'd seen you.'

'I thought he needed some time with his new family.'

'Is that all, sir?' Arceisius asked. Though young, he was not blind to his master's anguish.

Eperitus stood and looked down at the wine-dark sea, washing the jagged skirts of the mountain far below with its ceaseless rocking.

'No, Arceisius. No, it's not. I'm thinking of leaving Ithaca.'

'But Ithaca's your home.'

'Ithaca's my prison,' Eperitus retorted, instantly regretting his sharp tone. 'I'm sorry, Arceisius. It's just that, suddenly, everything's changing, as if I'm being reminded that my destiny lies beyond Ithaca. I've been thinking of my father for some time, wanting to wipe away the shame of what he did. Then there was the fight this morning. It was the first time I've killed a man in ten years, and I *enjoyed* it – not the killing, as such, but the thrill of danger and the pride of victory. It woke something inside me, a yearning for glory that's been dormant for too long, and a need to prove myself.'

'But you *have* proved yourself,' Arceisius protested. 'If it wasn't for you Ithaca would be ruled by Taphians.'

Eperitus shook his head. 'I'm still a warrior, Arceisius – Odysseus reminded me of that on the ship, and it was he who said Ithaca is a prison to me. But do you know what it was that made me decide to leave? The sight of that baby in Odysseus's arms. After all, a man needs a sense of his own eternity, something that will carry his memory beyond death. Telemachus will give that to Odysseus. But it made me realize that I'm slipping into obscurity. I need to get back out into the world and make a name for myself in battle – that's all I ever dreamed of when I was your age.'

The wind, which had been constant since Eperitus had reached the top of Mount Neriton, whipped at their cloaks and hair, bringing to them the sounds of the sea crashing against the rocks far below. The chariot of the sun had disappeared and in the cool of the evening they saw the first stars shining in the deep blue skies above.

'And now there's talk of war in the east,' Eperitus continued. 'A great war between Troy and the whole of Greece. Odysseus knows about it and is determined not to be drawn in. But for the likes of me – and you, if you're willing, Arceisius – it's an opportunity to become what we were always meant to be: warriors, killing and dying for the sake of glory.'

The squire took the skin from his master's hand and swallowed a mouthful of water. For a long time they watched the Peloponnese fade and the sea grow darker, then Arceisius broke the thought-filled silence.

'Let's go back, while we can still find our footing.'

'I'm leaving for the mainland,' Eperitus said. 'Once Telemachus has been dedicated to the gods I intend to ask Odysseus to release me from my oath. If he does, I will go to Mycenae and join the army of King Agamemnon.'

'Then I'll come with you, sir,' Arceisius replied. 'It felt strange killing that man this morning, but I know now it was only because I'd crossed a threshold into a new world. I'm a warrior now, and I don't think I'll ever find happiness on Ithaca again.'

Menelaus sat on his raised throne and eyed the Trojan prince with stern formality.

'Well, Paris, son of Priam, I'm told you want to see me as a matter of urgency. What is it you wish to discuss?'

A broad column of light plunged like a waterfall from a vent in the high ceiling of the great hall, illuminating the Spartan king as he waited for a response. Paris stood stiffly before him, with Apheidas and Aeneas on either side. The low flames of the hearth crackled behind them and they felt its warmth in the smalls of their backs, coaxing the sweat from their armpits and increasing their discomfort.

Paris cleared his throat and stepped forward into the golden, dust-filled light.

'I come with an offer of alliance from the king of Troy,' he began. 'My father is a great man, but his greatness lies in his desire for peace and friendship with his neighbours. With this wish at heart, he has sent me to speak with you and the other significant kings of Greece.'

'Priam rules over an empire of vassal cities that pay him homage and provide him with ships and armies to serve his will,' Menelaus interrupted. 'From all reports, the gods have already blessed your father with wealth and power far beyond the needs of any man. What could he possibly gain from an alliance with Sparta, or any city in Greece?'

'Peace, most importantly,' Paris answered. 'And the freedom to trade, the life blood of all truly civilized peoples.'

'But trade thrives, even though the Trojans have been demanding tribute from Greek merchants for some years now. Does your offer of alliance include the removal of this unjust taxation on our goods?'

'I will raise the matter with my father, if everything goes well.'

'You should grant this as an immediate concession if you expect any kind of profit from our meeting.'

'There will be no immediate concessions,' Paris countered. 'Priam wants cordial relations between Trojans and Greeks, to our *mutual* benefit.'

Menelaus leaned back in his chair and stroked his beard, eyeing Paris shrewdly. 'To our mutual benefit, but at a cost to Greece no doubt. And what does Priam want in exchange for the friendship of Troy?'

'There is something,' Paris nodded. 'My father's desire for peace and trade is genuine, but the plain truth is he's getting old, and old men are sentimental. He wants his family around him: he wants Hesione back.'

Menelaus looked at him through narrowed eyes.

'Telamon married Hesione thirty years ago,' he said. 'She was his by right of conquest, after he and Heracles sacked Troy. Do you refute this?'

'That is what the Greeks believe, but we Trojans say she was raped and kidnapped by Telamon.'

Menelaus raised a quizzical eyebrow. 'Shame and defeat often bring denial. But whatever the truth about Hesione, she has been Telamon's wife for many years now and has given him a son, Teucer the archer. And if I remember correctly, a Trojan delegation was sent to Salamis some time ago and rejected by Telamon himself.'

Aeneas stepped forward.

'Anchises, my father, was amongst them,' he said, angrily. 'The Greeks treated him like dirt and he and the others barely escaped with their lives!'

Apheidas placed a hand on the young warrior's shoulder and pulled him gently away from the Spartan king. Ignoring the others, Menelaus continued to fix his attention on Paris.

'I don't know what happened in Salamis and I don't know Telamon well enough to speak for his character, but as a husband I don't think I would have taken kindly to an attempt to rob me of my wife. Hesione's home is Greece, and no offer of alliance is going to change the fact.'

'Her home is Troy,' Paris responded sharply. 'Though Priam hasn't set eyes on his sister for thirty years, he still loves her and wants her back. All I request is that you send a message to Agamemnon, asking him to invite Telamon to meet with us at Mycenae. After the experience of the previous delegation we would rather discuss these matters on neutral ground, and I am sure Telamon will not be able to refuse a direct request from the sons of Atreus. In return for your help, we will lift the taxation on Greek trade in the Aegean. My father is also prepared to compensate Telamon generously for the return of his sister.'

'Priam seems to forget that his sister is now a wife and a mother!' Menelaus snapped. 'Do you Trojans care nothing for marriage? Is it your desire to rob a man of his wife?'

The accusation rang back from the walls of the great hall and at last Paris knew that Menelaus suspected him of coveting Helen. The cordiality of the evening feasts had gone and as he stared at the older man, the legitimate husband of the woman who had stolen his heart, he felt a rush of hatred. He wanted to spring forward and close his fingers about Menelaus's throat, but as he looked at the flush of grey in his hair and beard and the heavy lines about his eyes and forehead, he realized it was the fear of losing Helen that had aged him prematurely. Suddenly his anger turned to shame. Menelaus was not a man to be despised, but pitied, and yet for the sake of a woman's glance Paris was going to win his trust and then betray him. His scorn turned upon himself, and yet he knew there was nothing else he could do. What were honour and morality compared to his desire for Helen?

'Nevertheless,' the king continued, 'I am prepared to grant your wish and send a message to my brother, but I require something of you in return.'

'Name it, my lord?'

Menelaus narrowed his eyes at the Trojan prince. 'I do not know you, Paris. You are a stranger from a foreign land and your ways are unknown to me. Though you speak of friendship and alliances, how do I know you don't harbour evil or mischief in your heart? In a few days I will leave for Crete, but before I go I want an assurance that you will act honourably in my absence.'

'There's only one way to do that, my lord,' said Apheidas, standing beside Paris. 'You know the answer, too: a solemn oath of friendship.'

'Do Trojans respect the gods?' Menelaus tested him.

Apheidas did not respond. Instead, he gave Paris a subtle nudge in the ribs and stepped back.

'The gods are highly revered in Troy,' the prince replied. 'As you will see if you ever come to our homeland. Though we are foreigners in your eyes, an oath of friendship is as binding on a Trojan as it is on any Greek. If we give you our word, you can trust us to keep it.'

'So be it. While you are under my roof, let it be as a friend.'

Menelaus offered his hand, which Paris gripped firmly.

'Eteoneus,' the Spartan king shouted, 'bring me my best dagger.'

The herald, who had been waiting in the shadows of the great hall, snapped his fingers at a slave, who disappeared through a side door. A short while later he returned and, crossing the hall, placed a sheathed dagger in Menelaus's palm.

'I, Menelaus, son of Atreus, call on Zeus the protector of strangers to witness my promise of friendship to you,' he said, placing the weapon firmly in Paris's free hand. 'This dagger is a symbol of my oath, guaranteeing you my protection and help while you are in my kingdom, and ensuring that I will never be your enemy. Let this promise stand for myself, my children and their children until seven generations have passed, as custom demands.'

Paris scanned the ornately detailed gift without releasing Menelaus's hand – to do so before exchanging oaths would break the pledge under Trojan practice. Although the Spartan's promise sounded strange to his ears, its integrity was assured by the witness of Zeus. And yet Paris was unable to return the oath without a gift of his own. He looked at Apheidas, who in turn nodded to Eteoneus.

The herald reached behind himself and pulled a cloth bundle from his belt, which he handed to Apheidas. The Trojan, who had asked Eteoneus to retrieve the gift from the armoury, opened the swaddling to reveal a second dagger. Like the Spartan weapon, it had a black leather scabbard that was decorated with ornately worked gold filigree; but, where Menelaus's gift had a wooden handle with gold inlay and a gold pommel, the handle of the dagger that Paris now gave to the Spartan king was shaped from a single piece of ivory. It was almost twice as long as Menelaus's palm was wide and in it was depicted a scene of an archer hunting a stag, the intricate carvings inlaid with jet to make them stand out boldly. The blade was nearly double the length of the Spartan dagger and remained hidden beneath the scabbard, but Paris saw in his mind's eye the design it bore, of more huntsmen and their dogs described in gold, chasing in the wake of the archer and stag on the handle. It was a rich weapon indeed, designed to impress the wealth and skill of Troy on Menelaus's mind.

'With this dagger I swear to you, before Zeus and all the gods of Olympus, my friendship and loyalty.' As he said the words, Paris released his hold of Menelaus's hand, making his words meaningless. In doing so he knew he had crossed a threshold, from honour to dishonour, driven by the insanity of love. 'I will never bear arms against you, or bring harm upon your household in any form. I will honour and protect you when you visit my homeland. We will be allies until death takes us, or the words of this oath are broken – which can never happen.'

## Chapter Seven

# THE FLIGHT FROM SPARTA

The light was failing fast as Paris walked through the quiet avenues and alleyways of Sparta, heading for the temple of Aphrodite. He felt both nervous and elated at the thought of being with Helen again, this time alone and without any fear of disturbance. For the first time since seeing her in the great hall, he would be able to discover what her true feelings for him were. His heart told him that her display of sexuality the day before had not been a mere act, but that, amazingly, she wanted him as much as he wanted her. And yet there was a heaviness in his step too. His deception of Menelaus had appalled him, bringing into clear focus the fact he was not only intending to betray his host, but he was also on the verge of betraying everything he had ever believed in and stood for. His honour would be lost forever, and even if Apheidas was right and the gods were behind the madness that had driven him to this point, he would still earn their contempt for stealing a man's wife. Such was the way of the immortals. But despite the nagging voice of his conscience, he knew the only thing that could stop him now would be Helen's refusal to leave Sparta, and the older part of him still hoped he had misjudged her.

The directions he had been given by the armourer led him to a narrow side street that reeked sharply of dung and urine. Halfway down was an open doorway, from which a wavering orange light spilled out across the opposite wall. A tall, white-robed woman watched him from beneath the shadow of her hood, but as he quickened his pace towards her she ducked beneath the low lintel and entered the temple.

He followed her in and pulled the double doors shut behind him. The temple of Aphrodite was not what he had expected – a modest chamber with an avenue of slim, wooden pillars leading to a crude altar. Two sputtering torches cast a fitful glow over the plastered walls, where dozens of murals depicted the lovemaking of gods and mortals from a forgotten era. Once they would have formed a rich decoration, but now they were faded, smoke-stained and peeling – simple shadows of their former glory. Rows of alcoves stared like empty eye sockets from between the decaying murals; they had been made to contain images of the gods, but now the only effigy that remained was on a raised platform behind the altar. It was as high as Paris's waist, and was the crudest portrayal of a god he had ever seen – made of glazed clay, with huge breasts and a monstrous, leering face.

The contrast with the woman who knelt before it could not be stronger. Helen had shed her hooded robe to reveal a gauzy white chiton, clasped above her left shoulder by a silver brooch and bound around the waist by a thin purple sash. A narrow parting exposed the left flank of her body, from the slight furrows of her ribs down to the smooth, white flesh of her thigh. Her slender hands were laid flat on her knees and her feet were tucked beneath her buttocks, the dirt on the soles the only visible blemish.

Paris removed his sandals and walked across the cold flagstones to the altar. Taking some cakes from a bag that hung across his shoulder, he laid them down next to a similar offering that Helen must have placed there earlier. He then stepped back and knelt beside the Spartan queen, whose eyes were closed in silent prayer. Paris, though, had no thought for the gods. Instead he let his eyes rest on the perfection of Helen and imagined what it would be like to have her at his side for the rest of his life. The sight of her black hair tumbling across her forehead and cheeks, catching the red torchlight in its soft layers, filled him with an almost irresist-ible desire to reach out and run his fingers through its shining mass. But above all he wanted her long, curving eyelashes to part so that her eyes could meet his and read the strength of his love for her.

'Do you like what you see, Paris of Troy?' she said, her eyes still closed.

'You know I do,' he replied, gently.

She smiled faintly. 'And how do I compare to the women of your homeland?'

'The women of Ilium are beautiful, but next to you they would be like the stars that surround the moon. No mortal can match you, Helen. Even Aphrodite . . .'

'Shush!' she said, opening her eyes and placing a finger to his lips. 'My father may be Zeus, but it won't do to compare me to the goddess of love. She's jealous and can be cruel when angered.'

Paris laughed lightly. 'She might scare you, but I'm a warrior and a follower of Ares. In the world of men Aphrodite is among the least of the gods.'

'Then has she never blessed you with the love of a woman?' Helen asked, fixing him with her large, intelligent eyes.

The amusement drained from Paris's face and he looked away, frowning at the cakes on the altar as he composed his thoughts.

'As I said, I'm a warrior,' he answered. 'Though Aphrodite has visited me once. In a dream.'

'A dream?' Helen echoed. 'Tell me about it.'

'It was some time ago, when I was a shepherd on Mount Ida. I had been sleeping in the shade of an old tree when I sensed a great light pressing against my eyelids, far more brilliant than the sun. I opened my eyes and there before me were three women, each one naked and possessing terrible beauty. They told me they were Athena, Hera and Aphrodite and that I was to award a golden apple to the one I considered the fairest. Then, though their mouths did not open, I heard their voices inside my head, each offering me great gifts if I would but choose them over the others. But their promises meant nothing to me, for though they were all wondrous to look on, Aphrodite's beauty could not be matched. I gave the apple to her, heedless of the scowls of Hera and Athena, and the last thing I remember before waking was the smile on her lips, as if all the love in the world were given to me.'

Helen watched Paris's face intently as he spoke, then nodded her head knowingly.

'It was the goddess who brought you here to me. For years I've prayed for someone to take me away from Sparta, but when I saw you in the great hall I knew my deliverance was at hand. Have you come to take me back with you to Troy?'

Paris felt a nervous churning in the pit of his stomach. Strangely, it was the same sensation he felt before a battle, when he would sit on his horse trying to convince all around him that he was calm and unafraid, when his whole body was wracked with nerves. He looked at Helen and saw a similar helpless uncertainty, as if she too were standing at the threshold of a new world, wanting to step out but afraid of what she might find. She was no longer a great and beautiful queen, but a young woman, trapped and desperate for freedom and yet knowing that the price of her liberty was an end to everything she knew.

'I will take you if you're willing to leave,' he replied, his tone neutral, probing.

'But I'm a queen and the wife of another man,' she said, her voice shaking slightly. 'I . . . I can't just leave.'

Paris felt as if a blade of ice had been pushed into his stomach. 'But you *hate* Menelaus.'

'No. I've never hated Menelaus,' she protested. 'I couldn't have wished for a kinder husband or a better father to my children.'

'But you don't *love* him.'

'No,' she replied with a shake of her head.

'But you think you could love me?' he asked, unable now to keep the neediness from his voice.

'What does it matter? Did you not take an oath of friendship to Menelaus? Aren't you honour-bound never to harm him or his household? In fact, why did you even come here tonight? To tease me?' She looked at him and there was anger in her eyes. 'When I heard of the oath I cursed you for a fool, knowing he must have tricked you somehow. And yet I had to come, to see if it was true. Is it?'

'The oath was not carried out in the proper manner, according to the customs of my people.'

'Menelaus believed it was, and that's all that matters. If you break it you will lose your honour.'

Paris looked into her eyes, knowing the moment had come to choose between love and honour. He could concede that she was right, walk out of the temple and never see her again. There would be no loss of reputation; he would step back into his old life with no more damage than a broken heart and the thought of what might have been. Or he could step forward into a new world, a world of shame, danger and pursuit, but a world with her.

'Compared to you, the oath means nothing to me.'

She curled her fingers around his hand.

'Then I will come with you, and love you like no other woman ever could!'

He briefly caught the passion in her blue eyes, before she moved her face to his and kissed him. The press of her lips was warm and surprisingly tender, the scent of her perfume equally soft; the feel of her arms as they wrapped around his hard back was light and yet filled with urgency. He responded greedily, against his initial instinct, pulling her slender body against his and slipping his hand through the parting of her chiton, down to the flesh of her buttocks. Their embrace grew fiercer for a moment, and then she pulled herself free of his arms and moved back. She was breathing hard and there was a fire in her eyes as she stared at him.

'No more, Paris. I won't give myself to you – not yet, not even in Aphrodite's temple.'

'Then when?'

'I'm no prostitute, damn you! I'm a queen and the daughter of Zeus himself!' Her eyes were momentarily consumed by a terrible and beautiful fury, which subsided as quickly as it had appeared. 'My mother was an adulteress and I vowed never to be like her. I've only ever given myself to Menelaus, and all my children are from his seed. But I *can't* lead a life without love. I was made to love, Paris, and if you are prepared to break your oath then I will break mine. I promise I will love you with every beat of my heart, but if you want me you must take me away from Sparta first.'

'I will!' he said, reaching for her hand. 'I can have my men ready to go tonight.'

Again she stepped back from him, her eyes still alive with the passion that had been kindled by their kiss.

'Not tonight – not while Menelaus is in the palace.'

'Then when?'

'He leaves for Crete in a week,' Helen said. 'He won't want to go while you're here, but he can't change his plans now. Besides, he trusts in the oath you took.'

Paris sensed the challenge in Helen's words: she knew he was deceiving Menelaus, and that he could do the same to her.

'My words to you aren't hollow, Helen,' he assured her. 'I *will* take you back to Sparta with me. I'd have to be insane to refuse you, wouldn't I?'

'I have one condition, my prince.'

'Name it.'

'My children – they're to come with us.'

The sight of her irresistible face and the tantalizing glimpse of bare flesh where her chiton lay open filled Paris with the desire to do anything she commanded, but he knew what she was asking was almost impossible.

'I can get out of Sparta with you, Helen, but with four confused children our chances will be narrow.'

Helen stooped and picked up her robe, which she threw about her shoulders.

'Think of a way, Paris. If you want me to be yours, you must bring my children too.'

She turned and walked to the doors, pulling them open to reveal the twilight of evening in the narrow street beyond.

'I'll find a way,' he said. 'I promise – but stay with me a little longer. Helen!'

'Keep your word,' she said, and was gone.

❧

Paris yanked at the leather straps that held the two halves of the cuirass about his torso, pulling them taut before feeding them through the golden buckles. After nine days of feasting his armour was a tight fit, and heavy with the bronze plates that overlapped each other like fish scales from his neck and shoulders down to his groin. He looked around at his men, who were suffering similar agonies as they fitted their own armour and familiarized themselves with the feel and weight of their equipment. Greaves were tied about shins and leather or bronze caps – according to the wealth and rank of each man – were pressed onto heads.

'Hurry up!' Paris urged. He could feel the familiar sickness in his stomach that always preceded a fight, and just like the preludes to battle on the northern frontiers it made him irritable and quick-tempered. 'And pull your cloaks about yourselves – if the Spartans see our armour they'll get suspicious.'

'Much good it'll do us without weapons,' Aeneas grumbled.

'This'll do to start us off,' Paris said, holding up the dagger Menelaus had given him. Though the weapons the Trojans had brought with them lay stored in the palace armoury, Paris planned to dispatch enough of the guardsmen dotted about the corridors to provide some of his men with swords, spears and shields. It was a foolhardy plan, but his gut instinct told him it would work. 'Now, where in Hades is Apheidas?'

'Here, my lord.'

The tall warrior stepped into the room that had been the Trojans' quarters for over a week and strolled over to where his armour was laid out on a straw mattress. He sat down and began tying on his greaves.

'So, what did you find out?' Paris demanded.

'Menelaus left at sunset,' Apheidas announced. 'No fuss or fanfare, just him with his escort and a covered wagon.'

'A wagon?' Paris said, his heart rattling nervously in his chest.

'Don't fear – she's not with him. The slave I spoke to said she didn't know who or what was in the wagon, but she reassured me Helen is still in her quarters. Menelaus went up to see her before he left, but was told she was asleep so he had to do without his goodbye kiss.'

'Poor Menelaus,' one of the soldiers mocked, causing a ripple of laughter from his comrades.

'What about the rest of the palace?' Paris asked as Apheidas was helped into his cuirass. 'Are the guards at their usual posts?'

'The corridors and halls are quiet – there's no feast tonight and there's hardly a slave to be seen. But the guards are there, just like every evening. There's only one outside the great hall tonight, and he's virtually asleep already. I would have snapped his neck with my bare hands, if I didn't know you wanted all the glory for yourself.'

Paris frowned. His nerves were strained at the prospect of escaping from Sparta and he was feeling particularly surly.

'I'll kill him because I have to,' Paris said, turning to his men. 'But I want no unnecessary deaths. They may only be Greeks, but we are Trojans, not savages! Kill only guards or armed men; no slaves, no women, no one who does not stand in our way. Apheidas, Exadios – come with me. Aeneas, wait here with the rest of the men until we return; if you hear the alarm, make your escape as best you can.'

The three men made their way to the antechamber that led to the great hall, which was dark but for the restless glow cast by a handful of torches on the high walls. They waited in the shadows of a side corridor that ended only a short distance from where the solitary guard stood. They could hear his heavy breathing in the semi-darkness, and the occasional movement as he shifted his weight from one foot to the other and back again.

'He's still awake, then,' Apheidas whispered.

'Not for long,' Paris said grimly.

Wrapping his black cloak tightly about his armour to prevent it catching the light, he edged along the wall and caught his first sight of the guard. He was a young soldier with a wiry beard, wearing a bronze cap with cheekguards and a tall shield slung over his back. One hand rested on the pommel of a sword, while the other gripped the shaft of an ash spear. His head was tipped back against one of the ornate doors to the great hall and his eyes were fixed on the high ceiling, tracing the barely-visible murals that he already knew so well from long spells of guard duty. A moment later Paris slipped from the shadows, clapped his hand over the man's mouth and drew Menelaus's dagger across his exposed throat. The blade was so sharp it sliced through the flesh as if it were cutting into a leg of mutton. The guard gave a single, bloody choke before the life left his limbs and he collapsed against the door. Paris held him there until Apheidas and Exadios arrived to strip him of his spear, sword and helmet, then lowered him to the floor, when they also took the shield from his back.

'Put the body in there, Exadios,' Paris said, indicating the great hall. 'There'll be no feasting tonight. Apheidas – where's the next nearest guard?'

'By the wine store, but the only approach is in full view down a corridor. It's too risky: we should forget him and make for the rear entrance to the palace.'

'No – we need as many weapons as we can get, and as quickly as we can get them. How do I find this wine store?'

'Follow me,' Apheidas replied, smiling grimly as he clutched the unfamiliar Greek sword in his hand.

He ran through the gloomy corridors of the palace with Paris and Exadios close behind, until moments later they reached the mouth of a side passage where he signalled for them to stop. A low murmur of voices was coming from the corridor, and after pressing his finger to his lips Apheidas peered around the corner. A moment later, he gave a curse and drew back again.

'How many are there?' Paris asked.

'Two – the guard and a servant girl.'

'Are they . . .?'

'Not yet,' Apheidas grinned. 'But he's already got his hand inside her chiton. Give him a bit longer and he'll be too distracted to notice you creeping up on him.'

'No time for that – I'll have to bluff it.'

'But what about the girl?' Exadios protested. 'One scream from her and this place'll be teeming with guards.'

'Don't worry about her,' Apheidas whispered, giving Exadios a wink as he hid the sword beneath his cloak.

'Keep a lookout for us here, Exadios,' Paris ordered, before entering the side passage, closely followed by Apheidas.

There was just enough room for the two men to walk side by side. Though their weapons were concealed, neither man bothered to hide his armour with his cloak; by the light of the single torch at the end of the passageway they could see that the servant girl was now half-naked and the guard – who had already removed his armaments – was preoccupied with her. By the time he noticed the approach of the Trojans, Paris's hand was over his mouth and the point of his dagger was forcing its way between his ribs. Beside him, his lover opened her mouth to scream, but Apheidas's sword swept her head from her shoulders before the air could be forced up from her lungs. Without pausing, he opened the door to the wine storeroom, threw the body inside and kicked the head in after it.

'Damn you, Apheidas!' Paris hissed, dropping the corpse of the guard and stepping up to the older man. 'I said *no* unnecessary killing.'

Apheidas's pupils were wide with the exhilaration of the kill. He stared back at the prince for a defiant moment, then straightened himself up and lifted his gaze to the top of Paris's forehead, in the time-honoured manner of a soldier facing his superior.

'She was about to scream,' he began. 'But you're right, my lord, I overreacted. I'm sorry.'

Paris knew there was no point in saying more. He nodded curtly and signalled to the corpse of the guard. Together they threw it into the storeroom, before retrieving the discarded weapons and returning to where Exadios awaited them, nervously clutching the spear and shield of the first guard.

'Here,' said Paris, sliding a sword into the soldier's belt and handing him another spear. 'Take these to the rest of the men and have them meet us by the back entrance. Apheidas and I will wait for you there.'

When Exadios reached the rear doors of the palace with the rest of the party, Paris and Apheidas had already killed the guard and hidden the body. All that remained of him was a bloodstain on the wall and his weapons, which the prince was holding. He quickly ordered the redistribution of the captured armaments so that three men had swords, three carried spears and three more at least had the protection of a shield each. Paris refused all weaponry for himself, except the dagger Menelaus had given him.

Apheidas opened one of the doors and peered out at a small, moonlit courtyard. Other than two guards by the small gate that led out to the city streets, there was nobody to be seen.

'I doubt anyone will want to come through this way tonight,' he said, shutting the door again. He picked up a beam of wood from against the wall and slid it into the iron brackets on the back of the doors. 'And if they do, that'll hold them for long enough.'

'When will they change the guards?' Aeneas asked.

'Not before we're beyond the city walls and riding back to the ship,' Paris answered, his tone confident and reassuring to the ears of his men.

'That's assuming everything goes to plan,' Apheidas countered. 'Have you even let Helen know we're leaving tonight?'

With so much to be gained or lost, Paris felt more rankled than ever by Apheidas's insubordination. 'I told her maid I would come for her tomorrow night.'

'Tomorrow!' Apheidas exclaimed. 'We need her to be ready now – there's no time to waste if we're to get out of Sparta alive.'

'I have my reasons, Apheidas,' Paris warned.

But Apheidas was in no mood to accede – the drawing of blood had made him tense and quick-tempered. 'She should be in her room now, waiting for our arrival with her children dressed and ready to travel. It's madness to pull them from their beds in the middle of the night and expect them to ride with us to the ship.'

The men shifted uncomfortably, gripping the unfamiliar armaments and looking nervously at their two leaders. Paris stepped up to his lieutenant with anger smouldering in his dark eyes, his knuckles white as he gripped the handle of the dagger.

'Don't cross me again, Apheidas,' he warned. 'If we're to survive this night and take Helen back to my father, we've got to work together and under *my* orders.'

Apheidas stepped back slowly, his fierce, unbowed gaze still fixed on the prince. On this occasion there was no apology, but Paris knew that time was running out. Without wasting another moment, he signalled for Aeneas to join him and for the rest to follow on behind. As quietly as they could, using the cover of doorways and side passages, the group of soldiers returned to the antechamber before the great hall and then made their way down the central corridor towards the main entrance. The light from the few torches reflected warmly on the bronze of their weapons, but in the sleeping palace there was nobody to witness their silent progress. Then, just before they reached the ornate portals that led out to the main courtyard, Paris led them down a broad corridor to the left. Having become familiar with the labyrinth of passageways during their time in Sparta, they all knew that the royal quarters were up a broad flight of stairs only a short distance ahead, beyond a turning to the right.

It was usual for two soldiers to guard the stairs in the evenings. Paris hoped they would be fooled by the Spartan weapons his men carried, only discovering their error at the last moment, when it would be too late. Nevertheless, he felt his anxiety rise as he led his men down the shadowy corridor. He had not seen Helen since their meeting at the temple and their only contact had been through her maidservant, so his desire to see her again was increasing with every footstep.

As they approached the blind corner, Paris signalled for his men to stop before sending Aeneas ahead to check on the readiness of the guards. The young warrior came back at a run a moment later, his eyes wide.

'My lord, there're six men at the foot of the stairs – all of them armed and watchful.'

'Zeus's beard,' Apheidas cursed. 'Somebody must have alerted them.'

Paris shook his head. 'No. It's Menelaus's doing – he's not going to entrust the safety of his queen to two men while I'm still here, whatever oaths he believes may have been said. He must have tripled the guard as a precaution.'

'But now what will we do?' Aeneas asked.

'Entrust ourselves to the gods, of course,' Paris responded. 'No time for guile or caution now. Pray to Ares and follow me.'

He closed his eyes, kissed the bloodstained blade of his dagger, then ran around the corner towards the Spartan guards. The passageway was dimly lit, but at its end he could see six helmeted men with tall spears and swords thrust into their belts. Each was protected by leather body armour and a broad, oval shield. For a moment they did not notice Paris running towards them, his cloak billowing; only when the remaining Trojans turned the corner behind him did they wake to the fact they were being attacked.

They formed a hasty line, locking their shields together and lowering their spears towards their assailants, but it was too late. Paris leapt over the bronze-tipped shafts and crashed shoulder-first into a pair of shields, sending two of the Spartans sprawling backwards onto the stair behind. By good fortune or the blessing of Ares, he landed on one of the ox-hide shields and pinned its owner against the stone steps. He instinctively sank the point of his dagger into the man's exposed throat, killing him instantly.

The ringing clash of weaponry behind him signalled the arrival of his comrades. There was a brief cry of pain, followed by the grunts and shouts of men struggling against each other. Then the other man Paris had knocked down sprang to his feet and drew his sword from his belt. Not waiting to retrieve his shield from the steps, he rushed straight at the Trojan prince with the blade above his head and a vicious snarl contorting his features. Paris responded quickly, launching himself shoulder-first at the man's midriff and driving him hard against the opposite wall. The sword flew from his opponent's hand and clattered noisily down the stone steps to where the others were locked in a fierce battle. Ignoring the fists now raining down on his exposed back, Paris tightened his grip on the man's waist and pushed him to the steps. The Spartan cried out in pain as Paris fell on top of him, but in the confusion his hands found Paris's throat and his thumbs began to push into his windpipe. His grip was strong and painful for a moment, but quickly slackened and fell away as Paris pushed the point of his dagger into the man's heart.

The struggle between the four remaining guards and the Trojans led by Apheidas was quickly over. Paris was pulled to his feet by Exadios, whose eyes were wide with exhilaration.

'I can hardly believe it,' he grinned. 'They just seemed to collapse before us, and them fully armed as well.'

'It was Apheidas,' Aeneas added, stepping over one of the bodies. 'He was like a Titan, cutting them down like nettles.'

'Don't talk nonsense,' Apheidas said from behind them as he stooped to strip the weapons from one of his victims. 'We'd have been spit like pigs if Paris hadn't broken their line while they were still forming. Are you hurt, my lord?'

'I'm fine,' Paris replied, pleased that Apheidas's animosity appeared to have been forgotten. 'What about the men?'

'Mestor's dead,' Apheidas said, handing a sword to one of the unarmed Trojans. 'Got two spears through the belly.'

'And Dolon's lost half his leg,' Exadios added.

Paris's eyes fell on the young warrior, who was propped up against a wall. His face was screwed up with pain, though he somehow managed to stop himself from crying out. He had pulled one knee up to his chest, whilst his other leg was stretched out before him to reveal a bloody stump just below the knee. Two of his comrades were at his side, but stood up and moved back as Paris walked over.

'We've seen a few battles together, Dolon,' he said, kneeling down and placing his hand on the man's shoulder. 'Fighting on the northern borders.'

The wounded soldier smiled and nodded. 'Yes, my lord. The best days of my life.'

'But we'll never get you out of Sparta with us.'

Dolon's smile stiffened and faded.

'No. Not with this leg. And yet I don't want to be left to the mercy of these cursed Spartans,' he added, spitting on the floor and wincing with pain. He picked up a dagger from beside him and presented the hilt to Paris. 'If you understand me, my lord.'

Paris nodded and took the dagger. Placing it against the wounded soldier's chest, he waited for him to look away then pushed the blade into his heart. Dolon's eyes opened wide for a moment, then his head lolled onto his chest. Pulling the weapon free again, Paris stood and tossed it across the flagstones, feeling sick. He had lost two of his best men already and suddenly he realized that the price of his love for Helen would not just be the loss of his honour and possibly his life, but the lives of all those around him. There would be more bloodshed and more death, and as he looked at the bodies sprawled across the steps he knew it would not end in the corridors of Menelaus's palace.

The others, who had stopped to watch their comrade's demise, now looked expectantly at the prince.

'We shall mourn Dolon and Mestor when we return to Troy,' he told them. 'Until then every thought must be on our mission. Strip the dead of their arms and share what weapons we have evenly. Apheidas and Aeneas, come with me. Exadios, guard the stairs until we return – nobody's to come up or down.'

With the realization that nothing now stood between him and Helen, Paris took the steps three at a time to the next floor, where he found himself in a large antechamber surrounded on all sides by open doors. Several half-dressed women stood in the doorways with alarmed looks on their faces. Two more were sitting on straw mattresses in front of the only door that remained closed, brushing the sleep from their eyes and staring at the Trojans in confusion.

'What do you want?' one of the slaves asked. 'You Trojans aren't allowed up here.'

'Where's Helen?' Paris demanded.

The same slave – a woman of over fifty years – crossed the antechamber and stood before the closed door. 'When Menelaus hears of this outrage you'll wish you'd never lived.'

'We'll be halfway to Troy by the time your precious king gets back,' Apheidas laughed, striding towards the old woman with his sword poised in his hand. 'And your mistress will be coming with us.'

'I wouldn't be so sure of that,' she smiled.

The circle of slaves let out a loud scream as Apheidas struck the woman across the face with the back of his hand, sending her sprawling to the floor. In the same moment the door behind her opened to reveal Helen. Though just woken from sleep, her natural beauty was undiminished and Apheidas felt his anger fade before her. Her frightened slaves fell silent, unwilling to abandon their mistress and yet too afraid to throw themselves between her and the tall Trojan. Helen looked down at the nurse who had suckled her as a child – still groaning from the blow to her head – then at Apheidas and Paris.

'My maidservant said you would come tomorrow night,' she said, sternly.

'I lied to her,' Paris replied. 'I couldn't risk anyone guessing our plans. If you didn't go to bed, or if you kept the children up, dressed for a journey, then someone would get suspicious. It would only take one servant loyal to Menelaus to inform the captain of the guard and everything we hoped for would be lost.'

'Besides,' Helen added sardonically, 'you didn't trust me not to change my mind. Well, I'm not going to, despite your doubts about me and the violence of your men. Neaera, go and wake the children and dress them in warm clothes. I'm leaving Sparta with Paris, and the children are coming with me.'

There were gasps of disbelief from the women, some of whom began to weep. One, a young girl in a brown woollen chiton, shuffled across the antechamber – carefully keeping her distance as she passed Apheidas – and disappeared down a passageway to the right of Paris and Aeneas.

'Go and tell the men to be ready,' Paris said, stepping forward and placing a hand on Apheidas's shoulder. 'As soon as the children are dressed we'll be leaving.'

'And have you thought about getting us all through the main gate yet?' Apheidas asked, staring hard at the prince.

'Leave that to me. Now go.'

As his lieutenant disappeared down the stairs, Paris crossed the antechamber to Helen and pulled her into his broad chest. She wrapped her arms about him and held him tightly, unable to disguise her relief that he had come for her. The five days since she had last seen him had seemed interminable, filled with doubt, worry and a longing to be with him. Then he kissed her and the anxieties that had plagued her melted away.

Suddenly Neaera returned, holding the small form of Pleisthenes in her arms.

'Mistress,' she said, her voice trembling. 'Mistress!'

'What is it? Where are the others?'

'They're gone, my lady. Their beds are empty – they haven't even been slept in! Only little Pleisthenes was there, so I brought him immediately.'

Helen slipped free of Paris's arms and ran across to her youngest boy. Kissing him gently on the forehead and holding his face in her hands, she looked deeply into his sleepy eyes.

'Pi, my baby, can you tell mummy where Aethiolas and Maraphius are hiding? Where's your sister, Hermione?'

'I don't know,' the child answered, rubbing his eyes with the back of his withered hand. 'They went to say goodbye to father, but I was too ill to go.'

'And they're with him now,' said the old nursemaid, getting to her feet and holding a hand to the wound on her forehead where Apheidas had struck her. Her face was sad and fearful. 'The king asked me to bring the children to him as I was about to put them to bed – he told me he wanted to say goodbye to them before he went to Crete – and then he sat them in a covered wagon and said they were going with him. He would have taken Pleisthenes, too, if he'd been well enough.'

Helen looked at her with her mouth open and tears bonding her long eyelashes together.

'Oh, forgive me, my lady!' the maid cried, running across and kneeling before the queen, wrapping her arms about her legs. 'Menelaus said the children were his only guarantee you wouldn't run off. And how could I stop him – he's their father and I'm only a slave? Besides, mistress, I don't want you to leave us . . .'

'That's not your choice, Myrine,' Helen announced. 'It's mine.'

Paris moved towards her, realizing that Menelaus had outwitted him and seeing his hopes falling away.

'Helen,' he said. 'This is your only chance to be free. If you don't leave now you'll be doomed to live the rest of your life as Menelaus's prisoner. You know you can't do that – come with me!'

'No, my lady!' Myrine protested. 'Think of your children. You have freedom through them.'

Helen lifted Pleisthenes out of Neaera's arms and kissed his hair. She looked at the circle of her maids, most of whom had served her since she was a child, or since they had been children themselves. Some, filled with fear as their world was collapsing about them, held each other, while all were damp-eyed. The tears were flowing unchecked down Helen's cheeks, too, as she thought about her children and her life at Sparta, the only life she had ever known. She pictured the faces of her two older boys, Aethiolas and

Maraphius, both brave and strong like their father; and of her beautiful daughter, Hermione, who was as wilful and independent as she was. Then she looked at Paris and saw the passion that his eyes held for her, a passion that mirrored her own. Here, at last, was the one she had waited for all her life, a man who could free her from her gilded cage to lead a life of freedom; a man who she could love with all her heart. For his sake she would – *must* – surrender everything she had. She moved to him and pressed her lips against his.

'Neaera,' she said, eventually turning to her faithful body slave, 'fetch Pi's cloak and sandals. When Menelaus returns, tell Aethiolas, Maraphius and Hermione I love them, and that I will never forget them. Kiss each of them for me.'

As Neaera ran off, sobbing openly, Helen hid her face against Paris's shoulder and cried, overwhelmed by the sudden realization that she was giving up her children.

Seven fully armed Trojans stepped out into the moonlit courtyard. The guards by the gate gave them an inquisitive glance, but as the men carried Spartan shields and wore Spartan helmets they soon forgot them and returned to their game of dice.

'This way,' Paris said, leading the others to the royal stable where the strong smell of straw and dung filled their nostrils. They could hear horses shifting restlessly in the darkness, disturbed by the sudden presence of so many men.

'Lipse!' Paris whispered.

There was a corresponding snort a few stalls to his left. Paris greeted the horse warmly as if they were old friends, before opening the triple-barred gate and entering the stall.

'That's my girl,' he said, rubbing the mare's neck and placing his face against her nose. He led her out and told the others to bring ten more horses.

'But there're thirteen of us,' Aeneas reminded him.

'Helen will ride with me and Pleisthenes with you. Now hurry up – the alarm will be raised at any moment.'

They worked as quickly as they could in the faint light from the stable door, releasing the best animals they could find and throwing blankets over their backs. As Paris was fitting a leather harness to Lipse, Aeneas placed a hand on his shoulder.

'We should hamstring the others, my lord. It's the only way to stop pursuit.'

But Paris simply shook his head.

In quicker time than they had hoped – mostly due to the prince's reassuring influence on the unsettled beasts – the Trojans emerged from the stables and led the train of horses towards the palace entrance. This time the gate guards were less ready to ignore them.

'Hey!' one of them shouted. 'You there – where do you think you're going with those horses?'

'Mount up,' Paris ordered.

Realizing something was not right, the Spartans pulled on their helmets and lifted their shields onto their shoulders. Their leader gave a harsh shout and more men came spilling out of a nearby guardroom.

At the same moment, Apheidas led the rest of the party out of the palace and across the courtyard to where the others awaited them. Helen was with them, carrying Pleisthenes in the folds of her green cloak. Paris directed Lipse to her side and plucked the child from her uplifted arms. He passed him to Aeneas then pulled Helen up onto the mare's shoulders.

'Menelaus won't be happy if you steal his favourite horse,' she said, throwing a leg over Lipse's neck before turning and kissing the prince on the mouth. 'But I expect that'll be the least of his worries.'

As he watched his men jump skilfully on the backs of their mounts, Paris turned and saw a fully formed line of three-dozen Spartans barring the silver-sheathed doors that were the only way out to the city streets. The ten remaining Trojans gathered about their leader and looked at him with a mixture of desperation and – from those who knew him better – expectation.

'Forgive me, my love,' he said, and with a flick of his heels sent Lipse dashing towards the waiting ranks of men. The Spartan spear-points dipped in anticipation, while behind him he could hear the shouts of his own men calling him back. Then, as Helen threw her arms about Lipse's neck, Paris turned the reins and brought the animal to a sliding halt, spraying the triple line of guards with dirt.

He threw his arm around Helen, pulling her tightly against his chest, and with his other hand pulled the dagger from his belt, pressing it softly but menacingly against her white neck.

'Open the gate,' he commanded. 'Do it now or I'll slit your queen's throat!'

The Spartans hesitated.

'For pity's sake!' Helen screamed, realizing Paris's plan. 'Do as he says or he'll kill me.'

Moved by love of their queen and respect for her authority, the Spartan ranks melted away before them. A short, muscular soldier, whom Paris recognized as the man who had disarmed them on their arrival at the palace, ordered four of his men to remove the bars from the gates and swing them open. Within moments, all eleven horses had dashed through and were racing down the empty, moonlit streets of the city.

'Don't risk the main gate,' Helen shouted over her shoulder. 'There are three times as many guards to convince and I doubt they'll all fall for the same trick.'

'Can these horses fly over the city walls then?' Paris laughed, enjoying the wind in his hair and the warmth of Helen's body enclosed within his.

'Of course not, but there's another way: a gate on the east wall that leads out to a small road. It was made for trade to come in from the eastern hills, so it isn't very wide – we'll have to go through in single file – but it also means there'll only be a handful of guards at best. Turn to the left down here.'

Paris followed her orders, keen to escape the claustrophobia of the city and know the freedom of the plains once more. The others kept close behind, the sound of hooves on flagstones echoing noisily between the narrow walls as they made their way through the city. Eventually they entered a final, short avenue where the dirt had been heavily rutted by the wheels of innumerable carts. This led to the high city walls and a slender gateway, which stood open to reveal the gentle blue hills beyond. Three guards were drinking wine and swapping stories, hoping to fend off the inevitable assault of sleep that always threatened the midnight watch. As the clatter of hooves approached, though, they snatched up their shields and spears and ran out into the road.

Paris halted Lipse and signalled the men behind to attack. Couching their captured spears under their arms, three Trojans sprang forward. One of the guards threw down his arms and ran up a side street, his cowardice preserving his worthless life for another day. His braver comrades were barely able to raise their weapons in time to meet the charging horsemen: the first was spitted through the throat and fell beneath the hooves of a tall grey stallion; the second died instantly with a spear through the bridge of his nose, splitting his head open.

The victorious horsemen did not wait to exult in their victory, but with deft flicks of their heels drove their mounts on through the open gate, drawing their swords to deal with any guards that might be waiting on the other side. When one of them returned to signal that the path was clear, Paris led the rest of the party through in single file. Suddenly they were looking at the rolling plains on all sides, at the broad Eurotas River at the foot of the slope, and at the cloudless, star-speckled firmament above. Some were breathing deeply, enjoying the fresh air of their freedom; others were laughing. Helen simply laid her head against Lipse's neck and gazed out to the Taygetus Mountains in the west, their familiar outline black against the deep blue of the night sky.

'Say goodbye to it all,' Paris said, running his hand down the middle of her back. 'Soon you'll be on a fast ship, listening to the hiss of the waves before the prow and tasting the salt spray on your lips. There's nothing like it.'

'And then Troy,' she whispered, closing her eyes and trying to imagine what the foreign city would look like.

'Not straight away,' Paris said. 'Any pursuit will go there first, and I can't risk that. No, we'll head south, to Egypt, then work our way back up the coast. It'll take longer, but there's no hurry and it'll be much safer. Think of it as a honeymoon, if you like.'

Helen opened a single eye to look at him. His tanned skin looked paler in the moonlight and the scar that ran down his face and into his beard shone white. It was a brutal face, but there was also strength and independence in it, a wild undercurrent that reached out and touched something deep within her. It was a quality she could feel throbbing through her like a heartbeat, and with a contented sigh she knew she would be happy with Paris. If only Menelaus would let her go.

'My lord!'

Paris turned to look at Exadios, whose urgent shout had startled them all, and with an angry curse he realized they had lingered too long. Towards the west, a large troop of horsemen was leaving the main gateway to the city and forming up before the hump-backed bridge that crossed a tributary of the Eurotas River. There were at least fifty of them, and more were still emerging from the gate.

Suddenly, one of them gave a shout and pointed towards the party of Trojans. Then the whole troop were galloping towards them, losing any semblance of order in their eagerness to save their queen and have revenge on the foreign thieves.

'There's a bridge in the trees at the foot of the slope,' Helen said. 'It's wide enough and strong enough for a wagon, so we'll get across if we're quick.'

'And have your countrymen pursue us to our doom?' Apheidas snorted. 'I'd rather stand and fight.'

'There's no need,' Exadios told him. 'Take the woman and her boy across the bridge and ride as fast as you can. With you and Aeneas for protection, you should all make the ship before dawn. The rest of us'll buy you the time you need.'

'Don't be stupid, Exadios!' Paris said. 'They'll slaughter you.'

'No time to argue,' the warrior smiled, and with a series of orders formed his comrades into line. Moments later they were drawing their swords and trotting out to meet the approaching onslaught of the Spartan horsemen.

Paris turned the head of his horse to go after them, but Apheidas leaned across and grabbed his arm.

'Exadios is right,' he hissed. 'It's the only way any of us will escape. Now, don't let their sacrifice be wasted.'

'Come on then,' Paris said angrily. 'I'm sick of this damned country.'

He watched as the two lines of horsemen charged towards each other, hoping that the woman seated before him was worth the deaths of his men. He had surrendered his honour for her, risking the wrath of the gods and the avenging fury of Menelaus; and for a moment he wondered whether he had done the right thing. Then she looked up at him, the wind whipping strands of black hair across her face, and like countless men before him he knew no price was too steep to possess her. Unlike them, though, he knew Helen wanted his love. He had given her her freedom and she was giving it straight back to him.

He turned Lipse's head towards the bridge and dug his heels into her flanks. She covered the remaining distance at a gallop, followed closely by Apheidas and Aeneas.

## Chapter Eight
# ON HERMES'S MOUNT

It was a bright morning and the blue skies were filled with the harsh cawing of seagulls. They swept about the rooftops of Odysseus's palace and the surrounding houses, landing and taking off, and fighting with each other over the scraps of food the townsfolk had thrown out for their livestock. A cooling breeze swept across the channel from Samos, washing away the stink of fish from the day's catch and carrying in the smell of pine from the thinly wooded slopes of Mount Neriton.

The large expanse of open ground before the palace walls was thronged with people. Slaves bartered at the stalls of the many fishermen or haggled noisily with farmers who stood atop carts filled with grain or vegetables. A pair of herdsmen were driving in a score of pigs, using their sticks liberally on the pink backsides and shouting instructions to their dogs. Under the shade of a large olive tree a group of old men were watching the progress of a board game, giving advice or deriding unwise moves; colourful birds sat beside them in willow cages, singing cheerfully to each other. Young children were everywhere, clinging to their mothers or playing games that involved an unending flow of chasing and hiding.

Underneath the palace walls, not far from the folding gates, sat a semicircle of four boys and nine girls. They did not seem to mind the nearby dung pile, which had not been collected for three days and stank horribly; instead, their attention was fixed on a short, chubby boy with curly brown hair and large, staring eyes. He sat against the wall on an upturned basket and looked round at his audience.

'When the resourceful Odysseus realized Penelope had been captured by Polytherses and his Taphians, he devised a plan to get into the palace and free her. With Mentor and Antiphus, he hid in a large clay pithos filled with wine and was carried through the heavily guarded gates on the back of a cart.'

'How did they breathe?' said a sandy-haired boy with skinny limbs and a long neck. 'I mean, how did they breathe if the pithos was full of wine?'

'They waited until the last moment, and then when the long-speared Taphians stepped forward to check the shipment, they ducked their heads under the surface of the dark wine and breathed through straws.'

'See!' said a fiery-eyed girl with dark skin and long hair bunched up on top of her head. 'Now, why don't you shut up and let Omeros tell the story?'

Omeros held up his hands.

'Thank you, Melantho-of-the-pretty-cheeks,' he said, making the girl blush coyly. 'Now, after the cart had passed through the gates – those very gates to my right – and night had fallen, Odysseus, Mentor and Antiphus slipped from their hiding place and began their butchers' work, slitting the throats of the sleeping Taphians until the courtyard was awash with their blood. Fully a hundred were dead by the time rosy-fingered Dawn appeared, and then the mercenaries woke and discovered what was going on. Up they leapt and, seizing their bronze-tipped spears and leather shields, set upon the three Ithacans with a great fury.'

Omeros scowled and thrust an imaginary sword towards one of the girls, making her fall back with a squeal.

'At that moment a horn blew from beyond the walls. Out of the mist, striding across the plain came godlike Eperitus, leading an army of stout-hearted Ithacans.' Omeros stood and pointed to the broad terrace behind the other children. Every head turned, and in their minds' eyes the throng of slaves, peasants and tradesmen became an army, marching resolutely towards the palace walls. 'Halitherses of the great war cry was with them; Eumaeus the swineherd and Arceisius, Eperitus's squire, too. With a great shout they ran towards the gates, from which hundreds of Taphians were already issuing, eager to meet them in battle.'

Eperitus and Arceisius stood unobserved by the gates, listening to the story.

'There you go,' said Arceisius, his mouth full of apple. 'Why go to the mainland to seek glory when we've already been immortalized in song at home?'

'Omeros is eleven,' Eperitus replied, snatching the apple from his squire's hand and taking a large bite. 'Besides, the boy's imagination knows no limits – where'd he get this "godlike Eperitus" from, for instance?'

'Now then, sir, you can't lust after fame one moment and get embarrassed when you receive it the next.'

Eperitus tossed the apple-core on the dung heap. 'Come on, let's find Odysseus. We don't want to miss Telemachus's dedication, and afterwards I will ask the king's permission to go.'

'I was beginning to think you'd changed your mind about that,' Arceisius said. 'It's been a month since Telemachus was born and you haven't mentioned anything more about leaving Ithaca.'

'I meant what I said, Arceisius. Did you?'

Arceisius nodded, firmly but without enthusiasm. Then, as Eperitus made to go, he threw his arm across the captain's chest.

'Wait a moment, sir,' he said, pointing into the crowd. 'Here come Eupeithes's boy, Antinous, and his cronies. They'll be looking for trouble, or I'm a Taphian.'

'They mean trouble, all right,' Eperitus agreed, eyeing the newcomers with distaste. 'We'd better see what they're up to.'

A group of three boys strutted up to the circle of children, just as Omeros was describing the moment when Odysseus shot dead the traitor Polytherses. Antinous, a tall, slim boy of fourteen with an arrogant face and a pampered air, scoffed at the story.

'That oaf couldn't hit a horse's arse at point-blank range, let alone shoot a man through the eye in a darkened hall. You should take your ridiculous songs and tell them to the seagulls, Omeros, for all the truth that's in them.'

'Everyone knows Odysseus shot my father in the back,' rumbled Ctessipus, a large boy with a single eyebrow and a flattened nose. 'And if you tell any more lies about him, I'll chuck you on that dung pile and you can sing to the flies and worms, if you like.'

The boys stared menacingly at Omeros's audience, who began to slink away until only Melantho was left. She scowled at the third boy, a rather slow-looking lout who was trying desperately to avoid her eye.

'Melanthius,' she spat, 'if you don't clear off at once and take these two vultures with you, I'm going straight to Pa and telling him you've been up to no good again.'

Melanthius shifted uncomfortably, but was saved from answering his sister by Omeros.

'It's all right, Melantho. Perhaps they would like to sit down and listen to the rest of the story.' He turned to the three boys and indicated the recently vacated spaces before him. 'I'm afraid you've missed the part about how Eupeithes usurped the throne, then was himself betrayed by Polytherses – but as they were your fathers, I expect you already know the story. Maybe you'd like to hear of how Odysseus found Eupeithes in a storeroom, still chained up where Polytherses had left him?'

Both Antinous and Ctessipus leapt at Omeros, brandishing their fists and preparing to give him a beating. But before they could reach him they were pulled back by two pairs of strong arms.

'Steady now,' said Eperitus, hardly able to suppress his laughter as Antinous struggled against his firm grip. 'Or you might hurt yourself.'

Arceisius, who was not as powerful as Eperitus and only a little bigger than Ctessipus, had already lost patience with his prisoner.

With a grunt, he threw him over his shoulder, carried him to the dung pile and tossed him on it. At the sight of this, Antinous ceased his thrashing and fell limp, whilst Melanthius quickly disappeared into the crowd pursued by his sister, who was berating him loudly as she chased after him.

'Be on your way, lad,' Eperitus said, cuffing Antinous's mop of blond hair, 'and don't let me hear you've been in any more trouble.'

Antinous turned and scowled at the captain of the palace guard, tears of anger and embarrassment flooding down his cheeks. He bit back the words he wanted to say and, ignoring Ctessipus's plea to help him out of the dung heap, stormed off into the throng of people.

'You shouldn't provoke them, Omeros,' Eperitus warned the young storyteller. 'You're nothing more than a whelp compared to them, and one day they'll give you the thrashing you deserve.'

'Perhaps they will,' Omeros answered, jumping off his basket and following the two warriors as they navigated their way through the crowds. 'But it's precisely because they're bigger than me that I'm always baiting them. I can't defeat them physically, so I might as well humiliate them with my words.'

'Which is why Odysseus likes you so much,' Arceisius said. He took three barley cakes from a basket and gave the seller a wink. The man shook his head resignedly and continued haggling with a fat, red-faced woman.

Omeros took a bite of the cake Arceisius handed him, then caught up with Eperitus.

'Sir, the king was looking for you earlier.'

'And I've been looking for him ever since I finished my duties this morning. Do you know where he is?'

'He was on his way to Hermes's Mount, with the queen and their baby. He said to tell you that he has gone ahead to make everything ready and will be waiting for you there.'

'Then perhaps you should have been looking for me rather than lazing about and telling your friends stories,' Eperitus said, looking at the boy with as much sternness as he could muster. 'But I suppose I can't blame you. Odysseus shouldn't entrust his messages to daydreamers.'

'I won't always be a daydreamer, sir,' Omeros responded, looking hurt. 'People *need* stories – and bards to tell them – or where's the enjoyment in life? If we didn't give them tales of love, war and glory then no one would have anything to live up to.'

'And if you left us all alone, we could lead contented lives and not be blighted by impossible dreams,' Eperitus countered. 'Anyway, I'd be wary of becoming a bard if I were you. Most end up as little more than tramps, wandering from palace to palace to earn scraps from the tables of the powerful.'

'Some say that about warriors, too, sir,' Omeros suggested, stepping back a little as Eperitus gave him another stern glance. 'But I don't intend to be a wandering storyteller – I will be bard to the court of King Odysseus himself, and King Telemachus after him.'

Eperitus turned to Arceisius and signalled for him to catch up. 'Well, if that's what you want, then you should start telling things as they really were. How many times have I had to remind you Odysseus didn't enter the palace in a pithos of wine? He was disguised as a wine merchant.'

'But it doesn't *sound* as good, sir. Too much truth can ruin a story, and, besides, the king says he prefers my version.'

'Odysseus has never been a great respecter of honesty, and you should be careful of following his example,' Eperitus warned. 'He was born with the cunning of a fox and knows more than most men about how to live by his wits; but even for him there's a fine line between trickery and dishonour.'

Omeros was about to reply, but was silenced by the arrival of Arceisius.

'Odysseus is waiting for us at Athena's sacred grove on Hermes's Mount,' Eperitus informed his squire. 'We should go and find him now, and leave this young rascal to evade Antinous and his cronies.'

The two men turned and walked in the direction of the low, wooded hump of Hermes's Mount, which lay to the north-west of the town, but as they moved free of the crowd and began along the dirt track that led to the hill Omeros called after them.

'Don't forget that warriors need bards, too, sir. Without us, your acts of glory are worthless.'

'He's right, you know,' Arceisius laughed.

Eperitus said nothing. He was already thinking of what he had to say to Odysseus after Telemachus had been dedicated to the gods, and what the cost of his own search for glory would be.

A strong wind blustered up from the sea, flattening the blades of grass that clung to the exposed flank of Hermes's Mount. Eperitus and Arceisius held their cloaks about them as they walked towards the lonely thicket of pines that stood tall and dark in the centre of the sloping meadow, enduring the gusts that howled through its interlocked branches. Many years before, Odysseus's grandfather had met Athena walking through the grove, where she had given him her blessing; since that day it had been considered a sacred place by all Ithacans, and especially the rulers of the island.

As they approached, they could see Odysseus standing beneath the eaves of the small wood. His auburn hair was blowing wildly in the wind as his keen eyes looked out over the Ionian Sea, oblivious to their approach. He was mouthing a silent prayer in preparation for the dedication of his son, and from time to time would close his eyes and bow his head.

Behind him stood Penelope, the knuckles of her fists white as she gripped the edges of her cloak. Her eyes, narrowed against the gale, were fixed upon her husband. At her right shoulder was her nurse, Actoris, whose back was turned against the squall to protect the baby in her arms. Eurybates, Odysseus's squire and herald, was also with them; he held a struggling lamb in his arms and carried two skins over his shoulder, one filled with wine and the other with water.

Then Odysseus spotted the two figures coming across the meadow and waving at him in the bright sunshine. He waved back, and then, cupping his hands over his mouth so that the wind would not snatch away his words, called out, 'Where've you been? Didn't Omeros find you?'

'*We* found *him*,' Eperitus said as he and Arceisius reached the relative cover of the grove. 'Telling stories by the dung heap, as usual. If he'd given us your message straight away we'd have been here a long time ago.'

'No matter,' Penelope smiled. 'You're here now, and the gods are waiting. Odysseus, are you ready?'

'I'm ready,' he replied. 'Actoris, give Telemachus to his mother. Eurybates, make sure the sacrifice is willing.'

The squire knelt and placed the lamb on the ground, holding it fast by the scruff of its neck. He pulled a wooden bowl from the woollen bag at his hip and placed it on the ground in front of the gently bleating lamb, then filled it with a slop of water from one of the skins hanging from his shoulder. After a moment of uncertainty, the animal bowed its head to drink. Satisfied it had indicated its consent to be sacrificed, Eurybates removed the bowl and passed the skin to Odysseus.

After the king had washed his hands, he drew a dagger from his belt and beckoned for the animal. Pinning it against his muscular chest so that it could barely move, he cut some of the coarse black hair from its head and held it fast between his thumb and the blade. Holding it in the air above his head, he released it into the wind and watched it sail off towards the grey mass of ocean to the north. Eurybates took the lamb again as Odysseus turned to receive the swaddled baby from Penelope's arms. The boy woke and began to cry as his father removed the double-layer of white wool and lifted his naked red body over his head. Penelope instinctively raised a hand, fearful for her little Telemachus, then forced it down again.

'Mistress Athena!' Odysseus called. His voice, stronger than the wind, carried out towards the maddening waves. 'Proud lady of Trito! Virgin daughter of Zeus! Most glorious and great goddess, I call on you to accept the dedication of my son, Telemachus. Bestow on him your protection and guidance, just as you honoured my father's request for me. Make him strong and courageous, teach him the crafts of war, and endow him with wisdom. Seek for him the blessings of the other Olympians, so that he will be loved and honoured among men. And Mistress,' he added after a pause, 'allow me to remain on Ithaca and watch my son grow to manhood.'

Odysseus lowered Telemachus into his mother's waiting arms. As Penelope wrapped the baby in the thick woollen cloth, she gave her husband a questioning look. Odysseus, who had never told her about the doom predicted for him on Mount Parnassus, did not hold her gaze.

'Give me the lamb, Eurybates,' he commanded. 'And mix the wine.'

The animal began to kick out, as if it knew what was about to happen, but Odysseus held it tighter and drew the blade across its throat. Vivid red blood began to pour from the opening and Odysseus let the lamb fall into the thick grass by his feet, where it twitched and continued to kick until the last of its life had pumped out of its body. A moment later, he turned to Eurybates, took the krater of wine he held and poured a little on the ground in a silent libation. Then he took a sip and held out the krater to Eperitus.

'Do you still consent to be Telemachus's protector?' he asked.

Eperitus paused. Odysseus had asked him years before to be the protector of his children, should anything happen to him, and he had agreed without hesitation. Even as the king had reminded him of his promise during Penelope's pregnancy, he had confirmed he would accept the duty. But since the birth of Telemachus and his realization that his destiny lay beyond the safe and homely shores of Ithaca, Eperitus had questioned whether he was still the right man. Though he said nothing of his doubts to Odysseus, he had considered asking Mentor – Odysseus's friend since boyhood – whether he would take the role. In the end, though, Arceisius persuaded him to keep to his original promise. Even if they joined Agamemnon's army and went to war with Troy, they would still be able to return to Ithaca from time to time, and Penelope would know where to send a message should anything happen that would require Eperitus to fulfil his vows. With this in mind, he took the proffered krater and poured a dribble of the dark liquid onto the grass.

'I consent to protect Telemachus from any who would do him harm, and provide for him if his parents cannot; and I call upon all the gods of Olympus to bear witness to my oath.'

He raised the krater to his lips and drank. The ceremony was over.

Penelope moved past her husband and kissed Eperitus on the cheek. 'Here,' she said, placing Telemachus into the captain's hands and standing beside him, looking down at her son and smiling with contentment. 'We want you to be a second father to him.'

Eperitus knew the time had come. He looked at Arceisius, who returned his gaze with a slight nod.

'I'm proud to be his protector,' Eperitus said, turning back to Penelope. 'But I can never be a second father to Telemachus.'

'Nonsense,' Odysseus scoffed. 'You've so much to offer him, and it won't be long before he learns to love you like a parent.'

Eperitus shook his head. 'You don't understand. He won't see enough of me to love me. Unlike you, I won't be around when his needs are greatest. The truth is . . . the truth is I'm leaving – today – and Arceisius is coming with me. I'm asking you to release me from my oath to you, Odysseus.'

Penelope stepped back as if she had been struck. In the same instant Odysseus moved forward, his expression incredulous. He placed his large hands on Eperitus's arms and looked him in the eye.

'I know I challenged you about this on our return from Samos, because I've always feared you would wish to leave one day, but why do you want to go now? Didn't you tell me you had no intention of leaving? Besides, if it's because of what the goddess said . . .' He glanced out of the corner of his eye and lowered his voice. 'If that's the reason, we don't even know yet that this war will happen. Until it does, you should stay here where you have friends and a position of authority, everything you need.'

'But I *don't* have everything I need!' Eperitus rejoined. 'Yes, I have good friends, a home in the palace, my own slaves and more wealth than I know what to do with, but what's the point of it all? What I want is something lasting, something to be remembered by when my flesh and bones have rotted in the ground or been turned to ash. You have Telemachus, a bloodline to carry forward your memory. I have nothing.'

'Then find a wife here,' Penelope said, holding her hands towards him. 'There are hundreds of beautiful women on these islands who could bring you happiness and children of your own. You could have married Odysseus's sister, but you never returned her interest and in the end her father let her go to that merchant in Samos, fearing she would get too old to marry.'

'But I don't want a quiet family life,' Eperitus replied, gently. 'I want to make a name for myself with my spear. I used to think I could live on this island and be happy, but in recent days I've come to realize I can't. I just hope you will forgive me, both of you.'

As he said these words, he caught a movement in the distance behind Odysseus's shoulder and stared out at the grey sea, where a large warship was cutting through the turbulent waves. Its deck was crowded with armoured soldiers, their weapons glinting like gold in the sunlight as they stared up at the rocky, inhospitable slopes of Ithaca. Above their heads, a gigantic purple sail snapped repeatedly in the strong wind. It bore the device of a golden lion pinning a deer beneath its huge paws as it tore out its throat with its teeth.

Odysseus, seeing the alarm on the faces of Eperitus, Arceisius and Eurybates, turned to watch for himself the swift progress of the galley as it rounded the headland.

'Arceisius,' Eperitus said, his voice calm but urgent. 'Run back to the palace and call out the guard. Send the townsfolk to their homes and assemble the men on the terrace; Odysseus and I will follow shortly.'

'Wait!' Odysseus countermanded. 'They're not enemies: that sail belongs to the royal house of Mycenae. It's Agamemnon!'

'Agamemnon!' Eperitus repeated. 'But what's he doing here?'

'I don't know, but I've a nasty feeling it's to do with what Athena warned us about.'

Eperitus turned to the king and was surprised to see fear in his eyes. 'But if that's the case, what have you got to worry about? If Agamemnon is seeking recruits for war with Troy, then tell him it's nothing to do with you. It's just as you told Athena: you owe no allegiance to Mycenae or its king.'

'Not him,' Odysseus replied. 'But I do to Menelaus. I've been pondering the goddess's words to us, Eperitus, and I think I may have been caught out by one of my own tricks!'

'What are you two talking about?' Penelope asked, looking concerned as she rocked Telemachus gently in her arms. 'What's all this about Troy and Menelaus, and tricks?'

But Odysseus did not hear: he was looking around as if searching for something. His eyes narrowed in thought for a moment, and then he snapped his fingers and looked urgently at Eperitus.

'Was that old farmer still ploughing on the other side of that hill when you came over from the palace?'

'Yes, and he'll be there all day at the rate he was going.'

'Excellent! Arceisius, run to the palace and get Eurylochus to call out a guard of honour for Agamemnon – and possibly his brother, Menelaus. Then I want you to bring an ass and a bag of salt to where that farmer was ploughing, as quickly as you can. Is that clear?'

'As milk!' Arceisius smiled, before setting off at a sprint up the hillside.

*Chapter Nine*

# THE MADNESS OF ODYSSEUS

King Agamemnon, son of Atreus, stood at the edge of the broad terrace before the palace walls, his tall, muscular form still swaying slightly from having spent several days at sea. He wore a short tunic of the purest white wool and a golden breastplate that gleamed savagely in the sun. A red cloak, fastened by a golden brooch at his left shoulder, flowed over his back and around his calves like a river of blood. His smooth brown hair was tied into a tail beneath the back of his head, and his reddish-brown beard was short and meticulously trimmed. At only thirty-five years of age, his face was still young and handsome, but it was also stern and authoritative, as befitted the most powerful man in Greece.

His emotionless blue eyes scanned the Ithacan guardsmen paraded before him, instinctively noting the good condition of their dated weaponry and the well-oiled shine of their leather armour. Though their clothing lacked any sense of uniformity, the practised way in which they moved suggested to Agamemnon that they worked well together as a unit of men. He also approved of their physical condition – whether young or old (and there were many greybeards) the development of their muscles indicated long practice with their armaments. If all the men on Ithaca were to the standard of the hundred before him, they would be worth five times their number in levied soldiers.

Things had clearly changed since Odysseus had visited Sparta ten years before, when the soldiers he brought with him had been a spirited but bedraggled band. In those days they had been led by a captain called Halitherses, as Agamemnon recalled – an old warrior who liked to keep his men fit and well trained. But Halitherses was nowhere to be seen, and it was unlikely that the man who stood before the line of Ithacan spearmen now was responsible for their battle-readiness. Nevertheless, he signalled to the two men beside him and crossed the terrace towards the line of waiting soldiers.

Eurylochus bowed low as the men approached, momentarily taking his small, piglike eyes off the powerful visitors. His round face, with its pug nose, fat lips and broad jowls was covered with sweat from his balding pate to the layers of his chin.

'Greetings, my lords,' he announced. 'Welcome to Ithaca, kingdom of Odysseus, son of Laertes. My name is Eurylochus, cousin of the king.'

'I am King Agamemnon of Mycenae. These men are my brother, King Menelaus of Sparta, and my friend and adviser, Palamedes, son of Nauplius.'

Eurylochus bowed again. Menelaus turned his stony, tight-lipped face and troubled eyes towards the Ithacan and nodded briefly. Palamedes, a small, black-haired man with a thin, pointed face and clever eyes, simply looked away.

'We are honoured by your presence, my lords,' Eurylochus continued unperturbed. 'A feast is being prepared, but perhaps you and your men would like to wash off the salt spray first?'

'We're tired and will be glad of a hot bath, but first I need to speak to your cousin. Where is the king?'

'On the other side of that low hill, my lord, but if you're happy to wait for him in the palace I'm sure he'll be back soon.'

'Our business won't wait,' Menelaus snapped. 'We want to see him now.'

'As you please, my lord. I'll take you to him.'

'That won't be necessary, Eurylochus,' Agamemnon said. He nodded towards the thirty armed warriors behind him, who were formed in lines on the road that climbed up from the harbour. 'It would serve us better if you saw to the needs of my men, whilst Menelaus, Palamedes and I go to find King Odysseus.'

Eurylochus, who had been instructed by Arceisius to delay Agamemnon for a short while only, felt his duty had been adequately carried out. He turned and pointed at the dirt road that led to Hermes's Mount. 'Follow that track up into the woods until you come to an area cleared for farming. Over the other side of the hill is a grove sacred to Athena; you'll find Odysseus and Penelope there, dedicating their newborn son to the goddess.'

'I'd heard they were without children,' Agamemnon said, his cold expression darkening momentarily. 'Nevertheless, I'm pleased to learn Odysseus has a boy. A king needs an heir to take up his legacy, just as Orestes – my own lad – will take up mine.'

He beckoned a man from the escort and gave him quiet instructions, then led his brother and Palamedes up the track Eurylochus had pointed out. Before long they entered the wood, where the trees were densely packed and tall. The thick canopy of branches strangled out the sunlight and left only a brown gloom that smelled strongly of pine and damp earth. Though they occasionally heard sounds from the undergrowth and were twice surprised by the clatter of wings overhead, no birds were singing, which gave the wood a lonely, unwelcoming feel.

After a short while the narrow, overgrown path straightened and they saw an archway of yellow daylight not far ahead. In it was framed the diminutive figure of a man, walking towards them. He was muttering angrily to himself, and when Agamemnon spoke he leapt with surprise.

'We seek the king. Have you seen him?'

The old peasant blinked several times as his eyes adjusted to the murky half-light, then he craned his head forward to scrutinize the speaker and his comrades. His sunburnt skin was like leather, but his forehead was as pale as if it had never seen the sun. His black hair was thin and hung in greasy clumps, and the stench of stale sweat that emanated from him was almost unbearable.

'In the name o'Demeter!' he exclaimed. 'Where'd yer all come from, then. Are yer gods?'

'If we were,' Agamemnon began, trying to contain his revulsion at the figure before him, 'we should have blasted you down to Hades by now for your lack of deference, or turned you into something inhuman – though that already appears to have happened. As it is we're mere mortals, but it won't stop me from knocking your eyeballs into the back of your head unless you answer my question: have you seen Odysseus?'

The old man took no notice of the threat, but at the mention of Odysseus stamped his foot and shook his fists with rage.

'*B-loody* man!' he shouted. 'I divn't care if he be the king or no, but I won't tolerate bein' robbed o' me cap. That's bin on my 'ead since I were a lad, protectin' me brain from the sun, and he jes walks up and whips it off me crown as if it were 'is own. I tell yer, the man's lost the command o' his senses. The sun's sent 'im mad and 'e's taken me cap to protect 'is own brain.'

'Zeus's beard, man,' Menelaus said, his face dark with anger, 'will you stop your ranting and tell us where he is?'

'In field up yonder. And it ain't me who's rantin' – it's 'im, gibberin' on like an old maid who's lost 'er mind to the sun's rays, stealin' people's caps and . . .'

Menelaus strode past the fool and continued up the path, followed by his brother and Palamedes. Soon they were free of the wood and standing at the edge of a broad, sunlit field that was dotted here and there with solitary olive trees. A third of the soil had been freshly turned to hold some of the overnight rain, and the dark furrows sloped up in long, straight lines towards a ridge. At the point where they ended, a plough stood silhouetted against the skyline. Attached to it was the strangest team any of the men had ever seen: on one side was an ox, the normal beast of burden for such a task, but next to it stood an ass, its tall ears skewed at odd angles as it brayed loudly under the weight of the yoke.

'Why would anyone team an ass with an ox?' Palamedes asked.

'Perhaps we should ask him,' said Agamemnon, pointing to a

short, heavily built man with a dirty felt cap crammed on his head. His back was turned to them as he walked beside the furrows, sowing seed from a bag over his shoulder.

But as Agamemnon was about to call out, he noticed a knot of people sitting or standing under one of the nearby olive trees. At the sight of the newcomers a woman left the group and came running towards them, waving her hand and shouting for their attention. As she came nearer, they could see she was holding a baby to her chest and that she was clearly in distress.

'My lords,' she panted, kneeling before them and facing the ground. 'Thank the gods that you've arrived. It's my husband . . .'

'Penelope,' Menelaus interrupted. He offered her his hand, which she took, and pulled her to her feet. 'Penelope, it's me, Menelaus. And here's my brother, Agamemnon. Surely you haven't forgotten us so easily?'

Penelope looked blankly at the Spartan king, then at Agamemnon, before allowing recognition to spread over her pleasant features.

'Is it really you, Lord Menelaus? And you, King Agamemnon? Then Father Zeus has answered my prayers for help.'

As she spoke, she concentrated her thoughts on the time when Polytherses had captured her and told her that Odysseus had been slain. At once, tears welled up in her eyes and began rolling down her suntanned cheeks, which she then hid in the palms of her hands.

'Don't cry, my dear,' Agamemnon said, his voice calm and soothing as he took Penelope into his arms and held her. 'Tell us what's upsetting you. Menelaus and I are the most powerful kings in all of Greece: if Odysseus is in trouble or danger, we can help him.'

'Dear Agamemnon,' Penelope said, looking up into his cold blue eyes. 'I'm so grateful you've come now, of all the times you could have come. But even your great power can't save a man from madness, can it?'

'Madness!' asked Palamedes in his high, slightly squeaky voice. 'Do you mean the gods have robbed him of his wits?'

'I mean just that, sir.'

The three men exchanged concerned looks.

'But how?' Menelaus asked.

'Who can guess the will of the gods?' she replied with a sob. 'We were dedicating Telemachus here to Athena one moment, and the next Odysseus was rolling his eyes and talking nonsense. Now he's ploughing this field with an ox and an ass, and sowing salt in the furrows.'

'I've heard of Cadmus sowing serpent's teeth,' Agamemnon said. 'But he was acting on the orders of Athena, and each one became an armed warrior. What can Odysseus expect to reap from a bag of salt?'

'Nothing, sir. He's mad, and the mad do as they please,' Penelope answered.

'But he was one of the cleverest men in Greece,' Menelaus said, ruefully. 'Why, of all the oath-takers, did Odysseus have to lose his mind?'

Palamedes rubbed his chin speculatively and looked over at the Ithacan king, who had reached the ridge and was already returning, dipping his hand in the bag of salt at his side and casting it with skilful flicks of his wrist over the dark earth.

'Let's not be too hasty to dismiss him, my lords. We should speak to him and see whether this sickness is temporary or more long-lasting. Here he comes now.'

They turned to look at Odysseus, who was whistling cheerfully as he sowed. His belt was stuffed with pine branches and he only wore one sandal; the other was tied by its thongs around his neck, and in it was the partly decomposed body of a squirrel. Agamemnon waited until he was almost at the end of the furrow before drawing back his red cloak and stepping forward, his armour flashing in the sun.

'Odysseus!'

Odysseus stopped and looked at the king of Mycenae and his companions. An instant later his face was filled with recognition and joy, and he immediately ran towards them with open arms.

'My lords!' he cried.

'See,' Agamemnon said, turning and winking to his brother. 'A momentary madness, brushed aside at the sight of his old friends.'

Suddenly Odysseus was on his knees before them and touching his forehead to the ground. Agamemnon's look of satisfaction turned rapidly to consternation.

'Get up, Odysseus,' Menelaus said. 'There's no need to prostrate yourself like this, and you're embarrassing us.'

Odysseus peered up at them from between his fingers. 'But no mortal – even a king – can dare to look on the faces of Zeus and Poseidon and expect to live.'

'Zeus and . . .' stuttered Agamemnon. 'Odysseus, stop this nonsense at once and get to your feet.'

'As you wish, Father Zeus.'

'Don't you recognize us?' Menelaus asked, genuine concern on his face. 'Menelaus and Agamemnon? And Palamedes, who you met at Sparta.'

Odysseus looked at Palamedes and screwed his face up.

'I don't remember meeting any satyrs in Sparta. I've heard it said they're the ugliest beasts a man could ever have the misfortune of setting eyes on, and now I know it's true.'

'Stop this blasphemy, Odysseus!' Agamemnon commanded, checking Palamedes's anger with a hand on his chest. 'We're mortal men, not gods.'

'Of course, my lord. But why did you leave Mount Olympus to set foot on this humble rock, where I was king before my son took the throne from me?'

Agamemnon looked questioningly over his shoulder at Penelope, who shrugged forlornly and held Telemachus closer to her chest. Menelaus, now standing beside her, tapped his finger to his forehead and raised his eyebrows.

'Have it your way, Odysseus. We come on a mission of the

greatest importance: a crime has been committed against my brother – indeed, against the whole of Greece – that needs immediate retribution! A new enemy has raised his head, and if we don't unite against him now then our wives, our families and our homes will never be safe again.'

Odysseus folded his arms and scratched his chin while focusing intently on Agamemnon's right ear. 'A new enemy, you say? Committing crimes against Greece?'

'Yes.'

'And you want my help?'

'If you think you're well enough,' Menelaus added.

'Never felt better, sir. But you'll need an army! Every king from every city in the land must dust off his spear and shield – ornaments for too long – and call their subjects to arms.'

'Yes, yes – exactly,' Agamemnon enthused. 'I knew you'd be the first to understand, Odysseus. How many men can you bring, and how quickly?'

Odysseus's eyes lit up with a sudden fervour. He opened the mouth of his satchel and showed the salt to Agamemnon. 'Thousands! *Tens* of thousands. But not until harvest time.'

'Harvest!' Agamemnon cried. 'But that's over half a year away.'

Odysseus looked at him as if he had gone mad. 'Even you gods can't hurry nature, my lord. I've only just sown them,' he added, indicating the ploughed field with a sweep of his arm. 'They won't be full grown warriors until the late autumn. Why, they won't even be boys for at least two months.'

'By the name of every god on Olympus,' said Menelaus, storming past his brother and seizing Odysseus by the shoulders. 'Odysseus, I don't know if there's any part of the old you left in there, but you *must* listen to me. This is no joke – it's important, urgent! We – *I* – need every bit of your fighting skill and your cunning. I'm at my wits' end, Odysseus! It's Helen. She's been kidnapped and taken to Troy.' Tears rolled down the king's cheeks and fell in large droplets to the ground. 'Being without her is destroying me. Unless you can shake off this madness and help my brother and me get her back, then *I'll* be the one ploughing with an ox and an ass and throwing salt in the furrows.'

Odysseus looked at him for a long time, during which nobody spoke. Eventually, his eyes turned away to rest on Penelope.

'I know what it's like to love someone so much that you can't bear to be apart from them. For that reason, Poseidon, I shall tend and water these crops every day until they're ready. You'll have your army by the summer, even if they're only lads. And I'll get back to the plough this instant – there are thousands more warriors in this bag and I need to get them sown before evening.'

He patted Menelaus's arm sympathetically before sprinting as fast as his short legs would carry his ungainly bulk towards the waiting plough. As he reached the top of the ridge, he slipped the leather harness over his shoulders and picked up a long stick, which he applied to the backs of the two animals. The ass brayed angrily and immediately struggled against the yoke, whilst its slower companion took three more cracks of the stick and several shouts of 'Hah! Hah!' before it would agree to move. Though unhurried in its movements, its solid bulk prevented the ass from pulling away, and before long the plough was being dragged back down the slope with only Odysseus's great strength keeping it straight. Every now and then he reached into his satchel and tossed a handful of salt over his shoulder.

'By all the gods,' Palamedes said suddenly, snapping his fingers. '*Was* one of the cleverest men in Greece, you say Menelaus? I think he still is; but he doesn't fool me, and I'm going to prove he's not mad.'

As the plough came nearer, they could hear Odysseus singing a popular farming song, the words of which he had twisted to a martial theme.

> *'I sows 'em when it's frosty,*
> *The ground as hard as bronze,*
> *I waters 'em when it's sunny,*
> *My beautiful warrior sons.*

*I reaps 'em in the summer,*
*'Cos foreign wars demand,*
*Then sends 'em in the autumn,*
*To die on foreign land.'*

Suddenly, Palamedes turned to Penelope and snatched the baby from her arms. Rushing across the field, he laid the child before the oncoming hooves of the ox and ass, with the iron blade of the plough following behind. Telemachus, hearing the cries of his mother (who Agamemnon had seized and was holding fast), began to scream and kick. Odysseus threw his weight to the right and at the last possible moment steered the team past his son, the hooves of the ox trampling the ground beside his head. In an instant he had thrown off the harness and, abandoning the plough, picked up Telemachus to hold him in the protection of his arms.

Agamemnon released Penelope, who ran over and received the bundle from her husband. Odysseus then rushed at Palamedes with a terrible fire in his eyes, his insanity forgotten. Palamedes was so pleased with his own cleverness, he only realized his danger when Odysseus's fist came swinging into the side of his skull. He stumbled backwards and fell into the ploughed soil.

As soon as Menelaus realized that Odysseus's madness was feigned, he felt his own anger take hold of him and with a growl slid his sword from its scabbard. Eperitus, Arceisius and Eurybates, who had been watching the events from beneath the olive tree, drew their own swords and ran to protect their king.

'Menelaus!' Agamemnon shouted. The authority in his voice was so compelling that even Eperitus and Arceisius stopped and looked at the Mycenaean king. 'Brother, put your sword away. Odysseus was only doing what he had to do for the sake of his family.'

Menelaus looked at his older brother and realized in a moment that he was speaking the truth. The anger drained from him and he slid his sword back into its scabbard.

'Now then, Odysseus,' Agamemnon continued. 'My patience is

at its end, so let's have no more of this charade. Palamedes has outfoxed you, and you'll just have to accept it. We're forming an expedition of Greek kings to rescue Helen, so give us your answer: will you come with us to Troy?'

'Why should he?' Penelope interjected. Her cheeks were flushed and her eyes dark with anger as she clutched Telemachus to her chest. 'He's not beholden to you, Agamemnon. He's a king in his own right, and now he's a father. Although I have every sympathy for you, Menelaus – Helen is my cousin and this news is like a dagger in my heart – you've no right to ask a man to leave his family and go to war on the other side of the world. Odysseus has every reason to stay on Ithaca, and every reason not to go on this expedition of yours.'

'But Menelaus does have the right to ask Odysseus to come to Troy,' Palamedes said, propping himself up on one elbow and rubbing his reddened cheek. 'To *demand* that he comes, even. Isn't that so, Odysseus?'

The Ithacan king placed his arm about his wife's waist and kissed her on the cheek. He looked at the baby in her arms and touched the tip of his nose with his nail-bitten finger, smiling as the sight of his child momentarily eclipsed the troubles that were about to overtake him. Then, with a sigh, he turned to Penelope and looked her in the eye.

'My love, he's right. Ten years ago, those of us who wanted to marry Helen were made to take a secret pledge. Her father was so terrified her looks would cause a fight, I helped him out by suggesting a sacred oath.'

'What oath, Odysseus?'

'To protect the successful suitor and come to his aid if anyone threatened their marriage.'

Penelope looked away. 'And as Menelaus was the successful suitor, you're honour-bound to help him.'

'I never dreamed my own ruse would come back to bite me,' Odysseus said softly, stroking his wife's hair. 'But the moment I recognized Agamemnon's sail I instinctively knew it had. If it was only a matter of honour, I wouldn't care. But it's not. It was an oath sworn before all the gods, and if I refuse Menelaus's request I'll be a cursed man; the immortals will make my life a misery, and yours too. My only hope was to feign madness so Menelaus wouldn't call on me to honour my word, but I failed.'

'I understand, Odysseus, and I don't blame you for suggesting or taking this oath. But if the Trojans refuse to return Helen to Menelaus then it'll mean war. You could be killed, and then Telemachus would grow up without ever having known his father.'

'He won't,' Eperitus said. 'Not if we can prevent it.'

'And what can you do?' Penelope asked, looking at Eperitus and his squire with scornful anger. 'Aren't you and Arceisius deserting him to go and make names for yourselves?'

Eperitus felt the sting of her words, but gave her the most reassuring smile he could muster. 'We still intend to leave Ithaca in search of glory, my lady. But it looks as if Troy's going to be the place to find it, so we'll go there at Odysseus's side.'

'Besides,' said the king, looking pleased as he slapped Eperitus and Arceisius on the shoulders, 'I've no intention of releasing either of these rogues from my service. They need somebody responsible to keep them out of trouble.'

'That's the spirit I'm looking for,' Agamemnon interrupted. 'Eperitus, isn't it?'

'Yes, my lord,' Eperitus answered, as Odysseus hooked a hand around Arceisius's elbow and led him away. The last time Eperitus had seen Agamemnon was ten years before in Sparta, when the Mycenaean king was among a group of nobles who had sentenced him to death for assaulting Penelope in her bedroom.

'I'm glad to see you escaped execution,' Agamemnon continued. 'Especially as Odysseus was the one in Penelope's room that night.'

'We worked that out for ourselves in the end,' Menelaus said, putting a friendly arm about Eperitus's shoulder. 'And when we realized you'd offered your own life to save Odysseus's, Eperitus, the shame that had been attached to your name was wiped away and replaced with honour. Don't you agree, brother?'

Agamemnon turned his gaze on Eperitus and scrutinized the lowly warrior with his cold, passionless eyes for a long moment. Then the king's face broke with a smile that was surprisingly warm and inviting as he took Eperitus's hand.

'Men of your quality are hard to come by,' he announced. 'With the likes of you and Odysseus with us at Troy, Priam will soon learn that his days are numbered. And I can tell you, as sure as any oracle, the honour you've already earned will be nothing compared with what the gods will heap on you in Ilium. I'll be proud to have you at my side.'

Odysseus, who was busy unyoking the ass with Arceisius and Eurybates, looked over his shoulder at these words.

'We don't know there'll even be a war yet, Agamemnon. The Trojans might still be persuaded to return Helen unharmed, which will save us all a lot of time and effort, not to mention further heartache for Menelaus.'

'Satisfying my heartache is one thing,' Menelaus growled. 'Satisfying my anger will be quite a different matter altogether.'

Odysseus left the animal in Eurybates's care. 'That may be so, Menelaus,' he said, 'but wars need fleets and armies, and the time and wealth to bring them together. If you want Helen back, a peaceful solution is quickest and best. But let's not get ahead of ourselves. I suggest we return to the palace, enjoy a few kraters of wine and a roast hog, and discuss what needs to be done.'

book
# TWO

## Chapter Ten

# LEAVING ITHACA

The great hall was filled with conversation as the men seated around the burning hearth discussed the events of recent days. Only Eperitus remained silent, lost in thoughts and memories as his gaze wandered about the high-ceilinged chamber for what he mused might be the last time. He looked at the bright, active murals that ran the circuit of the lime-washed walls and recalled a time when the hall had been a dark and decrepit place, the plaster peeling away and the old frescoes lost beneath layers of smoke and grime. Odysseus had changed that. The walls had been replastered and new murals painted. These were kept clean by an army of slaves, and as Eperitus looked at them now they were almost as vivid and colourful as they had been when they were first laid down nine years before.

Most depicted wars of legend — between the gods and the giants on the north wall, the centaurs and lapiths on the west wall, and the gods and the Titans on the south wall. On the east wall, however, was the battle for the liberation of Ithaca. It was a celebration of Ithaca's recent history and the achievements of its king, and for that reason was filled with careful detail. Even Eperitus was shown, leading the attack on the walls — or so he was told, as each figure looked the same to his eyes — while Odysseus was at the centre, an oversized figure fighting the Taphians inside the palace.

Eperitus, though quietly satisfied that his part in the battle had been so generously recognized, nevertheless felt embarrassed by the mural. His bullying and critical father had never allowed him to develop anything other than a modest image of his own value, and the resulting humility was unusual for a warrior. Ironically, it was also the fuel that fed his desire to prove himself.

He turned his eyes from the mural to the numerous alcoves in the walls, which housed clay statuettes of the different gods. They bore a variety of tokens and symbols that distinguished them from each other: Zeus held a thunderbolt, Poseidon his trident and Apollo his lyre; Hermes had his winged sandals and carried the caduceus, while Hephaistos, the smith-god, held aloft his hammer as if ready to strike; Ares and Athena were both armed with helmet, shield and spear, and Artemis the huntress had her bow and quiver; the flowering branch of a chaste tree was held by Hestia, and a head of corn by Demeter; the naked figure of Aphrodite held a dove in both hands, and finally Hera, the wife of Zeus, was depicted offering an apple. Eperitus felt as if their stern eyes were fixed on him in judgement and turned his face up to the pine-beamed ceiling, where a deep-blue firmament was filled with celestial bodies, clearly picked out in gold and silver as they circled the vent in the centre. Even the crimson of the four soaring pillars that supported the roof was hardly dimmed by the trail of smoke that filtered slowly upwards from the hearth.

An increase in the clamour of voices brought Eperitus's gaze back down to the other members of the Kerosia, the council of the king's advisers. Opposite him was Eupeithes, the former traitor who had been placated with the position of counsellor for trade. He was a fat man with thin, dangling limbs that made him look like a beetle. His ageing head was completely bald, but for a wisp of grey hair above each ear, and his skin was pale and covered with moles. Though defeated and pardoned by Odysseus, his face showed little humility; instead he wore the arrogant, self-assured look of a wealthy man who felt his opinion was superior to all others.

He was holding a discussion with Eurylochus, who Odysseus

had made a member of the Kerosia to placate him after Eperitus was given the captaincy of the royal guard. In Eperitus's opinion, Eurylochus was a fool and his worthless contributions were a waste of the council's time, but the king always gave the impression that he valued his cousin's viewpoint.

On Eurylochus's right was the oldest member of the Kerosia, Phronius, a figure so bent with age that the carved back of his chair was visible as he leaned forward on his stick. Next to him was Halitherses, who had been captain of the guard for many years during Laertes's reign. The wounds he received fighting the Taphians had forced him to resign the post, though he remained a tall, heavily built figure with an imposing presence. Between him and Eperitus sat Mentor, Odysseus's boyhood friend who had lost his left hand to a Taphian sword.

Other than the king and Laertes, only one other member of the council was missing: Penelope. When Eperitus had first attended an Ithacan Kerosia ten years before, he had been shocked that Anticleia, Odysseus's mother, had been allowed to partake in the debate. It was strange in the extreme for a woman to discuss politics with men, but Eperitus had soon learned that Ithaca was a kingdom of strange customs and ideas. So when Odysseus succeeded his father as king he was not surprised that Penelope took Anticleia's place on the council, where her abundant wisdom quickly made its mark. But there were traditionalists on Ithaca, too: as a mother Penelope was now expected to turn her attentions from politics to Telemachus, the future king. Ever wise to the opinions of her subjects, she had temporarily excused herself from attending the Kerosia, much to Eperitus's disappointment.

Phronius, Mentor and Halitherses were having a heated discussion about the number of men they could afford to send to Troy, and how many should be left behind for the defence of the island.

'Over two thousand men answered the call to arms,' Mentor said, 'of which the king's taking eight hundred.'

'And they're all fools,' Phronius croaked, the feathery white strands of his moustache puffing out as he spoke. 'This ain't no local scrap with some boneheads from the mainland. It's a full-scale war on the far side of the civilized world – if you can call Ilium civilized. Any man who sails today won't be seen again in these islands for at least a year – you can count on that. So I say the same now as I said when I first heard mention of this so-called expedition: Odysseus should take sixty good men in a single ship and be done with it. That's more than he needs to do to fulfil this cursed oath, and it'll leave the islands well-enough manned for their own protection, not to speak of the day-to-day business of farming and fishing and so on.'

'That's as may be,' said Halitherses, 'but it won't be the way Odysseus sees it. If I know him at all, and I know him better than you do Phronius, he'll want to show Ithaca in the best light possible. We may not be a rich or powerful kingdom, but we've come a long way since Laertes's day. Just look at this hall, for example, or the number of slaves and guards there are now compared with ten years ago. If the other kings are bringing large numbers of ships and warriors, as Agamemnon says, then Odysseus won't make Ithaca a laughing stock by turning up with a mere boatful of soldiers. He's leaving more than enough men at home for Ithaca to take care of itself, though if he could've begged and borrowed more than a dozen ships I'm sure he'd have taken as many as could fit in their black hulls.'

'It's more than just a matter of pride,' Mentor added. 'Odysseus may be a king, but he's a husband and father first. His heart is here with Penelope and Telemachus, and he wants to get this war over as quickly as possible so he can come back to his family. The more men he takes, the bigger the Greek army and the better the chance of a speedy victory.'

'Whatever the reason, I'm just glad he's taking a good number of men with him,' said Halitherses. 'I wouldn't want to think of Odysseus facing a Trojan army with just a handful of Ithacans around him, no matter how many other Greeks there might be. At least his own people will stick by him if things get rough. And Eperitus'll see that he comes home safe – won't you, Eperitus?'

Eperitus, who had been watching the flames twitching in the hearth, looked up.

'Aren't you forgetting something, Halitherses? You were there when the Pythoness spoke her words of doom. Haven't you given any mind to what she said?'

'Of course I have!' Halitherses hissed, lowering his voice. 'And I mean to remind Odysseus of it, too . . .'

Before he could say any more, the door at the back of the great hall opened and Odysseus entered with his father. They were followed by slaves bearing tables laden with bread and cold meat, which they hurriedly placed around the circular hearth before retreating into the shadows. More slaves brought kraters of mixed wine for the members of the Kerosia as they stood for their king. Finally, a troop of four fully armed soldiers entered and stood guard at the door, which they closed behind them with a bang.

Odysseus took two kraters from a slave, handed one to his father, then approached the hearth and poured a libation into the flames. The others did the same, uttering quiet prayers as each slop of wine was welcomed with a hiss. Then Odysseus retreated to the granite throne and sat on the embroidered cushion that had been placed there by one of the slaves. Taking a tall staff of dark wood from another slave, he signalled for the others to return to their seats.

Laertes lowered himself into the vacant chair beside Eperitus, releasing a pained sigh as his joints bent to accommodate the simple movement. He turned his rheumy eyes on the captain of the guard for a lingering moment, then passed his gaze one by one to the other members of the Kerosia. When, finally, it was the turn of Eupeithes, his eyes narrowed and his stare remained fixed on the fat merchant. Eupeithes, however, had become used to this treatment some years ago and had learned to simply ignore it.

Odysseus leaned back into the throne and faced the council. Two large, grey dolphins decorated the wall behind him, their bodies arced over his shoulders and their noses almost touching. Odysseus had adopted the creature for his coat of arms long before he had become king, but now the image was found all through the palace and even on the sails of the ships that were waiting in the harbour below the town, ready for the long voyage to Troy.

'Agamemnon has been sighted coming up from the south,' he announced. 'He promised us a fortnight to prepare our forces, and that's exactly what we've had – there can be no further delay. Have the men who were chosen arrived, Eurylochus?'

'Yes, cousin, and many more besides. Most have come pleading to join the expedition, and some have even offered money to the lucky few to take their places. Several others were caught trying to stow themselves away on the ships. We were forced to drag them off and there were more than a few quarrels about it.'

'Their enthusiasm encourages me,' Odysseus said, though there was little sign of it in his face.

'Their spirits may be willing,' Phronius grunted, 'but any lunatic can rush off to war if they've never raised a spear in anger. I want to know what the abilities are of the men you've picked. How many of them have seen battle? What training have they had? Can they fight as a unit? These are the sorts of question we need to ask now if any of them are to come back.'

Eperitus stood and received the staff from Odysseus.

'You're right to ask these questions, Phronius. You saw your fair share of fighting when you were our age and you know what it can do to a warrior. But I'll be honest with you: most of these men are untrained and almost none have seen battle. I can vouch for the two hundred men that are being released from the guard, of course – Halitherses and I have trained them hard over the years, and they're fit and well used to working together as a unit. About a quarter have seen combat, too: the men who came with us to Samos recently, and those who fought to liberate Ithaca years ago from the Taphian invaders. But we chose the eight hundred as much for their fitness, strength, courage and willingness to fight, and I have complete faith that they will not let Odysseus down.'

Eurylochus stood and looked at the captain of the guard with contempt. 'No more than a dozen have ever been in a *real* battle,' he sneered. 'And only the guards have had any formal military training, or know how to manoeuvre as a disciplined unit. The rest will be a shambles if they go to war. They barely know how to use their weapons, let alone how to work together as an army.'

'That'll be taken care of,' Eperitus responded, ignoring Eurylochus and facing the other members of the council. 'We've already started giving the volunteers rudimentary weapons training and teaching them a few moves and basic tactics. There's been no time to make them into warriors or a functioning army, but Odysseus and I have worked out a proper training schedule, which we'll have enough time to implement when we reach Aulis.'

'Aulis?' asked Mentor.

'It's a sheltered bay in the Euboean straits,' Odysseus answered. 'Agamemnon has made it the muster point for the Greek fleet. We'll be there for weeks or even months while we wait for latecomers and make the proper preparations for war. Before we even think of sailing for Troy, the kings will need to agree on a leader for the expedition – which will almost certainly be Agamemnon – and then decide on strategies, tactics, reserves, supplies and so on.'

'As far as our own army is concerned, you can leave the problem of supply with me,' said Eupeithes, standing and sweeping his yellow cloak over his shoulder with a flourish. He received the speaker's staff from Eperitus and turned to look at the members of the Kerosia. 'In fact I've already made arrangements for corn to be shipped from Dulichium and wine from Samos – and all at a reasonable discount, considering the cause is a patriotic one. As for the army's other needs – clothing, replacement weaponry, not to mention lesser trifles such as pots, pans, bedding, and so on – I've discussed this with local merchants and we've agreed . . .'

'Sit down, you fat fool,' Laertes interrupted, glaring contemptuously at his old enemy. 'Don't you know Agamemnon and Menelaus have offered to provision the whole Greek army?'

'But . . . But nobody told . . .'

'Oh stop stammering and get back to your seat,' Laertes

snapped, walking around the hearth and snatching the staff from Eupeithes's hand. 'Now, *this* is the question I want to ask: what about the Trojans? We know the Greeks should be able to provide a large army – if the oath is honoured and each king brings his fair share of soldiers – and that a good core should be well trained, properly equipped and experienced, but what do we know about the enemy? Well, when I was the king of Ithaca I wasn't as idle or ignorant as some of my subjects thought,' Laertes glared at Eupeithes, 'so I'll tell you what *I* know. Priam, they say, is a womanizer with more brains in his penis than his head, but he has – or at least he had – a particular son who effectively rules in his stead. His name is Hector, a violent brute of a man with a sharp mind when it comes to fighting. He rules over an empire of vassal states and allied cities, which he keeps on a tight rein through the ruthless application of violence and fear. The Trojan army is considerable in size and battle-hardened through its unending border wars, and they can call on large numbers of warriors from the rest of the empire. These foreigners breed like dogs, so even with the whole of Greece against them they'll easily be able to match us man for man. I can't speak for their quality, but when a man is defending his home and knows the only thing between a vicious enemy and his wife and children is his spear, he will fight twice as hard as any invader.

'What's more,' Laertes continued, turning his calm, knowing eyes on Odysseus, 'the Trojans boast that the walls of their city were built by Apollo and Poseidon. They're impenetrable. Even if you defeat their walls of flesh and blood, my son, you won't pass their walls of stone. As I see it, if you go on this mission to Troy then it'll be many years before you see the halls of your own palace again – if at all.'

At this point, Halitherses stood and moved towards Laertes, who gave him the speaker's staff and returned to his seat.

'Odysseus,' Halitherses began, 'your father speaks with the wisdom of a god. As soon as I heard of this proposed mission to rescue Helen – the moment I learned she was being held in Troy

– my heart sank. Did you think I'd forgotten Mount Parnassus and the oracle the Pythoness gave you? Indeed, could any man forget the sight of that poor girl, transformed as she was with the face and tongue of a serpent, speaking those fateful words? It's always been kept a secret between those of us who were there – you, Eperitus, Antiphus and I – but now the time has come to share it with the Kerosia. Give me leave to reveal what she said, so that the council will know the doom that awaits you.'

Odysseus looked pensively at the old soldier, then gave a quiet nod of his head. Halitherses turned to the others and, in a slow voice, began to repeat the words of the priestess.

'"Find a daughter of Lacedaemon and she will keep the thieves from your house. As father of your people you will count the harvests on your fingers. But if ever you seek Priam's city, the wide waters will swallow you. For the time it takes a baby to become a man, you will know no home. Then, when friends and fortune have departed from you, you will rise again from the dead."'

As he spoke the flames in the hearth sputtered and threatened to fail altogether, while the shadows about the hall multiplied and grew darker. A silence fell and it was only after the last words had died away that the fire began to spit and crackle again, and the fidgeting of the slaves could be heard once more in the background.

'It doesn't seem like any choice at all to me,' said Mentor. 'Stay at home and be cursed by the gods for breaking an oath, or go to Troy and be doomed not to return home for two decades.'

'Which is why I say Odysseus should abandon this expedition and risk the fury of the Olympians,' Halitherses replied. 'The alternative is unthinkable.'

'Don't be foolish, Halitherses,' Odysseus admonished him. 'If anything in this life is certain, it's the vengefulness of the gods. We live by their blessing and provision, and suffer through their anger or fickle moods. No, I wouldn't willingly incur their wrath for anything – even when the alternative is being sentenced to twenty years at the other end of the world, away from my home and family. But there is still hope! The force Agamemnon is gathering is powerful indeed: Diomedes will be there; both the Ajaxes; Idomeneus of Crete; Menestheus of Athens; Nestor the famous charioteer. Even Achilles is to be asked.'

'Hope!' Phronius exclaimed, his voice cracking with disbelief. 'Hope? An oracle is the will of the gods, Odysseus – there can be no hope.'

'Then let me reveal another secret,' the king retorted. 'Ten years ago the Kerosia – yourself included, Phronius – sent me on a mission to compete with the best men in Greece for the hand of Helen. The odds were against me, but that has never stopped me from taking up a challenge. Then, before I had even reached Sparta, Athena herself told me that Helen was to be given to Menelaus. I believed her, of course, because the will of the gods cannot be changed by mortal action. Or that was what I had always believed. But then Helen offered herself to me, and her father was prepared to honour her wish.'

'What's that?' Laertes said, sitting up. 'If Helen offered herself to you, why didn't you take the chance and be sure of saving Ithaca?'

'If I had, then perhaps this expedition to Troy would have been for my sake instead of Menelaus's! As it is, I fell in love with Penelope instead and after that there was no question of marrying Helen. But my point is this: a goddess had told me that Helen was to be given to Menelaus, and yet it was within my power to make her mine. Do you understand? For a moment my destiny was in my own hands – not the hands of the gods or of anyone else, just mine. And if it was the case then, it can be the same now. I intend to fight this war as if that oracle had never been uttered. I'm going to use every bit of my cunning to finish it quickly, and if I have to I'll scrap like a cur until Troy lies in ruins and our black-hulled ships are speeding back home to Ithaca.'

At that moment, the guards stood aside and a soldier entered the great hall, his footsteps echoing from the walls as he marched up to the king.

'What is it?' Odysseus asked.

'Agamemnon, Menelaus and Palamedes have arrived, my lord. Their ship was moving into the harbour as I left to report.'

The king stood as the soldier left and, belatedly, received the staff from Halitherses's hand.

'This has been a difficult meeting and some things have been revealed that I would rather have remained secret. But there *is* hope, whatever Phronius says – maybe not of a swift victory, but we shouldn't dismiss the power of a united Greece to win this war in good time. It only remains for me to propose that Mentor takes charge of Ithaca until my return, deferring only to my father's experience and Penelope's wisdom. I have also asked Eperitus to be my second-in-command, a role that befits his position as captain of the guard and my friend. Are you in agreement?'

The members of the Kerosia – with the exception of Eurylochus – nodded, and the slaves began clearing away the tables and their untouched food. Odysseus signalled for Eperitus to join him, but before he could say a word to the captain of his guard Halitherses approached with a concerned look on his old face.

'Odysseus,' he said, 'Eperitus told me he offered to lead the army in your place, but that you insisted on going.'

The king nodded.

'Well, I'm your friend and you trust me,' Halitherses continued. 'Although your optimism in the face of the gods is admirable, don't forget Helen *did* marry Menelaus, whatever opportunities came your way. And my instincts are against you going to this war. Why don't you accept Eperitus's offer?'

Odysseus placed a hand on the old warrior's shoulder and looked him in the eye.

'Because I don't really have that choice, Halitherses. I was the one who took the oath, not Eperitus. Besides, I may not be as accomplished a fighter as Achilles, Diomedes or the greater Ajax, but I have more brains than the rest of them rolled up together. I'll think of a way to shorten this war when all their brawn and fighting skill fails, and when I come back home to my family in a couple of years the honour for the victory will be mine. I'll prove the oracle wrong yet, old friend.'

Halitherses embraced Odysseus and Eperitus briefly, the tears flowing openly down his cheeks as he bade them farewell. Phronius followed, silently taking the hands of both men before shuffling away, stooped over his stick. Eupeithes, in his usual aloof manner, shook the king's hand and wished him well.

'The last time you led an armed mission overseas,' he added in a quiet voice, 'a certain rich fool used the opportunity to seize the throne. Well, you've proved yourself a just and merciful king and I want you to know that rich fool has learned from his errors – he won't be making the same mistake again. That's all I wanted to say, Odysseus. Goodbye.'

He bowed low, then with a brief nod to Eperitus was gone.

'What was that all about?' asked Laertes after his nemesis had left.

'I believe that was the first heart-felt apology Eupeithes has ever offered me,' Odysseus answered. 'Will you and mother be coming to watch the fleet disembark?'

'Fleet?' Laertes scoffed. 'That's a very grand expression for a dozen ancient galleys pulled together at the last moment. If your Taphian friend Mentes hadn't offered to sell us six of his ships, half of the army would have been sailing in merchant vessels. Even now I doubt you'll make it to Aulis, let alone Troy.'

'Well, that would be one way to avoid my doom,' Odysseus replied, sardonically. 'But on the assumption the fleet makes it out of the harbour, will you and mother be there to see us off?'

'She said her goodbyes to you last night, Odysseus, and won't say them again. She already believes she's seen you for the last time, so I don't know how she'll take this oracle you've been keeping secret all these years.'

'She'll see me again, I know it,' Odysseus said firmly. 'And what about you father? Will you come to the harbour?'

Laertes took his son's hand. 'I don't like crowds, so I'll say farewell here. Look after yourself and come back as quickly as you can. Mentor and I will take good care of Penelope and Telemachus for you.'

With that, he turned his pale, watery eyes away and departed, leaving only Eperitus, Eurylochus and Mentor with the king. Odysseus took a last look around the hall he had known so well for all of his life, then turned and left.

The changeable weather had brought a sky full of grey cloud to cover the departure of the Ithacan fleet. Odysseus marched out of the palace gates with his three companions to a loud cheer from the waiting army and the crowds of Ithacans who had come to see them off to war. He waved his hand in acknowledgement and looked at the hundreds of faces. The soldiers stared back with something close to adoration, all of them eager to risk their lives for a war not of their making, in a foreign land none of them had ever seen. Each man wore a chelonion flower tucked into his belt or in a joint of his armour, to act as a reminder of their homeland. Odysseus knew almost all of them by sight and many by name, even amongst those who had come from the furthest corners of his small kingdom. As he stood before them, a wave of nervous energy burst through his stomach and filled him with a feeling of nausea. Every moment of the past two weeks had been consumed by preparation for the great expedition, but now he was finally able to understand that he was leaving his beloved homeland for a faraway country, unable to say when – or if – he or any of his men would return.

At that moment, a bark erupted from the crowd and Argus came bounding towards him.

'Hello, boy,' he said, bending down and patting the puppy vigorously as it licked his beard. 'I was wondering where you'd got to. Thought perhaps you didn't want to see me off.'

Argus barked and wagged his tail.

'I'm sure you'd love to come along for the voyage, youngster,' Odysseus said, holding the dog's face in his hands and looking into his eyes. 'And you'd be better company than most. But a ship's no place for a dog, and neither is a battlefield. Mentor's going to look after you until I come back.'

'That's right, boy,' said Mentor, bending down to pat Argus's head. 'We're being left at home while Odysseus and Eperitus go to reap all the glory. But at least we can hunt a few boar while they're away, eh?'

Odysseus grinned at his old friend, then turned to Eperitus.

'Time to divide the men into their units,' he said.

Eperitus nodded and stepped forward. 'Form up by your commanders,' he shouted, his voice rebounding off the walls and houses.

Suddenly the hum of conversation grew louder and more urgent as the men hurriedly kissed their loved ones goodbye and gathered their arms and belongings about them. This was followed by a disorderly stampede of warriors searching to find their nominated commanders, who in their turn were calling out their own names so that their men would be able to find them in the chaos.

'You'll have your work cut out getting this lot into shape,' Odysseus said in a low voice that only Eperitus could hear.

'We'll manage it,' Eperitus replied.

As he was the commander of Odysseus's ship, large numbers of men were now emerging from the mayhem and making their way towards Eperitus. They included the hand-picked warriors of Odysseus's personal bodyguard, Antiphus, Eurybates and the titanic figure of Polites among them. Arceisius was also with them, grinning in anticipation of his first great adventure.

'This is quite a rabble you've got here, Eperitus,' Antiphus sighed, looking about at the chaotic assembly.

'Anything we can do to help?' asked Eurybates.

'Yes. Organize our lot into ten rows of twelve, get rid of the women and make sure we haven't gained any stragglers,' Eperitus ordered firmly.

An instant later the old soldiers of the guard were barking commands and using the shafts of their spears to chase people into, or out of, the orderly ranks their captain had requested.

'Having trouble with your army, Odysseus?'

Odysseus turned to see Agamemnon standing behind him. Menelaus and Palamedes stood on either side of the Mycenaean king and an escort of a dozen well-armed men stood watchfully at their shoulders.

'If you're in a hurry, gentlemen,' Odysseus said, shaking the hands of the two brothers, though pointedly avoiding the hand offered by Palamedes, 'I can send them back to their homes and just take the one ship.'

He pointed to Eperitus's unit who, though still lacking a few men, were standing in orderly rows.

'We can wait,' Agamemnon replied, clearly enjoying the sight of hundreds of armed men running around with little semblance of order. 'I'm sure that once your men separate themselves from their families they'll make a fine body of men. Unless, that is, the women and children are coming too.'

Odysseus gave a tired smile and shook his head. 'Not yet. Now, if you'll forgive me, I have to say goodbye to my own family. Eperitus, get the men down to their ships a unit at a time, with ours last.'

Eperitus watched the king stride back through the palace gates with Argus barking at his ankles. Odysseus was about to face one of the hardest challenges of his life, but this time there was nothing Eperitus could do to help him.

Actoris gave Telemachus to his father and stepped back.

'Such a shame,' she tutted as Odysseus bent to kiss the child on his warm, red cheek. 'Such a shame. I hope this war doesn't last long, my lord, or you won't hear his first words or see him learn to crawl.'

'Don't make matters worse, Actoris,' said Penelope, her voice strained. 'Leave us now, and take Telemachus with you.'

Odysseus pressed a final kiss on the baby's forehead before passing him into the old nursemaid's waiting arms.

'Go with Telemachus, boy,' Odysseus ordered, looking down at Argus. 'Guard him until I return.'

He barked once and promptly followed Actoris out of the room, trotting along beside her with his head craned up at the white bundle in her arms. Odysseus watched them go, then shut the double doors behind them and walked over to the bed in the middle of the room. Each post had a thick girth and was inlaid with patterns of gold, silver and ivory that twisted and turned all the way up to the ceiling.

'Do you remember when I made this bed?' he said, sliding his palm like a plane over the smooth surface of one of the posts.

Penelope smiled and sat on the pile of furs that covered the thick straw mattress. 'Of course I do. You refused to sleep with me for two weeks until you'd finished it.'

'Ah, but it was worth the wait.'

Penelope lay back on the bed, her long, dark hair spreading over the light-coloured fleece like a fan. 'Yes, I couldn't forget that either.'

'I made this post from the bole of a living olive tree,' Odysseus continued. 'The others I just cut to size and fitted, but this one was from the tree that used to stand here before I built this part of the palace. Its roots still run beneath the bed we've shared for ten years – the best ten years of my life, Penelope.'

'Will you be away long, Odysseus? The talk among the slaves is that the expedition will take over a year – it's an awfully long time to be apart from you.'

'Who can say for certain?' Odysseus mused, sitting beside his wife and placing his hand on her warm stomach. 'The Trojans might give Helen back the moment they see our fleet anchored off their shores, or they might decide to fight it out. But I promise you I'll do everything I can to bring this quarrel to a quick end, even if I have to give up eternal glory and all the plunder in Priam's treasury to achieve it. There's nowhere I want to be more than back here with you and our son.'

'I know,' Penelope said, reaching up and touching his face. 'But

I'm going to miss you however long you're gone. It'll be lonely without you.'

'Don't say that. There are many people here who love you dearly, and you'll have Telemachus to look after. Besides, the war may not happen at all, and if it does victory should be swift.'

'Only the gods can say how and when it will end,' Penelope replied, sitting up. 'But I know this much, Odysseus: the Greeks won't succeed without you. Your intelligence and courage are already well known, but this war is going to reveal the *true* greatness that I know is hidden within you. I want nothing more than for you to be here, in this bed with me every night, but your potential can never be realized on this forgotten collection of rocks at the world's edge. So go to Troy and fulfil your oath, and let everyone see the kind of man you really are.'

She stood and took Odysseus's hands in hers, pulling him to his feet.

'The time is nearly upon us,' she said, her voice low to hide the emotion that was welling up inside her. 'But before you go, husband, I want you to have something to remember me by.'

She led him by the hand from the bedroom to the older part of the palace. There were no slaves in any of the corridors – everybody was outside, seeing Ithaca's army off to war – and soon they were alone in a torch-lit storeroom that smelled of wine and old leather.

'Here,' she said, taking a heap of cloth from a table and unfolding it. 'It's a double cloak. I made it myself.'

Odysseus unclipped his worn-out old cloak and let it fall to the dirt floor, then took the garment from his wife's hands and swung it over his shoulders. Even in the weak torchlight, the purple wool had a silvery sheen like the skin of a dried onion. The fine material felt soft and smooth on his upper arms, and despite its extra thickness was light and moved freely.

As he admired the feel of it, Penelope stepped up and fastened it over his left shoulder with a golden brooch. Odysseus looked down at it, but could not make out the design in the gloom.

'What does it show?' he asked.

'A dog killing a faun,' Penelope answered, putting her hands behind his neck and kissing him tenderly on the lips. 'I thought it suited you; it's like the motif on Agamemnon's sail, but more restrained. You're a greater king than he is, Odysseus, though your strength is more subtle.'

'I'll need subtlety if I'm to make my mark on this adventure. You remember the sort of men who paid court to Helen – powerful, rich, great warriors to a man. What am I compared to them? The only advantage I have is up here.' He tapped his head with his forefinger.

'Just make sure you use your brains to bring the rest of you back safely,' Penelope said, throwing her arms about his broad chest and leaning her head on his shoulder. 'I've heard terrible things about these Trojans, Odysseus. Is it true they're battle-hardened and show their enemies no mercy?'

Odysseus thought of his father's words to the Kerosia, as well as the things he had heard said at the failed council of war held by Agamemnon ten years earlier.

'They're good soldiers, I'm told – skilled with the spear, the bow and the chariot. Many Greeks will meet their deaths in Ilium, and I can't promise you I won't be one of them – that's for the gods to decide. But I'm no weakling, either, and there won't be many Trojans who can better me on the battlefield. If I die, though, or if I'm not home by the time Telemachus is old enough to take the throne for himself, then you must marry whoever you choose and start again. I don't want you to be lonely, Penelope.'

She opened her mouth to speak, but he placed a finger against her lips.

'Now I must go,' he said, kissing her on the forehead and holding her close. 'Look after my father and mother while I'm gone – they love you very much. And take good care of Telemachus. I've left him the horn bow that Iphitus gave me – it's in its box, hanging from a peg in the armoury. When he's able to string it, you can tell him he's old enough to be king in my place.'

'You'll be back long before then,' Penelope replied, then hid her face in her hands as the hot tears stung her eyes.

She felt Odysseus touch her hair with his large, gentle fingers, but when she opened her eyes again he was gone.

When Odysseus returned to the terrace, his newly donned armour gleaming in the grey light, most of the army had moved down to the harbour. The majority of the crowd had gone with them and the hubbub of their conversation could still be heard drifting up from the bay and over the wooded ridge to the town. Only the sixty men of the king's own ship remained, standing in rows awaiting his return. At their head were Eperitus and Mentor, talking to Omeros.

'Let's move,' Odysseus said, striding up to them. 'If I don't go now I might never leave at all. What are you doing here, Omeros?'

'He was caught hiding in a grain sack on one of the ships,' Eperitus explained. 'Apparently, he wants to come with us to Troy so he can experience war for himself and compose a song about our exploits.'

'Does he, now?' Odysseus asked. Then, sliding his sword from its scabbard, he turned and presented the handle to the angry-looking bard. 'I admire your spirit, lad – it's worthy of a true Ithacan, so I'll do you a deal. If you can strike any one of us – Eperitus, Mentor or me – with the flat of this sword, I'll take you with us. Fair?'

Omeros, his surly expression lightening a little, nodded silently and held his hand out for the sword. Odysseus laid the handle gently in the boy's palm, then let go.

The point fell straight into the dirt. Omeros placed both hands on the hilt and with all his strength was only able to lift the sword level with his knees, before dropping it again. Odysseus took the weapon out of his hands as if it weighed no more than a piece of driftwood, then slid it back into its scabbard.

'A warrior carries a sword, two spears and a shield made with at least four ox-hides sewn one on top of the other. He also has his breastplate, helmet and greaves. Without any one of these, Omeros, his chances in battle are reduced. He must be able to cast his ash spear as far as the palace wall is from us now, with enough power to drive the point through several layers of leather or bronze. Once his spears are used he must draw his sword and with one hand – the other is holding his shield, don't forget – fight his enemies to the death. All this with the sun on his back, the sweat in his eyes and the strength draining from his muscles with every passing moment. I'm not telling you this to humiliate you, Omeros, just to make you understand why you're not yet ready to come with us. If all a soldier needed was a stubborn will and a courageous spirit, I'd put you back in that grain sack myself. But it's not like that, son.'

'No, sir,' Omeros replied. 'But I can still sing for you. They say all the other kings have their own bards.'

'Terpius can sing well enough for my liking. And I know you think the man's an artless buffoon,' Odysseus added quickly as Omeros's mouth opened to protest, 'but he has the advantage of being a grown man who can throw a spear as well as anyone in Ithaca. Now, I won't argue about it any more – go back into the palace and sing something cheerful for my wife. I think she'd like that.'

Omeros, his head lowered, trudged back to the palace.

'You'd better go, too, Mentor,' Odysseus continued. 'I'm going to miss your counsel, but at least I can feel at peace while I'm away if I know you're running things here.'

He embraced his boyhood friend, then after sweeping the familiar town and the palace one last time with his eyes, he turned and led his men down the road towards the harbour.

## Chapter Eleven

# REGRETS AND HOPES

Helen sat in the soft, thick grass and looked across the bay towards the horizon. The sun was nearing the end of another day's journey, and in its final, magnificent moments the skies above were transformed into brilliant bands of magenta, orange, gold and indigo. As the shimmering orb dipped into the waters at the furthest edge of the world its reflection stabbed out like the head of a bronze spear, reaching the Trojan galley anchored at the broad mouth of the bay so that the ship's black silhouette seemed to be floating on a sea of yellow fire.

It was from these waters, off the western coast of Cyprus, that Aphrodite had been born. The legends told how the Titan Cronos castrated his father, Uranos, and cast his genitals into the sea. Aphrodite emerged from the foam they created and came ashore at Paphos, possibly even on the same crescent of beach that sloped away before Helen now.

Helen closed her eyes and rested her forehead on her raised knees.

'Goddess, my beloved Lady Aphrodite, have I ever failed to make pleasing sacrifices at your temple in Sparta, burning fat-covered thighs on the altar as the gods prefer? Since I was a small girl, haven't I always honoured you above the other Olympians? And yet, how have you rewarded my devotion? With disdain!' Helen sniffed and wiped an angry tear from her cheek. 'The beauty you gave me has been nothing but a curse. It's made me a prize for men to drool and compete over, and yet all it has ever brought me was marriage to Menelaus. Were you punishing me, my lady, or just mocking me? And the only things of worth to come from our wedlock, my beautiful children, have been taken from me in the cruellest manner – by my own choice. Only Pleisthenes was allowed to escape with me, and only then because his little, crippled form would be a foil to my own perfection. Why couldn't you have crippled me instead and spared him?'

She paused for a moment, sensing that the sun had finally disappeared below the horizon. A cool breeze drifted up from the sea, fanning her long feet and bare shins.

'And what is this choice I've made? Paris and I haven't even become lovers yet; we've sailed from one place to another – Egypt, Phoenicia and now Cyprus – and though I know I love him and he loves me, we've shared nothing more adulterous than a kiss. I know why. My mind has dwelt too long on what I've left behind: Hermione, Aethiolas and Maraphius; a safe and familiar home; even Menelaus's devotion and tenderness. And all that lies ahead are an unknown future with a strange man in a foreign city. Will his family and the people of Troy love me, or will they despise me if war and suffering follow in my wake? Will even Paris continue to love me, or will he tire of my fine looks and abandon me? Worse still, will he return me to Menelaus, an unfaithful and despised wife? Oh, why did you make me fall in love, turning my mind so that I deserted a loving husband and my beautiful children? I should have been a follower of Artemis or Athena instead!'

'Could anything be as dull as worshipping those old maids?'

Startled, Helen looked up and saw an ancient crone standing on the beach before her. She was dressed in a collection of brown rags that covered her from head to foot, leaving only her wizened, toothless face exposed. Her back was bent almost double and her leathery fingers were twisted about clumps of seaweed that hung down to the sand. Helen's faultless features soured in revulsion at the woman's appearance.

'You shouldn't eavesdrop on a person's private prayers, old hag.'

'Prayers is said to be heard, so they say. I might as well hear yours as anyone else.'

'Why would I pray to you?' Helen frowned. 'You can't answer prayers.'

'It sounds to me like your prayers aren't being answered anyway.'

'How long have you been listening to me?'

To Helen's disgust, the old woman began shambling up the sand towards her.

'Longer than you might think, my young beauty,' she said, sitting on the grass beside her. 'Much longer than you might think. Now, tell me about this young man – this Paris.'

'I'm not going to discuss Paris with an old sea-wife who stinks of brine and . . . and stale piss!'

The crone smiled and her eyes almost disappeared beneath a mass of brown wrinkles. 'Then I'll tell you something about him, my dear. Paris's passion has always been for fighting, and his loyalty has always been to Troy. But deep down he boils with a desire to be wanted – to be *loved*! He was rejected as a child, you see, and that has never left him, even if his warrior's self-discipline has helped him to control his emotions. But now you've entered his life and left him confused. You've torn him in half.'

'How do you know these things?' Helen interrupted, her revulsion momentarily forgotten.

'I know men, my dear. Look into his eyes and you'll see his heart belongs to you, but that male brain of his is still possessed by notions of duty and service. For years he has trained and fought and followed orders; every atom of his being has been polarized towards these trivialities. But ever since you opened his eyes to the world within – the world of the heart – he has struggled between two choices: a leap into the unknown or a return to what is familiar.'

'What do you mean?' Helen demanded, her face now filled with concern.

'I'm sorry, my sweet,' the crone replied. 'Have I upset you? Perhaps I should leave.'

'No! Stay, please. Are you suggesting Paris is *regretting* what he has done? Will he send me back to Sparta?'

'A few moments ago you were rueing leaving your loving husband and beautiful children.'

'Paris isn't the only one who is confused by all this, you know.'

'I know, I know,' the crone said, patting Helen gently on the shoulder and filling her with a strange sensation of warmth. 'It's such a shame for both of you. There's you on one side, wishing you were back in Sparta when all you've done since puberty is dream about escape – I would have thought the sight of the Nile and the Pyramids would have cured you of any desire to return home. And on the other side there's Paris, concerned about what his father and brother will think when he brings you back, and whether he was right to abandon his mission and risk war with Greece. Poor boy; all he has ever wanted is to love and be loved, and now he's discovered it he finds himself terrified and filled with uncertainty. Your own restraint and doubt isn't helping, either. But if you act quickly you can make him yours forever.'

'You mean there's still hope for us?'

'Hope?' The old woman smiled, and though her eyes were again almost consumed in folds of skin, the crescents that remained gleamed with an amused light. 'Who needs hope when you can have *certainty*? I can give you certainty, if you really want it. But do you, Helen? That's the question you have to answer. Do you want to be with a man you truly love, in a marriage that can fulfil you both, even though the future is uncertain; or do you want to go back to your children and be yoked once more to a man who has always shown you kindness and respect, but for whom your heart does not race?'

Helen looked into the crone's knowing eyes, only vaguely

wondering how she knew her name, and for a moment her thoughts and emotions seemed lost in a fog, inscrutable and beyond her capacity to decipher. Then the fog dissipated and the answer came to her clearly. She heard a scream of excitement, and looked over her shoulder to see Pleisthenes emerge over a high, grassy bank and run down to the beach, chased by Aeneas with whom he had formed a strong friendship since leaving home.

'I don't want to go back. Tell me what I must do to dispel Paris's doubts.'

'That's the simplest thing in the world, but I'll tell you all the same.' The crone leaned over and whispered something in Helen's ear. Despite the overwhelming stench of brine and stale urine, a knowing smile spread across the Spartan queen's full lips and she nodded. Then the old woman produced a vial containing a pearlescent liquid and handed it to Helen. 'A single droplet of this in his cup at tonight's meal, and another in your own if you think it'll help, and your problem will be solved.'

'If it's what I think it is, I doubt I'll need it,' Helen said, taking the small bottle anyway.

'Don't be ashamed, my sweet. The liquid can only work where love already exists, and the stronger the love the more irresistible the effect. No doubt you'll see for yourself. And now for my price.'

Helen, who had been staring at the swirl of strange colours trapped within the vial, looked up at the crone and made no effort to hide her scorn.

'For some foolish reason, I'd allowed myself to believe you were offering me your help out of kindness. But your advice has been sound and there's something of the witch about you – I should know, my sister is one – so I'll not quibble. We have plenty of gold.'

'I can have as much of that stuff as I desire, Helen. My price is not an earthly treasure – I want Paris for myself. And don't look at me like that, young girl. I want him to reject Ares and follow me, just as you already follow me. Do you understand me, Helen?

When the morning comes and you have succeeded in your task, make sure Paris builds an altar to me here in honour of what I have done for you both.'

The light was quickly fading and as the first star of the evening appeared, shining brightly above the horizon, Helen saw that she was no longer sitting next to an old crone dressed in rags, but a tall and beautiful woman whose naked skin shone in the twilight. Her loving eyes captured the light of the evening star and seemed to reflect it from a depth that was timeless. But before Helen could think to throw herself to the ground before Aphrodite, the goddess had faded into nothing.

As Paris lay alone in his tent, listening to the shushing of the waves in the bay, he knew he had been rash. In the heat of his passion for Helen he had risked the lives of himself and his men – many of whom had died as a result – and had brought the threat of war to Troy. What would Hector think of that? He had allowed Apheidas to persuade him of the merits of such an action, but in his heart he knew the only reason he had taken Helen was because he had fallen in love with her. Everything else was an excuse.

And yet, despite his longing to be with her, they had still not slept together. They had come close as they sailed from port to port and island to island, their lips meeting urgently in moments of passion and the closeness of their bodies filling them with a heart-stopping need for each other, but always she had backed away at the last moment. She excused herself by saying that she was not ready – that she was still mourning the children she would never see again – but with each new rejection Paris's doubts grew. Had he misjudged her? Despite her assurances to the contrary, was she regretting her decision to leave Sparta? Had she simply con-fused sexual desire for love? He did not know the answers, and part of him was left longing for a return to his safe, familiar life of duty and discipline.

But after tonight his doubts had weakened, driven back by a

renewed intoxication with Helen. They had spent the evening feasting on the beach and drinking wine until their heads swam, after which they had kissed with an intensity that had not yet left him. As he lay naked between layers of soft fleeces, looking up at the roof of the tent, his whole body was taut with the need of her. His mind was far from sleep and all he could think of was crossing the beach to where her tent was pitched, entering and taking her. On the northern borders, he had slept with his share of captured women before they were sent back to Troy as slaves. But he also knew that to take Helen before she was willing to give herself would damage the love she had spoken of as they had fled Sparta. And he wanted that love more than anything. He closed his eyes.

As he lay there, listening to the surf advancing and retreating endlessly over the sand, the flap at the front of his tent opened briefly and shut again. Paris leapt to his feet and reached for the sword that hung from the back of a nearby chair. In an instant he had tugged the blade free of its scabbard and was pointing it at arm's length towards the throat of the intruder.

The metal gleamed threateningly in the moonlight that penetrated the thin walls of the tent. Helen looked at it for a moment, then wrapped her fingers around the blade and gently pushed it aside, feeling the tension of her soft skin against the sharpened edge. Her large eyes were filled with longing, and as she looked at Paris he knew she was ready for him. He felt his own passions responding, churning hotly within him like waters gathering against the walls of a dam. But he made the walls hold for a little longer, moving the point of his sword to rest against the thick wool of her cloak.

'I acted foolishly,' he told her, hating each word that he forced from his lips. 'You love your children more than you can ever love me. Tomorrow I will return you to your home.'

'All lovers are fools, Paris, and I am the greatest. But I have finished mourning for my children; my heart and my body are yours now. You are my only home from now on.'

Again she pushed away the blade and this time Paris let it drop from his fingers. Then she unfastened the brooch at her left shoulder and, with a slight shrug, the cloak fell about her ankles. She stepped back from it and planted her feet apart in the mess of skins that covered the tent floor, enjoying the softness of the fur between her toes. Confident of her own nakedness, she leaned her head back and ran her fingers through her hair, revelling in the certainty that Paris's eyes were feeding rapaciously on her heavy breasts, the smooth, pale skin of her stomach and the vertical slit of her navel. She could almost feel his gaze flowing down her long legs and back up again to the triangle of black hair where his lust was concentrated.

Then she felt his arms fold about her, the firm muscles of his chest crushing her breasts as he ran his lips over her exposed neck. For a moment the strength of his passion stunned her, threatened to overwhelm her as he covered her ears, cheeks and lips with kisses. Then he lifted her easily in his arms and lay her down on the pile of furs, which were soft and yielding beneath the naked skin of her back and buttocks.

'I'll never give you up, Helen,' he told her, staring into her irresistible eyes. 'I love you!'

'Do you love me enough to leave your soldier's life behind and be a proper husband to me?' Helen responded, closing her legs against the probing of his hand. 'Will you reject Ares and follow Aphrodite?'

'Ares has never let me down,' Paris said, lowering his head to her breast and kissing her nipple. 'Even if I agree to give up fighting, what can Aphrodite do for me?'

'She can bless our marriage with eternal love. Isn't that better than anything Ares can give you?'

'Then, for your sake, I'll fight no more and worship Aphrodite. I remember her clearly from my dream on Mount Ida; I'd never seen a more lovely woman in my life, either sleeping or waking. Not until I saw you that night in Sparta.'

'You mustn't say that,' Helen half-protested, allowing Paris to slip his knee between her thighs. 'It was Aphrodite who brought us together, and tomorrow you must build a shrine to her.'

'I'll make one at home in Troy,' he said, kissing her ear lobe and neck. 'A proper one, with dressed stone and . . .'

'No. Make it here. To celebrate our becoming lovers.'

Paris smiled. 'As you wish. And when we're old and our children have found husbands and wives of their own, we'll sail back here and remember the time Aphrodite gave you to me.'

In response she felt a rage of passion well up from the pit of her stomach. It was stronger than anything she had ever known before, a surging intensity that flooded into every part of her body and made her light-headed as she lay beneath him. Suddenly, for the first time in her life, she was giving up control; and as she surrendered the restraint of a lifetime she felt an overpowering sensation of freedom, of becoming the wild creature the gods had created her to be. She stared up at Paris, at the lurid scar that split his face, and was greedy for the press of his lips against her again. She threw her arms about his neck and kissed him fiercely, and as he entered her the bonds of her former life – Sparta, Menelaus, her children – dropped away like locks of shorn hair.

The Ithacan fleet and the lone ship from Mycenae had reached the Cape of Malea by sunset of the third day of their voyage. The thirteen vessels were drawn up in a large bay along the eastern coast of the cape, where the crews threw their stone anchors overboard and made camp on the beach. Here they baked bread using stores of grain from the ship, or went up into the hills to hunt wild goats, rabbits and birds. That evening they feasted, drank wine and told stories until they fell asleep on the soft sand, whilst their commanders gathered in Agamemnon's tent and talked long into the night.

As Helen made love to Paris on Cyprus, her husband was pacing up and down and listening to the argument between

Odysseus on one side and Agamemnon and Palamedes on the other. After a while he could no longer hold back his thoughts.

'You're suggesting, Odysseus, that we send a single ship to Troy to plead for the return of my wife?'

'Not plead, Menelaus – negotiate. There's a difference.'

'I don't care if there is a difference. We're gathering the largest force of men and arms ever witnessed and you think we should *negotiate* for Helen like a pack of beggars? They kidnapped her along with my youngest son, don't forget! I agree with my brother – the Trojans need to be taught a stern lesson, one that will show the rest of the world we Greeks aren't to be toyed with. We should slaughter them to a man, reduce their city to rubble and bring Helen back to Sparta where she belongs.'

'I agree with everything you and Agamemnon have done so far,' Odysseus replied. 'Calling in the oath; gathering the armies as quickly as possible; preparing for a quick strike. But an embassy to Troy could save hundreds of Greek lives – even thousands – as well as the possibility of a long and expensive war paid for from Mycenaean and Spartan coffers.'

'We all appreciate your desire to return to your wife and son as quickly as possible, Odysseus,' Agamemnon said. 'I, also, have no desire to spend long months away from my lad, Orestes. He'll eventually take my place on the throne and needs his father's example to follow. Then there's my daughter, Iphigenia; without my influence to check her feminine nature, I fear she will become rebellious and gain ideas above her station. But how can we consider our needs more urgent than those of my brother? Menelaus has had his beloved wife torn from him and taken to Troy! He wants nothing more than to return her to the loving safety of her own home, where her children weep constantly for the loss of their mother. *That*'s why the Greeks are gathering in Aulis as we speak, eager as hounds to be at Trojan throats. Of all those called only Achilles has not yet responded, though if he's even half the warrior he is said to be then it won't be long before he joins us. But these negotiations you suggest could take months and will dampen the ardour of the army. So why don't you forget this noble but hopeless notion and turn your brilliant mind to thoughts of winning this war?'

Agamemnon folded his arms across his chest and stared at Odysseus, challenging him to respond. But the Ithacan did not meet his gaze, turning his eyes instead on the king of Sparta.

'Menelaus, my friend, Agamemnon is right – our sympathies lie with you first and foremost. You're the one who has had his family broken apart. It's you who have suffered the loss of a matchless wife and a devoted son, so you should be the one to decide on the matter.' He looked at Agamemnon, who was the most powerful of them and the one most opposed to a peaceful resolution. The Mycenaean king nodded and Odysseus continued. 'But first, listen carefully to what I have to say on the matter. Teach the Trojans a lesson, you say; wipe them out and destroy their city. Who can say they deserve any less? But ask yourself this – do you want revenge or do you want your family restored? If it's revenge, then let's all head for Aulis and rouse the Greeks to war. And don't tarry there – sail to Troy at once and launch our attack without delay, for this won't be a quick war. The Trojans will be defending their homes, and that alone will give them twice the stomach for a fight than our men will have. They're well trained and battle-hardened, and with their allies they can at least match us in numbers; they will have the safety of their walls to return to each evening and a sure supply of food and reserves, whereas we will sleep in tents or on our beached galleys, exposed to night attacks and relying on ships for our provisions. This won't be a speedy raid, Menelaus, and Troy is not some minor city with a weak army and no defences. Even with names like Diomedes, Ajax and Achilles – if he comes – in our ranks, this war won't be concluded until next year at the earliest, and not without the loss of much Greek blood. And all the time we must worry about attacks on our own kingdoms while we are absent.'

He paused and caught Menelaus's eye, holding his gaze for a long moment as if the others in the tent were not there.

'But if I were you,' he continued, 'I would forget revenge. If you want Helen back at all, then you need to act quickly – and with much more speed than the mechanics of war will allow.'

'What is *that* supposed to mean?' Menelaus asked, his eyes narrowing.

'Be realistic, Menelaus. Helen may have been able to keep Paris at bay thus far, but for how much longer? He took her because of her beauty. He wants to make her his lover and wife, and the longer she is kept prisoner behind the walls of Troy the greater the risk he will succeed. He won't be above forcing himself upon her either. Do you want Paris to violate Helen? Do you want her to bear his children?'

Menelaus's eyes widened and his face turned red. Suddenly the fury burst free and he smashed his fist down on the table, sending the cups and plates leaping into the air. Wine, meat and bread spilled over the fleece-covered floor.

'*How dare you*!' he shouted, grabbing a handful of the purple robe Penelope had given Odysseus and pulling the Ithacan king towards him. 'How *dare* you speak of such an outrage!'

Odysseus placed his hand on Menelaus's wrist and calmly forced it back down to his side.

'I dare to speak of these things, Menelaus, because I'm your friend. Palamedes there has spent the evening goading you with talk of revenge, provoking your anger by reminding you of the injustice Paris has committed against you. That's because he thinks that's what you want to hear, and he doesn't have the courage to tell you the painful truth. But what I'm telling you *is* the truth, whether you like it or not. And unless you're prepared to put aside your desire for revenge, then Paris and Helen *will* become lovers. That much I can guarantee. Your only hope – and my only hope of returning to Penelope and Telemachus – is to allow me to go to Priam and speak with him. I can make him see reason and let Helen go, especially if he knows about the army that's being gathered against him.'

'An embassy to Troy is a waste of time,' Agamemnon said,

icily. 'We'll lose the element of surprise if you tell Priam about our preparations. We can't afford to risk an opposed landing on the beaches of Ilium. And I know my sister-in-law better than you do, Odysseus. Helen won't betray Menelaus. She'll be expecting him to come with an army, and that thought alone will help her to resist Paris.'

'No it won't,' Menelaus said, shaking his head slowly. 'Odysseus is right. But there's something else he hasn't said, whether he thought it or not. I know Helen doesn't love me. She respects me and enjoys my friendship, but I don't consume her thoughts or fill her with desire. That I can live with, and have done for ten years. What I will not be able to bear is if she falls in love with another. I can't risk laying siege to Troy and knowing that, as each day passes, Helen is closer to giving her heart to Paris. It won't do! Agamemnon, you agreed the choice should be mine, and so I say Odysseus should get his chance. What's more, he should be given the power to make any bargain he thinks is necessary, as long as it results in the rapid return of my wife.'

'Think about what you're saying, brother . . .'

'I have, Agamemnon! I want Odysseus to go to Troy and bring Helen back before . . . before it's too late.'

Agamemnon sighed and shook his head. 'Very well,' he said reluctantly. 'There's none better than Odysseus to win a man over, and even a proud old fool like Priam might be persuaded.'

'That's settled then,' Odysseus said, standing as if to leave. 'Eperitus and I will leave at dawn tomorrow, while the rest of the fleet will be placed under my cousin Eurylochus. They'll escort you to Aulis, Agamemnon, and train in the full expectation of war.'

Palamedes stood. 'One more thing, my lords. I'd like to be part of this embassy – I've always wanted to see the famous walls and towers of Troy – and I think Menelaus should come too.'

Odysseus opened his mouth to protest but Agamemnon held up his hand to silence him. 'I agree that you should go, Palamedes – after all, two great minds are better than one. But not Menelaus.

The Trojans pretend to honour the customs of guest-friendship, but we've already seen Paris break one sacred oath – I can't risk my brother falling into their treacherous hands and being held hostage or killed.'

'Paris is not a king, my lord,' Palamedes said. 'But Priam is and he won't dare lose face by mistreating his guests. For one thing, no other nation in the civilized world would ever trust his word again, so you can rest assured Menelaus will be safe. What's more, if Priam hears from Menelaus himself the grief that Paris has caused him, that will be far more effective than any argument Odysseus or I could make.'

He gave Agamemnon a look, which the king appeared to understand.

'Very well,' Agamemnon announced, signalling for the guards to open the entrance flaps of his tent. 'Menelaus and Palamedes will board with you in the morning, Odysseus, and may the gods speed you on your voyage to Troy. The rest of us will sail to the gathering at Aulis.'

ဧ

They rose at first light the next day and set off before sunup, rowing the ships out of the bay to find a breeze, then hoisting the cross-spars and letting the sails fall. Eperitus stood in the prow of his galley as it rounded the cape, watching the cotton and flax sail flap and sputter several times before catching the wind and bellying out. The dolphin motif swelled in the orange light of the rising sun and for a moment seemed like a living creature, hauling the ship forward across the troughs and swells of the restless sea. In a flurry of activity, the sailors adjusted the leather ropes to distribute the wind pressure before returning to the crowded benches, their weight acting as ballast to make the ship ride evenly across the waves.

Although he had spent the past ten years living on an island, Eperitus was no sailor and was happy to leave the running of the ship to the crew. They were drawn from the islands of Ithaca,

Samos, Zacynthos and Dulichium, so had spent their entire lives travelling on boats of some form or other, whereas he had not even seen the sea before he met Odysseus. Despite that, he loved the oceans with a passion that could rival any of the veteran seamen. He had never forgotten the first time he had smelled the unfamiliar reek of brine, heard the cawing of the great white gulls and then, supremely, stepped aboard a ship and taken his first, swift voyage over the ceaseless waters. It had been the strangest and most exhilarating experience of his life to feel himself afloat on the powerful and shifting body of the ocean, its dark mass impenetrable and full of primeval mystery. That first experience had sparked a love that had never left him, and as he looked down at the waves breaking over the red-cheeked bows of the ship – each one painted with a large eye that stared fixedly at the horizon – he felt his joy of life renewed by the prospects of a long voyage to Troy.

He turned and leaned against the prow, enjoying the feel of the waves slapping against the thin planking beneath his feet and the wind whipping through his hair. He looked across the rows of benches at the faces of the warriors who would be under his command. Each craft had been constructed to carry sixty men in basic comfort, but with all their war gear and provisions for a long voyage the ship was horribly overcrowded. The two hundred men of the palace guard who had been chosen to form the backbone of the expedition had been divided to provide fifteen trained fighters per ship, with an additional twenty to act as Odysseus's body-guard. These included the most experienced and longest-serving soldiers, whom Eperitus was happy to see dotted in twos or threes on the benches. Some caught his eye and gave a nod or a smile of recognition, while others were busy in conversation, playing dice or just looking out at the waves, where groups of dolphins raced the great wooden vessels and occasionally leapt out to eye the men that sat in them.

At the helm were Odysseus, Eurybates, Menelaus and Pala-medes. Eurybates, one of the best sailors in the guard, stood with his hands on the twin steering oars, his eyes narrowed as they watched the sea ahead and read the wave caps to find the best current. Odysseus was beside him, looking displeased at the presence of Palamedes, yet with an indomitable glint in his eye. After leaving Agamemnon's tent, the king had confided to Eperitus that he suspected Palamedes would try to thwart his attempts to bring Helen back to Greece, but that he was determined not to allow him. Eperitus agreed to keep a careful eye on the Nauplian prince.

Before long, the king called down to the crew and ordered a change in the sail. Slowly the ship began to move away from the fleet, no longer shadowing the coastline but heading out towards the cluster of islands that formed the gateway to the Aegean Sea, which lay hidden beyond the haze of the horizon. Suddenly a cheer began to rise up from the crews of the other galleys, which was echoed by the men of the lone vessel. Eperitus, too, stood on one of the rowing benches, waving and calling to his adopted country-men with wishes for a speedy voyage to Aulis and the protection of the gods. How long would it be, he wondered, before they met again? Would it be a triumphal reunion, as they returned from Troy with Helen, or would they come back with thoughts of a long and bitter war ahead of them? It would depend on the ability of his friend and king to work his charm on the Trojans, but in his heart Eperitus hoped for war.

## Chapter Twelve
# TROY

P rogress had been good since leaving the Cape of Malea. Strong winds kept the sail full most of the time, whilst the waves were rarely steep enough to hinder the speed of the galley. Though not one man had ever sailed to Troy before, or even passed the belt of islands that separated the Cretan Sea from the Aegean, Agamemnon had provided them with a map showing the way. This had been drawn at the king's command by a Mycenaean merchant who was a frequent visitor to Troy. Though rough, it showed the coasts of Euboea, Attica and the Peloponnese on the left, all the major islands in between, and the shores of Asia on the right. The positions of significant ports and cities had been recorded, and in a northerly bulge of the Asian coastline were the words *Ilium* and *Troy*.

For seven days the crew had risen before the first light of dawn, eager to set the sail and forge on to new waters and new sights, but by late afternoon every man would be looking for a safe mooring before the approach of evening. To sail in darkness was to invite peril, with no lights to mark the shoreline and no way to spot reefs and other dangers. It was just as important – with the level of overcrowding on the ship – to camp on land, where the men would make themselves comfortable, light fires and cook their food. But Odysseus and Eurybates, who took turns at the helm, also insisted on finding a port or a bay with a fishing village. As helmsmen on galleys are only able to navigate from one headland to the next, they were keen to find sailors who could give them the benefit of their experience for the next day's voyage.

Using this method, they sailed eastward through the islands of the Cyclades, stopping at Melos, Myconos and Icaria, before turning north towards the Asian seaboard. Here the strong offshore wind took them past the islands of Chios and wooded Lesbos until, on the afternoon of the eighth day from Malea, they came within sight of another, much smaller island close to the mainland.

Odysseus was the first to spot it. He was leaning with one hand against the prow and the other gripping the bow rail, watching the features of the alien coastline as it slipped by on the starboard side. Eperitus was next to him as usual, his arms folded over the bow rail as he watched the waves sliced open by the blue beak of the galley, sending a constant sea spray over the bulging red cheeks and the ever-watchful eyes that adorned them. The light of the lowering sun was still bright and created circular rainbows in the fine mist. Suddenly Odysseus placed a hand on his friend's forearm and pointed. A moment later, Eurybates cried out from the helm, 'Tenedos! Tenedos on the northern horizon.'

There was a surge of activity on the benches as the crew crowded to the sides or stood to catch a glimpse of the still-distant island. Tenedos itself was of no significance, but every man knew it stood opposite a spur of land that protected a large inland bay, and on a hill in the plain to the north-east of the bay was Troy. At each stop there had been contact with sailors and merchants who had described to them its tall towers, high, sloping walls and strong gates, building in their minds a vivid mental picture of a city bulging with wealth and ripe for sacking. Despite their mission of peace, not one warrior on board wanted a bloodless resolution to their adventure. They had volunteered to fight, some inspired by dreams of glory or the desire to restore Greek pride, but all of them hoping to return to Ithaca laden with the spoils of war. After a while, when it was clear the lofty towers of their enemy's city were not yet visible, they returned to the benches.

Last to return was Menelaus. His anguish over the loss of his wife had all but disappeared since leaving the Cape of Malea, either because he had learned to disguise his grief in front of the common soldiery or, as Eperitus believed, because of his growing confidence that he would soon be reunited with Helen. He had shared his time cheerfully between the commanders – Odysseus, Eperitus, Eurybates and Palamedes – and the Ithacan warriors. When he was not plaguing Odysseus with questions about how he would deal with the Trojans, he would sit on the benches with the men, casting dice and losing lots of money (deliberately, as Eperitus and Odysseus suspected), or sharing experiences of battle and fighting techniques. This had won over every one of the Ithacans to his cause; if glory and plunder had been the motives that drew them to the expedition, restoring Menelaus's wife and his honour were now equally important. There was not a man among them who did not want to kill Trojans and raze their city to the ground. Yet as Eperitus watched the Spartan king look longingly northward, then turn away and go to sit despondently next to Palamedes in the helm, he knew the man's torment had not lessened.

'Won't be long now,' Odysseus said as the low, broad bulk of Tenedos drew nearer. 'The merchant we spoke to last night said the bay is crawling with Trojan warships, but we should be able to find ourselves a mooring before last light. Then we can set off to the city and seek an audience with Priam.'

'And if they attack us?' Eperitus asked sceptically.

'We're not at war yet, Eperitus. They won't harm us.'

'I wish I shared your confidence about that.'

Odysseus gave a relaxed shrug. 'Trojans are said to treat visitors the same as we do in Greece. If nothing else, they'll welcome us as guests and protect us while we're within the borders of Ilium.'

'But you heard what happened to Menelaus,' Eperitus said, lowering his voice and indicating the Spartan with a jerk of his thumb. 'Paris is no respecter of *xenia*, so why should any of the rest of them be? They're foreigners and barbarians, after all.'

Odysseus gave him a knowing look. 'I suspect Paris clapped

eyes on Helen and all his notions of honour turned to dust. You can hardly blame the man for that, can you?'

'You know I can. A man without honour is worthless.'

Odysseus laughed at the uncompromising look on his friend's face. 'You're a warrior in the old-fashioned style, Eperitus – principled, dependable and as hard as iron. There aren't many of your kind around any more.'

'Some warrior I'd have been if Agamemnon's sail hadn't appeared that day on Hermes's Mount,' Eperitus sniffed, arching his eyebrows. 'I'd have left you in search of glory and missed the greatest war in history!'

Odysseus shook his head. 'You'd still have got there, just under another king's banner.'

'Then you think it'll be war?'

'I can't say,' Odysseus replied. 'Not until I've spoken to Priam. But he's old enough to have seen three or four generations, so he won't be as hot-blooded as men of our age. He also has a kingdom to think of – will he want to sacrifice everything he's built for the sake of a woman? I hope not. I hope he'll give up Helen so that we can go back to our homes and families.'

'And more years of peace,' Eperitus sighed despondently.

'Peace is the most precious thing we have!' Odysseus said, his face serious. 'I used to dream of adventure and fame, too, but nowadays all I care about is persuading the Trojans to release Helen without a blow being struck. If men are still honoured for success in debate as well as battle, then I'd rather win renown that way than in a war that could last for months – or years.'

'I hope you'll get your wish,' Eperitus said, sincerely. 'It would make me happy to know you were safely back on Ithaca with Penelope and Telemachus. I'd be pleased for Menelaus, too – did you see his face a few moments back, when Eurybates spotted Tenedos? I've never seen such a melancholy look in a man. But my heart tells me our mission *won't* succeed, and that Agamemnon will have to resort to war to get Helen back.'

'Agamemnon doesn't give a damn about Helen,' Odysseus said,

shaking his head and looking towards Tenedos. The eastern side of the island was already in shadow, though the detail of olive groves and small farmsteads could now be seen as the galley sailed closer to its shores. 'All he wants is to conquer Troy, and Helen is just a convenient excuse to unite the Greeks under his banner. I doubt his ambitions have changed since the failed council of war in Sparta ten years ago.'

'Maybe,' Eperitus replied. 'But he also says that if we don't teach the Trojans a lesson now, they'll think the Greeks are afraid of them. Before long they'll be sailing across to steal our women whenever they feel like it. Then it'll be our homes and our land. What if he's right about that, Odysseus, and this embassy of yours is just putting off the day when we have to fight them anyway?'

'Then at least you'll have your chance of glory!' the king snapped. A moment later he dropped his gaze to the deck and wiped the sweat from his brow. 'I'm sorry, Eperitus. The truth is, I don't know what Priam or his sons have in mind, but I *do* suspect what Agamemnon wants. He wants to make Troy a Mycenaean colony.'

'That's ridiculous!'

'No it's not. You know Agamemnon: he's ruthless and ambitious, and won't stop at anything to have his way. You remember what he did to Clytaemnestra?'

'Of course I do,' Eperitus replied, his mind suddenly filled with the memory of Clytaemnestra's naked body, thin and hard as he made love to her on a Spartan mountainside. That was ten years ago and he had not seen her since, but he could still recall her pale skin glowing like bronze in the firelight, the sweat glistening on her ribs and small breasts. She had given herself to him that night because of her hatred for Agamemnon, who had murdered her first husband and infant child so that he could make her his wife. Yes, Eperitus thought, he knew how ruthless Agamemnon could be.

'Think about it,' Odysseus continued. 'If Agamemnon could eliminate Priam and make Troy into a Greek stronghold, the whole of the Aegean would be his. That would mean control of the trade in gold, silver, copper, timber, oil, cinnabar, linen, hemp and Zeus knows what other goods. He'd have the wealth to subdue the whole of Greece to his will, and maybe even oppose Egypt and the other great powers before long. If he defeats the Trojans it'll lead to one war after another, until even you'll be sick of the glory. The age of heroes has gone, Eperitus; we're entering a time of kings, men ruling empires that cross oceans and who have power over hundreds of thousands of lives. I've been thinking about this ever since that night on Malea, and I don't like it. I don't want Ithaca to be part of a single Greece ruled by Agamemnon, or part of an empire that stretches into Asia. I want it to remain peaceful and free, its own domain at the edge of the world. That as much as anything else – Penelope and Telemachus included – is why I want peace.'

Eperitus wanted to reply, but did not know what to say. He had always been a simple warrior with little understanding of politics, and yet the truth of Odysseus's words was inescapable. Perhaps the world *was* changing: the era of heroes, monsters and gods was fading, to be replaced by the cold, hard reality of power. Was his personal search for glory and a name that could cheat the totality of death already a thing of the past, like the bones of Heracles, Perseus and Jason? Would this war he so desired actually bring an end to the very values for which he was fighting?

As he struggled to comprehend the things that Odysseus had seen almost from the first appearance of Agamemnon's sail nearly four weeks before, the galley slipped slowly into the straits of Tenedos. To their right was a large bay that had been scooped from the gentle, wooded hills of the mainland, and on their left were the low humps of the island, behind which the sun was now sinking. Though Tenedos was an insignificant-looking rock – about the same size as the southern half of Ithaca – it was the last marker in their long journey to Troy. Eperitus felt a thrill of anticipation course through him as the strong coastal wind filled the sail overhead and pushed the ship forward against the prevailing current. The straits were soon left behind and new, much larger islands became visible. Odysseus, standing at the bow rail beside him, pointed at each one in turn and named them – distant Lemnos to the west; Imbros ahead of them to the north; and rising out of the blue haze beyond it, the high peaks of Samothrace. Then the reclining cliffs to their right fell away to reveal a wide, north-easterly gulf, into which Eurybates steered the ship.

Almost immediately, the coastline to their right opened out into a large bay that penetrated the plain beyond like the head of a spear. It was fed by two rivers – the greater emerging from an area of green marshland to the south and the lesser running down from sloping pastureland to the north-east – and the calm waters in between were crowded with fishing vessels, merchant galleys and an ominously large number of powerful-looking warships. Standing back from the plain, on a high plateau between the two rivers, was the city of Troy. Its sloping walls caught the last light of the setting sun, staining the great blocks of dressed stone a vivid pink and striking awe, wonder and fear into the hearts of the Greeks. The crenellated ramparts were lined with guards, who stood with their tall spears and flashing armour, staring down at the foreign ship that had come creeping into their waters. Rising above the level of the battlements were numerous tall, broad structures that were clearly the palaces and temples of the Trojans. Knots of people were gathered on the flat roofs, causing Eperitus to wonder whether Paris and Helen were among them. If Mene-laus's wife *was* watching their arrival, he thought, she would surely recognize the shape of a Greek warship and know they had come for her.

The galley slipped through the assortment of different craft, the majority of which were warships – over fifty of them, with their spars removed and stowed to leave the masts naked. Without their crews they were but peaceful shells, drifting at anchor on the quiet surface of the bay; and yet the power of such an armada, when armed with a full complement of warriors, was easy to imagine. The Ithacans looked in awe at the Trojan fleet, discussing in hushed voices the curiously curved bows and sterns, the double-banked oars and the second decks that ran the length of each ship to provide raised fighting platforms. The long, sleek form of their own craft fell into shadow as it glided between them, giving the crew a sense of how puny their vessel was in comparison.

On the yellow sands between the two rivers were the unfinished hulks of a dozen more ships. These were propped up on wooden platforms that kept them above the waves, and were hung about on all sides with spars and ropes where teams of workmen had been busily finishing hulls, fitting benches, adding masts and fastening rigging. They were abandoned and lonely now – the workmen having returned to their homes for the evening – but still seemed to echo with the noise and activity of the day just ended.

Beyond the rolling beaches, between the city and the mouth of the smaller river, a multitude of tents flapped noisily in the gale. A strong smell of smoke and roast meat drifted across the water from them, and large numbers of men – many of them armed – had left the cooking of the evening meal to watch the arrival of the newcomers.

The Ithacans stared back, curious and eager to see their first Trojans. None of them could look upon the fleet that was being created, or the army camped beside the bay, and not realize that Troy was preparing for war. But were they simply getting ready to defend Paris and Helen from the possibility of pursuit, or had they already heard of the planned gathering at Aulis? Whichever it was, the Greeks felt their stomachs sink at the sight of the organized and capable enemy before them, and as their eyes stretched eastward across the plain towards the well-built city of Troy their enthusiasm for war diminished even further.

'Is it true Troy's walls were made by Poseidon and Apollo?' Eperitus asked, glancing across at Odysseus.

'I'm sure of it,' the king answered. 'How could mere mortals build walls like those? When I saw them in my dream I knew they were strong, but now I see them with my own eyes they make the defences back on Ithaca look like a child's sand palace. Even Sparta's walls look weak in comparison.'

Eperitus stared at the city and could not help but be filled with admiration for its grandeur, might and sheer beauty. The north-west circuit of the walls stretched in an unbroken line that followed the contours of the steep-sided plateau. No gate or tower punctuated their smooth, reclining flanks. Then, where the hill dropped away to the south, the citadel ended and the city began. Here, flooding out across the plain, were the homes of the ordinary Trojans. Few structures could be seen beyond the high walls, which continued down from the citadel to surround the lower town in a vast loop, but the innumerable trails of grey smoke drifting over the towering battlements testified to the size of the population within.

As his eyes feasted on the vastness of the city, Eperitus was already probing the fortifications for weaknesses. The walls of the citadel benefited from the additional height of the plateau and were insurmountable. Even the walls of the lower city stood as tall as three men above the plain, and the western circuit that faced the bay was protected by three strong towers that could pour archery down on attackers from all sides. With his sharp eyes, Eperitus could see that the battlements were well made and in good repair, which meant the only vulnerable spot would be the single gate that opened onto the plain at the southernmost point of the walls. This was reached through a narrow defile that was protected by the tallest and broadest of the towers. In the event of an attack, the surrounding parapets would be crammed with archers who would send down a hail of arrows on any assailants as they squeezed into the gap that led to the gate.

'We'd better succeed, Odysseus, or we'll be a long time knocking *those* walls down.'

Odysseus and Eperitus turned to see Menelaus standing behind them, with Palamedes at his side. Both men had donned their breastplates, greaves and helmets and had slung their shields across their backs. Their swords were ready in the scabbards that hung from their shoulders, and naked daggers had been tucked into their belts.

'A very long time, if we manage it at all,' Odysseus replied. 'But if you *do* want us to succeed, Menelaus, then I suggest we don't start by marching into the city dressed like conquerors. You will have to leave your armour and weapons here.'

'But that's lunacy,' Menelaus snorted, tightening his grip on the ivory handle of his sword. 'I'm not going to walk up to Paris and demand my wife back armed with nothing more than my fists. If anything goes wrong up there, they'll slaughter us like lambs.'

'We'll be their guests,' Odysseus insisted. 'They won't dare harm us, not unless they want to bring the wrath of Zeus down on themselves.'

'Those foreign dogs have no respect for *xenia* or the gods – *if* they worship the gods at all,' Menelaus retorted, his face reddening with anger. 'Paris broke his oath when he was a guest in my house! What'll stop him from killing us all in cold blood?'

'Nothing, my lord,' Eperitus commented. 'Nothing at all. But once we're up in that citadel, surrounded by ten thousand Trojans and penned in by their god-built walls, what difference will a sword and some armour make anyway?'

Palamedes, who seemed irritated by the delay, stepped forward. 'They're right, Menelaus. The Trojans won't dare mistreat us and dishonour the gods, but we shouldn't risk provoking them either.'

Menelaus huffed in response, then lifted the shield off his back and threw it on the narrow decking of the prow, following it with his dagger, sword, and one by one the different elements of his rich armour.

'Bring in the sail!' Eurybates called from the helm.

There was an instant flurry of activity and within moments the sail had been furled and the spar detached. Odysseus looked on with pleasure as his crew demonstrated their excellent seamanship to the watching Trojans. Then there was a large splash from the anchor stone being cast overboard, followed by a jerk as the slow motion of the galley was brought to a sudden halt.

'Looks like they're sending a welcoming party,' Palamedes said, raising his chin towards the beach as he unbuckled his breastplate.

They turned to see an old man and two fully armed soldiers walking along the road that wound down from the city gate to the bay.

Odysseus peered over the bow rail.

'It's shallow. We can jump down and wade ashore from here. Eurybates,' he called, 'you're in charge while we're gone. I want half the men to camp on the beach and half to remain on the ship, just in case we need to leave hastily. No one is to steal any goats or sheep; there's enough food onboard, and I don't want you lot causing an incident while I'm trying to talk peace. Do you understand?'

'Yes, my lord,' Eurybates replied.

'Antiphus,' Odysseus said, beckoning the archer forward from the benches. 'I want you and Arceisius to come with us. And bring Polites with you; if we *do* get into trouble, someone of his size will be useful.'

Antiphus nodded and went to find the others. Odysseus seized the bow rail and, with surprising agility for his size, leapt overboard to land with a splash in the water below. The others followed and soon they were wading ashore to where the Trojan greybeard and his armed escort were awaiting them.

'My name is Antenor,' the old man announced in perfect but heavily accented Greek. His head hung down between his shoulders as if it had sprouted from his breastbone, and as he looked up at them – pronouncing each word with a slight nod and a flourish of his right hand – they could see his left eye was blind and looked away at a slight angle. 'King Priam has asked me to welcome you to Troy.'

'I am King Menelaus of Sparta, son of Atreus. These men are my companions: King Odysseus of Ithaca, son of Laertes;

Palamedes, son of Nauplius; and Eperitus, who keeps his lineage to himself but has the honour of captaining Odysseus's guard. We're here to speak with King Priam about a matter of the gravest concern.'

'Good, good. And my brother-in-law is equally keen to see you, King Menelaus,' Antenor assured him, with another series of nods and flourishes. 'He's intrigued to learn what business could bring a Greek warship to our shores, and has asked if you will eat with him in the morning.'

'What's wrong with now?' Menelaus said, his forehead gathering into a dark frown.

'I'm afraid the king is predisposed,' Antenor answered. 'He is with one of his wives.'

'*Wives!*' Menelaus repeated, looking aghast. 'You mean he has more than *one*?'

Antenor gave the angry Spartan another smile. 'Of course – he's the king, after all – but my sons and I will be greatly honoured to entertain you and your escort in our home tonight. It's just outside the walls of Pergamos, by the gates.'

'Pergamos?' Odysseus asked.

'The citadel,' Palamedes explained, pointing up at the lofty buildings on the raised plateau.

'Then we will be happy to accept your hospitality, Antenor,' Odysseus continued, ignoring the Nauplian. 'And as your Greek is so good, perhaps you can teach us a little about your country as we walk? We're unfamiliar with Ilium and her customs.'

And so Antenor led them across the windswept plain to the city. Herds of goats and sheep could be seen wandering freely across it in the dusky twilight, while here and there were large, circular corrals where groups of well-fed, strong-looking horses chewed at the grass or peered over the bars of the wooden fences that penned them in. Many stone-built farms and settlements sat nestled between olive groves and clumps of poplars, which seemed permanently bent over by the unceasing north-easterly wind that swept the open flats. Odysseus and Eperitus strolled either side of the old man who, despite his age and crumpled posture, was quick on his feet; Menelaus and Palamedes followed close on their heels, both staring at the city walls with undisguised interest, and the three Ithacan guards tramped behind them. The two Trojan soldiers, their spears sloped lazily over their shoulders, brought up the rear. The evening sky above them was now a deep violet sprinkled with a few early stars, and as the copper glow on the western horizon faded it was impossible for the Greeks not to envy the Trojans the beauty of their land.

The large river to the south of the city was the Scamander, Antenor informed them, which had been named for its crooked course. Its smaller cousin to the north was the Simöeis. The area around both deltas was notoriously marshy and had grown more so since the cutting down of large numbers of oak trees in recent months, something the old man regretted. But when Odysseus asked if they had been felled to build the fleet of ships in the bay he quickly forgot his sadness and pointed out the peak of Mount Ida in the south-east. It was sacred to the goddess Demeter, but several of the immortals were rumoured to frequent its wooded slopes. He went on to confirm that the city walls had been made by Poseidon and Apollo a few years before he was born, though some of the younger men in the city questioned the truth of the claim.

'It's because they've never had the privilege of seeing a god in human form,' he added.

Odysseus and Eperitus looked at each other, but said nothing.

'It didn't stop Heracles from sacking the place, though,' Antenor continued. 'I remember watching from the citadel walls, just a frightened youth quaking inside my inherited armour as he and Telamon breached the defences of the lower city. I can picture him as easily as if it was happening right now – he was as tall as a young tree, with muscles sticking out all over the place. But he was no brute to look at. He had flowing hair and a thick beard, yet his face was the handsomest you could ever hope to see. A true son of Zeus, he was.'

'Where did he breach the wall?' Eperitus asked, trying to sound only mildly interested.

'Just over there, by that fig tree – you can still see the repairs now. Shoddy work in comparison to the rest, but we Trojans aren't gods, after all.'

'Yes, I see it,' said Odysseus, sharing another quiet glance with Eperitus. They looked at the repaired breach with its ill-fitting stones that gave ample foot and handholds, and for the first time noticed the broad ditch that surrounded the walls of the lower city. Further along, at the foot of the plateau below the walls of the citadel, a group of women were filling jars with water from a two small pools, one of which was wreathed in steam.

'And this is the Scaean Gate,' Antenor said, pointing to the entrance they had seen from the galley. 'One of the four ways into Troy. The others all face inland.'

It had been a long walk from the beach to the city walls, and a hazy half-moon was already rising over the citadel as they reached the defile that fed into the Scaean Gate. A dozen spearmen stood watching them from the ramparts, dressed in the same curious style of armour worn by Antenor's guards. Each had a leather tunic covered in overlapping bronze scales that ran from the neck to the groin or upper thighs. The fish-like armour was supplemented by a tall, rectangular shield of ox-hide – sometimes with a layer of bronze over the top – that curved in at the sides, and a bronze cap with a horsetail plume that hung down at the back or side. Two more soldiers leaned against the trunk of a solitary oak tree to one side of the dirt track. They nodded to Antenor, but eyed the Greeks with undisguised hostility as they passed by.

The old man led his guests between the high walls of the salient to the open doors of the Scaean Gate. These were tall, made of thick wood and fitted closely with the surrounding stonework. Any attempted assault through them, Eperitus now felt sure, would be suicidal.

As they passed beneath the majestic, menacing battlements they heard a clamour of voices and suddenly found themselves surrounded by a great crush of onlookers. It was as if the whole town had rushed down to see the foreign warriors, and the armed escort now moved in front of Antenor and began using their shields in a brutal manner, herding the crowd back against the walls of the closely packed stone houses to clear a route. But the more people they thrust back, the more seemed to emerge from the doorways and side streets, swelling the multitude and pressing closer on all sides in their eagerness to see the Greeks.

Eperitus looked about himself at the sea of strange faces. All had dark skin, shining black hair and large brown eyes that stared at the newcomers with mistrust and even hatred. Why they should hate them Eperitus did not know, but the tension was palpable and he feared the tiniest spark could turn the mob violent. Some called out in their abrasive foreign tongue, the words unfamiliar but the meaning clear, and only the towering presence and withering gaze of Polites seemed to keep their anger from spilling over. Eperitus instinctively clutched at the hilt of a sword that was not there, and felt suddenly, horribly vulnerable.

'They'll not harm us,' Palamedes assured him, standing at his shoulder and looking calmly around at the many faces.

Eperitus said nothing as more soldiers barged past them to help disperse the crowd with the butts of their spears. Instead, following his protective instinct, he moved closer to Odysseus as Antenor led the way up the broad, paved street towards the citadel. The babbling voices on either side drowned out all other sounds and seemed to close in on him like a swarm of angry bees. His nostrils were full of the smells of roast meat and cooking fires, mixed with the sharp stench of a mass of unwashed bodies. Beyond the staring faces, the buildings on either side of the street were low – none of them more than a single storey high – poorly built and small in dimension. They reminded him of the slums in his home town of Alybas: tightly built shelters where families were crammed together in one or two rooms, taking their warmth at night from each other's bodies as they slept in a mass on the dirt floors. They were places where privacy – the preserve of the nobility – was unknown, and hardship and deprivation were a certainty. After ten years in the idyllic island kingdom of Ithaca, the experience of lower Troy revolted him.

Then, as they struggled up the cobbled road towards Pergamos, Eperitus noticed a young man elbowing his way through the crowd. A flash of clean white robes from beneath his black cloak marked him as wealthy – possibly even a noble. He would also have been taller than the rest of the throng, but his crooked back and stooping gait robbed him of any advantage, obliging him to fight for a position at the front of the press. All the time he maintained an unfaltering watch on the Greeks, his nearly black eyes gleaming out of the shadow cast by his hood as he scrutinized them one by one. The others hardly seemed to notice him in the noise and bustle, but Eperitus found himself fascinated by the pale, skull-like face. Then their eyes met and Eperitus was drawn helplessly into the man's gaze, which was deep and at the same time edged with a fierce intensity, like spots of sunlight trembling on the surface of a lake. At first he felt as if the Trojan was looking through him, and then he realized he was looking *into* him, searching his thoughts with a freedom Eperitus could do nothing to resist. It took all his strength to just close his eyes and force his head away, but even this, he felt, was only possible because the hooded man had already taken what he wanted. When he opened them again, the man was gone.

Eventually the crowds thinned and the guards were able to form a holding line across the road, allowing Antenor to proceed unhindered with his guests. They still found themselves watched from numerous doors and windows, but the higher they climbed up the winding road the larger and better built the houses became, and the less threatening the attention of the city dwellers. Before long they were at the walls of the citadel, where the white crescent of the moon looked down at them from above the high-toothed battlements. A tall tower stood away to their right. At its base were six carved figures mounted on stone plinths. They were clearly depictions of the gods, but their strange forms were unrecognizable to the Greeks, who drew no comfort from the sight of them and felt more distant than ever from the homes they had left behind.

'My house is just down here,' Antenor announced, indicating a two-storeyed, square building halfway down a side street to their left. Two young men stood at the open doorway, the light from within pooled at their feet. 'My wife, Theano, and our sons have been preparing a feast in your honour. Come inside, now, and put your weariness behind you. Whatever tomorrow brings, tonight I want you to taste real Trojan hospitality.'

## Chapter Thirteen

# PERGAMOS

'Is this any way to treat guests, Antenor?' Menelaus was red with anger. He sat on a stone bench outside the soaring, highly decorated portals of Priam's throne room and looked at the old man sitting opposite. Antenor shrugged his sloping shoulders in resignation and gave the Spartan king a reassuring smile.

'My brother-in-law is a busy man, my lord. I'm sure he'll be as quick as he can, but these affairs of state demand much of his time.'

'You mean he's with another of his blasted wives!' Menelaus retorted, gripping his knees until his knuckles turned white. 'Well, we've been waiting here all morning and I'm getting tired of it. If those doors don't open soon I'm going to go in there myself and teach him a few manners!'

'We're not in Sparta now, Menelaus,' Odysseus chided him. He sat between Antiphus and Polites on one side and Eperitus and Antenor on the other, slouching back against the wall with his arms folded across his chest. 'Trojan ways aren't our ways, but as long as we're in their country we'll just have to put up with them.'

'I don't believe Trojans *do* treat their guests like this,' said Palamedes, who was sitting between Menelaus and Arceisius. 'Antenor and his sons were perfect hosts last night. You and Menelaus were given the places of honour, and Eperitus, myself and the others were seated on either side of you; when the animals were sacrificed, the gods were given their due and then you both received the long chines, just as we give the choicest parts to the guests of honour at home. Whenever any of us spoke, Antenor and his sons listened respectfully and without interruption. So if Trojans know as well as any Greek how to care for their guests, then Priam is *deliberately* snubbing us. He wants to provoke our anger and force us to fail in our mission. In my opinion, he has no intention of giving up Helen at all.'

'*Palamedes*!' Eperitus hissed.

Antenor raised his head inquisitively. 'Who's Helen?'

'Nobody to concern yourself about, friend,' Odysseus replied, patting the old man amicably on the shoulder. 'A matter between us, that's all.'

Antenor seemed to accept this and returned his bored gaze to the doors of the throne room, but Eperitus could sense Odysseus's anger as he stared across at Palamedes. Only the night before, as they had bathed in preparation for the feast in Antenor's house, the Ithacan king had insisted that none of them should reveal the purpose of their mission until they were standing before Priam. Palamedes, Eperitus felt, had deliberately defied him, and the brief look of triumph on his pinched, rat-like features suggested Odysseus's suspicions about the Nauplian prince were true.

Eperitus turned to look through the open doorway of the antechamber, where the wide courtyard of the palace was bright in the sunlight, and trawled his mind through the events of the night before. Odysseus had left none of them in any doubt as to why he believed they should not speak to anyone about their mission. Despite the readiness of the Trojans for war, his instincts told him things were not as they seemed. People were bemused or angered by their arrival, but not afraid. If they had thought the Greeks were there to reclaim Helen, they would have known the threat of war was not far behind them. But their faces did not show anxiety or fear, and because of this Odysseus was convinced the ordinary Trojans did not know Helen had been brought to their city – if she was even within the walls of Troy at all. For this reason, he said, they should not speak of their mission until they had tested Priam on the matter.

Although Menelaus scoffed at the idea that Helen might not be a prisoner in the city – and Eperitus had been quietly doubtful – both men were quickly forced to agree that her presence was at least a closely guarded secret. Antenor and his eleven sons certainly seemed ignorant of the fact: they had even enquired about their guests' families – a bold question to ask, had they known the true reason for their visit.

Though normally suspicious of non-Greeks, Eperitus had quickly grown to like his hosts. Their household shrine was well maintained and treated with reverence by the entire family, even if the depictions of the gods were strange to Eperitus's eyes. He was also pleased with the honourable way they treated their guests, which was especially surprising for foreigners. However, it soon became clear that Antenor was an admirer of the Greeks and had passed this love down to his sons. As a buyer and seller of pottery and silver and gold artefacts, he had had dealings over many years with merchants from Mycenae, Sparta, Athens, Crete and other Greek kingdoms. This had led to an understanding of their language and an appreciation of their culture, for which reason Priam had sent him to Salamis to request the return of Hesione. Despite the poor reception he had received there, Antenor stayed long enough to intensify his fondness for all things Greek and become fluent in the language. This, as far as Eperitus was concerned, explained Antenor's excellence as a host.

'Does Priam speak any Greek?' Odysseus had asked, as they said goodbye to Theano and Antenor's sons at the threshold of the house that morning, before leaving for their audience with the Trojan king.

'He speaks several languages, but Greek only passably,' Antenor replied. 'I've been teaching him myself, at his insistence. But he will probably only speak in our native tongue when you come before him. He likes foreigners to think he can't understand them, then listens in on their private conversations. I shouldn't have told you that, of course.'

'Of course. What about his sons?'

'Hector speaks your language with a fluency equal to my own. He's thirsty for knowledge of all things Greek and has his own tutor – a man from Pylos – who instructs him daily in Greek language, culture, politics, warfare . . .'

'Warfare?' Eperitus interrupted.

'Yes. Hector has always loved anything to do with war, and you'll not find a more formidable fighter anywhere.'

By then they had reached the tower they had seen the evening before. Its soaring walls sloped to the height of two tall men, then continued vertically, up and up until they reached the crenellated battlements, from which the helmeted head of a guard was peering down at them. In the broad light of morning they could see the walls were constructed from massive limestone blocks, so finely fitted together that they did not need mortar. At the foot of the tower, facing south, were the six statuettes they had noticed the night before, deliberately placed so that all newcomers to the citadel would see them. Whether they were intended as a sign of welcome, or simply to warn visitors that the place they were entering was holy, was unclear, but their crude features and roughly formed bodies were unrecognizable as any gods the Greeks knew, and their lifeless eyes seemed only to offer the visitors hostility.

The great bastion jutted out from the walls and it was not until the party had passed the strange gods that they saw the gateway to the citadel, hidden in the shadow of the tower. Its carved wooden doors were already open and the two guardsmen stepped aside at a word from Antenor.

'And Paris?' asked Menelaus sternly, eyeing the black, rectangular mouth of the gateway. 'Is he a fighter like his brother, or a womanizer like his father?'

'Paris is a warrior, too,' Antenor said, choosing not to defend Priam or Paris against the Spartan's insults. His voice echoed slightly as they walked beneath the thick walls, where the air was cool and smelled of damp. 'Not of Hector's calibre, but he is known for his ferocity in battle and his strong sense of duty. And to further answer your question, Odysseus, Paris also speaks Greek, though he and Hector are unique in this among Priam's fifty sons.'

They emerged into the sunlight again and for the first time set their eyes upon the might and glory of Pergamos. On their left the walls fed out in a line to the west, while on their right they curved up and back to the north-east. Their thickness had already been made clear as they walked through the gate into the citadel, but now the visitors were able to see the wide parapets on top – where four fully-armed men could walk abreast – and the steep flights of steps leading up to them. At the foot of the walls were long wooden huts, where scores of heavily armed guards stared with hostile curiosity at the newcomers.

Beyond the gates, the citadel rose up in three distinct levels. Each new tier was separated from its predecessor by a sloping wall and the only way up was via a succession of stone ramps. Although the entrance to Pergamos was barely wide enough for one wagon to squeeze through at a time, the road beyond it was broad and well paved with flat cobbles. Indeed, as Antenor led the Greeks up the busy road, they could see two wool-laden wagons climbing the hill ahead of them, drawn easily abreast of each other so that the drivers could chat freely.

Lines of poplar trees stood on either side of the road, providing shade for the numerous townsfolk as they went about their daily business. By their dress, a quarter of them were wealthy nobles and probably lived or worked in the many tall, well-built and highly decorated buildings of the citadel. The rest were merchants, tradesmen, warriors and slaves, an even mixture of men and women from every craft and profession imaginable. From farmers to washerwomen and priests to prostitutes, the many different roles and trades flowed together to form a great stream of humanity that swirled and eddied through the wide, teeming streets of

Pergamos, as powerful a demonstration of Troy's wealth as the great buildings that filled the citadel.

Eperitus had never imagined such greatness could exist and stared open-mouthed at the two- and even three-storeyed structures that rose up all around him. The others shared his awe, particularly Palamedes, who gazed about himself with a look of wonder and joy on his face. Even Menelaus – who had seen the most powerful cities in Greece – looked with reluctant admiration at the dozens of mansions and temples crowded together on either side of the road. Antenor, who had seen them almost every day of his life, pointed out each building with pride, eager for his guests to appreciate the glory that made Troy famous throughout Asia and the Aegean.

'This mansion,' he said as they mounted the ramp to the first tier, indicating a palatial building over their left shoulders, 'is home to some of Priam's sons, where they live with their wives, children and slaves. There are many houses like it in on the lower tiers of the citadel, where other members of the royal family and high-born nobles live. Those buildings ahead of us are the temples of Athena and Zeus.'

Eperitus looked to the second tier, where on either side of the lines of poplars were two of the largest constructions he had ever seen. Both were fronted with marble columns and had wide, dark entrances reached by narrow flights of steps. The one to the right was tall and long, and on the plinth before it stood a large wooden statue of a male god, scaled to twice the size of a man. It had been painted with bright colours – though the once vivid hues had been faded by years of sunshine and rain – and its clothing was picked out with flashes of gold. A beard was visible on its chin and its right arm was raised in readiness to strike, though its hand was empty. By these tokens, Eperitus guessed the statue was meant to represent Zeus, though it did not clutch the customary thunderbolt.

On the opposite side of the ramp, which the party was now

mounting, stood the temple of Athena. Though not as high as the temple of Zeus, it was wider and more square in shape. On a plinth before it was an oversized figure of Athena, dressed in a chiton though not sporting her usual helmet, spear and aegis. The wood had been recently repainted and now the purple clothing with its gold hem gleamed in the early morning sun, while the goddess's brown eyes looked down her long nose at the passers-by. Unlike the temple of Zeus, a dozen armoured warriors stood or sat on the bottom steps, their spearheads and helmets flashing viciously in the sunlight.

'I'd like to pay my respects to the goddess on our way back, if I may,' Odysseus said.

Antenor smiled. 'Of course. No visitor to Pergamos should leave without seeing the temple of Athena. Along with the temples of Zeus and Apollo – which lies in the western corner of the citadel – there are no more sacred or awe-inspiring sights in the whole of Ilium. It also holds the famous Palladium, on which the fate of Troy depends.'

'The *Palladium*?' Eperitus enquired, trying to make his interest sound purely casual. 'What's that?'

Antenor looked at him with genuine surprise. 'You mean to say you haven't heard of our precious Palladium?'

Eperitus shook his head.

'Me neither,' said Odysseus. 'What manner of thing can carry the fate of a city with it? No, let me guess. It holds Priam's treasure and funds his armies?'

'Oh, no,' said Antenor, shaking his head dismissively. 'It has no value. In fact, it's nothing more than a small wooden effigy, about . . . *so* big, and with no legs.'

Eperitus caught Odysseus's eye and gave him a questioning glance.

'That's ridiculous,' Menelaus said, gruffly. 'How can Troy's safety depend on a lump of wood?'

'Because it's no mere lump of wood, my lord. They say that it fell from heaven when the city was first built. The temple was nearing completion when the Palladium came down through an unfinished gap in the roof and landed before the altar, where it sits to this day. Ilus, the founder of the city, was told in a dream that the image had been made by Athena herself, in memory of her dead friend Pallas, and as long as the image was preserved then Troy would be preserved with it. Some say it's just a legend – the same voices that say the walls were not built by Poseidon and Apollo – but most believe the story to be the truth. That's why Priam keeps guards there day and night.'

They had reached the ramp to the final and highest tier of the city, where a dozen warriors stood in a line with their shields and spears at the ready. They eyed the approach of the Greeks with suspicion and, unlike the other guards they had met, did not move aside at the sight of Antenor. Instead, their officer stepped forward and questioned the old man in a hushed voice, before ordering his men back and waving the visitors brusquely up the ramp.

And so, they had finally reached the palace of King Priam. As Eperitus sat in the cool, high-ceilinged antechamber to the throne room, waiting to be summoned into the king's presence, he pondered the size and magnificence of the palace as he had first seen it from the top of the ramp. Odysseus's home in Ithaca could not compare; neither could the palace in Alybas, where he had spent his youth. Although Menelaus's palace was similar in size, even that lacked the sheer beauty of the building that crowned the highest tier of Troy. The tall marble colonnades soared up to the heavens and left the visitor feeling daunted, whilst the many alcoves and stone plinths with their painted idols made certain that no one could doubt the reverence in which Troy held the gods. But most magnificent of all were the limestone walls and their large, richly decorated murals. These depicted many scenes from Trojan life: warriors fighting shield to shield; ships floating on seas full of dolphins; forests alive with bears, lions and all manner of creatures; but above all, the murals were filled with images of horses. Some were with riders and others without; many ran free, while more were being trained or were tethered to chariots. Antenor, when asked, explained all Trojans had a passion for horses, and Eperitus – who had loved horses since his childhood and had always rued the lack of them on Ithaca – was beginning to regret that war might be necessary against such an accomplished civilization.

At that point, the doors to the throne room swung open with a heavy wooden creaking to reveal a short, grey-bearded man in a long robe. In his right hand he carried a staff, which he beat importantly on the stone floor three times.

'His magnificence, King Priam, ruler of Troy, emperor of Ilium and all its protectorates and vassal states, guardian of the east and favourite of Zeus, bids you welcome. Those who wish to be humbled by his presence will please follow me.'

## Chapter Fourteen

# THE HOUSE OF KING PRIAM

Leaving Antiphus, Polites and Arceisius in the antechamber, the others followed the herald through the doors into a long, high-ceilinged chamber that echoed their footsteps as they entered. A rectangular hearth stretched before them, filled with purple flames that shivered on a bed of grey coals. Six black columns stood on either side of it; on a low dais at the far end was an empty stone seat with a high back, partially obscured by the haze of smoke and heat that trailed up from the fire.

The Greeks approached the four chairs that had been provided for them, while Antenor went to one of the many seats that lined each of the long sides of the hearth. Other than the throne and a single stool at the foot of the dais, every chair was now occupied and there was a large commotion of unintelligible voices as the Greeks took their places. The seats were of carved wood with a thin covering of silver plate and, despite the cushions, were uncomfortable. This and the scores of foreign faces that were now staring at them gave them a feeling of being criminals brought to trial, rather than honoured guests.

Eperitus sat on the far left next to Menelaus, whose eyes were scanning the crowd for sight of the hated Paris. Odysseus, sensing the Spartan king's growing anxiety, took the seat next to him and placed a large, reassuring hand on his shoulder. Palamedes, on the far right, lowered the palms of his hands towards the fire, enjoying the sensation of the heat on his skin. As soon as they were seated a dozen slaves rushed to pile food on the tables of Greeks and Trojans alike – baskets of bread, selections of nuts, cheeses, olives, grapes and fruit, platters of mutton or skewered fish – and pour wine into silver goblets for the assembled nobles.

Menelaus, stiff-backed, refused to either eat or drink. Palamedes also refrained, whilst Odysseus – after washing his hands in one of the bowls provided – helped himself to bread and mutton. Eperitus poured a small libation onto the flagstones at his feet, before raising the wine to his lips. It was the best he had ever tasted, and after a mouthful of the sweet, heady drink he felt refreshed and light-limbed. He looked about at Priam's throne room. It was unusually light, compared with the great halls of the Greek kings, with a broad column of blue daylight coming in through the lozenge-shaped vent in the ceiling, as well as several other shafts of light from openings high up on the walls. This was an innovation Eperitus had never seen before, and he could only guess that ducts had been built to pipe daylight from the roof into the hall. There were also numerous large torches fastened to the walls, which ensured that the magnificent murals that lined the room were not lost in shadow.

As with the architecture, dress and customs, the Trojan murals were very different from those of the Greeks. One whole wall was filled with a religious procession, featuring lines of priests, nobles and sacrificial animals. Another was painted sky blue and filled with depictions of men fighting bulls and other animals. The next wall showed fishing boats on a sea of wavy blue lines that teemed with fish, while on the hills behind (with Mount Ida in the distance) were flocks of sheep and herds of wild horses. On the fourth side a golden-skinned shepherd played a lyre as another golden-skinned man was fitting great blocks of stone into a high wall. Beyond the unfinished battlements were scenes of everyday life: people spinning wool, smiths working glowing bronze rods over an anvil, a potter removing vases from a kiln. Both men and women were depicted, distinguishable by the way they wore their hair or the colour of their skin: the men were brown because they led active, outdoor lives, the women were white, reflecting the ideal of a life spent indoors.

Around the walls were a number of guards wearing the strange, scaled armour of the Trojans. The spears at their sides and the swords that hung in scabbards over their shoulders reminded Eperitus of his vulnerability, and he prayed silently for Athena's protection and a safe return to the ship. As he finished his prayer, a door opened quietly in a dark corner of the chamber and a stooping figure entered. His black cloak made him inconspicuous amidst the activity that filled the room, and as he moved along the southern wall below the mural of the religious procession only Eperitus's watchful eye seemed to notice him. He walked with a faltering hop, his left hand hanging limply at his side while his right dangled before his chest, like a child riding a pretend horse. Then, as he drew level with Eperitus, he turned and his pale skin and dark, sunken eyes became visible under the shadow of his hood. Eperitus recognized him at once as the man who had pushed his way through the crowds the night before.

'We must speak, Eperitus,' he said in perfect Greek, whispering so that only Eperitus's supernaturally sharp hearing could distinguish the words. 'Come to me.'

Eperitus felt as if his legs had been kicked from under him. How could this stranger have discovered his name? More disturbingly, how could he know that he would be able to hear a whisper across a crowded room? Eperitus turned and stared into the hearth, as if hoping the hiss of the flames would drown out his confusion.

'Priam will be here soon,' came the same whisper in his ear. 'We don't have long. Leave your friends and come to me. Now.'

Eperitus backed his chair away from the table and stood.

'I need to relieve myself,' he told Menelaus, who nodded briefly before returning to his scrutiny of the crowd.

Eperitus crossed to the back corner of the throne room, where a large amphora reeked of urine. He lifted his tunic and emptied his bladder, then sensed the presence of the hooded man behind him.

'Who are you?' he said, lowering the hem of his tunic and turning. 'How do you know my name?'

The man stared at him from beneath the shadow of his hood. His face was contorted by a constant series of twitches, but his dark eyes remained firmly fixed on Eperitus.

'I know many things, my friend. For example, I know you've come to seek the return of Menelaus's wife.'

'Then she's here – in Troy?'

The man smiled. 'I did not say that, and if she is then I am not aware of it. Yet I know your mission all the same, and many other things besides. Perhaps you will be more convinced,' he added, seeing the look of scepticism in Eperitus's eyes, 'if I tell you that you were once brought back from death by Athena. Or if I say that I know you are ashamed of your past, and even now hate the mention of your father. I also know you are torn between your desire for war and your loyalty to Odysseus, who is keen to secure the peaceful return of Helen and go back home to his own family. And if that is not enough, then how about this: Odysseus has given you a powder to pour into Palamedes's wine that will – now, what were his words – that will have him emptying his bowels by the second gulp. Am I right?'

'You can't possibly know that – *any* of that.'

'But I do, and much more. I know things about you that even you don't know – *yet.*'

Eperitus felt his impatience growing. 'Stop talking in riddles and speak plainly. Tell me who you are and how you know these things, or by the name of Athena I'll knock you down where you stand.'

'My name is Calchas, son of Thestor, son of Idmon the Argonaut,' he announced, making Eperitus's eyes widen as he realized this was the man Athena had said would find him. He drew his hood back to reveal his shaven head, then opened his cloak to expose the white robes beneath. 'I'm a priest of Apollo. The god speaks to me in dreams – sleeping and waking. It's a gift, a wonderful, terrible gift. It shows me things that few can see, and few *should* see.'

Calchas pulled the hood forward to cover his hairless scalp and fixed his gaze on Eperitus once more. The pain and the madness glistered like sunken treasure beneath the surface of his eyeballs.

'And yet even *I* only see the shadow of things. Apollo allows me glimpses of the past, the present or the future, but I never see the complete picture. That's for the gods only. But I do know we live in momentous times, Eperitus. Our world is heading into a great terror – a war that will choke Hades's halls with the dead and bring a lasting darkness in its wake. Apollo has revealed it to me, and it is horrifying.'

'But what's that got to do with me?' Eperitus asked, uncertain that he wanted any part of the priest's awful visions. 'I'm a warrior, not a prophet.'

'It has everything to do with you, Eperitus. War is inevitable, but the choices you make today will decide which of our nations will survive and which will be destroyed. Odysseus gave you that powder to pour in Palamedes's drink because he knows Palamedes is acting for Agamemnon and will try to prevent a peaceful agreement for the return of Helen. One dose of that, though,' the priest said, tapping Eperitus's leather pouch with his finger, 'and Palamedes will be spending the rest of the day crouched over a latrine somewhere, leaving Odysseus free to use his powers of persuasion on Priam. But we have to stop him succeeding; although Odysseus does not know it, the safety of Greece depends on Agamemnon laying siege to Troy.'

'And why should a *Trojan* care what happens to Greece?' Eperitus scoffed.

'I may be Trojan by birth,' Calchas responded, 'but my loyalty is to Apollo, not Priam. I do whatever the god tells me to do, and he has ordered me to abandon Troy and join the Greeks.'

'But Antenor says Apollo has always favoured Troy.'

'And he still does. But Zeus is intent on war between Greece and Troy, and out of obedience to his will Apollo has ordered me to offer my services to Agamemnon. You are to take me back with you to the gathering at Aulis – yes, I know all about it – so that I can speak with him. But first we must prevent Odysseus's attempt at peace.'

'If you think I'll disobey Odysseus for your sake, Calchas, then you're as mad as you look,' Eperitus said, angered by the priest's presumption. He was beginning to wonder whether Athena had been right to say he should listen to the man at all. 'I'm going back to my seat.'

'Hear me out, Eperitus!' Calchas hissed, grabbing his arm. 'If your king succeeds the war will still come, but on Trojan terms, not Greek. Why do you think there's an army camped on the plain? What about the warships in the harbour? Don't you understand? The Trojans are planning to attack Greece. And it'll be no raid, either – it's going to be an invasion!'

Eperitus shook off Calchas's bony hand. 'Priam wouldn't dare.'

'No, he wouldn't. But *Hector* would. He's the real power behind Troy, not Priam – as you'll soon see. If Agamemnon doesn't attack Troy first, then Hector will conquer Greece city by city until he makes it part of Priam's empire – the empire *he* will inherit. Even Ithaca will fall, in the end. Do you believe me, Eperitus?'

Eperitus looked across the throne room to where Odysseus was sitting, pointedly ignoring Palamedes while trying to persuade Menelaus to eat some food. His friend had been optimistic about obtaining a peaceful resolution from the start, but was he just avoiding facing up to the inevitable? Ever since they had arrived in Troy Eperitus had sensed a threat; not just the curses and spitting of the crowd, but a deeper undercurrent. There was something sinister about the half-built war fleet and the gathering army camped on the plain, followed by the unwelcoming treatment they had received from Priam (or was that Hector's doing?). Even the large gathering of Trojan officials in Priam's throne room felt like a jury, waiting to decide the fate of the Greeks.

'Whether I believe you or not – and I'm not saying I do – how do you suggest I should prevent Odysseus from obtaining a peaceful solution?'

'Palamedes must be allowed to speak,' Calchas answered. 'If you don't pour the powder into his drink, he has the cunning and intelligence to upset Odysseus's plans. Odysseus will be angry, of course, but when he hears what I have to say he'll realize that war is inevitable anyway and will see reason.'

'You're assuming I'll do what you want me to.'

Calchas looked at him carefully, reading the thoughts behind his eyes.

'That's your decision, Eperitus. But remember this: one way or another, the fate of all Greece is in your hands tonight. The army you saw on the plain is but the first crop of a mighty harvest. Before long other armies will join it, just as other ships will swell the Trojan fleet to an armada. If Odysseus gets his way he could be back with his family in a matter of weeks, but his happiness will be short-lived. Within a year or two Hector's conquering armies will have reached Ithaca, and then Odysseus will see his precious wife and son butchered by Trojan swords and his people enslaved. Think on that when you let your king negotiate a peaceful end to this matter.'

Eperitus looked thoughtfully at the stooping priest. 'You're asking me to defy him when he needs my loyalty most,' he said. 'And in other circumstances your impudence would earn you a beating, priest or not. But I've seen the Trojan army you speak of, and the fleet in the harbour, and something tells me you're right. So I'll think about what you ask, Calchas, and if Odysseus *does* fail, for whatever reason, I'll make sure that you return with us to Aulis.'

'Then I will go and wait for you by your ship – Priam has already left his chamber and is on his way here with Hector. But first there is one other thing I have to say. It concerns you personally, Eperitus.'

'Go on,' Eperitus said apprehensively.

'I said I know things about you that you don't,' Calchas began, 'secret things that have been deliberately kept from you. I am forbidden to reveal what little I know about them, but the first is the answer to your heart's desires and will tempt you to stay away from the coming war – *you must not let it*! Troy has to fall to the Greeks, and that cannot happen without both you and Odysseus. But the second is darker and equally compelling, and would draw you back to Ilium whether there is a war or not.'

'What are these things – these *secrets* – you speak of?' Eperitus urged, staring hard into Calchas's half-crazed eyes. 'Does Odysseus know?'

'Your friend is as ignorant of them as you are,' Calchas reassured him. 'Go to Agamemnon's city, Mycenae. One who lives there can reveal the first secret to you. More than that I cannot say.'

With that, the priest turned and slipped back out the way he had come. Eperitus waited for him to leave then returned to his seat, watched by Odysseus.

'Who was that?' the king asked. 'Didn't I see him in the crowd yesterday?'

'I'll tell you about it later,' Eperitus replied. 'This must be King Priam.'

At that moment, a large door to the side of the throne opened and two warriors in golden armour entered. They stood either side of the door and bowed their heads as a third man swept past them into the room. King Priam was tall – a head higher than his escorts – and dressed in a richly embroidered tunic and a crimson cloak that dragged along the floor behind him. His hair was a shiny black and his fringe had been carefully plaited in the same fashion as the younger Trojan men; but, though he must have been handsome in his youth, his quick brown eyes were now sunken with age and the skin of his long neck hung in folds beneath his chin. Even the thick layer of orange powder he wore could not hide the labyrinth of wrinkles that were etched across his face.

He was followed by his eldest son, Hector, whose dark,

menacing eyes swept the room as he entered. He was nearly as tall as his father, but where Priam was lean, Hector was broad and powerfully built. Behind his thick black beard, his face was stern, hard and uncompromising, giving him an air of intimidating natural authority. This was accentuated by the simplicity of his clothing: a black, knee-length tunic and a woollen cloak, swept back over his shoulders to reveal a plain leather cuirass and a belt with a silver dagger.

Upon reaching the throne, Priam turned and raised his hands in an extravagant greeting, a broad and pleasant smile on his face. From the moment he had entered, the chamber had been filled with the scraping of heavy wooden chairs as the Trojans – regardless of age or rank – threw themselves to the flagstones to grovel like dogs before their master. Now, as Priam surveyed the large, bright chamber, only the four Greeks dared to look back at him. Though they had stood out of respect, their pride forbade them to prostrate themselves before any man, king or not.

'Get down on your knees, you foreign swine,' said the old herald who had called them in from the antechamber. He was kneeling beside them with his forehead to the floor, talking from the side of his mouth and desperately trying to swipe at Eperitus's shins with his staff.

'Peace, Idaeus,' Priam commanded in his own language, his strong, clear voice ringing from the walls. 'Our guests can't be blamed if Antenor failed to instruct them in our ways. Besides, they no doubt believe themselves my equal – I've heard there's no respect amongst Greeks, only pride and insolence. Now, my sons and friends, raise yourselves and let us hear what these people have to say. Antenor, please be so kind as to visit me in my personal quarters after this is over.'

The king lowered himself into his throne, while Hector sat on the stool at the foot of the dais, resting his chin on his fist and glaring at the assembly. As the rest of the Trojans lifted themselves from the floor and retook their seats, a bard ran his fingers skilfully across his lyre and began to sing. The sound of his voice was soft and clear, though unintelligible to the Greeks, and as he sang a crowd of slaves appeared with platters of food and cups of wine to replace those that had already been consumed. Priam rose again to pour the first libation to the gods, then lifted the shining golden goblet to his lips and took a mouthful.

'That's good!' he said with a smack of his lips. 'Idaeus, tell our friends to tuck in. If they're here to talk, they might as well do it on full stomachs.'

'King Priam says you should eat,' Idaeus informed the Greeks curtly.

Odysseus, seeing the eyes of every Trojan upon them, stood and poured his own libation, before taking a large gulp of wine and following it with a handful of goats' meat. Immediately the rest of the room began drinking and eating, and soon the smoky air was filled with the sound of voices and feasting.

Menelaus, however, continued to refuse all food and drink. As the cacophony continued – and Priam showed no sign of asking the names and lineage of his guests or the purpose of their visit – the Spartan king's impatience grew. Eventually, annoyed by what he saw as Priam's deliberate efforts to frustrate him, he slammed his great fist down on the table and stood up.

'You!' he said, pointing at Idaeus as the noise fell away and all eyes turned on him. 'Tell your king that the time for feasting is over. If he won't ask our names, as *polite* custom requires, then I'll give them to him: I am King Menelaus of Sparta, son of Atreus. This is King Odysseus of Ithaca, son of Laertes. Our two companions are Palamedes and Eperitus. We have sailed for many days on a mission of vital importance to both our peoples – as, *no doubt*, you are fully aware – yet since our arrival, Priam has treated us with nothing less than contempt. Are we dogs, that we should be kept outside the citadel walls until the king has finished toying with his women? Or are we kings, to be treated with the respect that our rank commands? However he regards us is immaterial to me, but I warn him to listen to what I have to say, or the whole of Ilium will have to face the consequences.'

Idaeus took a moment to comprehend what Menelaus had told him, then turned and translated it to his king. An angry murmur broke out from the gathered nobles, but was silenced by a barked command from Hector.

'Tell King Menelaus we are fully aware of who he and his companions are,' the prince replied in a gravelly voice, leaning on his knees and staring directly at the Spartan. 'And that, since Anchises and Antenor were sent to request the return of my father's sister, Hesione, and were almost murdered for their efforts, we do not feel inclined to be lectured on matters of hospitality by *Greeks*. However, we respect the code of *xenia* and will gladly listen to the purpose of his mission, if he will share it with us.'

'Menelaus!' Odysseus hissed as they listened to Idaeus's translation. 'Curb your temper, man. Do you want Helen back or not?'

Menelaus glowered at his comrade, but took a deep breath and turned once more to face the royal dais.

'Very well, then, we can dispense with the formalities. If Hector wants to pretend he doesn't know the purpose of our visit, that's up to him. But as this matter concerns his brother, I demand that Paris is brought before this council so that all the facts can be heard and properly debated.'

Menelaus watched as Priam and Hector exchanged looks and hushed words. It was Priam, this time, who answered.

'Paris is not here,' he said, a look of concern in his eyes. 'I sent him to Greece to bargain for the return of Hesione, hoping my own son would succeed where all previous envoys have failed. Surely you've seen him?'

'That's a damned lie!' Menelaus shouted. 'I know he's here, and my wife's here with him!'

He gave a cry of rage and seized the edge of the table before him, tipping it over so that its contents spilled across the stone floor. The younger Trojans on either side sprang to their feet and made towards him, but were stopped by another bellowing command from Hector. Odysseus and Eperitus were up in an instant and had to use all their strength to drag Menelaus back to his chair.

'Eperitus,' Odysseus whispered, catching his friend's eye and nodding towards the cup on Palamedes's table. 'Do it now. He's been drinking like a horse all afternoon – building up his courage, I expect. If you're quick, he won't even notice.'

Menelaus flopped back onto his chair and sank his face into his hands. Odysseus immediately left him and took two steps towards the hearth, so that all eyes were focused on his squat, triangular form.

'My friends,' he said, holding up his hands and looking around at the assembly, their faces glowing angrily in the light from the fire. Idaeus translated from behind his left shoulder. 'Honourable Trojans, I beg you to forgive my long-suffering comrade. If you knew what this man has been through these past few weeks, you'd understand his torment and look on him with pity, not the fury I see in your eyes now.'

Odysseus continued to stare from face to face, giving his words time to sink in and waiting for the angry murmurs of the Trojans to subside. Behind him, Eperitus pulled the small vial of powder from his pouch and held it in the palm of his hand, his eyes switching from Palamedes to Odysseus and back again.

'What's this all about, Odysseus?' Hector said, unable to tolerate the silence any longer. 'What does Menelaus want with my brother? Didn't Paris visit him in Sparta? He had intended to go there first.'

'My lord Hector, things haven't started well between us. There's been too much distrust on both sides, but if our peoples are to be saved from a great tragedy then we must agree to be open and honest with one another. Do you give me your word, as a warrior and a man of honour, that Paris is not in Troy, and that you haven't seen him since he left for Greece?'

'My brother hasn't been seen or heard of for weeks, and may Zeus strike me down if I lie. Now tell me what you know of him, Odysseus.'

'Is he dead?' Priam interrupted, leaning forward slightly and curling his fingers anxiously over the armrest of his throne.

'He lives, as far as I know, my lord,' Odysseus answered, 'unless the gods have avenged the dishonour he brought on your house. Because Paris *did* visit Sparta, and the last anybody saw of him he was fleeing the city with Menelaus's wife as his captive.'

This time Hector and Priam did not pretend to wait for Idaeus's translation.

'What?' Hector exclaimed in Greek, standing and staring at Odysseus through the haze thrown up by the hearth. 'He wouldn't dare!'

A moment later he was joined by the rest of the assembly, who after listening to Idaeus's translation again left their seats and cried out as one in protest against the accusation.

'No son of mine would do such a thing,' said Priam, also in Greek, as he stepped down from the dais to stand next to Hector. 'Kidnap a royal queen? He's a prince and a warrior, and he is loyal to the will of his father. It's just not possible!'

'It's true,' said Menelaus, lifting his face from his hands and talking with deep despondency. 'He was a guest in my home and swore a sacred oath of friendship to me, but the very night I went on a journey to Crete he stole Helen from me and took my lad, Pleisthenes, too.'

'By all the sacred gods of Ilium!' Priam exclaimed, leaning against Hector. 'He can't have!'

'He has,' Odysseus confirmed. 'And throughout Greece the storm clouds are gathering. Unless Helen is returned, there will be war.'

This statement was greeted by more angry muttering from the Trojans, and in the buzz of voices Eperitus signalled to one of the slaves to bring wine. As the man began refilling his half-empty goblet, Eperitus moved to the seat beside Palamedes.

'Fill this, too,' he ordered, taking Palamedes's goblet and passing it to the slave. Palamedes, who was growing more agitated as his eyes flicked between Odysseus and Priam, hardly seemed to notice Eperitus's presence beside him.

'Paris is not here,' Priam said again, in a loud voice. 'How do we know you're telling us the truth until we speak to him? For all we know, Helen may have left willingly.'

Menelaus lifted his head sharply and there was anger in his eyes, but Odysseus spoke first.

'We have taken you at your word, my lords, and accept that Paris has not yet returned to Troy; you must also take our word and believe that Menelaus's wife was abducted by your son. I can understand why you might doubt me – a foreigner who comes to your city with the threat of war on his tongue – so instead I ask you to look at this man.'

Odysseus moved to stand behind Menelaus's chair. His eyes rested briefly on Eperitus, who raised Palamedes's goblet and poured the powder into it. Odysseus smiled and gave a subtle wink, before turning and placing his hands on the Spartan's shoulders.

'I've known this man for ten years,' he told the assembled Trojans, 'ever since the best of the Greeks gathered to pay court to the most beautiful woman in the world – Helen of Sparta. And of all the great men she could have chosen from – Diomedes, Ajax, Idomeneus and many more – she picked the greatest of us all, Menelaus. But look at him now, a ruin of his former self, destroyed by the loss of his wife. Could a man feign the rage and despair you yourselves have witnessed in him?'

He paused for Idaeus to translate his words, and as the Trojans discussed what Odysseus had said, Eperitus placed Palamedes's goblet of wine on the table before him.

'What do you think?' he asked in a low voice. 'Will they agree to return Helen?'

Palamedes's eyelids were heavy with wine and his eyes unfocused. 'Can't be sure, but Hector's certainly angry with Paris. He told Priam this is going to ruin everything he's planned for.'

'How could you know that?' Eperitus asked, suddenly attentive. 'Every word they've spoken to each other has been in their own language.'

'My nursemaid was a Trojan slave, captured in a raid,' Palamedes answered. 'She taught me her language when I was a child, and I've been able to understand almost every word I've heard since arriving here.'

'Then why didn't you tell us that before?' Eperitus snapped, feeling his temper rise at the sight of Palamedes's smug grin.

But at that moment Odysseus held up his hands for silence. 'Even if you don't care for the suffering of this man,' he continued, patting Menelaus's shoulders, 'even if your desire is to support Paris, regardless of whether Helen was taken from Sparta or left willingly, then think of the wider consequences. You're all noblemen and many of you have royal blood in your veins. If you condone the abduction of a queen – Helen was not taken as a spoil of war like Hesione was, remember – you are saying that such acts are acceptable. Then where will you be? Moral standards will falter. The gods will abandon you. If in times of peace men are allowed to think that royal women are there to be plucked like apples from a tree, or women come to believe they are free to choose their lovers, how will you protect your own families? What's more, how will you ever be sure that your children are truly yours? Do you want to raise the bastard sons of others as your own and let them inherit what is not theirs? If you do not give Helen back to Menelaus when Paris returns, then *you* will be responsible for the doom that follows!'

Odysseus's final sentence rang ominously through the silent hall. Eperitus could see by the looks on the faces of the Trojans that his words had hit their mark, but in the moments of quiet that followed all he could think of was the warning given to him by Calchas. What if the priest was right and peace now would only open the way to a Trojan invasion of Greece? Were these the plans Palamedes had overheard Hector talking of? And if so, would they ultimately lead to the conquest of Ithaca and the destruction of everything Odysseus held most precious? He watched Priam and Hector leaning into each other and whispering urgently, and wondered whether the fearsome Trojan prince was thinking of how to keep the Greeks from attacking Ilium before his own plans could come to fruition.

'Your king speaks well,' Palamedes said, reaching for the drugged goblet. 'Too well for the good of Greece.'

Eperitus watched the man's fingers curl around the stem of the cup. He thought for a moment then hooked his foot around Palamedes's chair and pulled it backwards. Palamedes grabbed the table in an attempt to regain his balance, knocking the cup to the floor with a clang. Odysseus turned to see the dark wine spreading over the flagstones, and the confident gleam in his eye wavered. A moment later Hector spoke.

'My father and I have come to an agreement. In view of Menelaus's anger with my brother we think it wise that he returns to Sparta as soon as practical. However, as we intend to give his wife back to him' – Menelaus raised his head at these words, his eyes wide, almost disbelieving – 'we invite you, Odysseus, to remain here until Paris returns so that you can escort her back to Greece. Regardless of why Helen is with Paris – and we do not yet accept she was taken against her will – we agree with Odysseus and don't want to set a precedent. Is this agreeable?'

'No,' said Palamedes, rising unsteadily to his feet. 'No it isn't. My friend has spoken truly, for it's a vile crime to steal a man's wife, but there is also the matter of compensation.'

'Sit down, you fool,' Odysseus commanded, his voice stern. 'Sit down before I knock you down.'

'Yes, sit down Palamedes,' Menelaus agreed.

'I will *not* sit down! You may think, Hector, that Troy can escape its crime by returning Helen, but Agamemnon, Menelaus's brother and the most powerful of all the Greeks, does not. He demands that Priam pay compensation.'

There was an ugly muttering from amongst the ranks of Trojan nobles. Priam's face was like stone, and Hector's expression was dark and menacing.

'Go on,' he said, slowly. 'Name your demands.'

'There are no demands,' Odysseus insisted.

'Agamemnon feels that, as Paris will almost certainly have violated Helen and made the atrocity more heinous, Menelaus's suffering cannot be measured by financial compensation alone. He therefore demands an annual tribute in copper, timber, wool and slaves – the exact amounts to be negotiated – as well as the handing over of three Trojan cities: one for himself, one for Menelaus and the third for Odysseus . . .'

'You lying dog!' Odysseus shouted, springing towards Palamedes with his fists raised.

Eperitus quickly flung himself between the two men.

'Fighting Palamedes won't help!' he hissed, placing the flats of his hands against the king's chest as Palamedes retreated behind him.

'So that was your intention all along, was it?' Priam crowed, standing on the royal dais and shaking his fist at Odysseus. 'A city of your own in payment for the return of Helen and the humbling of Troy. Do you think we would ever have agreed to such terms?'

A silver cup was thrown from amidst the mob of angry officials, hitting Odysseus on the back. Another glanced off his arm, followed by a torrent of abuse. Eperitus stepped in front of his king and looked quickly about the room as more cups, plates and pieces of food were thrown at them. An armed warrior stood at each exit, but the remainder were already closing in on the Greeks, their spear-points lowered threateningly. It would still be possible to rush the soldiers before they could bring their weapons to bear, Eperitus thought, but even if they overpowered them and took their spears and shields, it was unlikely that they could fight their way out of the city and back across the plain to their ship. Escape was impossible.

'I say we should kill them,' said a short man with a crooked nose and pointed beard. 'If Paris has taken this man's wife, then let's do away with him now and at least then the Greeks will have no further claim on the woman!'

There was a murmur of agreement, but then a voice called out from the crowd.

'Peace, my friends! Sit down! Don't let Antimachus's words add fuel to your anger. Remember these men are our guests and under the protection of Zeus himself. If you harm them, you defy the gods and bring judgement upon yourselves!'

It was Antenor. He had forced his way through the closing circle of Trojans to stand with his arms aloft between them and the outnumbered Greeks. His countrymen shouted at the old man and told him to stand aside, but advanced no further. Then Hector appeared, clearing a passage through the throng to stand face to face with Odysseus.

'You insult us with your deceit, Odysseus. If I was free to do as I pleased, I'd tear you to pieces right now with my own hands. But Antenor is right: you remain guests here, and I'll not bring the wrath of the gods down on Troy by killing you.'

Odysseus met the Trojan's stormy gaze without flinching. 'You're a fool, Hector. We came to offer you the chance of righting the wrong Paris has done, but from the moment of our arrival you chose to treat us with hostility. Now, if you really respect the will of the gods, you'll let us return to our ship unmolested.'

'I'll make sure you're escorted back in safety,' Hector replied, sternly. 'Have no fear of that. But once you've left our waters, I advise you never to return. If you do, you'll find us ready for you.'

*Chapter Fifteen*

# THE GATHERING AT AULIS

They all knew they had been fortunate to escape from Troy alive. The hostility in Priam's throne room was nothing compared with the anger that awaited them on the streets of the city. By the time they had rejoined Antiphus, Polites and Arceisius and marched out of the citadel gates, they found a large mob had already assembled beyond the walls, armed with rocks, lumps of wood and even a few spears. Only the escort of a hundred warriors enabled the Greeks to reach the Scaean Gate unharmed, and it was not until they felt the gentle motion of the Ithacan warship beneath their feet once more that they could finally relax.

The relief of being free of Troy gave each of them a sense of calm. Palamedes sat in the prow, his arms crossed over his knees and his chin resting on his forearm staring blankly ahead of himself. Menelaus joined the three guardsmen on the benches and took hold of one of the polished oars, pulling quietly in time with the rest of the crew as Eurybates steered the ship out of the harbour. What he was thinking as he looked over his shoulder at the high citadel no man could tell. Odysseus and Eperitus withdrew to the stern, from where they looked back in silence at the broad plain with its scattered farmsteads and flocks of sheep, its corralled horses and the city of tents by the mouth of the Simöeis. It all seemed so peaceful as they watched the walls of the citadel turn pink in the light of the lowering sun.

As the ship slipped back out to sea and Troy was lost behind the wooded headland, Antiphus brought Calchas to the king. He had arrived shortly before Odysseus's return and surrendered himself to the crew, insisting he had information that would be of use to the Greeks.

'What information?' Odysseus asked the hooded priest, whom he had recognized immediately.

'What I have to say is for all the kings of Greece together, or none at all.'

'Why don't you tell it to the fish, then,' Odysseus responded, grabbing a fistful of Calchas's robes and almost carrying him to the side of the ship. The man's hood slipped back to reveal his bald head and pale, drawn features.

'Wait!' Eperitus shouted, rushing over and grabbing Calchas's arm, fearing that in the mood he was in Odysseus would cast him overboard without a second thought. 'If he says he has information then we should trust him. When he spoke to me in Priam's palace he told me things about myself that only you and I know. He knew about the powder you gave me, Odysseus, and he even knows about the gathering at Aulis. He's a seer like none I've ever come across, other than the Pythoness herself. Calchas,' he added, turning to the cowering priest, 'I don't know what this other information you have is, but at least tell Odysseus what you told me in the throne room.'

Odysseus pinned Calchas against the side of the ship, where clouds of spray soaked his clothing and formed into watery beads that trickled off his hairless scalp.

'Tell me what you know, Trojan, or you can swim to Greece instead.'

'Hector has been preparing Troy for war against Greece,' Calchas stuttered. 'The galleys you saw in the bay, the army camped on the plain – they're just the beginning.'

'Then he knew we were gathering our forces for an attack, even before we arrived?' asked Menelaus, who had overheard the conversation from the benches and come to stand behind Eperitus.

'No, my lord, he had no idea you were coming. But he has

dreamt of invading Greece for many years, waiting patiently while his father's power waned and his own influence grew. Now, with peace on the northern borders, he feels his time is approaching.'

'But why would Hector want to invade Greece?' asked Odysseus.

'For the same reason Agamemnon wants to conquer Troy,' Calchas replied. 'A stranglehold on the Aegean and all the trade that flows across it.'

'My brother wants the return of Helen,' Menelaus said, with slow menace in his voice.

'Don't delude yourself about what your brother wants, Menelaus,' Calchas retorted, his face convulsing unconsciously under the glare of the Spartan king. 'For years Mycenae has been spreading its trade routes like a web across the Aegean; and where merchants lead the way warriors eventually follow.'

'Why tell us this, Calchas?' Odysseus asked, releasing his grip on the man's robes and helping him to stand as upright as his stooped form would allow. 'You're a Trojan, after all.'

'Because Apollo has ordered it,' Calchas said with a shrug. 'And now, if you're satisfied, I'd like a drink.'

Odysseus ordered a skin of wine to be brought for the strange priest, who sat facing the benches and staring at the sailors as he drank. His unflinching gaze made them uneasy, and even with their backs turned they could feel his eyes boring into them.

'He's an odd one,' Odysseus commented later, as he sat with Eperitus in the stern and watched Calchas get progressively drunker.

'But useful.'

Odysseus gave a sidelong glance at Menelaus, who lay snoring against the side of the ship.

'What else did he say to you in the throne room, Eperitus?'

Eperitus felt a sudden sensation of guilt overwhelming him, as if Odysseus knew every detail of the conversation with Calchas and was aware that the captain of his guard had betrayed him. But Eperitus also knew from long experience that Odysseus often tried to give the impression of knowing more than he did – a trick by which he would draw his victims out and make them reveal all sorts of secrets to him. It was impossible that the king could know Calchas had asked Eperitus to foil his plans for the peaceful return of Helen, and that he had caused Palamedes to spill the drugged wine. Odysseus was clever, of course, and knew there must be a reason why the priest had spoken to Eperitus first, but Eperitus guessed he was simply casting a line and seeing whether he could get a bite.

'He said there are two secrets about me that I don't yet know. He didn't tell me what they are – and I don't think he fully knows – but he said one will make me want to avoid war, while the other would compel me to return to Troy.'

'Hmm,' Odysseus mused. 'I can't imagine anything that would make *you* want to miss out on a chance of glory, but if such a thing exists then at least we'll both be working to the same goal – a quick and peaceful resolution to this mess.'

'Then you still think war can be stopped, even after what has just happened?'

Odysseus leaned back against the rail and looked towards the western horizon. The sun had already slipped behind the outline of Lemnos and a pale moon was rising in the purple sky.

'I'm only mortal, Eperitus. I don't know what the Fates have in store for us, and as long as I remain ignorant of that then yes, I *do* believe this war can be averted. Things look dark right now, but opportunities will always present themselves. We just have to be ready for them.'

'I don't know where you get your optimism from,' Eperitus rejoined, shaking his head. 'What about the fleet in the harbour and the army on the plain? Calchas says that Hector will attack Greece sooner or later, and that eventually his armies will reach Ithaca too.'

Odysseus laughed heartily, as if he were sharing a joke with friends in the great hall back on Ithaca, not on a ship on the far side of the world. 'I'd say Hector is the optimist if he expects to conquer Greece. If the different states can unite for the sake of a woman, however beautiful, then we can join together to repel a common enemy. But aren't you forgetting the biggest problem of all?'

Eperitus raised his eyebrows and shrugged.

'The oracle said I'd be twenty years away from home if I ever went to Troy,' Odysseus continued with a wry smile. 'Well, I've been to Troy now, so I'm doomed anyway. Unless,' he added, raising a cautionary finger, 'I can cheat destiny, like I had the chance to do ten years ago.'

'Then we'll both have to wait and see what happens,' Eperitus concluded, looking at Odysseus's smiling face and getting the distinct feeling there was something hollow about his bravado – as if, deep down, he knew he would not see his home for a very long time.

The remainder of the voyage to Greece was slow and tedious. As they retraced their route southward past Tenedos, Lesbos and Chios to Icaria, before turning west to find a passage through the Cyclades, they were beset by unseasonably rough weather. On three occasions they were unable to leave the different ports and coves where they had taken shelter the night before, not daring to risk the raging seas and blustering winds. Then, in the second week out of Troy, they made sacrifices to Poseidon and the storms eased away. Soon, a westerly wind was speeding them towards Euboea and the gathering of the Greek kings. On one occasion they were approached by pirates – who quickly turned and fled at the sight of a deck crammed with armed men – but the rest of the passage was smooth and unhindered.

Finally, three weeks after leaving Troy, they reached the island of Euboea and spent the night in the bay below Mount Ocha, where Zeus and Hera were said to have fallen in love. In the pre-dawn light of the next morning their oars were already gliding through the calm waters as the sailors took their craft out into the wide triangle of sea between Euboea and the western mainland. Before long they had picked up a mild breeze and Odysseus, leaning his weight on the twin rudders, steered them to the northern apex of the triangle, where the two opposing landmasses closed to a narrow point. By mid-morning, with the sun's heat bearing down on them from the naked blue sky, they passed between the small islets that guarded the mouth of the straits and saw a handful of masts in the distance ahead of them, clustered near to the shore where the hills of the mainland sloped into the sea.

The sight of these ships caused an excited rush to the prow, upsetting the ship's balance and forcing Odysseus to order his crew back to their places. For days, the conversation on the benches had been filled with speculation about which kings would answer the call to arms, and what force of men and ships they would bring with them. Now, with the first glimpse of Agamemnon's assembly, the galley was suddenly a cacophony of competing voices. Even Odysseus could barely disguise his excitement.

'How many can you see, Eperitus?' he asked, squinting at the ships that were framed between the lines of the halyards and the billowing sail above.

'Six?'

'There's a dozen at least,' said Eurybates, whose sailor's eyes were not as sharp as Eperitus's but were more accustomed to counting ships at a distance.

'There must be more than that!' Menelaus exclaimed. 'There *have* to be!'

'There are,' said Calchas, his bald pate gleaming in the sunlight as he remained sitting on the planks of the main deck. 'Hundreds upon hundreds of them. I saw them in my dream last night.'

'Pah!' Menelaus sniffed. 'You were drunk, as usual.'

But Menelaus's distrust of Calchas – which had grown greater each time the Trojan drank himself senseless – proved to be unfounded. As they followed the curve of the coast around to the west they passed fleet after fleet, each one belonging to a different king. Some numbered just a handful, while others had as many as two or three dozen vessels; and opposite each mooring were large numbers of tents, where hundreds of soldiers stood watching the lone galley slip by. But even these were just the vanguard. Eventually, the straits closed to form a large bay where the mountainous flanks of Boetia and Euboea almost touched, their independence maintained by a narrow strip of water leading north. Here, finally, they saw the massed might of Greece.

This time even the combined voices of Odysseus and Eperitus could not drag the men back to their seats, as each warrior moved to the prow to gaze in stunned awe at the great armada before them. The whole bay was filled with warships, their black hulls anchored so closely together that a man could almost walk from one shoreline to the other.

'Zeus's beard,' Menelaus whispered, his eyes filling with tears.

'There must be *hundreds* of them,' exclaimed Eurybates.

'It's just as I saw in my dream,' Calchas added, standing with the others and surveying the forest of masts.

'Look at the hillsides,' Eperitus said. 'All those tents. There must be thousands of soldiers up there.'

'Tens of thousands,' Odysseus corrected. 'And look! There're the dolphin sails of Ithaca. Bring in the sail!'

A great cheer greeted them as Odysseus steered the ship into a gap between the other eleven galleys of the Ithacan fleet. Men flooded out from the camp on the hillside, rushing down to the sandy beach where the beak of the ship slid to a halt. Suddenly men were leaping down from the sides of the galley and dashing through the knee-deep water to greet their comrades.

As Odysseus and Eperitus waded through the surf to the shore – their countrymen cheering them and slapping their shoulders as they passed – they saw Eurylochus waiting beneath the shade of a sycamore tree. He was pink with the heat of the late-spring day, and his fat jowls and forehead glistened with a film of sweat.

'Thank the gods you've returned,' he said, embracing his cousin and ignoring Eperitus. 'It's been five weeks since you left for Troy – we were beginning to fear the worst.'

'It's simply a long way,' Odysseus answered, sitting down against the broad trunk of the tree and accepting a krater of wine from a soldier. 'Has much happened in our absence?'

Eurylochus pointed to the ships in the bay. 'Only the gathering of the greatest fleet of ships in history! We were almost the first – only King Nestor of Pylos was here before us – and there's hardly been a day since that some contingent or other hasn't swelled our numbers. And you should see the men who've come! More warriors than I've ever seen before, and all the great oath-takers are among them. Great Ajax is here, with Little Ajax and Teucer, of course. Diomedes arrived last week, bringing Sthenelaus and Euryalus the Argonaut with him. Idomeneus alone brought eighty ships from Crete! Then there's Menestheus, Tlepolemos . . .'

'What about Achilles?' asked Palamedes, striding confidently up the beach with Menelaus. He had been a subdued presence during the voyage from Troy – even though Odysseus had made no mention of the events in Priam's throne room, realizing that the Nauplian had been acting under Agamemnon's orders – but seemed to be rapidly regaining his old arrogance and self-importance now that he was back on land.

'Not yet,' Eurylochus replied, giving Palamedes an equally haughty stare. 'And nobody knows where he is. Some say he is in hiding, but others say he didn't take the oath so isn't under any obligation.'

'They're wrong on that point,' said Menelaus. 'His cousin Patroclus took the oath on his behalf.'

'And if the rumours about him are true, he'd come whether he was bound to or not,' Eperitus added. 'One thing's for certain: he won't be hiding.'

'We'll see about that,' Odysseus said, shutting his eyes and resting his head against the gnarled bark. 'Is my tent ready, Eurylochus? And how about something to eat for Menelaus, Eperitus and myself – not forgetting Palamedes, of course?'

'We've just sacrificed a goat. It'll be cooked by the time you've washed the brine from your limbs and changed your clothes.'

'We'll refrain,' Menelaus said, though the smell of meat roasting over a nearby fire brought the saliva flooding into his mouth. 'I have to find my brother and let him know we're back. Where's his camp, Eurylochus?'

'On the highest point overlooking the bay – you can see his banner on the hillside, up there.'

'And don't be long yourself, Odysseus,' Menelaus called over his shoulder, as he and Palamedes headed towards a path that led up the wooded hillside beyond the beach. 'He'll want to speak to you, too, no doubt.'

Odysseus simply shut his eyes and thought of a plate of freshly roasted goats' meat.

News of the return from Troy spread rapidly and soon the Ithacan camp was besieged by soldiers from every state in Greece, seeking information about the Trojans and their fabled city. As the different Greek armies had spent the previous weeks practising their drills and tactics alongside or against each other, many of the men were greeted as friends and encouraged to share the Ithacans' food and wine. And thus the rumours grew of the unassailable walls of Troy, with its beetling towers and vast armies, and of the great riches that lay within for any who could raze it to the ground.

Before long, Agamemnon's squire, Talthybius, arrived at the camp with a summons for Odysseus and Eperitus. They were to leave their weapons behind and come to a council of the Greek kings, where the news from Troy was to be discussed and decisions made on what action to take. Odysseus asked Calchas, who had remained with the Ithacans, to come with them.

The path up the hillside was a steep one, but by now it was late afternoon and the heat of the day could no longer be felt under the dense canopy of trees, where the air was cool and fresh with the smell of pine. This made for a pleasant walk, though Eperitus quickly found Calchas's company irksome: he often fell behind, and when they waited for him to catch up he would mutter endlessly under his breath. Before long they could smell the smoke from numerous cooking fires, drifting down the hill from the main camp above, and almost taste the roast pork on their tongues. A hubbub of conversation followed it, growing steadily louder until the woodland gloom gave way to patches of slanted light and, suddenly, they were free of the trees and standing atop a high, rocky plateau with a marvellous view of the vast fleet below them to their right. Even Talthybius, who had seen the sight many times by now, had to stop and admire the black silhouettes of the ships floating like coals on a sea of fire. In the west the sky was a brilliant, unblemished sheet of copper, glowing fiercely in the light of the bloated, dying sun. Beneath it, stretching over the boulder-strewn hilltop, were hundreds upon hundreds of white tents, reminding Eperitus of the flocks of seabirds that would gather on the craggy cliff faces of Ithaca. They snapped and fluttered in the wind, as did the flags and pennants of the many different kings that streamed out above them.

'This way, my lords,' said Talthybius, leading them down an avenue that drove through the middle of the canvas city.

There were soldiers everywhere. Some wore armour, though most did not, and all carried weapons of some kind – spears over their shoulders or swords hanging from baldrics or tucked into their belts. The majority were cooking or eating, though some were busily burnishing their bronze armour to a high sheen, or drawing whetstones up and down blades to sharpen them to a deadly edge. Occasionally, the laughter or cry of a woman indicated that prostitutes were plying their trade amongst the army.

Talthybius, however, did not take them deeper into the camp as they had expected, but suddenly led them down another wide avenue that went back towards the straits. As they were passing a crescent of large tents, Eteoneus, the squire of Menelaus, emerged, followed by three others.

'Odysseus?' said one of the men. 'Odysseus, is that you?'

Odysseus turned to see a tall man of thirty years or so,

athletically built and dressed in a grey tunic and dark green cloak. His long, auburn hair was pulled back over his scalp and tied at the nape of his neck, revealing a handsome and intelligent face. Despite the fact that he wore no armour and did not carry any weapons, the brown scar across his clean-shaven cheek marked him as an experienced warrior.

'Diomedes!' Odysseus exclaimed, breaking into a broad smile. He seized the man's hand and pulled him into a fierce embrace, which they held for a long time as they thumped each other's backs and exchanged friendly greetings.

'I hear you and Menelaus have been in Troy, talking peace and other such nonsense,' said the king of the Argives. 'Tell me you failed!'

'You'll hear my report when I give it to the council – you're heading there, too, I assume. Have you been in this place long? What's the hunting like?'

'Good – plenty of woodland beyond the camp, full of deer. But stop trying to change the subject. Tell me about Troy – what's it like? Will we take it at the first assault, or is Priam going to put up a fight?'

'Forget Priam. It's his son, Hector, we need to worry about. Anyway, you'll have to wait until . . .'

'And what about Helen?' Diomedes continued, his voice assuming a more serious tone. 'Did you see her?'

Diomedes had lost his heart to Helen when he first set eyes on her ten years before, and despite taking a wife since then it was clear he still loved her.

'No, Diomedes, I didn't see her. Now, will you stop heaping questions on me and introduce your companions?'

Diomedes gave an apologetic nod and stepped between the two men, placing a hand on each of their shoulders.

'This is my friend, Sthenelaus, son of Capaneus,' he began, indicating the man to his right. 'We sacked the city of Thebes together in vengeance for our fathers, and now I've asked him to rule the Argive army in my place, if I should fall.'

Sthenelaus's hair was a mass of black curls and his thick beard covered half of his hardened, bitter-looking face. He gave a curt nod in response to Odysseus's smile.

'And this is Euryalus the Argonaut, son of Mecisteus. He was also with us when we conquered Thebes.'

Euryalus was a small man, several years older than his companions, with long, white hair and a closely cropped beard. His red face broke into a pleasant smile as he shook Odysseus's hand.

'You remember Eperitus, captain of my royal guard,' Odysseus said, turning back to Diomedes.

'Glad you're with us, Eperitus,' Diomedes said, taking his hand. 'And your other companion?'

'I'm afraid *that* introduction will have to wait until the council,' Odysseus said. 'And we shouldn't keep our royal comrades waiting any longer. Talthybius?'

The Mycenaean herald, who had been talking patiently to Eteoneus, gave a small bow before turning and leading the way through the field of flapping canvas. Diomedes walked beside Odysseus and threw a muscle-bound arm about his shoulders.

'So, I hear you're a king now. You look like it, too: majestic appearance, powerful bearing, grey hair . . .'

'Thanks. I wish I could say the same for you, but you look as young and handsome as you did ten years ago.'

'Listen, have you spoken to Agamemnon yet?' Diomedes asked, lowering his voice confidentially.

'I spoke to him the night before we left for Troy,' Odysseus replied, surprised by the sudden change of direction. 'But not since we arrived at Aulis. Is something wrong?'

'I'm not sure. I've been his friend for a long time and I know him well, but since all this business started with Helen and Troy . . . well, he seems different.'

'Concerned, perhaps?' Odysseus suggested. 'Or pressured? It's understandable.'

'Perhaps. But you'll be able to judge for yourself soon.'

And with that he would say no more.

## Chapter Sixteen

# THE COUNCIL OF KINGS

They heard the clamour of voices long before they reached the edge of the camp. After they passed the last tent, Talthybius and Eteoneus led them through a belt of sycamore trees to a pair of tall, grim-looking standing stones, placed there by an ancient people long since forgotten. These formed the gateway to a large, natural amphitheatre that opened out to the east, giving a view over the crowded bay far below. They walked out into the midst of at least a hundred kings and other nobility, who were crammed on benches around the rocky slopes of the arena, talking noisily.

Odysseus, Diomedes and Eperitus recognized many of them from the courtship of Helen in Sparta. Most prominent was Great Ajax, the king of Salamis, whose vast bulk took up most of the bench he was sitting on. On his left – the antithesis of the giant warrior – was his half-brother, Teucer the archer, who sat twitching and blinking like an owl and constantly wiping his large nose on the back of his hand. To Ajax's right was his namesake, Little Ajax, so called for his short stature and to distinguish him from his titanic friend. To Eperitus's disdain, he saw that the man's pet snake – a hideous brown serpent with a long, pink tongue that constantly darted from its scaly mouth – was coiled about his shoulders. Its master fixed Odysseus with a sneering look and spat into the dirt.

Odysseus, who had not forgotten their contest for the hand of Penelope, chose to ignore the Locrian king and looked about at the other familiar faces on the benches. Menestheus, king of Athens, was seated beside Idomeneus of Crete; both were handsome and richly dressed, with noble looks that befitted the great power each man wielded. King Elphenor was there, who ruled over the island of Euboea on the opposite side of the straits, as were Agapenor, king of Arcadia, Tlepolemos, king of Rhodes, Iolaus, king of Phylake, and many other renowned names. Among the lesser men were Palamedes, seated on the bench nearest Agamemnon, and Philoctetes of Malia, son of Poeas. The last time Odysseus and Eperitus had seen the latter, he was a young shepherd boy who had been awarded the magical bow and arrows of Heracles for agreeing to light the great hero's funeral pyre; now he was a tall, lean young man with a chaotic mop of light brown hair and a wispy beard on his chin. But he was not the only one who had changed in the past decade. Some of the former suitors to Helen had aged visibly; others seemed to have grown in stature; still more had grown in other ways, allowing their bellies to expand through overindulgence and too little fighting.

At the far end of the basin were the Atreides brothers, Agamemnon and Menelaus, seated on high-backed wooden chairs. Unlike the rest of the council, they watched the newcomers in stony silence. Agamemnon, to Eperitus's surprise, looked as if he had not slept for days: there were dark circles under his eyes, which were bloodshot and heavy-lidded, and his usually meticulous hair was unkempt. More shocking was the way his rich clothes seemed to hang about him. Agamemnon had always boasted a well-fed, athletic physique, similar to the other warriors gathered about the arena, but in the time they had been away on the mission to Troy the Mycenaean king had become drawn and thin.

Standing at Agamemnon's shoulder was an old man wearing a purple cloak and a golden belt that glittered in the warm evening light. King Nestor of Pylos wore his grey hair short and kept his beard neatly trimmed; though not a tall man, he boasted a powerful physique and the hard-bitten aspect of a seasoned warrior. His nose had been broken in some battle or boxing match of the past, and the top of one of his large, disc-like ears had been sliced off many years before by an opponent's sword. Like the Atreides brothers, he had his eyes fixed on the newcomers as they stood in the centre of the arena.

Though not one member of the council had been allowed to bring their weapons – a wise precaution in view of the arguments that often occurred between nobility – a dozen heavily armed soldiers stood behind the Atreides brothers, with one more by each of the standing stones, guarding the entrance to the meeting. They were clearly an elite, probably from Agamemnon's personal guard, who were dressed in ceremonial armour of an antiquated style unfamiliar to Odysseus and Eperitus. Their highly polished bronze breastplates were supplemented by further bands around the stomach and waist, as well as shoulder-pieces and neckguards that rose above the chin. On their heads they wore domed leather helmets with cheekpieces tied beneath the chin. Horsehair plumes sprouted from the top and fell across the back of the neck, while rows of boars' tusks covered the helmet to give both ornamentation and protection. They wore inlaid greaves over their shins and carried tall, ox-hide shields with an outer layer of polished bronze that gleamed fiercely in the light of the setting sun. Their spears, swords, axes and daggers stood as a reminder to the gathered kings that, though this was a council of equals, Agamemnon still held the greatest wealth and power.

Agamemnon nodded to Talthybius, who beat his stave three times on the ground.

'My lords,' the herald announced in a strong, clear voice that commanded silence from everyone gathered, 'I present King Odysseus of Ithaca, son of Laertes, and King Diomedes of Argos, son of Tydeus.'

'Please take your seats,' said Agamemnon, pointing to an empty bench by one of the standing stones. 'Talthybius – the wine, please.'

The herald nodded to a steward, who clapped his hands twice. Immediately a swarm of slaves appeared from the line of trees that topped the lip of the amphitheatre, bringing kraters of diluted wine to the members of the council. As soon as each man had been served, Agamemnon stood and raised his cup in both hands, tipping a small amount into the dirt at his feet.

'Most glorious and mighty Zeus, Lord of High Heaven, father of the gods, grant us clear minds as we debate the future of Troy, and if this mighty fleet is to sail with vengeance to the shores of Ilium, give us the wisdom to choose a single leader, one who will unite the Greeks against our common enemy and lead them to certain and uncompromising victory. Now is the time for men to act, for better or worse, and I call upon you to witness the oaths that we take today and see that they are kept.'

Agamemnon drained the rest of the wine and handed the krater to his steward. The other members of the council stood as one and poured their own libations, offering silent prayers to whichever of the gods they honoured most. Eperitus, like Odysseus and Diomedes next to him, prayed to Athena, and after his few words asking the goddess to ensure there would be war against Troy sat back down.

He adjusted the thick cushion that had been handed to him by a slave and turned to look at Agamemnon. The king sat back in his chair and rested his chin on a fist, his golden breastplate reflecting the purple skies above and his red cloak turning scarlet in the dimming twilight. His tired blue eyes surveyed the faces of the men crowded on the rows of benches, dispassionately assessing whether they were for the war or against it. Agamemnon's cold demeanour had not thawed in the ten years since Eperitus had first met him, and the shadow of exhaustion resting on him did not seem to have reduced his ability to disguise his feelings beneath a remote exterior.

'Brother,' Agamemnon said, turning to Menelaus. His voice was soft but clear, and the few conversations that continued quickly died away at the sound of it, leaving the amphitheatre hushed and expectant. 'Brother, for the sake of those who don't yet know, take the floor and recount for us what happened in Troy.'

'With pleasure,' Menelaus growled, walking out to the middle of the arena and facing the gathered Greeks with his fists firmly on his hips. 'Palamedes, Odysseus and I have just returned from Troy. Against my better judgement, I allowed Odysseus to persuade me into seeking the return of my wife and son through *diplomacy*, even though I've been itching to wash my spear in Trojan blood ever since Paris stole my family from me.' The Spartan king held his shaking fists out before him and received a murmur of approval from the benches. 'But despite our peaceful intentions, they treated us like a pack of curs. Priam – this fornicating old lecher the Trojans call their king – made us wait a whole day before he'd see us. *Us* – kings and princes of Greece! We slept the night outside the walls of the citadel, in the home of a Trojan elder, and when Priam finally allowed us into his presence, he didn't even ask our names or our business in Troy. I had to tell him the purpose of our mission myself, and then they nearly killed us!'

'Foreign dogs!' Ajax boomed, giving rise to a chorus of angry shouts from the other kings and nobles.

'If I'd known how these Trojans treated their guests,' Menelaus continued, raising his voice above the others, 'I wouldn't have listened to all this talk of diplomatic solutions. As far as I can see, the only diplomacy the Trojans understand is at the end of a bronze-tipped spear!'

There was a great roar of approval from the audience, a sound that brought a smile to Eperitus's lips and made the blood pound through his veins. Powerful voices were shouting for the fleet to sail immediately and for Troy to be crushed, though as the Ithacan captain looked around at the many faces he saw some that were silent and thoughtful. Then Odysseus rose from the bench beside him and walked out to stand beside Menelaus, who, after revelling in the tumult for a few moments longer, eventually returned to his seat.

Odysseus waited patiently for the last cheer to die away, then held his hands up.

'Well, friends,' he began, 'I think we can put any ideas of a peaceful solution behind us. I may have been the one who suggested a tactful approach, but let me say this – there are none among you keener for war than I am now!'

Eperitus looked at his king with surprise, wondering at his sudden and suspicious change of mind. All around him the benches erupted once more with belligerent glee, as great-voiced kings vied to outdo each other in their anti-Trojan fervour. Again Odysseus waited for silence to return before holding out the palms of his hands.

'And why should a man of peace suddenly want war? Well, a peace mission can have more than a single purpose. Menelaus – our great friend who beat us all to the hand of Helen – may think I was wasting my time with all this talk of diplomacy, but can he deny that we now know the strength of Troy's army? Or the number of her warships waiting in the great bay before the city walls? Or the size of that bay and its openness to attack? What about the breadth of the surrounding plain, and its capacity to support an invading army? Not to mention the ability of the walls, towers and gates of Troy to withstand a siege? Who of you would know the strengths and weaknesses of that city, and how best to attack it if we hadn't been there already and sized the place up for you?'

Odysseus paused as the men before him murmured among themselves, some nodding in quiet approval of the Ithacan's great foresight. Eperitus, of course, knew differently, and could only admire his king's ability to turn a situation to his advantage.

'And let me make it clear to you, Troy will not fall in a day, or a week, or maybe even a year. The city's walls are strong, tall and in good repair – they won't fall to anything less than the most determined of attacks. Those of you who think we'll storm in like Heracles with his six ships are going to be disappointed. And the armies of Priam and his allies haven't allowed their swords to rust or their bellies to expand as we have. While we Greeks have been enjoying the fruits of peace, the Trojans have been mustering their forces to *attack us*!'

Odysseus paused for a third time, waiting for the shock of his news to die away before continuing.

'But let no man think these Trojans will prove easy opponents. They'll be ready for us, and what's more, they'll be defending their homeland. If we attack too soon, without proper preparations, then we'll pay the price. My advice is that we should treat them with respect and caution, and build up our forces slowly and professionally over a year or two . . .'

'To Hades with caution!' thundered Ajax, making Teucer jump beside him. 'I say we launch at dawn and take bloody revenge to their walls! Look at the army we've gathered! Look at the fleet at anchor down there! What reason do we have to be cautious? Let's slay the men and take their women and gold for ourselves. Nothing else matters!'

The ranks of warriors, who had fallen silent at the thought of long preparations, now gave a huge shout of enthusiasm, but before Odysseus could respond a man stood on one of the higher rows and wagged his finger accusingly at the gigantic warrior.

'I'd heard you were a buffoon, Ajax, and now I know it's true.'

Suddenly the arena fell silent and every face turned to look at the speaker. Last of all, Ajax turned his head and looked up with disbelieving eyes. But instead of finding himself opposed by a powerful king, he was greeted instead by the deformed features of a hunchback. One eye was lost in a tight squint, but the other bulged out in a ferocious stare that roamed from face to face.

'In fact,' the hunchback croaked, 'judging by all the oafish cheering, I'd be surprised if there are enough brains in this arena to fill a helmet.'

'Shut up!' called a voice.

'Sit down, Thersites!' cried another.

But the hunchback was not to be deterred. 'All this talk of war! If Agamemnon and Menelaus want to fight the Trojans, then let them! And they can take that great yob Ajax with them.'

Ajax stood, his face flushed and his bunched fists shaking with anger, but Agamemnon signalled for him to resume his seat.

'What need do the rest of us have for war?' Thersites continued, scratching the tufts of hair on his cone-shaped head as if confused. 'What do we care for Troy? Don't we have our own homes and families to protect?' At this there was a rumble of agreement from some of the benches. 'And what will our reward be if we go? Have you asked yourselves how the plunder will be shared? Then let me tell you – the richest pickings to the Atreides brothers, and the scraps for the rest of us!'

'Silence, you deformed fool!' Agamemnon shouted, jumping to his feet, his cool facade suddenly and shockingly broken. 'This is a council of kings, not of commoners, and if you can't hold your tongue in front of your superiors then I'll have it cut out and fed to my dogs. *Do you understand?*'

Thersites's whole body quaked before Agamemnon's unexpected rage, and his vulture-like eye twitched in fear as he shrank back down among his Aetolian countrymen.

Agamemnon now waved Odysseus back to his chair and walked out into the middle of the arena. He had regained much of his usual composure, but Eperitus felt there was still a darkness about his face that hinted at his ruffled emotions.

'Fellow Greeks!' he said, his voice calm once more. 'Have we not already heard from my brother how he was thrown out of Troy like a beggar, and from Odysseus of how the Trojans have been preparing to bring war to our shores – news even to my ears? Are we not here today because a Greek queen has been abducted from her bed by a Trojan prince? These things alone are enough to *demand* war, and yet there remain voices of dissent. I don't talk of the protests of one ignorant man, but of the nods and the mumbled agreements that accompanied them. Why, then, should you leave your homes to fight a distant foe, beyond the reasons I have already stated? Let me tell you.

'First, no Greek state has made war on another since the Epigoni laid waste to Thebes ten years ago. As a result, our industries thrive, our merchants sell Greek goods all over the known world, our people are well fed and peace reigns. But such peace brings its own problems, as I said it would when I first proposed a raid against Troy a decade ago. We pay our armies to do nothing, and they in turn are restless. They want war – what warrior doesn't thirst for the very thing that defines him? And they want plunder, the true wages of a fighting man. So should we return to the old days of fighting each other – brother against brother, father against son?'

'No!' a chorus of voices shouted.

'No, of course we shouldn't. And then there's the problem of resources. Every king here knows the pressures of running a state – the constant calls for more copper to make our bronze, more timber to build our homes and our ships, more wool for textiles, more this, that and everything else. But above all?'

'More slaves!' Diomedes called out, firmly.

'After all,' Agamemnon continued, 'who spins the yarn, or turns the clay, or mines the silver, or tills the field, or mills the grain, or nurses the babies? Slaves, of course, the beating heart of our agriculture, our industry, even our domestic life. Slaves are the one true product of war. We can buy slaves from Asia, but the constant demand and the high cost are crippling. A war would solve that problem, for a few years at least. Mycenaean merchants tell me that Troy is a rich city – filled with gold, bronze, copper, wool, horses, livestock, timber, spices and, above all, people. If you make war with me against Troy, you and your armies can all have your fill of the plunder. And whatever that fool Thersites might say, I won't deprive an army of their rights.'

A great cheer rose up from the benches and many stood and applauded the king of Mycenae, or shook their fists triumphantly above their heads as if the hulls of their ships had already been filled with the loot of a ransacked Troy.

'But I said all this before – ten years ago in Sparta – and no one would listen. The riches of Troy were on offer to us then, but only a handful of you were prepared to leave the safety of your palaces for the promise of glory on foreign soil. Even you, Ajax, though your mighty voice calls for war now – even you said it was impossible to unite the Greeks and raid Ilium. So I come to my final reason why you should leave your families, your homes and your kingdoms to fight a bitter war in a distant place. Stand up, Menelaus.'

The Spartan king, who had been watching the faces of the council as they reacted to the rhetoric of Agamemnon, looked up in surprise. Slowly, he rose to his feet.

'My brother's wife has been taken from him,' Agamemnon continued, walking to where Menelaus stood. 'He trusted a foreign prince with the most beautiful woman in Greece – you've all seen her – while he went off to Crete. The kingdom of Sparta was only his because he married the daughter of its former king. Now that she's been taken from under his very nose, he has allowed his own authority to be brought into question.'

As the last word left his lips, Agamemnon struck his brother across the face with the back of his hand. Menelaus reeled backwards, as much with shock as with the force of the blow, and stared at Agamemnon with surprise and a burning rage. His nostrils flared and his lips curled back from his teeth, but he said nothing. The crowded kings and nobles, staring down from the tiered benches, fell silent.

'Fortunately for him,' Agamemnon continued, turning to face the council, 'a sacred oath was taken to protect Helen and her husband from any who would try to come between them. *You* took that oath! That's why you've come here to Aulis, because not one of you would dare to offend the gods before whom you gave your word. So, as I very much doubt the honour of Greece, the threat of Troy and the prospect of plunder are enough to ensure your support for war, I call upon you to honour the oath you swore. Stand, damn it, and put your hands on your hearts if you mean to sail with us. Or if you haven't the guts to fight but would rather face the persecution of the gods, then leave now — through those ancient stones that mark the sacred nature of this place — so that we can all look upon your shame as you go!'

The first to stand were Diomedes and Eperitus, followed more slowly by Odysseus. Ajax and his companions were next, and after them the entire assembly. Not one man — not even Thersites — left the spot where they were standing, and only Calchas, the Trojan renegade, remained seated, covering his face with his hood and looking down at his sandalled feet.

Suddenly, Ajax stepped forward and punched the air.

'Death to Troy!' he bellowed, and his voice carried out across the harbour so that the few sailors craned their necks towards the hilltops.

'Death to Troy!' echoed the combined voices of the council.

They were not exuberant, as if a great victory had been won and they stood over the piled corpses of their foes. Instead, they were hard and determined. As the ringing echoes of their war cry died away over the straits and between the stony hillsides, Nestor stepped forward and indicated for the grim-faced kings, including Agamemnon, to sit.

'We are equals,' he began, his voice strong and smooth despite his great age. 'We are kings of *Greece*, not slaves like the vassals of Asia who stoop down before Priam. We go to war against Troy as free men, honouring our sacred duty. And yet all armies must have leaders.'

'That's clever,' Odysseus whispered to Eperitus. 'I could learn something from this old dog.'

'An army without a leader is a disorganized rabble. A strong gust of wind could blow it away. But an army that chooses its own leader is greater than any. The different elements retain their freedom and individuality, without subjugating themselves to a tyrant. *We* must choose a leader, if we're to attack Troy as a coherent force.'

'You're the best tactician amongst us, Nestor,' called a voice from the benches. 'You lead us.'

'Aye, you lead us!' echoed other voices.

'Not me,' the king of Pylos replied, shaking his head and smiling. 'I'm too old.'

'Agamemnon should lead us.'

Every eye turned to Odysseus.

'Who has brought the greatest force of men and ships?' he said, standing and turning once more to face the assembly. 'Who first proposed war against Troy, when we were too busy worrying about our own palaces? Not one of us had the foresight to see that one day Troy would threaten us. Only Agamemnon did. I say *he* should lead us.'

Agamemnon watched from his high-backed chair and said nothing, but his expressionless eyes were fixed intently upon the king of Ithaca.

'I agree,' said Diomedes, rising to his feet. 'Agamemnon to lead!'

'Me, too,' Menelaus said, his face still red where his brother had struck him.

'And me,' smiled Nestor. 'Agamemnon should lead. Does anyone oppose?'

Thersites stood and raised another accusing finger, but was pulled back down before he could speak. One by one the other kings and leaders of the Greek armies nodded their consent, some with more enthusiasm than others.

'So be it,' Nestor announced, snapping his fingers at a slave who stood behind the chairs of the Atreides brothers. The slave ran over and handed the old man a tall item wrapped in purple cloth. 'Agamemnon, you are elected king over the Greek army, for the duration of the war against Troy. Free men chose you, and their choice will be bound upon them by an oath. But first, stand and receive the symbol of your power.'

With a flourish, Nestor tore the cloth away to reveal a golden staff, beset with jewels that gleamed in the twilight and topped by a silver bird in flight. It was as tall as the old king and was a work of great skill, greater than anything most of the council had ever set their eyes upon, whether commoner, noble or king.

'You know this sceptre well, Agamemnon,' Nestor announced. 'It was made by Hephaistos for Zeus, the king of the gods. He gave it to Hermes, who then gave it to your grandfather, Pelops. Pelops passed it down to your father, Atreus, and you would have seen it many times in his hand. As he was dying he entrusted it to your uncle, Thysetes. It was your father's wish that this rod of empire be given to you when you had reached the heights of greatness you were destined for. Come, receive that which is yours.'

Agamemnon stood and crossed the arena to where Nestor was waiting. He stretched out his hand to take the sceptre, but Nestor withheld it from his grasping fingers.

'This sceptre represents immense power, Agamemnon. You must use it with wisdom and humility; crush your enemies, but listen to counsel when it is given and never forget to honour the gods.'

He offered the golden staff to the Mycenaean king, now king of all the Greeks, who snatched it from his hand and stared at it with adoration and amazement. He turned it around and around, loving the way its jewels sparkled like the stars on a winter night, enjoying the feel of the cold metal in his palm and revelling in the sense of power that it gave him.

Nestor signalled to the waiting slaves, who rushed to refill the kraters of the kings.

'Stand now and swear your loyalty to Agamemnon, whom the gods have guided you to choose as your leader,' Nestor commanded, raising his own cup and pouring a libation. 'Oh, Father Zeus, and all you Olympians, bear witness to this oath that we freely give, to submit to the leadership of Agamemnon until the lovely Helen is restored to her husband and her kidnap avenged in Trojan blood. If any here disobey the commands of the properly elected king of the Greeks, then punish their iniquity and bring dishonour on their name so that they will bear the shame for eternity.'

'And let no man here return to his homeland until our mission is complete,' Agamemnon added. 'And as a symbol of his commitment, let each man vow not to cut his hair until Troy lies in ruins and my brother's wife is back in his arms again. So be it!'

'*So be it!*'

Agamemnon drained his cup and was followed by the members of the council, who then retook their seats.

'So,' said Little Ajax, looking crossly from Agamemnon to the rows of faces on either side of him. 'When do we sail? When am I going to get a chance to kill some Trojans? That's all I want to know.'

'That isn't a decision to be taken here and now,' Agamemnon replied. 'We need to consider the information Menelaus and Odysseus have brought back with them before settling on a course of action.'

'We can't tarry here much longer,' said Menestheus, the Athenian king. 'The men are getting restless. There've already been several raids on nearby islands, where this fleet or that have thought they'd found Ilium. Unless we're careful they'll be attacking each other before long.'

Eperitus suddenly rose to his feet, no longer able to hold back the question that had been nagging at him since he first arrived in the amphitheatre.

'I may be speaking out of ignorance,' he began as every eye turned upon him, 'and I hope you'll forgive me, my lords, as I only arrived back from Troy today, but how can this expedition think of setting off without Peleus's son, Achilles? I'd heard the oath was binding on him, too, though Patroclus took it on his behalf, yet no one here has even mentioned his name. Isn't it true his mother,

Thetis, dipped him by his ankle in the River Styx to make him invulnerable? And that he can beat any man in battle, hunting, sport or debate? As I see it, we can't afford to start for Troy without him.'

'We have no choice, Eperitus,' Diomedes responded. 'There isn't a man here who wouldn't want to fight alongside a warrior of Achilles's reputation, but he hasn't responded to any of our summonses.'

'The problem is that no one knows where he is,' Nestor took up. 'Thetis had a vision of his death at Troy, so I've heard, and has hidden him so he can't be persuaded to join the expedition. But we can't wait forever, and unless he turns up soon we will have to trust to our own strengths to defeat the Trojans.'

'Without Achilles you will never defeat the armies of Troy.'

Calchas, who had remained silent and innocuous throughout the debate, threw back his hood to reveal his bald head and pale, sunken features.

'Odysseus,' said Agamemnon, 'who is this skulking character you've smuggled in under the hem of your cloak? He has the appearance of a corpse, though there's clearly breath in his lungs.'

'His name is Calchas, son of Thestor, a priest of Apollo. We brought him back with us from Troy.'

The council burst into new life, animated by the news that a Trojan had been with them through the whole of their debate.

'A prisoner, you mean?' Agamemnon asked.

'No, brother,' said Menelaus. 'He demanded to come back with us. Says he's a seer and that he had some information for us from Apollo, who ordered him to help the Greeks.'

'What rubbish,' laughed Ajax. 'He's a damned spy. Let me wring his scrawny neck and be done with him.'

Agamemnon held up his hand and Ajax sat back down, looking disappointed. 'Let's hear what he has to say before we decide what to do with him. What's this information you have for us, priest?'

'A dream,' Calchas replied.

'Go on.'

'I was asleep on the temple floor when Apollo woke me with a vision of Greek victory.'

'That's a good start,' Agamemnon said, scrutinizing Calchas with his icy blue eyes. 'Any more?'

Calchas stood and crossed to the centre of the arena. His stooping gait provoked a ripple of gentle laughter from the benches, but as soon as the priest's eyes fell on Agamemnon the king's own smile fell away as he felt his thoughts opened up and probed, as if by a skilled surgeon.

'Don't mock me, Agamemnon. You can listen to what I have to say and benefit from it, or you can cast me over the side of the cliff to the deep waters below, but do not dismiss me as a fool because I look like a ghost or walk like a cripple. Apollo showed me the sack of Troy – its fine houses burning, its men struck down in the streets by bloodthirsty Greeks, its women raped in the temples and its children thrown from the walls. He also showed me the end of Priam's house – Hector brutally slain, Paris shot down, and the old man himself beheaded by a Greek sword in the temple of Zeus. All these things he showed me, and more, and they can come true if you listen to the prophecies of the gods.'

Agamemnon stepped back, his eyes wide as he clutched the golden sceptre in his sweating hands. Then Little Ajax hawked loudly and spat in the dust.

'He's a spy, all right. What better way to win favour than by telling us all about his great vision of the destruction of Troy and the death of Priam? Well, let me tell you something, priest – *we've* been dreaming about that for weeks!'

There was a howl of collective laughter from the tiered ranks of the Greeks. Calchas turned on them with anger, but they only laughed the more. It was Eperitus who came to his rescue.

'Listen to the man!' he shouted, angrily. 'In Troy, he told me things about myself that only the gods could have known. I say we should give him a chance.'

'Test him!' called a voice.

'Ask him how many sons I have,' shouted another.

'No, ask him what my wife's favourite sexual position is,' said Thersites, causing more hilarity on the benches.

'I have a test for you, Calchas,' said Nestor, facing the priest and studying him with his pale-grey eyes. 'You say we can't defeat the Trojans without Achilles. Then tell us where he is.'

Calchas, his face twitching with anger and nerves, focused his gaze on the old king. The noise on the benches died down as all eyes looked at the Trojan, waiting to see whether he could answer the question that had frustrated all the efforts of the Greek army. For a moment it looked as if he would pull the hood back over his face and lower his head in defeat. Then his whole body gave a fierce spasm that would have thrown him to the floor if Eperitus had not caught his elbow. Suddenly he looked at the Ithacan captain and dug his fingers into the hard flesh of his arms as a white film spread over his eyes.

'*Seven*!' he gasped.

'Seven what?' Eperitus asked him, clutching his elbow so that he did not slip to the floor.

'Seven sons. The man has seven sons,' Calchas said, pointing into the crowded flanks of the amphitheatre. 'He believes he has eight, but one is a bastard. The other man – his wife prefers him to come at her from behind, so that she does not have to look at his repulsive face.'

'Forget about those fools. What about Achilles?'

Calchas blinked and his body went limp, so that Eperitus was forced to take his whole weight in his arms.

'Achilles is on Scyros, in the court of King Lycomedes.'

## Chapter Seventeen

# ACHILLES DISCOVERED

Odysseus, Eperitus and Nestor were the only members of the council who believed Calchas. Nevertheless, Agamemnon agreed to let them go to the island of Scyros in search of Achilles, and just before first light the following morning the three men were standing in the stern of Odysseus's ship waiting for the crew to fit their oars into the freshly oiled leather loops. Then, as the anchor stone was hauled aboard, Eperitus was surprised to see Great Ajax come running out of the tree line behind the Ithacan camp, waving his muscle-bound arms and shouting that he was coming with them to Scyros. He and Achilles were cousins, he explained as they strained to haul his bulk onto the listing galley, and as they had never met he was prepared to test the verity of Calchas's second sight for the chance of meeting the son of his uncle Peleus.

Once aboard, the king of Salamis was surprised to see three caskets in the prow, overflowing with brightly coloured dresses, necklaces, headdresses, mirrors, sashes, bracelets and a host of other trinkets that would please the vainest of women.

'What's all this, Odysseus?' he rumbled, picking out a sky-blue chiton and holding it across his armoured chest. 'Hoping to *charm* Achilles out of hiding?'

Nestor, who had noted the caskets in silence as he had boarded earlier, now followed Ajax to the prow and began casually picking through the various items of bronze and silver, studying each one briefly then replacing it and choosing another.

'I'm interested, too,' he said. 'Is it some sort of gift? And if it is, what would a great warrior want with chests full of feminine baubles – unless you're intending to offend him?'

The thirty crew members ceased their chattering and turned towards Odysseus. Eperitus was also keen to know why the Ithacan king had sent his men out the night before to barter for clothing and jewellery from the numerous prostitutes in the camp.

'It is a gift, but not for Achilles,' Odysseus replied, nonchalantly looking up at the sail with its dolphin motif as it caught the westerly wind. 'The caskets are for Lycomedes's daughters, of which he has many.'

'Renowned for their beauty, or so I've heard,' Nestor commented, stroking his grey beard. 'But unless you're hoping to recruit *them* to the army, I don't see the point . . .'

'If Achilles is hiding on Scyros, I've a feeling Lycomedes won't tell us where he is, no matter what gifts we bring him. But maybe his daughters will. They're sure to know everything that's going on in the palace, and with a little persuasion,' he added, picking up a pair of earrings from the pile and dangling them by his ears, 'they'll take us straight to him. Now, how about a bit of cold breakfast?'

Scyros lay less than a day's voyage away on the other side of Euboea, and by sunset they were cruising into a wide bay crammed with fishing vessels and a few larger ships. Eperitus was leaning against the bow and looking up at the high, craggy hill that dominated the harbour. Halfway up was Lycomedes's palace, shrouded in shadow as the sun sank behind the island. It faced east across the Aegean, and from its lofty seat visitors could be seen long before they pulled into the bay below. Indeed, by the time they had anchored and climbed up to the copper-plated gates of the citadel, the king was waiting to welcome them.

He was a tall man with a pinched nose and close-set eyes, and from the moment he saw the forced smile on his bearded lips Eperitus knew he could not be trusted. After giving his name and his lineage, Lycomedes invited each of the three kings to do the same; and though his eyebrows arched a little – especially as Nestor and Ajax declared themselves – he showed little surprise at receiving such renowned guests. He also politely asked the names of the men who accompanied them – Eperitus first, then Arceisius, Antiphus and Eurybates – before inviting the whole party to a feast in the great hall. First, though, he ordered his squire and an entourage of slaves to show the guests to a wing of the palace where rooms had been prepared for them, and where they could refresh themselves before the feast.

After they had bathed and changed their clothing they were taken to a small, dark chamber – which reminded Eperitus of Laertes's hall in Ithaca as he had first seen it – where Lycomedes was waiting for them. Several nobles and courtesans were seated on either side of the hearth and a bard sang about the exploits of Heracles from beside the throne, while the guests were brought wine and newly sacrificed meat fresh from the spit.

'Scyros rarely receives a visit from men of your rank or calibre,' the king admitted as he tore the fat from a leg of lamb with his teeth, leaving his wiry beard glistening with the grease. His shrewd, light-green eyes came to rest on Nestor. 'And we are greatly honoured, of course. But now that you're bathed and fed, hopefully to your satisfaction, I'm intrigued to know the purpose of your journey here. An insignificant island like Scyros can offer little of military worth to the expedition against Troy. Besides, I wasn't one of the oath-takers, being happily married with five daughters when the courtship of Helen took place, so there's no obligation upon me . . .'

'Nor me,' Nestor responded. Being an old warrior with many notches on his spear, he could tell a coward when he met one and it made the taste of the meat and wine sour in his mouth. 'I was at home in sandy Pylos with my wife and children when the oath was taken, though I have joined the expedition out of a belief in its wider cause – to avenge the dishonour done to Menelaus and to ensure that such outrages are not tolerated in the future. But we have not come to call upon your armies, Lycomedes. We are here to find Achilles, who is rumoured to be on Scyros, and invite him to join us against Troy.'

There was a pause as Lycomedes laid down his leg of lamb and looked at the kings, smiling calmly and patiently.

'Unfortunately, my friends, Achilles has never been to Scyros,' he informed them confidently. 'Therefore I regret to say you have travelled in vain. But if you want to stay the night and search the palace in the morning, then you're more than welcome.'

Eperitus sensed that Lycomedes was challenging them. He was lying of course, and was fully aware his guests knew it, but he was so sure they would never find Achilles that he hardly seemed to care.

'We accept,' Odysseus said, raising another krater of wine to his lips. 'Who knows what we might find tomorrow? Besides, it's too dark now to sail back to Aulis, so we should enjoy the chance to sleep in proper beds covered in sheepskins and furs. And with your permission, I will go to mine now.'

Odysseus stood and was followed by the others, who were keen to return with him to their quarters and discuss what they had seen and heard. But as Lycomedes stood with them, Eperitus could see that his gaze was focused entirely on Odysseus, perhaps sensing that the least of the three kings would prove the most troublesome.

❧

They woke late the next morning and took their breakfast on the flat roof of the palace. From here, with the sun already hot in the sky above them, they could pick out the Ithacan sailors on the galley in the harbour below. Other vessels – fishermen and merchant ships – were visible further out on the white-capped waves of the Aegean.

Ajax leaned back in his chair, which strained to contain his huge torso.

'What a waste of time,' he said, the disappointment in his voice clear. 'The fleet could be on its way to Troy by now.'

'We won't be ready to sail for three or four weeks yet,'

Eperitus said. 'You've seen the levies most of the kings have brought – half-trained at best, and many have never held a shield and spear in their life. They're farmers and fishermen, Ajax, not soldiers; they need to be trained if they're to stand a chance of survival in Ilium.'

'Ach, they'll soon learn how to fight on the battlefield,' Ajax sniffed. 'Ares has a way of sorting the men from the girls, when the arrows are flying and the ground is thudding with approaching hooves. Besides, what's the point of these levies anyway? *We're* the ones who do the real fighting – the kings and nobles, and the trained warriors like your lads there.'

He nodded towards Arceisius, Antiphus and Eurybates, who forgot the joke they had been sharing and tried to look as serious and warlike as they could.

'You're too harsh, Ajax,' said Odysseus. 'Every man has to be given a chance to survive, or who will farm our fields when we get back home? There's not much glory to be had in steering a team of oxen all day long, or tying up wheat sheaves at harvest time.'

'Odysseus is right,' Nestor added. 'Besides, whatever you may think about our levies, Ajax, we can't leave without sorting out the provisioning of the army. The walls of Troy won't fall in a day, so we need to arrange supplies of food, wine, clothing, replacement armaments, horses, timber, canvas, and a thousand other things. War isn't just about lopping men's heads off and taking their armour: we need to assess the information Odysseus, Menelaus and Eperitus brought back with them; calculate the best way to attack; decide on our tactics if things go against us – all the mundane groundwork that will prevent the Trojans from routing us as soon as we land on their beaches. I remember my first fight against the Eleans after I stole their flocks and cattle. I was a teenager then, and when I saw their army ranged against us I thought it was going to be a glorious day's killing. But they out-thought us and, for a while, they out-fought us, until I called on Ares and he stoked my blood up. I killed a fair few Eleans from my chariot after that, and I learned a few things about how to use my shield and spear, too. But that was nothing compared with what I learned about being prepared for a fight.'

'Pah!' Ajax replied with a wave of his hand. 'You still won, didn't you? And it doesn't change the fact that we've had a wasted journey. Achilles isn't here, and we might as well say our farewells to Lycomedes and get back to Aulis – the sooner we're back, the sooner you two can waste time training those hopeless peasants you set so much store by.'

'Surely we're not giving up yet?' asked Eperitus. 'For one thing I think Calchas is right, and for another it's obvious Lycomedes is lying. If you ask me, Achilles is right here under our noses, but in a place few would expect to find him.'

'Of course he is,' Odysseus agreed. 'The very fact Lycomedes is desperate for us to search his palace proves it – after all, a man with nothing to hide wouldn't need to prove his innocence, would he? And when we don't find Achilles, Lycomedes thinks we'll go back to Aulis and not trouble him again. But I think his overconfidence will be his undoing.'

'Don't underestimate him,' said Nestor. 'He can't be trusted, that's for certain. Rumour says he murdered Theseus a few years back, when he was a guest in his house. There was a dispute over some land Theseus had inherited on Scyros, so Lycomedes pushed him off a cliff.'

'That's one way of settling a dispute,' said Ajax. 'But do you mean to say you're going to hunt through the palace looking for Achilles inside *pithoi* of grain and such nonsense? Well, spare us the bother and humiliation. When I came here I expected to find my cousin in Lycomedes's care, somehow ignorant of this war that the rest of Greece is talking about. I've heard the tales about him, just like everyone else: taught by Chiron the centaur to kill lions and bears with his own hands and feed off their raw offal; to use his cunning and speed to catch stags; to ride, play the pipes, heal, sing and a hundred other things. So I was expecting him to leap at the chance of a fight and come with us to Troy. Instead, he's nowhere to be seen, probably skulking away in some hole, too afraid to reveal himself and fulfil the oath Patroclus took on his behalf. If he is here – and Eperitus there seems convinced Calchas isn't wrong – then why doesn't he prove himself to be the man everyone says he is?'

'Perhaps he doesn't even know of our arrival,' Nestor suggested. 'Like you, Ajax, I can't believe he'd refuse the opportunity to reap glory in Ilium and make a name that would last forever.'

'Whether he knows or not, why do we need him anyway?' Ajax responded, smashing his fist down on the arm of his chair. 'We have the greatest army ever assembled in the history of warfare, and the fiercest warriors in the world at its head. And *I'm* the best fighter of the lot of us! I'd defer to Heracles if he were still alive, but he's not and now there's no one who can match me for sheer power, brutality or skill in combat! If you must know, I came here with you to see whether Achilles was all he was made out to be, to see whether he could rival me. But he's had his chance to prove himself and failed. Now the rest of the Greeks will have to acknowledge that I am without equal. Troy will have to fall to my efforts alone.'

'Be careful, Ajax,' Odysseus warned him. 'You may be the greatest fighter we have – no one is disputing that – but you shouldn't forget the gods. Even if you smash down the gates of Troy single-handedly and skewer Hector and Paris on your spear while you're at it, it won't have been without the help of the immortals.'

'That may be the case for you, Odysseus, but not for me. Any coward or clod-brained peasant can win glory with the help of the gods; Troy will be mine without them.'

Nestor drew a deep breath and looked at Odysseus, who arched his eyebrows in response. Antiphus, Eurybates and Arceisius looked into their cups, not daring to criticize a king, but Eperitus shook his head.

'Only a fool thinks he can do without the gods, Ajax. It just angers them. If you want my advice, you'll take those words back and promise a sacrifice to each of the Olympians.'

'What's said is said, Eperitus, and I'll say it again to any man who asks me – or any god for that matter. As for Achilles, he's clearly more of a little girl than a man. If you still want to lure him out of hiding, Odysseus, perhaps you should use those dresses and pretty trinkets you brought with you from Aulis.'

'Zeus's beard, Ajax,' Odysseus said, sitting up sharply. 'Perhaps that's it!'

Ajax roared with laughter and slapped the arms of his chair, just as Lycomedes was climbing the steps that led to the broad roof of the palace.

'I'm sorry to interrupt your joke,' he said as he joined them, an oily smile on his lips. 'But perhaps now that you've enjoyed a good night's sleep and a filling breakfast, this would be a good time to conduct your search of the palace? After all, you said you were going to have a look around for Achilles before you went.'

'Why should we?' said Ajax, balancing his chair on its back legs and looking at the king of Scyros. 'You should know whether a *great* warrior like Achilles was hiding in your own palace, shouldn't you? Besides, we've got a war to prepare for and the sooner we return to Aulis the sooner the day will come when we can sail for Troy.'

'Well, if you insist . . .' Lycomedes began, feigning disappointment.

'There is something I'd like to see before we leave, though.'

'Yes, King Odysseus,' said Lycomedes, his smile becoming suddenly forced. 'Whatever you wish.'

'So far our journey has proved fruitless,' Odysseus said. 'But I wouldn't call it wasted if we could set eyes on your daughters. I'm told their beauty is unrivalled, so to have seen them would at least sweeten our return to Aulis.'

'Most gracious of you to say so, but I'm afraid . . .'

'Come now, Lycomedes,' interrupted Nestor, who quickly sensed that Odysseus may have another motive. 'Modesty isn't becoming for a king and we won't accept any excuses. As for myself, I've been eager to see these fabled maidens for some time, and if we can't see them now then perhaps we can see them tomorrow. Or another day, if that isn't convenient – after all, we're in no particular hurry.'

'And we've brought gifts,' Odysseus added.

Lycomedes looked at his guests in turn, then gave a resigned shrug of his shoulders.

'Of course. They're in the gardens with my grandson Neoptolemus but I'll have them brought here . . .'

'Oh, don't trouble them,' said Odysseus, rising from his chair and turning to his squire. 'Eurybates, take Antiphus and Arceisius and bring the gifts to the king's gardens as quickly as you can. And . . .'

He walked over to Eurybates and whispered something in his ear, which only Eperitus with his supernatural hearing could pick up.

'Yes, my lord,' Eurybates replied, looking uncertain for a moment before dashing down the steps and back into the palace. Antiphus and Arceisius followed, their faces equally confused. Eperitus caught the familiar glimmer of a smile on Odysseus's face – the look that always signalled a plan had come to him – but it was beyond him to understand the strange order he had just given to his squire.

Lycomedes was soon leading them across the palace courtyard to the gardens, wringing his hands anxiously as he marched several paces ahead. The sweet fragrance of blossoms filled their nostrils as they reached an arched gateway in a high wall, where Lycomedes threw back his robe from his arm and knocked three times.

There was a murmur of whispering from the other side, then a female voice said, 'Who is it?'

'It's me, Deidameia, and I've brought guests. They want to see for themselves the famed beauty of my daughters, but I hope they'll find you modestly covered.'

Another rustle of lowered voices followed, punctuated by a giggle before the door swung open. A girl of perhaps seventeen or eighteen years bowed her head as she gave way before them. She had long dark hair that was held up in plaits about her head, and though her face was veiled her dark eyes watched them carefully as they entered in single file.

Eperitus looked around at the walled garden, lined on each side by rows of blossoming trees. The lawn of coarse grass around each trunk was covered in fallen petals, though many more of the pink and white flowers remained on the thin, twisting branches above. Four cobbled paths stretched from the corners of the enclosure to the centre of the garden, where a circular pond was surrounded by flowers of every colour. Here, seated on stone benches or kneeling on the lawn, were a host of young women and girls. The eldest wore veils and all but one had dark hair and eyes. The exception was a tall, blonde girl standing at the back, whose blue eyes watched the newcomers closely. Sitting before them all, dangling his bare feet in the pond, was a young boy with light-coloured hair and a frown.

'Look,' boomed Ajax, pointing at the lad, 'we've found the great Achilles!'

'Unfortunately not,' Lycomedes replied, smiling weakly. 'This is Neoptolemus, Deidameia's son.'

'A handsome lad,' Odysseus said, strolling down the path to stand opposite the boy. 'He looks to have something of the gods about him. And his father?'

'Gone away,' said Deidameia, walking around the pond to pick up her child.

Odysseus looked at the girl, who could only have been twelve or thirteen when she became a mother. The thin gauze across her face did little to hide her beauty: her skin was fashionably pale, her nose pert and attractive, and her lips full and red. Her chiton was worn short, revealing long, shapely legs, and she had no cloak in the warm sunlight to hide the smooth flesh of her shoulders and arms. Some of her sisters were similarly dressed, though others were more modest in their appearance, wearing their dresses long and hiding their naked limbs beneath thick shawls or cloaks. Odysseus held his arms out and Deidameia brought her son to him.

The child looked sternly at Odysseus for a moment, then slapped his breastplate with the palms of his hands.

'I will be a warrior when I'm older,' he announced.

Odysseus smiled back.

'That's good, son. But who will train you to fight? All I see is a host of aunts – have you no uncles?'

'No, sir.'

'What about your father?' Odysseus asked, running his thick fingers through the boy's hair. He saw the eyes of the fair-headed maiden flash towards Deidameia, who quickly stepped forward and lifted Neoptolemus from Odysseus's arms.

'I told you, my lord, his father has gone away.'

'And is his father blond, also?' Odysseus asked. 'It's uncommon among Greeks.'

'He is, my lord, and a more handsome man you will never set eyes upon. Neoptolemus's father has immortal blood in his veins, though he himself is only a man, and as for all this talk of warriors – if you were to ever see my husband's anger the blood would run from your face and leave you pale, though your skin is as brown as leather.'

'Ah!' Odysseus smiled back. 'He must be a great warrior indeed, then. What's his name, and where might we find him? He would be a welcome recruit to our cause.'

From the corner of his eye he saw a movement among Deidameia's sisters, and at the same time Lycomedes stepped forward.

'The whereabouts of my daughter's husband are unknown, King Odysseus,' he insisted, his brow furrowed with barely concealed anger. 'Now, I hope you've found my daughters pleasing, but as they usually bathe at this time of the day I don't think we should keep them from their normal pleasures.'

'Of course, King Lycomedes, though I would ask them to wait a short while longer. You forget the gifts I promised.'

'Gifts?' said one of the younger girls. 'Oh, father, can't we wait a little longer?'

'Yes, father!' came a chorus of voices.

'Here they are now,' Eperitus announced, seeing Antiphus and Eurybates struggle through the arched gateway with a casket between them.

They were followed by Polites, whose size and strength allowed him to carry another casket unaided. Two more Ithacan sailors appeared with the last casket, which was dumped without ceremony on the lawn next to the other two. All the trunks were open, their heaped contents plain to see, but sitting on top of the dresses and pretty ornaments in the third – to the surprise of all but Odysseus and Eperitus – were a long spear and an ox-hide shield.

'Help yourselves to whatever you desire,' Odysseus announced as his men stepped back from the caskets.

Lycomedes's daughters surged forward to lay their hands on the mass of brightly coloured chitons and the sparkling collection of feminine baubles. As they squabbled with each other for this necklace or that sash, only Deidameia and the blonde maiden hung back. Eventually, Deidameia stepped forward and picked up an orange dress that had been tossed aside in the rush for gifts.

'Here, Pyrrha,' she said, handing it to her sister. 'We're the oldest and shouldn't be left without gifts, after all.'

Pyrrha snatched the garment and reluctantly held it against herself, in the same manner that some of her younger sisters were doing with the other dresses. As she did so she caught Odysseus's eyes watching her. The Ithacan king smiled and nodded at the shield and spear, which remained untouched. Pyrrha looked at the armaments, then stared back at Odysseus with disdain in her blue eyes. A moment later she tossed aside the orange dress and instead picked up a sky-blue chiton – the same one Ajax had mockingly pulled from the caskets the day before — and made a show of admiring its quality and beauty.

'Come here, Eurybates,' Odysseus ordered, then whispered something in his ear that even Eperitus could not hear over the clamour of Lycomedes's daughters. 'Now, take the men back to the ship and make ready to leave.'

Eurybates, with a bemused look on his face, led the sailors from the garden. Meanwhile, Neoptolemus had left his place by the pond and was attempting to pick up the spear, which was far too heavy for him. Odysseus laughed.

'Those are my gifts for you, lad. They may be big now, but you'll grow into them.'

Suddenly, a long horn-blast tore through the warm afternoon air, rising then falling away to silence. Another followed it, deep and lonely, causing everyone to look about themselves in surprise and shock. An instant later they heard the unmistakable clash of bronze against bronze and the shouts of men locked in combat. Antiphus came running in through the gateway, his sword drawn and his eyes wide with fear.

'We're being attacked!' he shouted, falling to his knees in front of Odysseus. 'Trojans have landed in the harbour — they're killing everyone.'

Eperitus instinctively fumbled for his sword, before recalling he had left it in the guest quarters.

'Where's the guard house?' Ajax demanded, seizing Lycomedes by the shoulders and staring at him with fierce eyes. 'Where do you keep your arms, man?'

'Damn it all!'

They turned to see the blonde maiden, Pyrrha, throwing off her cloak and chiton to reveal a naked and splendidly muscled body — the body of a man! He tore his veil aside and leapt to where Neoptolemus was still trying to lift the spear.

'Give me that, lad,' he ordered, gently easing the weapon out of the boy's hands. A moment later he had lifted the shield onto his other arm and was dashing out to the courtyard.

'Follow him, quickly!' Odysseus shouted to Eperitus and Antiphus. 'Stop him before he kills somebody.'

They ran out of the garden, followed by Nestor, Ajax and Lycomedes. Achilles – for there was no longer any doubt about Pyrrha's true identity – was running towards a knot of warriors by the gates. They were armed with swords and shields and were methodically attacking each other with slow, deliberate moves. As they saw the naked warrior running swiftly towards them they cast down their weapons and backed away, their arms held over their heads in submission.

'Achilles!' Odysseus shouted, his great voice carrying across the courtyard.

The warrior skidded to a halt in a cloud of dust.

'Achilles! Throw down your armaments. There are no Trojans, and Scyros is not under attack.'

Achilles turned to face the Ithacan king. His golden hair flashed in the sunlight and his rage-filled eyes were terrible to look at, even for seasoned warriors.

'I'm sorry, my friend,' Odysseus continued, holding his arms wide to emphasize his apology. 'I suspected Lycomedes had hidden you among his daughters – the last place anyone would look – and I had to find a way to make you throw off your disguise. And what better way is there of discovering a warrior than a call to arms?'

Achilles tossed the shield aside, but gripped the spear more fiercely as he walked towards Odysseus. Eperitus moved two paces forward, placing himself to the front of his king's right shoulder, ready to take any blow the warrior might deliver. Though Achilles did not have the bulk of Odysseus or Ajax, Eperitus had never seen such definition in a man's muscles. The skin was so tightly drawn over his limbs and chest that each small movement of the tissue beneath was visible. The heavy ash spear with its socketed bronze point, which Neoptolemus had struggled even to lift, was carried easily, as if its weight was trifling in the man's hand. And the intense look in his eyes as he approached was like a lightning bolt from Zeus, awe-inspiring and fearsome to look at. Nevertheless, Odysseus did not flinch as he waited for the younger warrior to come within a spear's length of him, where he stopped.

Achilles looked for a long moment at the king of Ithaca, and then at Eperitus who stood before him, unarmed but with his fists clenched. Then Achilles's severe expression was melted by a smile and his face became even more strikingly handsome. He offered Odysseus his hand.

'Your reputation for cunning is well deserved, Odysseus, son of Laertes,' he said. 'I *am* Achilles, prince of Phthia, son of Peleus, and perhaps you will oblige me with how you knew to find me here on Scyros. But first you can tell me the name of your friend, who thinks his fists can stop the point of my spear.'

'I can speak for myself. My name is Eperitus, captain of King Odysseus's guard.'

'It's strange that a man should name himself but not his father,' Achilles replied. 'But if it doesn't matter to you, then it doesn't matter to me either. I only hope Odysseus appreciates the loyalty of a man who is prepared to step between his king and the wrath of Achilles, which is to invite certain death.'

'Don't be so certain of that,' Eperitus said, offering his hand. Achilles took it with a smile.

'And by your grey hair and many scars of battle,' Achilles continued, looking at Odysseus's other companions, 'I guess you can only be King Nestor of Pylos, son of Neleus. I'd heard you had dusted off your armour one last time to help the expedition against Troy.'

'Then you must also know why we're here,' Nestor responded, accepting Achilles's hand.

'I'm not ignorant, old friend. Nor am I an idiot.'

'A coward then, perhaps?' said Ajax.

Achilles met the king of Salamis's angry gaze and held it.

'And this great brute must be my cousin Ajax. Even in sleepy Scyros they speak about you with fear in their voices. Some even say you're the greatest warrior in Greece, though not within my hearing.'

'Then I shall speak clearly, so that you can be sure to hear me: I *am* the greatest warrior in Greece.'

A sly smile crossed Achilles's lips as he locked eyes with Ajax, their gazes struggling against each other like equally matched wrestlers.

'I have my own claim to that title,' he said. 'Perhaps, cousin, we should compare the number of Trojans we slay. That will tell us who is truly the greatest.'

'That's a contest I would enjoy,' Ajax replied, unable to prevent a grin spreading across his bearded face. 'But first I'd like to know why you were hiding away in a girl's dress when you were oath-bound to come to Aulis.'

'I have a wife whose beauty can drive a man insane with lust, and a young son who needs his father to preserve him from the ways of a houseful of women,' Achilles said, looking across to where Deidameia and Neoptolemus stood beneath the arched entrance to the garden. 'And even Odysseus wasn't beyond a bit of trickery to get out of this war for the sake of his family, or so the rumour goes.'

Odysseus shrugged. 'We can console each other on the shores of Ilium. But do you really expect us to believe a warrior of your reputation would let such things keep you from the temptation of glory, not to mention break the oath that was taken in your name?'

'No,' Achilles answered. 'But I am bound by older oaths than that. Thetis, my mother, foresaw my doom on the day she brought me forth from her womb: that I could live out a long and peaceful life at home in Phthia, or seek death and everlasting glory on the fields before Troy. A year before Helen was married she made me swear never to seek Troy, though she did not tell me why in those days. And now I feel I have honoured my word to her: I have not looked for Troy, but Troy has found me. Now I am bound by the later oath that Patroclus took on my behalf, and though it will mean my death I will come to Troy with you. I choose the path of glory.'

He looked over at the archway again, but this time his family were gone and the gates were shut against him.

## Chapter Eighteen
# THE WHITE HART

A few days later Eperitus stood with Peisandros, the Myrmidon spearman who had helped save him from execution in Sparta ten years before. They were at the edge of a clearing in the wood that overlooked the Greek camp. At its centre stood a lone plane tree, and welling up from between its roots was a spring of clear water. It was said Artemis would stop there and drink by the light of the full moon while she hunted her prey, and aware of its sacred associations Agamemnon had ordered a circle of twelve marble altars – one for each of the principal gods – to be built around the spring. It was on these white plinths that the kings and princes, along with their priests and attendants, were performing the final sacrifices to the gods before the voyage to Troy.

As the fleet made its preparations in the straits below, ready to sail at first light the next morning, the warm, torpid air of the wood was filled with the sounds of prayer and slaughter. Animal after animal was butchered, flayed and jointed. The stench of blood from the gore-splattered altars mingled with the smell of charred flesh from the fires around the clearing, where the priests were burning the fat-wrapped thighs of the beasts in offering to the mighty Olympians. A thick pall of smoke hung over the treetops like a grey ceiling, blotting out the blue skies above, while in the shadow of the wood hundreds more dull-minded beasts tugged at their leashes or snorted impatiently as they awaited their turn to be sacrificed.

Agamemnon led the relentless procession of death, dressed in a lion's pelt that hung down to his ankles. The upper jaw of the once mighty animal was worn like a cap, and beneath the shadow of its sharp teeth the king's face looked pale and hard. In his bloody fist he clutched a silver dagger with which he mechanically sliced open the throats of the animals that were set before him, his lips moving in an unceasing prayer to Zeus. The familiar golden cuirass he had worn since becoming king of Mycenae was gone, replaced by a new breastplate sent by King Cinyras of Cyprus as a gift to the King of Men, as Agamemnon had now taken to calling himself. It was exquisitely worked with numerous bands of gold, blue enamel and tin; three snakes slithered upwards on either side to the neck, their outlines glittering in the light of the sacrificial fires. The other leaders were clustered around the remaining altars, where they were assisted in the various stages of sacrifice by an army of priests and slaves.

'There's going to be some feast tonight,' Peisandros said, grinning as he watched Achilles joint a goat he had slain only moments earlier in dedication to Ares. 'Just the thing we need to see us off to war.'

Peisandros was a thickset man with a large stomach and a wiry black beard, shot through with grey. Despite his fierce eyes and bushy black eyebrows, he had a carefree cheerfulness that had appealed to Eperitus from their very first meeting a decade ago. Their friendship had been renewed at the gathering of the Myrmidon army in Phthia, shortly after Achilles had sailed from Scyros with Odysseus, Nestor and Ajax, and since then they had spent much time together, training and retraining the troops under their command until they could teach them nothing more.

'Make the most of it, Peisandros,' Eperitus replied. 'It's a long voyage to Ilium and we'll be lucky to get anything more than bread and a few smoked fish on the way.'

'Ah, but when we've sacked Troy,' Peisandros said, wagging his finger, 'we can eat our fill in the ruins of Priam's palace. That's a thought that can tide over any man, even one with an appetite like mine.'

'Be careful you don't starve to death then, if that's what you're waiting for.'

'Come now, Eperitus, you need to be more optimistic. There's a fine army in the camp down there – a match for anything Ilium can produce. Besides, you haven't seen Achilles fight yet.'

'And *you* haven't seen the walls of Troy,' Eperitus responded, leaning against the bole of a tree and watching Odysseus sacrifice a lamb to Athena.

'It'll take more than stone to stop us Myrmidons,' Peisandros insisted, thumping his armoured chest proudly. Then his ardent expression faded and he cast a sidelong glance at the gathered kings. 'Still, there is one thing that could rob us of victory.'

'Agamemnon?' Eperitus asked. Peisandros had never hidden his low opinion of the king of Mycenae.

'Who else?' Peisandros confirmed with a sigh. 'The more I see of him, the more I'm convinced he's losing his grip. For one thing, he's becoming a ghost of his former self: pasty-faced, sunken-eyed, thinner; and if it's because he's losing sleep or his appetite, what does that say about his state of mind?'

'Perhaps he's working too hard. Making preparations for an army this big has to make its demands,' Eperitus said unconvincingly, watching as Agamemnon signalled for his priests to bring him a white heifer.

Peisandros dismissed Eperitus's argument with a flick of his hand. 'That doesn't explain his change of attitude though, does it?' he contended, his naturally booming voice uncomfortably loud amidst the muttered prayers and the whimpering of animals. 'I know he's always been more pompous than most, even for a noble, but look at him now! Who does he think he is with that lion's skin hanging off his back – Heracles? And I don't like this new title he's awarded himself, "King of Men". The Trojans might enjoy grovelling before their kings like gods, but *we're* Greeks, Eperitus. We're *free men*!'

'Odysseus says it's a fitting title for the elected leader of the Greek nations,' Eperitus said, though without enthusiasm. He felt as uncomfortable as Peisandros did about Agamemnon's new title, but if it was good enough for Odysseus then it was good enough for him, too.

'Odysseus is just being clever,' Peisandros said. 'He knows the best way to influence Agamemnon is to make a show of his loyalty – the voice heard clearest is the voice that's nearest, as we say back home. I just hope for all our sakes that he can keep his strange moods in check. You told me yourself how he hit his own brother in front of the whole assembly of kings.'

'Well, I'll be happier if he loses his altar-stone coldness altogether,' Eperitus responded. 'I can't read a man who doesn't show his emotions.'

'Nevertheless, it makes me feel uneasy,' Peisandros growled. 'Normally I'm like you – I'd rather have a man yell at me, punch me, or even throw his arms about my neck and kiss me. Achilles is like that: as proud and moody as a little child, but passionate and generous, too. But when I see what's going on inside Agamemnon, it tells me something's wrong. I'd have trusted the old him, but not this one.'

As they watched, the King of Men seized the white heifer by its gold-covered horns, pulled its head back and held his bloody dagger to its neck.

'Father Zeus,' he called aloft, his voice dry and cracking from the inhaled smoke of the fires. 'God of gods, I offer you the life of this unblemished beast and ask that you send us a sign of your support for us. Give us encouragement – let us know that victory will be ours.'

Calchas hobbled forward and scattered the sacrificial grain. Agamemnon had not allowed the priest to leave his side since he had been proven right about the whereabouts of Achilles, and even insisted on his presence at the nightly councils of war. The king's own seer had been sent back to Mycenae and all his privileges given to the Trojan instead, whom Agamemnon plagued with questions about Troy, Priam, Hector and Paris. The fact that

Calchas would not reveal more than Apollo had already allowed him to know only increased his credibility in the eyes of the king.

The heifer gave an impulsive nod of its head, which Agamemnon read as a good sign and immediately slit its throat. The strength left the animal's legs and it fell heavily to the ground, its dark blood gushing over the trampled grass. Suddenly a loud hissing shivered through the groans and prayers. Calchas turned and gave a shout of fear as he stumbled away from the altar of Zeus. The other priests also fell back in shock, whilst Agamemnon stared at the base of the plinth with wide, disbelieving eyes. Within moments, all the kings and princes had fallen quiet, their exhortations dying on their lips as they turned to look at the altar to the king of the gods, where a huge serpent had coiled itself several times around the gore-splashed marble.

It raised its triangular head and hissed at the mass of men, before unwinding its long, blue and red body from around the plinth. Eperitus looked at it and gave an instinctive shudder, his phobia of snakes gripping him even though the vile creature was some way off. Then, as the snake began slithering through the grass towards the plane tree, Diomedes drew his sword and moved towards it.

'Don't touch it!' Calchas screamed, rushing forward with his palms held out. 'Not unless you want to bring the wrath of Zeus down on you. Can't you see the beast has been sent by the gods?'

As he spoke the serpent coiled about the bole of the tree and moved up towards the topmost branches where, though barely noticed before in the noise of the sacrifices, every man could now see a nest of sparrows. The helpless chicks were calling loudly for their mother, unaware of the death that was creeping ever closer from below. Then the broad, flat head of the monster rose slowly over the edge of the nest, waving slightly from left to right as it eyed the unfortunate birds. A moment later it struck, snatching one of the screeching brood and devouring it whole so that the struggling shape was briefly visible as it slid down the neck of the snake. The kings and princes below left their sacrificing and formed a circle about the tree, watching awestruck as one by one the chicks were eaten, until the last one remained, chirping fearfully in its loneliness. In that moment its mother arrived, squawking with panic as she saw the violation of her family, but the snake lashed out and took her by the wing as she hovered above the nest, swallowing her whole as it had done the others. Finally, it closed its jaws over the head of the last remaining bird and plucked it from its moss-filled bed, silencing its cries with a single gulp.

Its divinely appointed task performed, the snake now began to return down the trunk of the plane, hissing at the crowd of men. The sight of its pink, forked tongue flickering out at them in warning was enough to make each man take an instinctive back-ward step, but as the circle widened something happened that rooted them to the ground where they stood.

'How can it be?' said Menelaus in a low voice.

'Calchas! Calchas, tell us what it means.'

Agamemnon turned to the seer and pointed at the bole of the tree, where the serpent now stared at them with dull, lifeless eyes.

Calchas stepped forward and looked up at the dead snake, whose soft flesh had turned to rigid stone before the eyes of the watching men.

'I . . . I don't know,' he stuttered. 'It's beyond me.'

As he spoke his whole body was seized by a strong convulsion that arched his spine and threw his head back, causing the hood to fall away and reveal his bald scalp. His arms shot out from his sides and his hands began to shake. Odysseus moved towards him, but Agamemnon waved him back. Then, as they watched, a silver light suffused the seer's dark eyes and the look of terror on his upturned face was transformed by a smile that seemed to mock the heavens above. Slowly the trembling stopped and Calchas, still smiling, let his head fall forward so that his chin was resting on his chest. Streaks of spittle covered his lips and cheeks, and as he turned his eyes on the watching crowd few could tolerate the look that was in them.

'This sign comes from Zeus himself,' he said, his voice suddenly rich and smooth. 'For each of the eight chicks, you will spend a year besieging Troy. The mother represents a ninth. But in the tenth year, if the prophecies that will be given are fulfilled, victory over Priam's city will be granted to you.'

The words reverberated around the clearing, dousing the confidence that had filled the hearts of the Greeks and replacing it with gloom. Menelaus thought of his wife, held in the lofty towers of Troy for ten long years, where her affections would inevitably turn to Paris. Agamemnon, who had made the commanders swear not to return home until the siege was over, now realized his boy, Orestes, would be left under the twisted influence of Clytaemnestra until he became a man. Odysseus and Eperitus both pondered the oracle that had condemned the king of Ithaca to be away from his home for twenty years, rather than the ten stated by Calchas. But of all the kings who now considered the long war they had committed to, only Achilles, whose death had been prophesied by his mother, took heart; whereas he had expected to live but a few months longer, he now had the prospect of enjoying life for years to come – a life spent in war, reaping souls and the glory that came with them.

For a while, Calchas turned his shining eyes on each of them, whether great or lowly. Then the brightness faded and a moment later he collapsed to the ground. The spell broken, Odysseus and Philoctetes, the archer, rushed to help the priest of Apollo as he lay panting in the grass, while all about them scores of voices rushed to discuss the prophecy that had been uttered.

'Come on,' said Eperitus, slapping Peisandros on the arm.

Together they ran to where Calchas was sitting, rubbing his head and drinking from a cup that Philoctetes had given him. But as they knelt down beside him, a new voice was added to the cacophony about them.

'My lord! My lord Agamemnon!'

'What is it, Talthybius?' Agamemnon snapped, shaking off the stupor brought on by Calchas's words.

The Mycenaean herald burst through the crowd of royalty, his breathing heavy and his face red from running in the hot weather.

'My lord, it's been seen again. Here in the woods. The white hart.'

Many of the voices stopped immediately, and the remainder soon followed.

'The white hart?' Menelaus repeated.

'Yes, my lord. One of the herdsmen saw it just now. I thought you'd want to know.'

'Is this the creature that was seen while I was away in Phthia?' Ajax asked, turning to the other kings. 'Then, by Ares's sword, what are we waiting for? Let's hunt it down before it disappears again. Teucer! *Teucer*, where are you, damn it! Bring me my spear, and don't forget your bow and arrows.'

Suddenly there was uproar as the kings and princes rushed this way and that, hollering the names of their squires or calling aloud for their various weapons.

'Peisandros!' said a tall, sinewy man with a long, pointed nose. His voice was high and pinched, which suited his arrogant face. 'Fetch my hunting hounds at once. They're tethered on the southern side of the wood.'

'Yes, sir,' the Myrmidon replied, and after a farewell nod to Eperitus ran off through the trees.

The arrogant-looking man remained for a moment, staring down his nose at the three men kneeling beside Calchas, then with a curt nod to Odysseus turned on his heel and walked away.

'What's up, Patroclus?' Philoctetes called after the commander of the Myrmidon army. 'Think you're too important to acknowledge your fellow commoners? Or does sharing Achilles's bed again make you somehow high-born?'

Patroclus wheeled about in an instant and drew his sword, but Odysseus was already on his feet and walking towards him. Seizing the Myrmidon gently but firmly by the wrists, Odysseus leaned forward and spoke quietly in his ear. After a moment, Patroclus shot Philoctetes an ugly glance, then turned and marched over to where Achilles was throwing a quiver of arrows over his shoulder.

'That was foolish,' Eperitus said, turning to the young archer with an angry look in his eye. 'Whether the rumour's true or not, if Achilles had heard you you'd be a dead man now.'

'I'm not afraid of Patroclus or Achilles,' Philoctetes hissed back. 'These arrows of mine would kill them both before they could so much as raise a spear against me.'

'Your weapons won't make you great, even though Heracles himself gave them to you – they're just a continuation of *his* greatness. If you want my advice, Philoctetes, prove your *own* worth before you think you can challenge a warrior like Achilles.'

'Looks like it's each man for himself,' said Odysseus, returning with a smile on his face as if nothing had happened.

Philoctetes paused to lift Calchas's hood back over his head, before helping the priest back to his feet. 'Then don't be too slow if you want a chance at the beast,' he warned, mirroring the Ithacan's cheerfulness. 'I've seen it myself and it's magnificent – pure white with antlers of gold – but as soon as I fire one of my arrows at it it's running days'll be over.'

He patted the quiver at his side, and with a last glance at Eperitus bounded off into the rapidly dispersing crowd.

'Take my spear, Odysseus,' Eperitus said. 'Yours are still down by the boats, and we'd better hurry if we're going to hunt this animal.'

Odysseus shook his head. 'Let the others run about as much as they like – only Talthybius knows where the animal was spotted, and he's over with the Atreides brothers. If we want a throw at this fabled hart, all we need to do is follow Agamemnon.'

Eperitus looked over his shoulder and saw the King of Men slip the lion's pelt from his back as he picked up a horn bow and a leather quiver full of arrows. Menelaus stood beside him with two spears in his hand, looking about surreptitiously to note the different directions in which the leaders were disappearing. He only saw Odysseus and Eperitus running towards him at the last moment.

'You do realize,' Odysseus called, 'that this white hart may belong to one of the gods. It could cost us dear if we kill it; all your carefully staged sacrifices could be wasted, Agamemnon.'

'Nonsense,' Agamemnon sniffed, throwing the quiver over his back and tightening the golden buckle. He circled his shoulders to test the fit. 'If it belongs to a god, then they shouldn't let their pets loose around so many skilled hunters. Besides, once you see the animal, Odysseus, you'll know why everyone's leaving in such a hurry.'

'Then we'll accompany you, if you have no objections,' Odysseus said, taking the spear Eperitus held towards him and moving into the undergrowth before the Atreides brothers could have a chance to refuse him. 'Lead the way, Talthybius.'

They set off at a rapid pace through the humid wood, leaping over fallen branches and crashing through knee-high forests of fern, all the time looking left and right through the columns of dusty light that penetrated the canopy of leaves above. Eperitus, whose supernatural senses far outstripped those of his fellow hunters, sniffed the languorous air, sifting out the different smells of damp earth, distant blossom and the sharp odour of human sweat until he could detect – though still faintly – the powerful musk of male deer.

'It was seen not far from here, in a glade to the east,' Talthybius informed them.

'No. It's moving north,' Eperitus announced, after a moment's consideration. 'That way.'

Agamemnon looked doubtful. 'Are you sure? This might be the only chance we get – we can't afford to follow whims.'

'He's sure,' Odysseus assured him. 'I'd trust Eperitus's senses above my own hunting dog's.'

Without any further hesitation, the five men set off in a north-easterly direction. The ground began to slope away before them and the trees grew denser, stifling the gauzy yellow light that had managed to penetrate the thinner woodland they were leaving behind.

'Look!' Eperitus said after they had been running for a while.

He pointed to a branch hanging from a tree. The shards of the broken stem were still fresh and white, indicating it was recently broken. There was no sound or sign of the other hunters, and with a flush of excitement they realized it could only have been snapped by a tall animal passing that way a short while before.

They increased their pace, moving deeper into the wood until they reached a narrow stream. They splashed across and followed its winding course for a while before Eperitus veered suddenly to the left. They followed in his wake, crashing on into the dense heart of the wood until Talthybius could hold the pace no longer and began to slow, gasping for breath.

'Shhh!' Eperitus hissed, suddenly slowing to a crouching walk and pressing his finger to his lips. 'It's close.'

Menelaus and Odysseus instinctively raised their spears, holding the shafts lightly in their cupped palms. Agamemnon slipped an arrow from the quiver and fitted it to his bow, drawing it to half-readiness as his eyes scanned the gloom. Eperitus sniffed the thick air, his eyes narrowing as he judged the different smells captured in his nostrils.

'*It's here*,' he whispered.

The hunters halted and slowly lowered themselves into the cover of the crowded ferns, so that their eyes were just above the curling fronds. For a breathless moment they heard nothing, not even a bird in the closely packed branches above, then a twig snapped and they turned to see a magnificent, pure-white deer trot into a small clearing ahead of them. It stood beside the upturned roots of a fallen tree, bathed in a single shaft of golden light that penetrated a gap in the canopy above. It looked about itself, completely unaware of the men only a stone's throw away, then bowed its antlered head to chew at the rich undergrowth.

'He's mine,' Agamemnon whispered, drawing the bowstring back to his cheek and preparing to stand.

But before he could move, his brother stood and launched the long spear from his hand. It spun through the air, its imperfect shaft twirling behind the bronze tip as it flew towards its target. A moment later it skimmed the shoulders of the hart and buried its point in the mud-caked roots of the tree.

The hart raised its head, saw Menelaus and bolted in the opposite direction. Odysseus stood and cast his own spear, aiming at the flashing white of the animal's hindquarters as they disappeared through the undergrowth. It fell short.

Agamemnon also stood, but unlike the two spearmen knew he had a few moments more to take aim and release his shot. Closing his left eye, he squinted down the shaft of the arrow and focused on the triple-barbed point, aiming it slightly ahead of the fleeing deer. Snatching a half-breath and holding it so that the movement of his lungs would not disturb his aim, he released the shaft.

The bow hummed and Agamemnon leaned his head to the left, hoping to see the white form stumble and fall, but the animal had already disappeared among the trees.

'Missed it,' Menelaus announced, almost gleefully.

'Thanks to you, you buffoon. I told you to leave it for me.'

'What? And let you take all the glory, as usual, *King of Men*?'

'Quiet,' Eperitus ordered, momentarily forgetting he was talking to the two most powerful men in Greece. 'I can't hear its footfalls any more. It's stopped running.'

'No man could hear that well,' said Talthybius.

'Come on,' Odysseus said. 'Let's see if you've hit your mark, Agamemnon.'

They dashed into the undergrowth; twigs snapped loudly beneath their sandals and brittle stems whipped against their shins. They ran past the spears of Menelaus and Odysseus and forged on to the place where they had last seen the hart's white flanks. The trees were thinner here, allowing more sunlight to illuminate the woodland floor, but they could see nothing.

'You were wrong, Eperitus,' Agamemnon said, with clear

disappointment in his voice. He stopped and looked about himself. 'It's gone. The glory will go to no man now.'

But Eperitus merely shook his head.

'No, my lord, I'd still be able to hear its feet beating the ground now. And I can smell fresh blood.'

Odysseus, who had continued following the course of the deer, suddenly called for them to join him. He stood near to the edge of the wood, where the trees filtered out into open fields and the light was almost unbearable to look at. As they ran to join him they saw the carcass of the white hart at his feet, shining like silver through the screen of ferns. Agamemnon's arrow still protruded from its neck.

Eperitus knelt and ran his hands over the soft, warm fur, feeling the ridges of the ribcage beneath his fingertips. This close, the animal was as magnificent in death as it had been when he had seen it in the small clearing, bathed in golden sunlight. He looked up and saw Agamemnon standing above him. The face of the sun glittered in the intertwined branches behind his head, and with the richly decorated breastplate he wore he looked like a god.

'A magnificent shot, my lord,' Eperitus said, reaching to stroke the still-warm flank of the hart.

Agamemnon laughed, a triumphant look gleaming in his sunken eyes as he smiled down at his prey. 'Artemis herself could not have done better!'

And as the words left his lips the sunlight about them seemed to flare out brightly for a moment, then shrink back again. Though they could not yet see it, grey clouds were massing rapidly on the eastern horizon. Before long they were rolling across the skies like a conquering army, swirling and twisting in their tortured agony as they crossed the blue expanse. By the time the men emerged from the wood with the dead hart over Agamemnon's shoulders, the first grey outriders of the approaching storm had blotted out the sun altogether. The hunters looked up in fear and the hills echoed with a boom of thunder.

book
# THREE

## Chapter Nineteen
# THE STORM

The rain lashed furiously against the forest of tents, drenching the flaxen sheets until they hung heavily upon the wooden poles beneath. Inside, men shivered against the unseasonable cold and pulled their woollen cloaks tighter about their shoulders, longing for the day when the unending storm would lift and allow them to sail for Troy. But if any man opened the flap of his tent, all he could see was grey clouds from horizon to horizon, pressing down on the camp like the belly of a great monster as the rain fell and the wind howled.

It had been this way for three weeks. Night flowed into day and day back into night, so that the only change was from Stygian blackness into melancholy gloom and back again. The only real light any man saw was the glitter of lightning inside the ever-shifting mantle of cloud, or the occasional bolt stalking across distant horizons. And all the time their ears were assailed by the monotonous groaning of the wind as it passed between the avenues of tents, tearing at pennants and tugging at guy ropes, a constant worry to the men inside. Many a shelter was blown away in the storm, and most others were made unbearable by the wind that whistled through the gaps in the walls. Once inside, it would drive out any warmth until the flesh of every soldier was chilled to the bone and each man was ready to give up the expedition and return home. But with their ships wind-bound in the straits below, they had no choice but to sit tight and pass the time grumbling against the gods and, above all, their leaders.

There were few who did not blame the slaying of the white hart for their present troubles. Agamemnon had shot a creature precious to one of the immortals, and now this unidentified god was making all their lives a misery because of their leader's sacrilege. The King of Men, keen to set sail, was the most frustrated of them all. He had offered repeated sacrifices to all the gods, but to no avail. On every occasion, as he had stared up into the rain with fresh blood streaming down the dagger in his right hand, his desperate prayers were met with deep rumbles of displeasure from the skies above. And as the fleet remained holed up between the mainland and Euboea, the pressure on its leader grew.

He sat on a heavy wooden chair with a high back. It was covered in a thin layer of tin and had been draped over with furs, which were soft beneath the naked skin of his thighs and calves. His new breastplate felt stiff and awkward, pressing into the flesh beneath his armpits and at the tops of his legs, but he refused to remove it because of his constant fear of assassination. The double cloak over his shoulders was warm and light.

Agamemnon drummed the fingers of his right hand repeatedly on the table before him, trying to drown out the constant pattering of the rain on the high roof of his tent. The thumb and forefinger of his other hand were busily massaging his aching temples as he studied the map Odysseus had placed on the table. It depicted a rough representation of Ilium and its surrounding islands.

'If this distance is correct,' said King Nestor, leaning across and tapping the point between the walls of Troy and the line of beach between the Scamander and Simöeis, 'then it's too risky to make the landing so close to the city.'

'Nonsense,' Menelaus said. 'If we land the ships here we can cross the plain in no time. The Trojans will be taken completely by surprise, and before they know it our army will be streaming through the city.'

The two men were among a handful that had joined Agamemnon in his tent after the nightly feast, a time when the leaders of the expedition would sacrifice to the gods and share food together. Tonight, though, the atmosphere was more affected than usual by the sombre weather. Achilles had departed with the Ajaxes and Teucer, all of them intent on brightening their mood with wine. Many others had returned to the familiarity of their own camps, hoping to wake the next morning and find clear skies. Only Idomeneus, Diomedes and Odysseus had joined Nestor and the Atreides brothers to discuss a strategy for the attack on Troy, and were now poring over the rough map that the Ithacan king had made from memory.

'Your eagerness to rescue your wife is blinding you to the realities of war, Menelaus,' Nestor countered. 'If the Trojans are prepared for us, they can meet us on the beaches and massacre us as we leap down from our ships. If they are not prepared but are able to meet us in force on the plain, they could check our advance and throw us back into the sea before we have time to organize a proper defence. And if we don't take the city in the first attack and have to lay siege to it, any determined attack they make could reach our camp with ease.'

'Do you doubt our army's ability to beat the Trojans?' Agamemnon asked, cocking an eyebrow towards his trusted adviser.

'No, but just as many battles are decided by the gods as they are by feats of arms. If the prophecy of the snake and the sparrows was interpreted correctly, then we can be sure the gods won't give us Troy in the first attack. And I've seen too many battles on open ground to want to risk our ships on that beach. If it's my advice you want, Agamemnon – and that was the reason you asked me to join this expedition – then you won't gamble everything we have in such a place.'

'Nestor's right,' Odysseus agreed. 'The plain is too exposed. If we attack there the war won't last ten days, let alone ten years.'

'Then where *do* we attack?' asked Idomeneus.

'Right here,' Nestor answered, tapping a point on the mainland north of Tenedos. It was one of the large bays Odysseus's ship had passed on its mission to Troy. 'It's wide and sandy, ideal for beaching a large number of ships, and it can't be seen from Troy because of the distance and this ridge. That means we can land unopposed and form up our armies before marching on Troy. Then, if the gods are against us and we are forced back, we can use the ridge as a line of defence.'

'That places the Scamander between us and Troy,' said Diomedes, running his finger over the line of the river. 'Even if there's a ford, it'll be easier for the Trojans to defend it against . . .'

He left the sentence unfinished as all seven men turned to look at the soldier who had just entered. His cloak was soaked through and his polished armour streamed with rivulets of rain that dripped onto the furs beneath his sandals.

'Sorry, my lords, but it's the Trojan priest. He wants to see the King of Men – says it can't wait.'

'Another one of his wine-induced dreams, no doubt,' Menelaus sniffed. 'Send him away, Ixion.'

'No,' said Agamemnon, shooting a glance at his brother. 'Bring him in. It might be important.'

The soldier disappeared and a moment later Calchas came hurtling in through the same elaborately embroidered flap of cotton, to land in a damp heap on the piled furs and fleeces. His customary hooded cloak was absent, and his white priest's robes were soaked through, revealing his nakedness beneath. He raised himself up on his hands and looked at the gathering of kings, swaying slightly and reeking of wine. His staring eyes were red-rimmed and filled with fear.

'What is it, my friend?' Agamemnon asked, forcing a smile to his lips. 'Do you have a word for us from the gods?'

'Yes, King of Men!' Calchas replied, raising himself to his knees and shuffling forwards with his hands clasped together like a suppliant. Then he looked around at the other kings, as if he was seeing them for the first time, and pulled back with an angry look on his face. 'No! I have nothing for *these*, only you. You must send them away.'

'Show some respect or I'll send you to Hades, you wretch,' Diomedes warned, putting a hand to the hilt of his silver-studded sword.

'Don't be offended, Tydeides,' said Agamemnon, using the familiar form of address for the son of Tydeus. 'He's half out of his mind at most times of the day, but even more so when he's had one of his visions.'

Odysseus looked up.

'Have there been others we haven't heard of?'

'Nothing of importance,' Agamemnon responded, meeting Odysseus's intelligent eyes. 'And nothing that has upset him as much as whatever's on his mind now.'

'In the name of Apollo, send them away!' Calchas implored, tears of anguish and frustration rolling down his cheeks. 'Lord Agamemnon, I *must* speak to you alone.'

Idomeneus thumped the table in frustration, the annoyance clear on his handsome features.

'Calchas may bring word from the gods themselves, but what we're discussing could decide the fate of the whole expedition. Send him to the guard tent, Agamemnon, and call him in when we're done.'

Diomedes and Menelaus voiced their agreement with the Cretan king, while Odysseus and Nestor both looked at Agamemnon in a way that left him in no doubt of their feelings on the matter.

Calchas turned on them in disgust. 'What good are your strategies and tactics if the fleet is stuck at Aulis? *I'm the only one who knows how to lift the storm*, and unless you listen to me your ships will remain here until their timbers rot and their crews die of old age.'

'Come now, my lad,' said Nestor, leaning down and patting the distressed priest's shoulder. 'If you know how to appease the god we've offended, then tell us so that we can do whatever we must.'

'Whatever, King Nestor?' Calchas replied with a mocking smile. '*Whatever*? Even a brave man like you would pale at what needs to be done. And that's why I can only tell the King of Men. *He* must decide whether to pay the terrible price that is demanded of him, or abandon his dreams of conquest and go back home.'

'You'd like that wouldn't you, you Trojan dog?'

'Enough, Menelaus,' said Agamemnon, though his eyes did not leave Calchas. 'If this vision is for me alone, and if it'll show me how to send these winds back to where they came from, then I must ask you to return to your tents. We can carry on our discussion at noon tomorrow.'

The kings paused and looked at Agamemnon for a moment, then Odysseus went to the table by the entrance and picked up his purple cloak, throwing it about his shoulders and fastening it together with the golden brooch Penelope had given him. The others followed, gathering up their cloaks and helmets before leaving without a word. Odysseus was the last to go, but before he lowered the embroidered flap of the tent behind him, he looked back to see Calchas with his arms around Agamemnon's knees, crying like a child.

❧

While storms raged over the Euboean straits, the skies above the island of Tenedos were peaceful and clear. Countless stars winked and shivered as if blown by a celestial wind, and a new moon hung low over the black silhouette of the hills. Helen lay on her back in the deep grass with her hand held above her face, the tip of her forefinger tracing the shapes of the heroes and monsters of old in the myriad lights before her. Her nurse, Myrine, had taught them to her from the window of her bedroom when she was a small child, telling her their names and the stories that had earned them their place in the heavenly firmament.

'There's Cepheus, the king of Ethiopia,' she told Paris, who lay beside her. 'And that's Cassiopeia, his wife. Poseidon set their images in the stars after Perseus had turned them to stone with the head of Medusa. Their daughter, Andromeda, is below them. And there's Perseus, reaching for her hand.'

'Hmm,' Paris replied uncertainly. He pressed his naked flank against hers, enjoying the warmth of her body as they lay beneath his double cloak. 'That's not what we Trojans call them.'

'Then how about that bright star a little further to the west? That's Capella, the she goat who suckled Zeus when he was an infant. Can you see the four bright stars about her? Athena put them there to commemorate Erichthonius, whose lower body was that of a snake. He invented the chariot, so they say, and that's why we call that constellation the Holder of the Reins.'

'The Holder of the Reins,' Paris repeated with mocking slowness. 'Well, I've never heard it called that before. When I was a shepherd on Mount Ida we used to name that the Crooked Stick, though I never knew why. And those two you call Perseus and Andromeda, they're Marduk and Istar in our reckoning.'

'Then Trojans must be stupid,' Helen replied.

Paris rolled on top of her and pinned her wrists to the ground. Helen struggled against him, smiling through the concentration as she wrapped her legs about his waist and tried to throw his heavy bulk to one side. But her efforts were in vain and she quickly lay still beneath him, looking up at his scarred face and into his dark eyes.

'You won't say that when you see my father's city tomorrow. Troy makes Sparta look like a pig farm.'

'I'm looking forward to seeing your home at last,' she replied. 'Though it scares me at the same time.'

'There won't be a person there who won't take you to their heart,' Paris promised her. 'The whole of Troy will love you. And if anyone doesn't, then my father will command them to.'

'You can't command someone to love a person.'

'The king can. In Greece, kings are merely respected and their word obeyed grudgingly; in Ilium, the king is worshipped like a god. When the king speaks, his wishes are carried out with love and fear. Your life depends on it.'

'Can no one question his authority?'

'Absolutely no one. He has his council of advisers, and a few of his sons can try to sway his decisions, but when Priam has given a command only a reckless man would dare speak against him. I know of only one who has.'

'Who?'

'Apheidas, of course,' Paris said. 'He's Trojan by birth, but he spent too many years in Greece and his foreign breeding has given him a rebellious nature. Fortunately for him, we've learned to tolerate his wilfulness because of his skill as a fighter. You're very similar to him, you know; you have a strong spirit, and perhaps that's why I love you.'

Helen placed a hand on his bearded cheek and smiled up at him.

'And one day your father's power might be yours,' she said, not sure whether the thought excited or terrified her.

'When the king dies Hector will inherit the throne,' Paris corrected, a hint of embarrassment in his voice at having to admit the fact to Helen. 'And then, when he eventually takes time away from war and politics to find himself a wife, he'll have children who will precede me in the royal line. Eventually I will become of no importance and fade away.'

The sound of reed pipes and a lyre floated up to them from the palace at the foot of the hill. Further out, in the bay where their ship was anchored, they could hear the sea washing over the shoreline, back and forth, back and forth, like a nurse shushing her infant charge to sleep. They had been guests of King Tenes for several days, and as a client king of the Trojan empire he was obliged to offer Trojan royalty the best he could provide. Somewhere in the modest collection of buildings below, where the yellow lights flickered from the windows, Apheidas, Aeneas and the rest of the crew would be enjoying the pleasures of food, wine and music, happy that their prince was in the arms of the woman he loved. Little Pleisthenes had been left in the care of a young nurse from the town, much as he had been left in the care of others ever since the flight from Sparta.

'It doesn't matter,' Paris continued. 'Power is of no interest to me. All I care about now is you. When we get home we'll be married, and then one of my younger brothers can have my shield and spears. I'll be giving up fighting for good.'

'You promise?' Helen asked, surprised by the unexpected admission.

'Of course! What interest will war hold for me if it keeps me away from you? The northern borders will just have to find a way to exist without me.'

He looked at Helen, whose skin had a ghostly pallor from the faint light of the moon, then lowered his face to hers and kissed her. She responded, folding her slender arms about his neck and pulling him closer.

'Never leave me,' she whispered, planting a kiss on his earlobe.

He kissed her again and ran his hand over her ribs, cupping her breast. She crossed her calves over his buttocks, kicking the cloak away so that their bodies were cooled by the night air, then pulled him into her.

❦

The relentless, soul-destroying rain had stopped, though the ceiling of turbulent cloud remained. It pressed down on the camp, keeping out the morning light so that the world seemed to be made of ash; the tents were but colourless shadows, their occupants spiritless wraiths. The only thing in this upper-Hades that told Menelaus it was day was the lonely trilling of a blackbird from the branches of a nearby oak, and the sense that, somewhere far above, the sun was creeping through an invisible blue sky.

Instinct had woken him at dawn, and since then he had been busy finding things to do, trying to ignore the urge to visit his brother and extract from him whatever it was Calchas had been so desperate to reveal. Eventually his resistance folded and he walked the short distance to Agamemnon's tent, stepping over the guy ropes and beneath the lines of clothing that had been hung out to dry during the reprieve from the rain. The heavily armoured guards bowed their heads at his approach, before stepping aside and letting him pass.

He found his brother alone, seated exactly as he had left him the night before – his elbows resting on the arms of his chair, his fingers laced together in his lap and both sandalled feet planted firmly on the fur-covered floor. His head was bowed and he did not seem to notice Menelaus enter.

'Agamemnon?'

The king remained still. His great chest, encased by its magnificent cuirass, did not stir, and immediately Menelaus felt panic claw at his throat. His flesh prickled and went cold.

'*Agamemnon*?'

'I hear you, brother.'

Agamemnon's voice seemed to come from a distance, as if he had indeed died and his soul was speaking from the Underworld.

'Ag . . . Agamemnon, what's wrong?'

The king of Mycenae lifted his head and faced his brother. Menelaus's nostrils flared briefly, the only sign of his shock at the sight before him.

'Brother, what's happened? You look – ill.'

If the preceding weeks had seen Agamemnon transformed from a healthy, vigorous and determined ruler into an exhausted shadow of his former self, the man who sat before Menelaus now was changed almost beyond recognition. His once smooth skin was lined with anguish and his dark-rimmed eyes had lost their shine, leaving only a glimmer of the tormented soul within. The hair above his ears had turned grey overnight.

'Calchas told me how to lift the storm, Menelaus. He told me what we must do if we want to sail against Troy.'

He let his gaze fall to the floor again. Menelaus rushed across to kneel before his brother, taking his hands in his own and looking up into his troubled face. Tears were rolling down Agamemnon's cheeks – something even Menelaus had never seen before – causing the Spartan king to shiver. He squeezed his brother's hands gently.

'What is it? What must we do? *Zeus's beard*, man, won't you tell me?'

Agamemnon shut his eyes tightly. When they opened again, the window into his emotions had been closed. Instead, there was a dark, hard glint, like the reflection of light from a piece of obsidian. He turned to Menelaus, his features drawn with a tense determination that made the edges of his nostrils tremble.

'I'll tell you, Menelaus, but first you must answer me this: are you determined to have Helen back?'

He seized his brother's wrists in a fierce grip and looked deeply into his eyes, as if the answer could be seen in the reflection from his eyeballs. Menelaus yanked his hands free and stood.

'You know I am,' he answered sharply, turning his back on Agamemnon and walking to the centre of the tent. Then something struck him about the way the question had been asked, and he turned and pointed his finger at the man who had been elected to lead the expedition. 'I want Helen as much as *you* want Troy!'

Agamemnon's shoulders sloped, as if the last taste of hope had left him. 'Then we must send for Iphigenia.'

'Iphigenia?' Menelaus asked, perplexed. 'Your daughter?'

It was then that Agamemnon told him what was to be done.

Menelaus sat on one of the other chairs and stared at his brother in silence. After a while he reached for a silver goblet on the table beside him, only to find it empty.

'And you'll go through with this?'

Agamemnon did not respond, but the grim look on his face showed his resolve.

'Well, *I* don't trust Calchas,' Menelaus stated, his voice seething with anger. 'He's a Trojan, after all, and a traitor to his people, which is even worse. He's always getting drunk and then having these supposed dreams from Apollo – how can you be sure he's right with this one?'

'You saw him when the snake turned to stone. It was a clear sign from Zeus, and he was the only one who could interpret it.'

'But you don't know he's right, yet.'

'He's been right about plenty of other things,' Agamemnon said. 'He's told me things that no other man could know. And I believe him with this, too.'

'Clytaemnestra will never allow it.'

'Do you think I'm stupid enough to tell *her*?' Agamemnon spat. 'I'll send Talthybius to fetch the girl on some other pretence. I'll say . . . I'll say I'm going to wed her to Achilles. Even Clytaemnestra won't prevent her precious daughter from marrying the best warrior in Greece.'

'Don't be too sure of it,' Menelaus responded, standing again. He began pacing the floor, trying to make the horror of what they were planning to do settle in his mind. But it was too awful, and as he spoke it seemed as if he was preparing some cold military strategy. 'She's a stubborn woman and she loves that girl more than her own life. We need to send somebody who can persuade her to let Iphigenia come to Aulis. Perhaps you should go.'

'No!' Agamemnon snapped. 'Never! Do you think she wouldn't be able to read it in my eyes? If I go, she'll sense something's wrong.'

'Send Odysseus then. Even if he can't convince Clytaemnestra to send the girl, he'll be able to devise some trick or other.'

A smile crossed Agamemnon's face, making Menelaus flinch with revulsion.

'Yes. Send Odysseus, then, with Talthybius as a guide. And make sure Eperitus accompanies him.'

'Eperitus?' Menelaus asked.

'Why not? My wife always spoke highly of him, and I've a gut feeling he'll be able to appeal to her now. We'll send for them immediately – they'll have to journey overland because of the storm, so we can't afford to waste any more time.'

Agamemnon stood and shouted for the guard and his body slave. His drive and energy were rapidly returning and he began to strip off his armour and clothing, eager to bathe and start the day.

Menelaus left his brother to his machinations. The price for releasing the fleet and sailing to the conquest of Troy had almost been too much for the King of Men to bear, but somehow – at a terrible cost – he had brought himself to accept it. The cost was another piece of his humanity fed to the cold fires of his ambition; but the thought that his preparations for war could continue seemed to console him and lend him new energy.

For a moment, as Menelaus filled his lungs with the cool, damp air outside the tent, he wondered whether it was right that his passion for Helen – and his desire for vengeance on Paris – should demand so much sacrifice from others. But he immediately knew that if he entertained such questions they would defeat him. He had to be determined to see the war through at all costs, to himself or anyone else. No, he had not asked Paris to offend his hospitality and steal his beloved wife. If there was a cause for the coming war, the blame lay firmly in the Trojan's lap, not his.

## Chapter Twenty

# GALATEA

Eperitus was woken the next morning by Arceisius, kneeling beside his straw mattress and shaking him gently by the shoulder.

'Is it time?' he said, his voice creaking with tiredness. The air beyond his thick woollen blanket was cold and damp, and he could sense the sun had not yet risen.

'Yes, sir,' Arceisius replied, standing and pulling away the blanket. 'Talthybius is outside with the ponies and King Odysseus is dressing in his tent. The gods have sent a thick mist to cover our departure, but it'll lift once the sun rises.'

Eperitus stood and pulled on his tunic. 'What about the others?'

'Still sleeping. I'll wake Eurylochus and Polites, sir, if you'll see to Antiphus.'

Eperitus dressed quickly and followed Arceisius outside, where Talthybius greeted them with a silent nod. Behind him, half hidden in the fog, were the dark shapes of eight ponies – one for each of the party and another for their supplies. Their handlers stood nearby, rubbing their hands against the cold and talking in low voices.

As Arceisius disappeared into the white mist, Eperitus walked up to one of the ponies and ran a hand over its neck. The animal raised its head, snorted and twitched its tall ears.

'Hello, boy. Ready for a long journey?'

'His name's Sophanax, sir,' said one of the handlers, breaking off from his conversation. 'He might not be quick, but he'll take you wherever you need to go.'

Eperitus had spent his youth with horses and knew at a glance that the pony was well fed, well treated and strong. He nodded at the handler.

'Keep this one for Polites. He doesn't know a horse's head from its arse and he'll need something strong to take his weight. Do you have a quicker animal for me?'

'Little Melite's fast on her feet, but she's spirited,' the man said, pointing to a small grey mare whose head was bent to the ground, busily tearing at the coarse grass.

'She'll do,' Eperitus replied, then went to wake Antiphus.

They started slowly. Though Eperitus, Odysseus and Talthybius were good horsemen, the others had lived their entire lives on a small, rocky island – with the exception of Polites – and were not used to anything larger or quicker than a mule. They struggled to control their mounts as they negotiated their way out of the camp, and even before the sun had nudged above the hills of Euboea behind them there were complaints of soreness, most notably from Eurylochus. But as soon as they reached the small town of Aulis they were able to pick up the road that led west towards the Peloponnese, and from there the going became easier.

Talthybius, who had travelled the route several times before, confidently informed them they would reach Mycenae by the fourth day. Eperitus did not share his faith in the abilities of their travelling companions, but as they crossed the lowlands of Boetia their progress improved and by afternoon they were passing the ruins of Thebes. Diomedes had laid waste to it in his youth, slaying or scattering its population with such ruthlessness that the proud city was still unoccupied over ten years later. Only bands of brigands and other outlaws lived amidst its broken walls and charred houses now, presenting a danger to all who passed by. Eperitus's sharp eyesight picked out their faces among the shadows, eyeing them greedily as they trotted past, but he knew they would not dare to challenge a party of seven armed warriors.

By evening they reached a line of low mountains, anchored at its western end by the broad peak of Mount Cytheron. Already the persistent rain and squally winds of Aulis had given way to clear skies and a gentle breeze that came down from the foothills, lifting their spirits as they made camp. Antiphus took his bow and went hunting, and by the time the chariot of the sun had disappeared beneath the peaks to the west they were eating roast goat and exchanging stories around a blazing fire. A ceiling of stars sparkled overhead and the miserable weather of the past few weeks was quickly forgotten.

It took them the whole of the following day to find their way across the mountains. The road that had made their journey easy up to this point now became a rough and poorly maintained track, often requiring them to dismount and lead their ponies along narrow escarpments or past perilous drops. The sun blazed down from a naked sky, slowing their progress even further as they toiled and sweated over and around the undulating contours of the hills. But Talthybius remained cheerful and undaunted, and eventually they saw the port of Eleusis below them, with the Saronic Sea glittering like gold beyond it. They reached the town by last light, and though it was small and unimpressive they were able to find an inn where they feasted on skewered fish and barley cakes, washed down with kraters of good wine. That night they slept under a solid roof for the first time in many days.

By dawn of the next morning they were mounted again and riding in single file along the coastal road that would take them to Megara and, ultimately, the city of Corinth in the north of Agamemnon's realm. The island of Salamis, where Great Ajax was king, lay on their left. As Eperitus watched the new sun rising over its low hills, his mind drifted back to the words Calchas had spoken to him in Priam's throne room. He had thought of little else since he and Odysseus had been summoned before Agamemnon three days before, when the King of Men had ordered them to fetch his eldest daughter from Mycenae to be married to Achilles. The fact she was only nine years old, and the Phthian prince was already married to King Lycomedes's daughter, Deidameia, should have warned him that all was not as it seemed. But Eperitus could only think that, against all his expectations, he would soon be in Mycenae. Here he would seek out the one Calchas had spoken of, a person who could reveal to him the secret that would make him reject the coming war. What could Calchas have meant? What could make him turn his back on battle and the chance for glory? Who would reveal this mystery to him, and how would he find him? And what was the second secret the priest had mentioned, that would compel him to return to Troy whether there was a war or not?

The answers were beyond Eperitus's capacity to think. In his frustration he was tempted again and again to share these things with Odysseus, whose thoughts were much clearer and deeper than his own. But Calchas's words seemed too private even for their friendship, and so he was forced to wait in lonely silence, anxiously chewing the mystery over and over again in his mind.

He heard hooves quickening over the stone road behind him and turned to see Odysseus coming alongside. The king gave one of his reassuring smiles.

'You've been very quiet since we left the camp, Eperitus,' he began, keeping his voice low so that the others could not hear him. 'What's troubling you?'

'This mission,' Eperitus lied, after pausing to consider his reply. 'I don't understand why Agamemnon has suddenly decided to marry his daughter to Achilles. She won't have reached puberty yet and he's already married, so why do we have to trudge halfway across Greece to fetch the poor girl?'

'Eurylochus asks that question with every step his pony takes,' Odysseus responded, looking back at his cousin's strained face. 'But you're right. There's something strange about this – something we haven't been told. And why wasn't Achilles allowed to know?'

'Would you be pleased if you were told you were going to marry a nine-year-old?'

'No, and I think they're afraid he would have stopped us from going if he'd known the purpose of our journey. The problem is, he's under no obligation to accept the marriage anyway and can just as easily say no to the girl when we bring her back as he could have done before we set off. So why would Agamemnon send for his daughter, only to have her sent home again if Achilles refuses to marry her? I can only think the important thing *isn't* the marriage: either he's looking for an excuse to get us out of the way – which wouldn't make sense – or he wants Iphigenia to be brought to Aulis for some other reason.'

'Such as what?'

Odysseus threw another glance over his shoulder, this time to ensure they would not be overheard. 'Insurance. He knows Clytaemnestra has no love for him, and I don't think he trusts her not to try to take the kingdom for herself while he's away. But she does love Iphigenia, so as long as he holds her he knows Clytaemnestra won't dare do anything foolish.'

Eperitus was impressed, though not surprised, by his friend's analysis of the situation. But he also wondered whether Agamemnon's sending them to Mycenae had anything to do with the secret Calchas said would be revealed to him there. He had a gut feeling that it did.

'Whatever the reason, though,' Odysseus continued after they had ridden in silence for a while, 'I'm glad to be away from Aulis. And it isn't just those unnatural storms – all that waiting around and doing nothing was slowly robbing me of my sanity.'

Eperitus nodded. 'Yes, it is good to be travelling again. The last long journey we took by road was when we went to Sparta, all those years ago. And we didn't have ponies then.'

'No, we didn't,' Odysseus laughed. 'But do you remember those pack animals? I've seen more flesh on a sparrow.'

'I remember trying to get the damned things across that river,' Eperitus said. 'But I remember the fights best. Do you think we'll have as much fun at Troy?'

'I hope we'll never get there,' Odysseus replied, as if to remind his friend he had not yet accepted the inevitability of war. 'But if a warrior can't enjoy a good scrap, then what can he enjoy? There are a lot of good men whose spirits will go down to Hades's halls before it's all over, though, Achilles among them.'

'It's hard to imagine there's a man alive who could kill him,' Eperitus said. 'You've seen his mock fights with the Ajaxes – they're both excellent warriors, but he's twice as quick as they are. If they were his enemies rather than his friends he'd have killed them both a hundred times over. And he can wrestle, box and run, too, better than anyone else I've seen.'

'And yet his own mother has predicted he'll die at Troy,' Odysseus said. He spat contemptuously on the road. 'There are too many prophecies about this war. Soon a man won't dare to lift his spear in anger for fear of bringing about his own death – or being doomed not to see his homeland for twenty years.'

Eperitus sensed his friend's pain as he thought of his family. If Penelope had been his wife and Telemachus his son, he wondered whether any oath would be able to separate him from them. But he also knew that Odysseus had the courage and endurance to do his duty if the war came, and go to Troy and fight until he was the last man alive if the gods demanded it.

At that point, Odysseus leaned forward and raised a hand to shield his eyes from the sun. 'What do you think's got into Polites?' he asked.

He pointed to where the giant warrior – the foremost in their party – had stopped his pony and was staring ahead of himself, also holding up a hand against the bright sunlight. The next instant, he jumped from his pony and ran towards a crumpled shape at the side of the road. Eperitus and Odysseus spurred their own ponies into a gallop, covering the distance in a few moments. They dismounted and ran to where Polites was scooping something large and heavy from among the rocks.

'What is it?' Odysseus demanded.

'Not *it*, my lord,' the Thessalian replied in his deep, slow voice. He stood and turned to face them. '*She*.'

Draped between his muscular arms was a girl. Her eyes were shut and her head hung limply across the crook of his elbow, a cascade of black hair flowing almost to the ground. Her young cheeks were smeared with blood and dirt, as were her long, suntanned limbs. One of her sandals was missing and her white cotton dress had been torn open to expose her pale breasts.

Polites's broad, flat face stared down at her with tender pity, and for a moment Eperitus thought she was dead. Then he saw a faint movement of her ribs and knew there was still breath within her.

'She's alive!' he exclaimed, reaching for the skin of water that hung over his shoulder and pulling out the stopper. 'Bring her here, Polites.'

He tipped some of the lukewarm liquid into the palm of his hand, then poured it over her forehead and rubbed away the dirt and blood with his thumb. Her skin was warm and soft, which gave him hope she was still far from death. He did the same to each cheek, then lifted the mouth of the water skin to her lips and, after pulling them open to reveal her bottom teeth and her tongue, allowed some of the liquid to flow into her mouth. At once, the girl choked and brought her head forward, coughing until the water ran back out over her chin and neck.

Her eyes fluttered open and she blinked up at Eperitus. A moment later she flung her arm across her face and turned her head away.

'Why don't you leave me alone!' she cried. 'You've taken all I have. What more do you want?'

'Don't be afraid,' Eperitus said. 'We're not going to harm you.'

'We found you by the road,' Polites added. 'You'll be safe with us.'

The girl was no more than twenty years old, and with the dried blood and streaked grime washed from her face her natural beauty was clear to see. She looked up at Polites with her grey eyes and smiled.

'Thank you. Who are you?'

'We're going to Mycenae,' Odysseus said, stepping forward and pulling the torn halves of the girl's dress across her breasts. 'King Agamemnon has sent us.'

The girl watched the other four members of the troop trot up behind him and dismount.

'Then you must have come from the army at Aulis,' she said, letting her eyes roam over Odysseus's bearded face and broad chest. 'And you must be one of the kings, judging by your looks.'

'Don't concern yourself about me,' Odysseus said, his hands on his hips. 'Tell us who you are and what has happened to you.'

'You can put me down now,' the girl instructed Polites. There was authority in her voice, though her simple dress and her suntanned skin indicated she was no more than a peasant girl or a slave.

Polites let her slip gently to the ground, and as she stood they could see she was almost as tall as the colossal warrior. She turned to Odysseus. 'My lord, whoever you are, my name is Galatea. I serve the goddess Artemis in her temple on the other side of that wood, and live with my widowed mother in a house nearby. Until recently I led a simple but happy life, tending to my mistress's shrine and offering her prayers and pleasing sacrifices. But, ever since the kings left for Aulis and took their armies with them, these lands have become a dangerous place. There are so many brigands roaming the countryside now, no one dares to venture far from their towns or villages. Then, last night . . .'

A pained look filled her eyes and for a moment the strength left her. Polites caught her as she fell, supporting her in his arms as if she weighed no more than a child.

'Here,' said Eperitus, handing her his water. 'Take as much as you need.'

She thanked him and lifted the skin to her lips, taking several mouthfuls.

'Then last night *they* came to the temple. There were four of them, standing in the shadows by the entrance, but I could see the torchlight gleaming on their bronze swords. I told them to leave –

ordered them to in the name of Artemis – but they just laughed. Then one slapped me across the face and tore my dress. Another stripped me bare – *me*, a virgin servant of Artemis!'

'They weren't afraid to violate the sanctity of the gods?' Odysseus asked, frowning.

'Or the sanctity of their servants,' Galatea said, tears suddenly filling her eyes. 'When they were finished they beat me and left me on the temple floor, where I think I just drifted into a sort of dream. Eventually I was woken by the dawn light spreading across the temple floor, gleaming red, warming me as it touched my skin. And then I remembered my mother.'

She stopped, unable to go on through her broken-hearted sobs.

'Why don't you sit down?' Eperitus said. He removed his cloak and laid it over a low boulder with a flat top.

'Thank you, sir,' she said, wiping the tears from her face and allowing Polites to help her to the seat. Polites, not to be outdone by Eperitus, removed his own cloak and threw it about her shoulders. Galatea continued her story. 'I returned to our house, where the door lay thrown from its hinges and in splinters, and I began to fear the worst. The brigands were nowhere to be seen, so I stepped through the doorway and looked about at what remained of our home. They had broken every pot we own – no doubt searching for anything of value – and the shards lay all over the floor. Our few bits of furniture had been smashed to smithereens, the floor had been dug up to find buried goods, and they had even shredded our mattresses. It was under one of those I found my mother.'

'Alive?' asked Odysseus, who was now seated cross-legged on the road to hear Galatea's tale, leaning across his knees towards her.

'Yes, thanks to the merciful gods. I patched up the mattresses and laid her down on them, with a leg of lamb I'd saved from yesterday's sacrifice. But it's the last of our food and we've nothing left to cook in or eat out of. They found the few precious things we had.' She gave an ironic laugh. 'And now I can't even bring back the leftovers from the sacrificial offerings.'

'Why not?' Eurylochus asked.

'Why?' Galatea repeated, looking at him with a raised eyebrow. 'Because only virgins are allowed to serve the goddess. Now I'll have to leave the temple and our little hut and wander the countryside, scratching about for scraps of food.'

'But when the winter comes you'll starve!' said Polites.

'Life is often hard, especially on unmarried women,' Galatea replied, struggling to her feet. 'And I can always turn to prostitution. But I thank you for your help, sirs, and bid you a safe journey to Mycenae. Maybe you'll see those brigands on the way, and if you do you can teach them not to disrespect the sanctity of the gods.'

'It won't be a quick death if I catch the swine,' Eperitus said. His anger had grown as each layer of Galatea's story had been unfolded, and he was silently praying to Athena that she would let him find the men who had committed such a violation.

Polites stood and went to his pony, returning a few moments later with a leather bag in his fist, which he pressed into Galatea's hand.

'I'll not see you forced into prostitution yet. It's only some dried meat and a bit of bread, but it'll keep you for a few days, if you're careful.'

The girl smiled at him, but returned the bag to his huge hand.

'Thank you, friend, but you might as well keep it. My mother and I will starve sooner or later, unless some man takes pity on us. But who'd take a pair of destitute women under their roof? Few men around here can afford to keep themselves, let alone a violated priestess and her mother.'

'Keep Polites's food,' Odysseus commanded, dipping into the pouch that hung from his belt and producing two bangles of pure gold (he always carried items of value for bartering with). They flashed in the morning sunlight and drew all eyes to them. 'A man will accept a dowry for a wife, regardless of her misfortunes. These should satisfy most men.'

He held Galatea's hand and placed the bangles in her open palm. Then he took Polites's leather bag and hung it from her wrist by its strap. The priestess looked at the gifts for a long time.

'Here,' said Eperitus, handing her his own food bag.

Talthybius and Antiphus followed with handfuls of bread and dried meat, which spilled from the girl's hands, forcing her to kneel and pick them up. Arceisius also gave what little he had, and finally even Eurylochus parted with a half-eaten leg of mutton; Eperitus, who had always known Eurylochus to be closely attached to his food, was surprised, but nonetheless gave him a look that forced him to part with some cakes of bread, too, before withdrawing from sight behind his pony.

'We must go,' Odysseus announced, checking the position of the sun then turning to his pony and taking the reins.

Galatea placed her hand on his shoulder. 'But how can I thank you?'

Odysseus smiled at her. 'Just return to your mother and bring some joy back to her heart.'

The men returned to their ponies. Eperitus was last, taking his cloak from the rock and throwing it over his shoulders before mounting. Galatea started to unfasten Polites's cloak, but he told her to keep it as he had a spare. Then he turned his pony and spurred it forward with a jab of his heel to its ribs.

'Wait!' Galatea suddenly cried. 'There *is* something I can do for you. I can place your weapons on Artemis's altar and ask her to bless them. I know I can't serve her in the role of priestess any more, but she'll remember the years I dedicated to her and answer my prayers, I'm certain of it. And maybe she will return your kindness to me by giving special qualities to your weapons. All I need is one item from each of you, just to show my gratitude. I remember a hunter who asked for his bow to be dedicated at the altar, and he later claimed he never missed a shot.'

The men halted and looked at her in silence as they pondered her words. It was difficult for any warrior to part with his arms, but somehow the prospect of having them blessed seemed appealing. Then Antiphus lifted his treasured bow from his back and handed it to her.

'You'll be quick?' he asked.

'Of course,' she replied with a smile, kissing his maimed hand where the fore and middle fingers had been docked.

Talthybius and Eurylochus were next, handing her their swords in their scabbards, which she threw over her shoulder with the bow. Polites placed his oversized helmet on her head and was followed by Arceisius, who handed her his spear.

'You're overloaded as it is,' said Odysseus, passing her his dagger.

'But I'm tall and strong,' Galatea replied.

Finally, she turned to Eperitus.

'And you, sir? What about that dagger in your belt – I can ask Artemis to make the blade sharp enough to cut through bronze.'

Eperitus laid a protective hand on the hilt of his cherished dagger. It had been given to him by Odysseus when they had first met, and he treasured it above all else, with the exception of his grandfather's shield. But Galatea came close to him and placed a long-fingered hand on his arm.

'Please, sir, let me repay your kindness.'

'Give her the dagger, Eperitus,' Talthybius urged him.

Eperitus reluctantly removed the prized gift from his belt and handed it to her. She tucked it into the sash about her waist, alongside Odysseus's blade.

'I'll have to ask you to wait here for me, as men aren't permitted in the temple,' she said, bowing to them as she backed away. 'It's just on the other side of the wood, so I'll be back soon. I'll bring my mother, too, if she has regained her strength yet. She'll want to thank you herself.'

The warriors dismounted again and watched the priestess disappear into the wood, Polites's dark green cloak blending easily with the undergrowth and quickly disguising her even from

Eperitus's sharp eyes. He sat on the rock from which Galatea had told her story and took a swallow from his water skin. Already he could feel the absence of the dagger, the handle of which normally pressed against the hard muscles of his stomach. He watched Odysseus haul a sack of grain down from the back of the baggage pony and order Arceisius to feed the animals, before walking over and sitting on the rock beside him.

'Unless Troy falls quickly,' the king said, 'I'm beginning to worry that we won't have any homes to come back to. The rule of law is already crumbling and we haven't even set sail yet.'

'Ithaca's safe,' Eperitus replied, taking a mouthful of water and handing the skin to his friend. 'Mentor and Halitherses will take good care of the place, and they've enough good soldiers under their charge to fight off any raiders.'

Odysseus wiped the sweat from his brow and squinted up at the sun. 'It may be safe for now, whilst Mentor is seen to be acting under my authority. But the longer I'm away, the weaker my authority will become and the less people will listen to Mentor's commands. Penelope is a good queen and the people love her, but she can't impose her will at the point of a spear. And Telemachus is only a baby.'

'And perhaps all the oracles and prophecies are wrong and we'll be back on Ithaca within a year, glorious conquerors of Troy, our names to be sung forever in the tales of the bards.'

'That would make me happy,' Odysseus nodded, looking at the others sitting under the shade of their ponies with the warm blue of the Saronic Sea behind them. 'And perhaps it would slake your thirst for adventure and renown, at least for a few more years.'

Perhaps, Eperitus thought, and with an unexpected pang of homesickness he found himself thinking of how nice it would be to be back on Ithaca with Odysseus and Penelope, safe from the threat of war and busy playing his own role in the upbringing of Telemachus. It occurred to him then that he was more like Odysseus than he had ever thought, or at least that his friend's love of home had rubbed off on him over their years together. But as pleasing as these thoughts might be, he also realized that happiness of that kind could not be attained until he had first answered his own questions about himself. He had always thought of it as a personal quest for glory, a name that would endure beyond his own death, but in truth it was simply a desire to find out who he really was. Odysseus, he felt sure, had no such need – though Troy might yet reveal parts of his character that he did not know about – and Eperitus envied him his contentment.

He glanced over his shoulder at the woods where Galatea had taken their weapons, but there was no sign yet of her returning through the trees. When he looked back it was to find Eurylochus's small eyes boring into him. He was quick to turn his head away, but the look served to remind him that Eurylochus's animosity had not gone away, and he had not forgotten their argument on Samos.

'Shouldn't she be back by now?' asked Talthybius after a while, craning his neck towards the wood. 'I know prayers can be a complicated business, but all the same . . .'

He trailed off as if reluctant to follow his question to its natural conclusion. Odysseus, however, sucked on his teeth for a moment then rose to his feet.

'I'm starting to believe that a mere girl may have tricked us out of our goods and weapons,' he began. There was a chorus of protest, which he stilled with raised palms. 'It's true: where a band of armed brigands would have failed, it seems a pair of plump white tits with some audacity behind them have succeeded.'

The looks on the faces of the others revealed their growing anxiety about the whereabouts of the priestess, but they were unwilling – or too embarrassed – to accept Odysseus's deduction. Polites, in particular, was adamant that Galatea had been telling the truth, and in the end it was agreed that Antiphus and Eurylochus should be sent to the temple to find her.

They returned quicker than expected, the hooves of their ponies kicking up a cloud of dust as they sped back across the fields from the wood.

'There isn't even a wooden hut, let alone a temple!' Antiphus cried.

'Odysseus is right, she's fooled us all,' Eurylochus added, panting as he pulled his pony to a halt.

'And I've lost the bow I had since I was a boy. If I ever see that girl, I'll . . .'

'Silence, Antiphus,' Odysseus commanded. 'We have a mission to fulfil, so we might as well forget our losses and move on. Mount up, all of you.'

Eperitus pulled himself lightly onto Melite's back, and as he turned her about saw Polites standing by his pony, looking wistfully at the wood.

'That old helmet of yours is long gone by now, Polites,' he said.

'I don't mind,' he replied, his voice deep and slow. 'She can barter it for some food. At least she won't have to offer her body. I couldn't abide the thought of that.'

'But she was . . .' Eperitus began, then thought better of it and spurred Melite forward with a jab of his heel.

*Chapter Twenty-one*

# GOLDEN MYCENAE

Eperitus had not seen Clytaemnestra for ten years, ever since they had made love in the hills overlooking Sparta. She had given herself to him out of her spite for Agamemnon, and though there had never been any love between the young warrior and the Mycenaean queen, Eperitus had always remembered their brief time together with affection. Yet, as they came ever nearer to Mycenae, he began to feel nervous at the thought of meeting her again. He was also concerned about what else he would find within the walls of golden Mycenae. At first he had been keen to find the person who Calchas had said knew the first of the compelling secrets that had the potential to change his life, but as they crept closer to Agamemnon's city a sense of caution grew in him – perhaps inspired by the disquiet he felt concerning their mission – and soured his enthusiasm.

'See those watchtowers?' Talthybius called back over his shoulder, pointing up at the high peaks on either side of the road where two wooden structures kept a silent vigil. 'They mark the northern border of Mycenae. A richer and happier land you'll never see, even if you live to be as old as King Nestor.'

Talthybius's pride seemed justified. It was late afternoon as they crossed the border, but while the sun remained in the sky their eyes were able to feast on a fat and bountiful country. Their tired ponies trudged through valleys covered with crops of wheat, rye and barley, in the midst of which lay numerous stone farmsteads, their white walls gleaming in the sunshine. Children chased each other through the fields, enjoying the relative freedom of life before the coming harvest, when they would be busy gleaning the fields in the wake of the reapers and sheaf-binders. At one point they passed a herd of straight-horned cattle, standing up to their hocks in a gabbling stream and feeding among the rushes that nodded and swayed on either bank. Each fertile valley they passed through was flanked with hillsides where great numbers of sheep and goats seemed to cascade down the scree-covered slopes, searching for patches of vegetation whilst their shepherds looked on, talking peacefully between themselves as they leaned on staffs or spears.

The broad, winding road also took them through numerous villages, where grubby children and their mothers would gather in packs to wave or stare at the party of warriors as they passed. Many offered food or drink at inflated prices, which Odysseus occasionally felt obliged to purchase for his men with the last of his trinkets. He explained to Eperitus that he felt guilty for letting them give the last of their own food to Galatea, when he should have realized they were being tricked.

Soon the road took them closer to the low mountains. A fiery sunset left a brief legacy of purple skies, promising another warm day to follow, but as Talthybius assured them his home city was close they gave no thought to stopping for the night. For some time now the road had been paved – another sign of the wealth of Mycenae – and the hooves of their ponies sounded sharp and hollow in the evening air as the stars opened out above them. Occasionally they crossed bridges over deep ravines, where far below, lost in the twilight, they could hear mountain streams that had been dried to a trickle by the summer sun. Eventually they saw the lights of a city emerge from the darkness to the south-east. They had reached Mycenae.

The road angled down a little towards the plain, where it intersected another that ran from east to west. At the crossroads, they turned left and headed eastward up the slope towards the city. As the moon sailed out above the black hills, its light painted the wide circuit of the walls and the high-sided buildings beyond them a ghostly white. Nestled on the rocky hill at the centre of the city was the royal palace, where dozens of lights gleamed from its many windows and lines of blue-grey smoke trailed up from vents in its rooftops. Behind the city were two cone-shaped peaks, one to the north-west and another to the south-east. The northern-most peak supported another watchtower, the top of which was framed by the underbelly of the moon. The armour of its occupants glinted in the silvery light as they stared out over the plain. Beside the watchtower was a mound of stacked wood, ready to act as a beacon in times of need.

Not that Agamemnon's city would ever find itself in desperate need of help. As their ponies approached the citadel, plodding slowly between the spread of shanties that surrounded it, Eperitus looked up in awe at the colossal walls ahead of them. Even though Troy's imposing defences were built by Poseidon and Apollo, with well-fitted stone and a much wider circuit than Mycenae's, the walls here surpassed them for brute strength and invulnerability. The blocks were crude but massive – surely beyond the capacity of men alone to lift and fit into place – and in places they were easily as tall as three or four men. Even the handful of bronze-clad troops that peered down at them from the ramparts would be able to hold the city against a besieging army for a very long time; Heracles and Achilles together could not have sacked such a place.

Soon they were under the shadow of the city wall, where the high battlements eclipsed the moon and left them in darkness. Despite this, Eperitus's sharp eyes noted a gateway up ahead, lost in the deeper gloom between the city wall on the left and another, shorter rampart to the right. The overlapping wall at first seemed pointless to Eperitus. Then, as it loomed up beside him and he instinctively imagined what it would be like to be in a press of attackers storming the gate, he realized that defenders on the shorter wall would be able to fire or throw missiles at him from his unshielded right side. Clever, he thought, and deadly.

Talthybius dismounted and signalled for the Ithacans to do the same. They led their ponies up to the tall oak doors of the gateway to the city and stopped. The gates were over twice the height of a man and flanked by two stone pillars of immense size, which had been built into the walls for added strength. Resting above them was a stone lintel, on top of which was the magnificent relief Eperitus had seen in his dream, depicting a pair of lions standing either side of a short column. Their forepaws were planted firmly on its low plinth and their snarling faces looked out over the approach to the gate, a fearsome and majestic reminder that Mycenae was the greatest city in Greece, and its ruler, Agamemnon, was the greatest king. Though the lions were only faintly visible in the darkness, Eperitus could see the dull gleam of gold in their eyes, a final reminder of the wealth of the city they protected.

Talthybius took his herald's staff and beat it three times against the doors. The wood was so thick, the sound of each knock boomed as if it came from the ground beneath their feet.

'Who's on the door tonight?' he called. 'Is it you, Ochesios? Open up quickly and let us in.'

A voice called down to them from the ramparts above. 'Talthybius? What are you doing back here? Is something wrong?'

'Open this damned door, Ochesios, will you? I'm tired, hungry and saddle sore from riding this beast for four days.'

There was a brief delay and then the doors swung slowly inwards, revealing the moonlit innards of the city beyond. They walked through quickly, the sounds of the ponies' hooves echoing beneath the solid walls, and soon stood on a raised roadway overlooking the lowest level of the city. A group of guards nodded to Talthybius, but eyed his companions with caution. To the left was another high wall, perhaps a form of inner defence, and ahead of them a ramp climbed up to the next level. Of more immediate interest to the Ithacans, though, was the large circular arena slightly to their right, where a collection of upright slabs cast long shadows across the floor. It was cordoned off by an outer circuit of slabs, each standing to the height of a man's chest, and was entered through a single gate. Talthybius smiled as he saw his companions' undisguised interest.

'The royal burial ground,' he explained. 'Atreus is entombed there with his queen, Aerope. And one day King Agamemnon will be interred there, too, alongside his forebears. If we had arrived before sunset it would've been proper to make a sacrifice here before going up to the palace, but perhaps we can show our respects tomorrow.'

Beyond the arena was a collection of well-built houses that filled the remainder of the lower level. They reminded Eperitus of the buildings that skirted the walls of Pergamos in Troy, which housed the numerous officials who served Priam's household. Their Mycenaean counterparts were less elaborate in their architecture, but that was not a reflection of Troy's superior wealth – it merely highlighted the different mindsets of the two opposing cultures. Though he had been impressed by the grandeur of Troy, Eperitus felt much more at home with the functional, honest architecture of Mycenae.

After his rustic guests had spent long enough gazing down at the royal cemetery, Talthybius led them up the ramp to the next level of the city. Here they could see the palace buildings looming ahead of them, their layered walls faced with silver by the moonlight. These were built on the third and highest level of the city and before long Talthybius had led them around to the left and up some steps to a double portico. In the narrow courtyard beyond they found more guards, chatting quietly among themselves as they drank wine and played dice on the flagstones. They rose at the sound of the ponies' hooves and the clank of bronze armour, and immediately levelled their spear-points at the approach of the newcomers.

'Talthybius,' said one of the guards, the surprise evident in his voice. 'The watchtowers sent word we would have visitors before long, but we weren't expecting you. Shouldn't you be in Troy by now?'

'I wish we were, Perithous,' Talthybius replied. 'But we're storm-bound at Aulis.'

'In the height of summer?' Perithous exclaimed. 'It can only be the will of the gods. But if Helen truly is the daughter of Zeus, he won't allow the fleet to be held up for too long. The good news for you is that the queen made preparations for your arrival as soon as she heard a group of warriors were approaching – a hot bath for every man, followed by a feast in the great hall. Who shall I tell her to expect?'

'King Odysseus of Ithaca, son of Laertes,' Odysseus answered, 'with five of his men.'

'Yes, my lord.'

Perithous, though he appeared unimpressed by the name or rank of the stocky warrior before him, gave a low bow before departing through a tall and richly decorated doorway. Shortly afterwards a dozen slaves appeared and took the ponies away to be fed and rested. As he stripped the last of his belongings from Melite's back, Eperitus looked out across the Argive plain stretching away towards the Gulf of Argos. The moonlight revealed a network of paved roads spreading out across the hilly plateau for as far as his sharp eyes could see. Farmsteads and villages were strung along the roads like beads on a webbed necklace; the hardworking populace would be up long before dawn, so not a single light could be seen burning anywhere on the landscape of silver and blue.

As soon as the tired travellers had gathered their effects, Talthybius led them into the palace. They entered a short, echoing corridor that opened onto a square courtyard, brightly lit by the moon now soaring in the sable skies above. Opposite was the pillared threshold of the great hall, overshadowed by the conical hump of one of the peaks flanking the city. In contrast to Priam's great home, the seat of Agamemnon's power appeared modest and almost homely to Eperitus. It had the disadvantage of being built on a steep hill and hence the architect had been forced to constrain his designs, but even the decorative reliefs on the walls – of

rosettes or spirals set between fanned palm leaves – were simple
and constrained in comparison with Troy. Four warriors in expensive armour stood guard at the entrance to the throne room, eyeing
the newcomers with curiosity and suspicion.

An elderly slave emerged from a doorway to their right. He
stretched out his arm, indicating that they should enter. From the
open door a wisp of steam curled out and the smell of hot water
and perfumed oil greeted their nostrils.

'After you,' said Talthybius, bowing to Odysseus.

'Mycenaean manners are justifiably famous,' the king replied
with a smile, before leading the way to the waiting baths. He was
already stripping the heavy armour from his shoulders as he disappeared through the door.

§

After being bathed and rubbed down with oil by slaves, the men
put on the fresh clothes that had been laid out for them and
stepped out into the courtyard. The four guards stood aside at
Talthybius's command, allowing the warriors to pass between the
twin pillars of the threshold and into the antechamber beyond.
Here they found a single soldier, who took a torch from the wall
behind him and – after satisfying himself that they were unarmed
– opened the twin doors and allowed the men through.

They entered a square, dimly lit room with high ceilings and a
wide, circular hearth at its centre. The air was stiflingly warm and
tasted of roast meat, while the red light of the fire pulsated against
the four wooden pillars and the heavily muralled walls. Eperitus
looked about himself and felt disappointed. This room was the
beating heart of the most powerful state in Greece, and yet it was
a pale shadow of the great halls of Troy and Sparta, and lacked
even the fresh vitality of Odysseus's throne room on Ithaca. The
once-colourful murals on the walls of the modest chamber were
fading, and in places had begun to peel away. A scene depicting
Perseus lopping off the snake-covered head of Medusa was so faint
and stained by smoke that it was difficult to see in the red light

from the fire. Perhaps there was little the greatest king in Greece could do to increase the dimensions of the hall, but to restore the murals would have been an easy thing for a wealthy ruler.

Unless that ruler was waiting to replace the murals altogether, Eperitus thought – maybe with depictions of his own glorious conquest of Troy? Eperitus smiled to himself and turned his eyes to the tables of food laid out around the hearth. The smell of the freshly roasted meat filled his nostrils, making his stomach rumble and his mouth salivate. To his left he could see a slave in the shadows, washing the blood of a recently sacrificed animal from a wooden altar. The altar stood before an alcove containing a glazed terracotta image of a goddess – Hera, the wife of Zeus, judging by the pomegranate in the palm of her hand. But the pomegranate was also associated with Persephone, the dark goddess of the underworld.

'Be seated, my lords,' said a voice.

The newcomers turned as one towards a large granite throne positioned against the right-hand wall of the great hall. A woman stood beside it, scrutinizing them carefully as she leaned with her elbow on the back of the chair. She had dark red hair that was tied back behind her neck, with a fringe of ringlets and a tumbling curl before each of her protruding ears. She had her fair share of the beauty that her sister, Helen, possessed in such abundance, but Helen's face was fair and pleasant, whereas hers was dark and hardened with bitter experience. As if to emphasize this, she wore a black chiton over her tall, bony figure, against which the pale skin of her face and arms stood out starkly.

'Please,' Clytaemnestra said, stepping into the glow of the fire and indicating the seven chairs that circled the hearth, 'sit and eat. I may only be ruling in my husband's stead, but I won't have it said that I don't treat my guests according to the customs of *xenia*.'

Odysseus and Talthybius sat, followed by the others. Eperitus was last, eyeing Clytaemnestra as he walked around the hearth to the only remaining chair. She did not return his gaze, but sat on a high-backed wooden chair opposite Odysseus.

'*Xenia* exists to protect travellers and allow alliances between men of power,' Odysseus said, taking a knife from the table beside him and carving a slice of mutton. He folded it into a piece of bread but did not eat. 'What use is it to a woman?'

'I'm not a woman, Odysseus. I am a queen. And while Agamemnon fights his wars abroad and his son Orestes is still only a boy, Mycenae is under my rule. Now, you and your comrades will have travelled far and must be hungry; I have provided food and wine; please, satisfy yourselves and then we can talk.'

She leaned across the arm of her chair and poured herself a cup of wine. The others, who were famished, immediately began to help themselves to the modest meal. Eperitus's appetite, however, had diminished and he satisfied himself with a barley cake and a swallow of the cool wine. Had Clytaemnestra forgotten him, he wondered? They had been lovers, and though some treated physical intimacy lightly, he could not believe she had allowed the evening they had spent together to die in her mind. And yet she ate and drank and smiled at the other men as if he were not there.

'It's been a long time, Clytaemnestra,' Odysseus said, after washing down a mouthful of food.

'Ten years,' Clytaemnestra replied. 'In which time I hear you've become the king of Ithaca, and fathered a son.'

'Telemachus,' Odysseus nodded proudly. 'A fine lad, but born at the wrong time. I only hope the war will be short so I can go home and watch him grow up.'

'It's a cruel fate that separates a parent and a child. They uphold our memory and make sure we are not forgotten – our only real hope of immortality.'

'A warrior's memory is upheld by his spear,' Eperitus contested, tired of being ignored. 'A child may pass his name on from generation to generation, until he becomes nothing more than another name in a list of names learned by rote. But if his achievements in battle are great enough, his name will be remembered forever, just like Heracles, or Perseus on that wall up there.'

Clytaemnestra looked into her krater of wine. 'Who am I to deny that a warrior can make his name on the battlefield or in the pile of bodies he leaves behind him? But corpses are cold and lifeless, and the stories they tell are full of blood and horror. A child, Eperitus, is warm and loving, and will carry on a man's legacy through the blood that is in their veins, not the blood that is spilled in the dirt of a distant country.'

Their eyes met at last, and instead of the confidence she had demonstrated before Odysseus, or the strength and power that befitted a queen of Mycenae, he saw only her weakness and longing. He was suddenly aware of her frail beauty and wanted to hold her slender body again, as he had done by the fire in the Taygetus Mountains so long ago. Then her staring eyes faltered and blinked, and she turned back to face Odysseus.

'I'm unfamiliar with practising the custom of *xenia*, King Odysseus, but once a guest's needs are met is it not time for the host to ask the purpose of his visit? I already know the fleet is wind-bound at Aulis, but perhaps you will tell me why you have left your duties to visit a lonely queen, four days' ride away by pony. Have you come all this way, only to feast your eyes on golden Mycenae?'

'No, though I'm glad to have seen this famous city,' the king responded. 'But I have not left my duties to come here, as you suggest; rather, I am carrying out the command your husband and his brother gave me, to come to speak with you in person about a matter of great importance and honour.'

Clytaemnestra shifted uncomfortably in her chair.

'And what does the great Agamemnon want you to say that he cannot say himself?'

'The king is busy marshalling the fleet and preparing for the attack.'

'Nonsense, Odysseus. The king knows the storm will not abate until the gods permit it. He could have come himself.'

'It isn't for me to know the mind of Agamemnon,' Odysseus countered, unfazed by the queen's shrewd questioning. 'But here I am, and the news I bring should warm a mother's heart. Especially one who talks with such pride of the immortality her children will bring her.'

'That all depends on what a warrior believes will warm a mother's heart, does it not? Perhaps my husband intends to give command of half the fleet to eight-year-old Orestes, and has asked you to take him back with you to Aulis?'

Odysseus smiled and shook his head.

'Shame,' Clytaemnestra sighed. 'The boy despises living among women, and me most especially. He needs a father's discipline. So what is it, Odysseus? I know Agamemnon has always valued your powers of persuasion and trickery, so whatever he's sent you for must be something I won't be willing to give easily.'

'We've come for Iphigenia,' Talthybius interposed, staring disdainfully at Clytaemnestra, who he knew did everything in her power to make his master's life insufferable. 'She's to be married to Achilles at Aulis, before the fleet sails for Troy.'

The queen's eyes narrowed quizzically and she turned to Eperitus.

'Is this true, Eperitus? At least I know I can trust you.'

Eperitus nodded.

'But she's *nine*,' Clytaemnestra protested through gritted teeth, turning her dark eyes back to Odysseus. 'And Achilles is already married with a child of his own.'

The king shrugged sympathetically.

'Achilles and Deidameia were never married in the official sense, before a priest and with all the appropriate sacrifices. And as for Iphigenia's age, what can I say? It'll be a political marriage, of course, so that Agamemnon can be assured of Achilles's support for the campaign against Troy. Nothing else matters as far as your husband is concerned. But don't be too hasty to condemn it,' Odysseus added, holding up his large hands and smiling amicably at the queen. 'I know it doesn't sound like the sort of arrangement a loving mother would want for her daughter, but if you see it the way I do then it will be nothing more than a minor inconvenience.'

'That depends on what you regard as a minor inconvenience?' Clytaemnestra said, eyeing Odysseus with suspicion.

'Most importantly, Achilles may be prepared to marry Iphigenia to show political goodwill to Agamemnon, but he won't have any interest in consummating his marriage to a nine-year-old. The word in the camp is that he and Patroclus share a bed, but I'm certain his sexual tastes don't extend to little girls. Then, after the wedding ceremony is over the fleet will sail to Troy and Iphigenia will return home to Mycenae, married but with her child's innocence intact. And while she's safe with you, Achilles will meet his doom before the walls of Troy – his own mother has predicted that much – so Iphigenia will become a widow and everyone will be happy.'

'Except Achilles, of course,' Clytaemnestra replied, wryly. 'The truth is, Odysseus, I don't trust Agamemnon where my daughter is concerned – he has never paid her any mind before and it seems strange that he should do so now. Your argument has its merits, though, and if there is nothing beneath what you say then I will give urgent attention to my husband's request. But it's late and we're all tired; I need to think this over and consult the gods. Until then, you and your men are welcome to enjoy Mycenae and all its pleasures.'

As she spoke her eyes touched on Eperitus. Odysseus noticed the glance.

'How soon will you let us know your decision, Clytaemnestra?' he asked firmly. 'You know Agamemnon doesn't like to be kept waiting.'

'Before the week is out,' she promised, rising from her chair. 'And you're to say nothing to Iphigenia, or anybody else, about this marriage until I say so. Goodnight, my lords.'

The queen turned and crossed the room to a side entrance, her black chiton blending with the shadows as she moved.

## Chapter Twenty-two

# HELEN OF TROY

A dozen guards stood by the Scaean Gate and a dozen more on the battlements above, their armour gleaming like silver in the moonlight. Helen gripped the chariot's handrail and put an arm around Pleisthenes's shoulders as Paris spurred the black horses on towards the city, eager to see his home again after so long. Beside them Apheidas and Aeneas urged their mounts to keep up with the prince.

'They've doubled the guard,' Apheidas shouted as the wind tore at his hair and threw his cloak out behind him.

Paris laughed and lashed his whip harder across the backs of the horses. 'It's a guard of honour for my return. They must have got news that we were on our way.'

'Then why are they forming a defensive line?' Aeneas yelled from the opposite side of the chariot. 'Slow down, Paris. There are archers on the walls and if they don't recognize us they'll fire.'

Helen looked in alarm at the line of men by the gates, their tall, rectangular shields planted firmly in the soil and their long spears levelled at the chests of the approaching horses. A dozen more soldiers were rushing out from the gates and making a second line behind them.

'Paris,' she hissed, placing her hand on his arm. 'Slow down, my love. You'll be home soon enough.'

Paris looked at the concern in her eyes and nodded. 'Whoaaa!'

he yelled, pulling back the ox-hide reins. 'Whoaaa, there. Slow down, girls. Slow down.'

The gold-covered chariot slowed to a trundle and the two riders on either side reined in their mounts to fall in beside it. Helen and Pleisthenes relaxed their grip on the handrail and looked at the wall of soldiers, whose spears were still levelled at them. The Spartan queen – or former queen, as she now regarded herself – looked in awe at the high ramparts with the spike-filled ditch below and the imposing guard towers that overlooked the plain all around. Paris had not exaggerated when he had said they would be safe inside his father's city. Even if Menelaus should be supported by his brother and come after her with the combined armies of Sparta and Mycenae, they would never prise her out of Troy. For the first time in weeks, she began to feel safe in her new life. Soon, she and Paris would be married and would live in the house he had promised to build for them.

'Is *this* our new home?' asked Pleisthenes, his tired eyes wide as he looked at the splendid battlements and the rows of exotically armed warriors. The limestone walls shone white and smoke trails rose from the city into the star-littered sky. 'Are we really going to live *here*?'

'Yes, son,' Paris answered, scruffing his hair with his large hand. 'This is Troy, city of the gods, and from now on we must all speak the language of the Trojans. You and your mother have been good pupils, but now's the time to test your learning. You'll find very few people who speak Greek here.'

'Who's that?' called a voice from the rank of soldiers. 'Name yourself and your purpose.'

'Don't you know me yet, Deiphobus?' Paris replied. 'After all, we share the same father and mother.'

'Paris? By the gods of Mount Ida, it *is* you!'

A short youth with long black hair left the line of soldiers he had been commanding and ran towards the chariot, holding his hands towards the team of horses.

'You've been gone an age,' he said, peering up at Paris from between the heads of the black mares, as if to be sure it really was his older brother. 'There've been all sorts of rumours about you and . . .'

At that moment, Deiphobus's eyes fell upon Helen and his words faltered.

'This is Helen, formerly of Sparta, now of Troy,' Paris announced. 'She's to be my wife.'

Helen smiled at the lad, pleased her beauty was as powerful a weapon against Trojan men as it had been against Greeks. She sensed she would need it in the coming days, if the people of Paris's city were to welcome her.

'Then the stories are true,' Deiphobus said, as if to himself. 'Welcome to Troy, my lady. I'm pleased we are to become brother and sister; to be able to look at such beauty every day is more than any man could hope for.'

'Thank you, Deiphobus. If all Trojans welcome me thus, I will find happiness here,' Helen replied haltingly, the harsh-sounding words strange but satisfying as she heard herself speak them. She had never known any language other than Greek and it excited her to pluck the correct Trojan words from her memory and arrange them in her mind before conveying them to her lips. In time, she expected that both she and Pleisthenes would think and speak fluently in their new language.

Deiphobus bowed low before her, revealing the back of his sun-tanned neck. This amused Helen, who was not used to seeing such gestures of subordination from the obstinate Greeks.

'See, Helen,' said Apheidas, 'the gates of Troy have already fallen to you. Now we must see what waits inside.'

He trotted towards the line of spearmen and ordered them to one side; each man's eyes were upon the woman in Paris's chariot as it rolled past. Helen, who was used to the stares of men, ignored the attention and looked through the approaching gateway at the upward-sloping street and its closely packed houses. The gateway walls echoed as they passed between them and out into the cool night air again.

So this was Troy, she thought to herself. Large, impressive and asleep. The streets that branched off the main route were all empty and few lights burned in the windows. Part of her wished they had arrived in the daylight, when the whole city would be able to rejoice at Paris's return and marvel at the beauty of the woman he had brought back with him. Commoners and slaves were easily won over by her looks, she had always found, and if she had been able to gain the approval of the rabble Priam may have felt unable to rebuff his son's choice of wife. That had become her greatest fear, to be rejected and forced to return to Sparta. Paris had assured her no such thing could happen, and if it did he would sooner turn his back on Troy forever and live with her on an obscure island, far beyond the reach of Menelaus. But Helen knew the ways of politics better than he did: Menelaus may have already visited Troy and persuaded, bribed or cajoled Priam into returning his wife to him. Something in Deiphobus's words at the gate, along with the strong guard there, made her suspect that her arrival would come as no surprise to the old king.

And yet she was glad they had not hurried to Troy. Instead of sailing into the large bay before the city, they had landed on the beach opposite Tenedos, intending to make their way overland so that Helen could get a taste of the rich and beautiful country she hoped would become her home. After disembarking the chariot and finding a team of horses, Paris ordered the crew to wait a day before sailing home – so that news of their arrival would not precede them – before setting off at a leisurely pace with Apheidas and Aeneas for company. Under cloudless skies they drove between wide fields of corn and barley, the chariot bumping and jogging over the pitted cart tracks. Little Pleisthenes constantly called his mother's attention to each new sight he saw, from the herds of wild horses that roamed the plains to the unfamiliar flowers that dotted the roadsides. After a while they reached a town where the market square was too crowded for them to pass through. Dismounting, they had forged their way through crowds of spectators to a cleared area where hundreds of youths were dancing together to the music of a lyre. The girls had on their finest dresses with garlands woven into their hair, and the young men wore close-fitting tunics and had rubbed oil into their brown skin. They stepped lightly around each other, the maidens resting their hands on their partners' wrists as they circled smoothly and kept time with the music. The soft shuffle of their dancing feet was too much for Helen, and taking Paris's hand she joined the lines of simple peasants and felt again the wonder of being young. And as she danced the crowds looked on in awe, believing a goddess had graced them with her presence. But her smile and her flowing black hair also filled them with joy as she danced late into the evening, Paris always at her side, until Apheidas had reminded them of the need to press on.

Another wall rose in front of them as they climbed the road through the city, pierced by another gateway. Beside it, a pale tower loomed upwards into the night sky, crowned by the white moon. They passed the strange idols that stood in a line at its base and continued through the gate to Pergamos, Apheidas and Aeneas lowering their heads to clear the low archway as the hooves of their mounts echoed around them. On the other side Helen stared in wonder at the richly decorated buildings, which cried aloud the wealth and self-importance of the city. It all looked so alien and exotic, making her feel both afraid and excited at the same time. More than ever she realized there could be no return to her old life now; she had cut all but one of her anchor stones, and only Pleisthenes was left to remind her of the woman she had once been. Paris, noticing her wide eyes, placed his hand on her wrist and smiled at her.

'Won't be long now. You'll like the old man, and I *know* he'll like you. He'll be angry at first, of course, but that'll be at me, not you. He'll curse me for failing to bring his sister back, and then when he learns I've brought a Greek queen with me he'll probably threaten to cut my head off and send it to Menelaus. But he'll forgive me sooner or later, if only for the sake of your beauty. Which reminds me, you should lower your veil.'

Helen had always hated veils and thought them demeaning. They also took away her greatest weapon. But this was a foreign land and she trusted Paris's judgement, so she unhooked the thin material from her hair and pulled it over her face, leaving only a faint impression of her perfect features visible through the gauze.

They reached the ramp to the final level of the city, where the marble columns of Priam's palace could be seen shining in the moonlight. Apheidas had ridden ahead and informed the guards of Paris's approach, so they were unhindered as the prince spurred his horses up the slope to the terrace above. Here the chariot slowed to a halt and Paris threw the reins to Aeneas before jumping down.

Helen looked at the ornately decorated walls and the many alcoves with their painted figurines of different gods, but her appreciation was cut short by voices coming from the threshold of the palace. She turned to see an old man crossing the terrace towards them. He was tall with long black hair and a handsome, but ageing, face; his pace was unhurried, but his long legs brought him towards them at speed, his purple gown flowing behind him. Hurrying at his side was an equally old woman, her short, plump body covered by a thin dress of what might have been a light green hue, though Helen found it impossible to tell the colour in the achromatic moonlight. She was wagging her finger at the old man and speaking with a fluidity that Helen's understanding could not follow, only stopping as they reached the chariot.

'Father,' Paris said, stepping forward and embracing the old man. 'How did you know I was here?'

'I'm the king,' Priam answered, placing his hands on his son's shoulders and staring into his eyes. 'Even the birds of the sky are required to tell me what is going on in my realm. But if you must know, King Tenes informed me over a week ago that you were under his roof, and this morning he sent another message to let me know you had landed on the bay opposite his island and were travelling overland by chariot.'

Paris leaned across and kissed his mother on both cheeks, which were wet with tears at the sight of her son.

'We've missed you, my dear,' she smiled. 'Or *I* have missed you, at least. Your father has done nothing but curse your name, ever since he heard you'd abandoned the mission he sent you on and brought back a foreigner.'

Paris turned to his father. 'Then Tenes told you about Helen also?'

'I heard long before he informed me,' Priam answered, looking up at the tall woman standing aloof and motionless in the golden chariot. 'Tenes only confirmed what I had already been told, though previously I had struggled to believe the news that had been brought to me.'

'Brought by whom, my lord?' asked Apheidas, bowing low before the king. Both he and Aeneas had handed their horses to slaves and now stood at Paris's shoulder.

'Ah, Apheidas. It is a comfort to have you back at Troy. Your prowess in battle may be called upon before long. But in answer to your question, a Greek embassy arrived several weeks back claiming you, Paris, had taken the queen of Sparta against her will.'

'That's a lie!'

'*Silence!*' Priam shouted, clenching his fists by his side. A moment later he was calm again. 'This is not a debating chamber, Paris, and you will not interrupt me until I have finished. The king of Sparta himself sat in my hall, along with Odysseus of Ithaca and Palamedes the Nauplian, threatening war if this woman' – Priam nodded towards Helen – 'was not returned immediately. Unfortunately for Menelaus, you had not yet returned and I knew nothing of your antics in Greece; as their tone grew more bullying I'm afraid I lost my patience with them and had them returned to their ship. Since then, however, my blood has cooled and I have had time to think. Though a Greek, King Odysseus spoke wisely and reminded us that it is an offence against the gods to steal a man's wife. So the matter now lies with you, my child.'

The king looked at Helen and offered her his hand. She took it and stepped down from the chariot.

'I do not know you, Helen, queen of Sparta, and my heart wishes you had never come to Troy. But here you are, and now our fate rests in your hands. It is in my power to send you back to your husband and prevent this war. If I do I may break my son's heart, but I will save many lives, both Trojan and Greek. But I will ask you one question, and if your answer satisfies my sense of honour and justice, then you can remain here and the walls of Troy – and the blood of her sons – will have to bear the consequences. Tell me, did Paris take you from Sparta by force, or did you come of your own free will?'

Paris had said he would tell her to remove the veil when the time was right. But Helen did not need to be told that the time had come, and lifting the veil from her face she looked Priam in the eye.

'Sir, I came here by choice. I was forced to leave three children behind in Sparta, because their father had taken them with him to Crete. But I was prepared to sacrifice them because of my love for your son.'

Priam stared at the incomparable face and his heart melted.

'That is the answer I was dreading, daughter. But now that I look on you, I know that I could never have sent you back to Menelaus, whatever your reply had been.' He leaned forward and embraced her with warmth and respect for her beauty. 'Now you must go with my wife, Hecabe. She will show you to your quarters. *You* are to come with me, Paris. It may be late, but Hector and I want to discuss the consequences of what you have done. You too, Apheidas.'

'And me, my lord?' asked Aeneas, as Priam turned with Paris and Apheidas at his shoulders.

'No, not you,' Priam answered without looking back.

Helen saw the young man scowl at the departing king, then turn and kick a stone halfway across the terrace.

'Will you bring Pleisthenes, Aeneas?' Helen asked, as Hecabe walked over and hooked an arm through her elbow. 'Please?'

Aeneas gave a surly nod and lifted the sleeping child from the gleaming chariot, before following the two women as they crossed the courtyard at a diagonal to the king.

'Poor lad,' said Hecabe without looking at Aeneas. 'Priam treats him like one of the dogs that lick up the scraps from beneath his table.'

'But isn't he the son of a king?'

'Yes: his father is Anchises, king of the Dardanians. Aeneas is kept here to ensure Anchises's loyalty, though the lad still has the freedom to come and go as he pleases.'

'Then why is he treated so badly?'

'Most think it's because Priam disdains any royalty that is not purely Trojan,' Hecabe said. 'But I know it has nothing to do with that. The old man's simply jealous because Aeneas's father slept with Aphrodite. Priam has always prided himself on the number and beauty of his lovers, you see, but he's never had the pleasure of the goddess.'

Helen was shocked at Hecabe's indifference on the matter.

'Doesn't it bother you?' she asked. 'That your husband has had so many lovers, I mean.'

'Not at all,' the old woman responded, pushing open a side door to the palace. 'He's the king, and the king does as he pleases. The more wives he has, the more sons there are – fifty at the last count – and the more sons there are, the stronger his base of power. He also uses marriage to secure ties beyond the walls of Troy.'

They entered a torch-lit corridor with a flight of stone steps to one side. Two women were sitting on a wooden bench and rose to their feet as Hecabe and Helen appeared, with Aeneas behind them.

'Take Leothoë here,' Hecabe continued, indicating the shorter of the two women. 'She is the daughter of King Altes of the

Leleges. Her father married her to Priam to seal an alliance between our two states. Now, if the Greeks are foolish enough to come after you, King Altes will be obliged to bring his army to our aid.'

Leothoë stepped forward and bowed. She was no older than Helen and had a face and body that would be the envy of most women.

'Welcome, Helen,' she said, her voice light and leaving almost no impression. 'I'm sorry you've been brought so far from your home. It must be difficult for you.'

'I came freely,' Helen replied.

'Such beauty,' said the other woman, reaching out and touching Helen's cheek as if to assure herself she was real. 'You must have the blood of a god in your veins. I am Andromache, daughter of King Eëtion of the Cilicians. My brother is a friend of Hector and brought me here to see the marvels of Troy.'

'Then this is your first time here, too?' Helen asked, looking at the tall, black-haired woman before her. Her face was beautiful and intelligent, though tinged with sadness.

'Yes. My home is Thebe, beneath the wooded slopes of Mount Placus. It's a lovely city, but very plain compared with Troy.'

'I've asked Leothoë and Andromache to help you get used to the palace,' Hecabe said. 'They'll show you to your rooms and make you feel at home. They'll also teach you our customs and help you learn our language, although Paris already seems to have taught you much.'

Helen took Pleisthenes from Aeneas's arms and wished him and Hecabe a goodnight, before following Leothoë and Andromache up the steps.

'Thank you both,' she said. 'I hope we can be good friends.'

'I hope so too,' said Andromache. 'Though I fear that great suffering will follow in your wake, for all Trojan women.'

## Chapter Twenty-three

# IPHIGENIA

'Do you think she'll agree to the wedding?' Eperitus asked.

He stood in the middle of the courtyard, looking up at the humped shape of the mountain behind the great hall. The early morning sun was still hidden behind its black bulk, but the sky above glowed like heated bronze. A few purple clouds scudded through the fiery skies, their bellies transformed to gold by the hidden dawn.

'I think I've convinced her there's nothing to be lost by allowing the marriage,' Odysseus replied, biting into the barley cake he had brought with him from the breakfast table. 'The problem is whether she believes that's the real reason why Agamemnon wants his daughter to go to Aulis.'

'But if the marriage is just an excuse, do you think Clytaemnestra knows what Agamemnon *really* wants Iphigenia for?'

'Shhh,' Odysseus said, nodding towards the sentries at the threshold of the great hall and giving his friend a wink. 'Come with me.'

He walked to the low, rectangular building that blocked off the southern edge of the courtyard, between the great hall and the guest house in which they had slept. Inside was a stone staircase that led them down to a garden of broad lawns, edged with fruit trees and flowering bushes. At its centre was a circular pond filled with white and yellow lilies and with a long, semicircular wooden bench on its southern side. A high wall enclosed the garden, and the only entrance from the city was an arched gateway in its western corner.

'I don't think Clytaemnestra knows what Agamemnon really wants with Iphigenia, any more than we do,' Odysseus continued. 'But if she wants to know, she has powers that can tell her. You remember all those rumours about her being a witch?'

'I remember them,' Eperitus replied, avoiding Odysseus's eye.

'Well, it wouldn't surprise me if she's . . .'

'Are you Eperitus?' asked a voice behind them.

They turned to see a girl with black hair and a stern, demanding look on her pretty face. She was staring at Odysseus and had her arms crossed tightly over her chest.

'You mean Eperitus the Great, Sacker of Cities and Slayer of Thousands?' Odysseus smiled, crouching down to face the youngster.

The girl narrowed her eyes and pursed her lips disapprovingly. 'I mean Eperitus of Alybas. And if that's you, sir, and you've really sacked cities and slain thousands, then I would like you to tell me about it.'

Odysseus shrugged his shoulders apologetically.

'Sorry, little princess. I am only Odysseus, the king of lowly Ithaca.'

'I've heard of you,' the girl nodded. 'But it's Eperitus I'm looking for.'

Odysseus flicked his eyes towards his companion and took a step back.

'I'm Eperitus. What do you want, child?'

Eperitus, who had always found young children irrelevant and irritating, looked down at the girl, and as their eyes met he felt a curious sense of recognition.

'I wanted to see what you looked like, sir,' she replied. 'My mother has told me lots of things about you. She says you are a strong warrior with a stout heart, and that you and she were friends long ago.'

'You're Iphigenia,' Eperitus said. The girl had Clytaemnestra's tall, thin frame and large ears, though there was also a shadow of Agamemnon in her authoritative mannerisms. But there was something else familiar about her, too, something elusive that he could not define.

'You don't look as I had imagined,' Iphigenia said, after pausing to scrutinize the man before her. 'But now I look at you, I think you are *better* than I imagined.'

'Forgive my daughter, my lords,' said Clytaemnestra, emerging from the doorway at the bottom of the staircase and striding confidently towards them. She had an elegant femininity as she crossed the lawns barefoot, dressed in a yellow gown that gleamed with the early morning light. 'She's naturally drawn to warriors. She's convinced she'll be one herself, one day.'

'I will,' Iphigenia protested, frowning at her mother's funmaking. 'Just like Eperitus. I want to roam Greece doing good – killing outlaws and slaying serpents and rescuing cities from tyrants.'

She made slashing motions with an imaginary sword as she spoke, while Odysseus laughed aloud and slapped Eperitus on the back.

'I had no idea you were so talented, old friend. Or so famous.'

Eperitus looked questioningly at Clytaemnestra, who replied with a sheepish smile.

'I apologize for Jenny's imagination. I've told her all about the great men at Sparta, but she seems to have a special liking for you, my lord. She also enjoys hearing about *your* exploits, of course, Odysseus.'

'Oh, yes – she tells me she's heard of me.'

'Naturally,' Iphigenia nodded, though her eyes did not leave Eperitus for a moment. 'Eperitus saved your life after you were caught in the women's quarters at Sparta.'

Odysseus arched his eyebrows. 'Well, there was more to it than just that. You see, what actually happened was . . .'

'Come now, Odysseus,' Clytaemnestra interrupted. 'You and I have more serious matters to discuss. I've been thinking about your proposal of last night, and perhaps you could answer a few questions to help my decision.'

'Certainly, if I can,' Odysseus replied.

Clytaemnestra hooked her arm through his elbow and steered his bulky, triangular form back towards the stairs. 'Perhaps you will keep Jenny entertained for me, Eperitus?' she said over her shoulder.

'Actually I was intending to go . . .'

'Don't be afraid,' Odysseus called back as they crossed the lawn. 'She's only a girl, after all, and you're a famous slayer of serpents and rescuer of cities.'

Odysseus and Clytaemnestra disappeared through the doorway. Eperitus turned and looked down at Iphigenia, who was still staring at him.

'Well,' he said, after a long pause. 'What do children do to keep themselves entertained nowadays?'

Iphigenia's face broke into a smile. She reached across and slipped her hand into his, her little fingers cold as they gripped his rough skin.

'I'd like to hear about your adventures. My mother tells me as much as she knows, but she's no bard and when I ask her questions about the names of the men you killed and how they died, and things like that, she doesn't know. And in return I will show you around the city and let you meet some of my friends. There's Thoosa, the goldsmith's daughter, and Tecton, who helps his father carve ivory trinkets, then there's . . .'

'Is that the way to the city?' Eperitus said, pointing at the west-facing gateway. He was already dreading the thought of being forced into the company of other children.

'You mean you're really going to let me show you around?' Iphigenia said, her eyes wide as she gripped his wrist with both hands and stared up at him. 'That's great! An adult all to myself, for the whole day!'

'I didn't say for a . . .'

'None of my friends will have an adult, and even if they did he wouldn't be a warrior like you. You're even better than mother says you are. You have to tell me about the serpent in the temple of Athena first. What colour was it? Did it have one head or many?'

She pulled him towards the gate, still chattering as Eperitus walked stiffly at her side, already imagining the humiliation of being seen in the care of a child. At first he tried to correct her about the fight with the serpent. It had happened in Athena's temple at Messene, but both he and Odysseus had been defeated by the giant creature and had to be saved from death by the timely arrival of Mentor. Iphigenia, however, was dismissive of Mentor's contribution, stating that the creature must already have been brought to the edge of destruction by Eperitus before anyone else could claim its life. As she was not far from the truth, Eperitus did not press the point.

They spent the rest of the morning and most of the afternoon together. As they walked the streets, he was forced to recount the various adventures of ten years before, which Iphigenia already knew for the most part. What she did not know she had guessed or made up, but she was keen to ask questions and prise out different details from him as each story progressed – what sort of shield did this man carry, or at which point was that man's leg severed, and so on. She would frequently interrupt to point out different features of the town, from smithies and lamp-makers' shops to the different places where a child could climb a wall or hide from pursuing adults. But she would immediately return to the part of the story where the interruption had occurred and either press for more detail or simply listen to what her warrior friend could remember.

After a while, Eperitus began to find the attention pleasantly flattering. He had never possessed any talent as a storyteller, but Iphigenia seemed to hang on his every word and her enthusiasm even made him forget his own natural modesty. Before long he found himself adding small embellishments to the tales of his past battles, perhaps recreating a sword thrust to an enemy's stomach or demonstrating how he would use his grandfather's shield to parry a life-threatening blow. People would look at them as they walked by, but he found he no longer cared about their stares: to his surprise, he had quickly warmed to the feisty girl and was more concerned about what she thought than the thoughts of the townsfolk around them. He had never before enjoyed the company of children, but in the simplest way being with Iphigenia took away his concerns about the past and the future and allowed him to feel complete once again, something he had not experienced since his own childhood.

The streets were crowded and full of the activity of buying and selling. Women weaved through the crowds with heavy amphoras on their shoulders, filled with precious oil or wine; others haggled for lengths of cloth or bags of grain. Young boys forced their way through the throng with trays of freshly baked bread or cakes on their heads, the shouts of those they had barged aside following behind them. As the sun cleared the top of the eastern mountain, though, the streets eventually became too hot for large crowds and Eperitus found it easier to keep up with the young girl whose hand had barely left his own for a moment.

She took him to the circle of graves by the city gate, where she said he should make an offering to honour the royal dead. Eperitus thought it would be most appropriate to buy a garland of flowers from a nearby seller, and together they draped it over the stone marking the grave of Atreus's wife, Aerope. At Iphigenia's request, Eperitus cut a lock of hair from her head, which she placed at the foot of the stone. Then they went and bought cakes, as they were both hungry.

At some point, when the stories of his adventures were finally exhausted – picked to the bone by Iphigenia's energetic questioning – they found a group of children crowded under the shade of a high stone wall. They were playing a game that involved throwing stones into a circle drawn in the dust, which Eperitus vaguely recalled from his own childhood in Alybas. The game stopped as they approached and suddenly he was surrounded by curious children, all of them looking up at him and asking Iphigenia a gabble of questions. She answered as many as she could, her tone proud but aloof, whilst Eperitus felt like a giant who had been captured by a tribe of pygmies.

Among the children was Tecton, who dragged them off to his father's house. Here they found a man with a long nose and small, close-set eyes, bent almost double over a dust-covered bench as he scratched away at pieces of ivory. He looked up as they arrived, though it was clear he could barely see much beyond an arm's length from his face, and greeted Iphigenia and Tecton warmly. Then he offered to fetch wine and barley cakes for Eperitus, and the afternoon was spent with Iphigenia telling the old man and his son all about Eperitus's various exploits. The warrior found himself deeply embarrassed, at first, but soon allowed himself a sense of satisfaction at their joy in listening to the girl. Before they left, Tecton's father gave Iphigenia a carved warrior. She immediately named it Eperitus and held it close to her chest all the way back to the palace.

After the evening's feast, again in the company of the queen of Mycenae, Eperitus found himself unable to sleep, and eventually he threw off his furs and dressed. Eurylochus and Polites were snoring in the darkness as he stepped over them, one exhaling as the other drew breath so that they sounded like a pair of giant grasshoppers. Outside the full moon was lost behind cloud, but emerged slowly as he reached the threshold of the palace.

A group of guards were playing dice by the double portico through which the Ithacans had led their ponies the evening before. They nodded to Eperitus, but when he made no sign of joining them they returned to their game, leaving him to lean against the low wall and look out at the moonlit plain of Argos. As before, there were no lights shining from the farmsteads or villages that dotted the plain, where a silvery mist lurked in the dells and straggled across the fields between the blue hills. Directly below him, the walls and houses of Mycenae gleamed like bones in the night. Then the moon was swallowed once more by cloud and the city turned to darkness.

Eperitus fell to thinking about Iphigenia and the day they had spent together, then about her mother in the yellow dress – he had never seen her before in anything other than dark and sombre clothing – and finally the words of Calchas, until a flicker of light in the corner of his eye caught his attention. He turned to his left, where a spur of the eastern mountain lay black against the star-peppered sky. As he looked, his sharp eyes discerning the shapes of rocks and trees, he saw it again: a burst of red light, arcing above the brow of the ridge. It disappeared quickly, though the impression of the fierce light lingered against the back of his retina for a moment longer. Then a second arc of light followed. This was green and flowed like a banner in the wind before fading. More lights scored the night sky, some high and clear, others low and dim or seen only as a reflection in the treetops.

After a while Eperitus walked over to the guards, whose eyes remained fixed on the flagstones as he approached, their game of dice almost forgotten. He recognized one of them from the previous night.

'Those lights, Perithous. Where do they come from?'

'What lights, my lord?'

'The lights over the brow of that hill. Red and green, mostly; like nothing I've ever seen before.'

'I didn't see them, sir. How about you, lads?'

The others shook their heads and began rolling the dice again. Eperitus turned and went back inside the palace.

'Where did you go to last night?' Eurylochus asked as they ate breakfast the next morning. He was unable to conceal the sneer on his lips at having to talk to Eperitus, but his curiosity had got the better of him.

'I thought you were asleep,' Eperitus replied, with equal disdain. 'Your snores were loud enough to wake the Titans.'

'There's little escapes my notice,' Eurylochus boasted, dipping a piece of bread into the pot of honey between them and cramming it into his mouth. 'I saw your outline in the doorway as you went.'

'I couldn't sleep, if you must know,' Eperitus replied, irritated. 'Though it isn't any of your business what I do at night.'

He pushed the wooden plate away and swallowed the last of his water before standing and walking out into the bright morning air. Odysseus and Arceisius were practising their swordplay, moving back and forth across the courtyard to the sound of bronze ringing against bronze. The king held up his hand as Eperitus emerged, then handed his sword and scabbard to Arceisius. The young squire took the weapons back inside the building where the Ithacans were being housed.

'Another beautiful morning, Eperitus. Sleep well?'

'I slept enough. Do you think Clytaemnestra will make a decision today?'

'Possibly,' Odysseus answered, indicating the doorway to the stairs.

He followed Eperitus down the broad steps to the garden, where a brief sprinkle of rain had freshened the aroma of the flowers. The branches on the trees and bushes nodded with the weight of the water, and let fall a cascade of droplets if brushed against.

'She certainly seemed full of cheer yesterday,' he continued. 'Do you remember seeing her in anything other than black before?'

'No – that *was* odd. Perhaps she'll let us take the girl today and we can get back to the fleet. The storm might have lifted by now.'

'I'd rather stay here until it does,' Odysseus said, sitting on the semicircular bench and looking down at his reflection in the pond. 'At least the sun is shining in Mycenae. How was your time with Iphigenia yesterday?'

Eperitus gave a shrug, trying to look as nonchalant as possible. 'It was bearable. She's amiable enough considering she's a child, and a girl at that. I'd wanted to supervise Arceisius at spear practice, though. He needs to improve his aim before we sail for Troy. Perhaps I'll get the chance today.'

'Perhaps,' Odysseus replied, with a knowing smile.

They remained in the garden until the sun crept over the mountain, discussing the various training needs of their warriors and how they were likely to fare in the coming war. It was an abiding topic that was never far from their thoughts as war loomed. One day soon they would find themselves on the plain before Troy, when their survival would depend on the effectiveness of the men under their command. Eventually, Clytaemnestra appeared again at the foot of the stair, though her jovial appearance of the day before had disappeared. Now her hair was worn loose and the yellow dress had been replaced by her familiar black garb. Her face was bloodless and her eyes red-rimmed as she walked towards them. The two warriors looked at her in silent surprise.

'My lords,' she said, greeting them with a small bow. 'You slept well, I hope.'

'Perfectly well, my lady,' Odysseus replied. 'And you? Did you consult the gods, as you promised me?'

'Still keen for your answer I see, Odysseus. Yes, I consulted my gods and . . . and they have consented that Iphigenia must go. Does that please you?'

'It makes no difference to me, but I am pleased for Iphigenia. To boast Achilles as a husband will earn her great honour, if short-lived.'

Clytaemnestra looked at him for a long moment, searching his expression. Odysseus met her gaze without wavering, until the queen gave up the struggle and lowered her eyes to the pond.

'If that's what you believe, then so be it. But I will not release my daughter immediately. Preparations need to be made – such a wedding cannot be left to men alone. And I must get myself ready, if I'm to come with you.'

Odysseus nodded. 'Of course. How long?'

'My husband is as impatient as ever, no doubt, but I would need at least two weeks.'

Odysseus clicked his tongue and narrowed his eyes. 'Any more than a week and he'll be arriving here himself, my lady, and I wouldn't want to be accused of failing in my task. If I disappoint Agamemnon once, he may never value me again.'

'A week then, Odysseus. But you must lend me your intelligence and help me with the preparations if I'm to have Jenny ready by then. And I want her to remain ignorant of this wedding until we reach Aulis. I was hoping you would watch over her for the next few days, Eperitus. She needs to be kept away from the rumours and gossip that are certain to spread through the city, and she so enjoyed your company yesterday. Her nurse tells me it was almost impossible to get her to sleep.'

'I was intending to give one of the men some additional training, my lady,' Eperitus answered looking down at the pool, where Clytaemnestra caught his eye in the reflection. 'With the war approaching, he needs all the advice and instruction he can get.'

'Of course he will,' Clytaemnestra sighed. 'No matter. I saw Eurylochus talking to Iphigenia as I came down the stairs. I'm sure he will look after her.'

'He can't take care of himself, let alone an independent and energetic girl like Iphigenia,' Eperitus protested. 'Arceisius's training can wait; I'll look after her.'

Clytaemnestra's pallid face warmed slightly as she gave Eperitus a smile.

Eperitus stood at the threshold of the palace, resting his forearms on the wet, cold stone of the wall and looking up at the moon. The guards were playing dice and drinking wine under the portico, the only place where the flagstones were still dry after the early evening rain. They had become used to Eperitus's nightly appearances by now, and were content to leave him to his thoughts.

Before arriving in Mycenae he had forgotten what it was like to be a child. He had regarded them as nothing more than ill-

disciplined nuisances living beyond the fringes of society – irres-
ponsible, loud and driven by impish desires. The four days he had
spent with Iphigenia had proved him right. And yet he had enjoyed
their time together more than any other since he and Odysseus had
fought the bandits on Samos. He had seen life through her eyes,
and it was a thing of excitement and adventure. Mycenae and the
surrounding country were her entire world, but it was a world full
of new experiences. At first he had been cautious, his nature hardened by years of military discipline and the need to preserve the
veneer of respectability that his position required. But by the third
day he was climbing trees with Iphigenia and joining forces with
her as they fought mock battles against Tecton and Thoosa, laughing and shouting as freely as the rest of them. They had roamed
the hills and roads of Mycenae together, seeking adventure and
swapping stories about outwitting adults or meeting goddesses in
disguise. Then, as they sat under the arch of a stone bridge earlier
that afternoon, avoiding another squall of rain, Iphigenia had told
the others about Eperitus's visit to the Pythoness at Mount Parnassus. All his life he had hungered after glory, and yet had never
gained a sense of what he had achieved; here, in the light and
cheerful voice of Iphigenia, he began to see himself from another's
perspective. Her world began and ended in Mycenae, but in him
she saw a world beyond that, where fear and danger were met with
courage, sweat and hard bronze. In this nine-year-old girl's eyes he
meant something.

Later, as they had returned to the city along roads that smoked
with evaporating rain, they were accosted by a young boy with
auburn hair and a handsome but serious face. He stepped out from
behind the wall of a sheep enclosure and puffed his chest up at
them, resting his fists importantly on his hips.

'Are you Eperitus?' he demanded.

'I am,' Eperitus responded.

'He's not so big,' the boy said, looking at Iphigenia. 'But you
always exaggerate things, anyway.'

'Go away, Orestes,' Iphigenia responded, eyeing her younger

brother with disdain. 'Find another corner to cry in until Pa comes home.'

'You'd better shut up, Jenny, or I'll give you a thump,' he snapped back.

'Calm yourself, lad,' Eperitus warned, 'or I'll tan that backside of yours and take you back to your mother over my shoulder.'

Thoosa giggled into her hand, but a sharp look from Orestes silenced her.

'Iphigenia may think you're someone special,' he sneered, giving Eperitus a dark look. 'But my father could kill you easily.'

There was a menace in the boy's tone that echoed Agamemnon's self-confidence and power. Eperitus looked at him and shook his head.

'Nobody can kill me easily, boy, including King Agamemnon. Now, get out of my sight before I strangle you and throw your body down a ravine.'

He took two steps towards the boy, who turned and ran back to the city, not stopping until he had passed from their sight. Eperitus felt Iphigenia's eyes on him and knew his reputation had risen higher still.

'I hope Jenny hasn't bored you these past few days,' said a voice, waking Eperitus from his thoughts.

He turned to see Clytaemnestra standing behind him, her white face given a blue tinge by the moonlight. She had tied her hair up behind her head again, leaving a spiralling strand to fall down by each ear.

'No,' he replied, containing his surprise. 'I've enjoyed our time together – I couldn't have wanted a better guide to the city.'

Clytaemnestra's sad face was lifted by a smile. 'I'm glad you like her. She *adores* you.'

'Thanks to you. You must have told her everything I've ever done.'

'Only what you shared with me that night . . .'

Clytaemnestra turned away in embarrassment, looking across at the guards and then up at the moon.

'You've changed a lot since then,' she continued. 'You're more experienced, more sure of who you are. I don't sense so much of that urgency to prove yourself any more, though you still lack fulfilment. You're still chasing after something.'

'Who isn't?' Eperitus said, squinting across at the Plain of Argos. 'It seems to me the only people who stand a chance of happiness are children. They have some freedom, at least, until they grow up.'

'Have you ever wanted children of your own, Eperitus? Perhaps that's what you're looking for, a child to leave your mark in this world.'

Eperitus was surprised by Clytaemnestra's boldness, but kept his eyes fixed on the plain below the city.

'When I saw Telemachus – Odysseus's child – in Penelope's arms, I felt envious. I knew the boy would carry on his bloodline and preserve his memory, whereas if I perished I would leave no one behind. Then the jealousy went. After all, I'm a warrior and I can win immortality through glory, whatever you may think on the matter, Clytaemnestra.'

'Sometimes you remind me of Agamemnon,' she said, suddenly cold. 'As hard as bronze and desperate to bathe in the blood of your enemies.'

'How can you compare me to him?' Eperitus responded. 'Your husband lusts after power, not glory.'

Clytaemnestra's gaze fell to the wet flagstones. 'I'm sorry, you're nothing like Agamemnon. At least you have a heart.'

Eperitus reached out and touched her shoulder. 'Besides, the king of Mycenae is losing his sanity.'

'Hush!' Clytaemnestra whispered, placing a finger to his lips and glancing over at the guards. She caught two of them watching her, but they were quick to look away again. 'It's not wise to criticize the king. Even when he's away he has spies everywhere, reporting everything that goes on. But you're right. Follow me, I know somewhere more private we can talk.'

She led him into the palace, passing the exit to the courtyard and on up a steep flight of stairs to the second floor. They continued past a series of closed doors until they reached an arched doorway where a maid slept on a bench outside. Clytaemnestra opened the door and walked through into the room beyond, beckoning Eperitus to join her. Reluctantly, he followed.

'This is my room,' she said, closing the door. 'We can talk safely here.'

'Safely?' he replied. 'If I'm caught here and Agamemnon hears about it . . .'

'Don't concern yourself about him. He stopped suspecting me many years ago. As far as he knows, I've never slept with anyone other than him and my first husband.'

Eperitus looked about at the richly decorated bedroom. The muralled walls and painted furniture were visible in the moonlight that poured in through the single window, and in the centre was a low bed covered in thick furs. A heady perfume in the air eased the tension from his muscles and at the same time stirred something deep inside him. He relaxed and slumped into a cushioned chair.

'How can you be sure he isn't having you watched? You told me long ago that he loved you jealously.'

'Agamemnon doesn't understand what love is,' Clytaemnestra answered sternly. She let the heavy black cloak fall from her shoulders and walked over to stand before Eperitus, the folds of her chiton stirring gently in a breeze from the window. 'When he killed my first husband, he simply wanted to possess me and was driven to distraction by the fact I would not give myself to him. That all changed after the children were born, especially Orestes. Perhaps he thinks he owns part of me through the boy, I don't know, but he's long since lost any passion for me.'

Clytaemnestra kicked off her sandals and sat down on the sheepskin rug at Eperitus's feet. She folded her arms about her shins and rested her chin on her knees, looking towards the window. After a few moments she began to talk again, almost as if to herself, explaining how Agamemnon had turned Orestes against her. By using their son, the king had repaid her for her coldness towards him over the years. Her only pleasure in life now was Iphigenia, and as she spoke of her daughter her whole being seemed to lift. She raised her face towards Eperitus and he could see the same happy light he had first glimpsed when they became lovers ten years before. The sadness that made her unreachable fell away and suddenly Eperitus felt the urge to stretch out his hand and touch her. The thought of who she was – the queen of Mycenae and the wife of another man – held him back, but at the same time his eyes were drawn to the pale flesh of her bare arms and feet, and the shape of her long legs and small breasts through the thin dress. His mind was filled with the memory of her naked body from so long ago, and as he stared into her eyes he knew she was no longer thinking of her daughter. He took a deep breath, filling his senses with the heady perfume, and looked away – part of him still trying to resist – but his gaze fell at once on the bed and only strengthened the desires that were coursing through him.

'Even if Agamemnon knew you were here,' Clytaemnestra said, placing a hand tentatively on his knee, 'I doubt he would care any more. Ever since Helen was taken, or chose to leave, he has been obsessed with war on the Trojans. And I think you're right, Eperitus: it *has* turned his mind. If he was ruthless in seeking power before, he will stop at nothing to achieve it now. He will have this war at any cost.'

Eperitus looked at her, sensing something in her tone. 'What do you mean?'

Suddenly, Clytaemnestra rose up on her knees and kissed him. Eperitus lifted his hands to the sides of her head, running his fingers into her thick red hair as her tongue forced its way into his mouth. She came closer, forcing his knees apart with her body until he could feel the softness of her breasts against his lower ribs, all the time pressing her mouth against his with a passion that was fierce and needy. Then she pulled away and stood up, taking his hands and pulling him from the chair. Quickly, clumsily, she unfastened his cloak and pulled his tunic over his head, revealing the hard, deeply etched muscles of his body to the moonlight. A moment later her dress lay in a dark pool about her ankles and she was pressing her naked body against his.

Eperitus's hands instinctively sought her thin waist, feeling the shape of her smooth flesh as she pressed her lips to his shoulders. He closed his eyes and felt the tip of her tongue moving gently up his neck to his jaw, then her mouth was on his again as she pulled him blindly towards the bed. Her ankles caught against the mattress and she fell backwards into the dense layers of fur, pulling him on top of her. As they lay there, their limbs locked eagerly about each other again, he stared into her smiling face and felt for a moment as if nothing else mattered. Her rich, shining hair spilled back across the bed and her dark eyes gleamed up at him with pleasure, momentarily freed from the concerns of her life. Then she folded her calves across his buttocks and held his body against hers, while he pressed his lips roughly to hers once more, eager to enjoy the welcoming sensation of her body.

## Chapter Twenty-four

# THE SECRET REVEALED

Eperitus opened his eyes to the dawn light and the sound of birds in the gardens below. It took him a few moments to realize where he was, but Clytaemnestra's arm across his chest and her hot inner thigh resting on his leg quickly brought back memories of the night before. Her head lay on his upper arm with her face half-hidden by the mess of red hair, making him reluctant to move and wake her, but the sound of slaves moving about beyond the bedroom door made him anxious to find his clothes and be gone before the rest of the palace awoke.

'Don't go,' Clytaemnestra said as he tried to slip free of her embrace. Her limbs tightened about him and she lifted her face to look at him. 'There's no hurry – the sun hasn't even risen yet.'

She must have been awake for some time, Eperitus realized as he brushed the hair from her eyes and kissed her on the cheek. It was hot where it had rested against his arm.

'I can hear slaves in the corridor. If they catch me here and Agamemnon finds out, you could pay for it with your life.'

'As could you,' Clytaemnestra responded. 'But my maids are loyal; they won't dare say anything that could incriminate me.'

Suddenly the door swung open and a young, heavily proportioned girl rushed in, carrying a folded black dress over her arm.

'My lady! My lady!' she began, before sensing at once that something was out of place. Her eyes fell on the garments strung out over the floor, then crept over the bed to rest on the man in her mistress's arms, his nakedness only half covered by the furs. Her round face was transformed with horror as she dropped the dress and clapped her hands to her mouth.

'Damn it, Polymele!' Clytaemnestra snapped, throwing the furs aside and rising naked from the bed. 'What do you mean by bursting in like this?'

'My lady,' the maid stuttered, eyeing Eperitus with a mixture of fear, confusion and desire. 'It's . . . It's your husband. The king is approaching the Lion Gate with an escort of twenty men.'

'Gods!' Eperitus exclaimed. He leapt from the bed and began gathering up his clothes, heedless of the maid's eyes.

'The dress, girl, quickly!' Clytaemnestra ordered, holding her arms wide as Polymele unfolded the garment and began draping it about her mistress. 'Are you sure it's him?'

'Yes, my lady.'

'Then something must be wrong. Leave the dress to me; I want you to fetch a hooded cloak – black, of course – and wait for me by the door. And not a word of what you've seen to anyone, do you understand? If Agamemnon finds out, Polymele, I'll put a curse on your womb so that you give birth to a litter of pigs.'

Looking terrified, the maid fled the room with a squeal and Clytaemnestra closed the door behind her. Finding her sandals, she slipped them on to her feet and began to knot her hair up at the back of her head. Eperitus, now fully dressed, rushed to the window and looked out towards the city gates, where there was a large commotion of people and horses.

'Come away, my dear,' Clytaemnestra said, putting a hand on his shoulder and drawing him back into the room. 'You don't want to be seen peering out of the queen's bedroom, do you?'

Eperitus turned to her and placed his hands on her thin hips.

'If Agamemnon's here, the palace is going to be teeming with life. How am I going to slip out without being noticed?'

'There's a back stair that leads to the garden. Polymele will take you. But tell me this, Eperitus, and quickly: if I leave with Iphigenia, tonight, will you come with us?'

'Leave?' Eperitus smiled. 'Assuming Agamemnon *doesn't* find out about us, why would you want to leave? This is your home, Nestra, and Iphigenia isn't your only child.'

'You don't know the danger she's in,' the queen replied.

There was a sharp knock at the door and they instinctively pulled apart from their light embrace, looking anxiously across the room.

'Who is it?' Clytaemnestra asked.

'Polymele, my lady. I have your cloak, and they say the king is on his way up to the palace at this very moment. I was concerned . . .'

Clytaemnestra pulled the door open and allowed Polymele to fold the cloak about her shoulders. She instructed her to take Eperitus down to the gardens then, without regard to the girl's presence, put her hand to Eperitus's cheek and kissed him.

'Think about what I said,' she whispered, then turned and rushed down the corridor, her cloak billowing out behind her.

Polymele led Eperitus down a narrow staircase that opened onto the gardens below the palace. She left him there without a word and returned by the same route, though her parting expression was enough to tell him what she thought of his presence in the queen's quarters.

The gardens were bright and fresh in the morning light and the pungent aroma of the many flowers reminded Eperitus of Clytaemnestra's bedroom, but he had no time to enjoy their peaceful beauty. A sudden commotion on the terraces above filled him with a sense of urgency and he ran across the dew-wet lawns to the main staircase, leaping up them three at a time to emerge on the courtyard before the great hall. As he stepped out into the chaos of slaves and guards, all running in different directions to prepare for the arrival of their king, a voice called to him. He turned to see Odysseus waving from the doorway of the guest house. Talthybius was at his side.

'Where have you been?' Odysseus asked as Eperitus pushed his way through the crowds to join them. 'I've had men looking all over for you. Agamemnon's here, in person!'

'I've been in the gardens since before dawn. I couldn't sleep. But why's Agamemnon here?'

'We don't know, yet,' said Talthybius, looking worried, 'but for him to leave the army and come here himself, it must be a serious matter.'

As he spoke a group of slaves spilled out of the passageway that led from the palace threshold, chased by a pair of soldiers with bronze body armour and plumed helmets – members of Agamemnon's personal bodyguard. The king emerged in their wake, his armour dusty and his red cloak travel-stained. His beard had grown longer and more unkempt since they had last seen him, but the blood-drained face and sunken eyes were alert and filled with purpose. At his appearance, every slave and soldier bowed their heads before him. Talthybius followed suit, but Odysseus and Eperitus remained upright as the King of Men approached. The stooping form of Calchas was at his shoulder.

'Welcome home, my lord,' said Talthybius. 'We weren't expecting your arrival.'

'Of course you weren't,' Agamemnon snapped, the blood rising to his cheeks. 'You were too busy dithering about here, enjoying the comforts of palace life no doubt.'

Despite Agamemnon's accusation of idleness, Odysseus seemed unconcerned and responded with a broad smile and a hand on the Mycenaean king's shoulder.

'You've arrived just in time, Agamemnon,' he said. 'Your wife has been busy making preparations for Iphigenia's marriage to Achilles, and if everything goes to plan we'll be setting out within two or three days. But how are things with the fleet? Have you come to tell us the storm has lifted?'

Agamemnon's icy blue eyes met the warm green of Odysseus's, trying to penetrate the thoughts behind them. After a few moments his severe expression melted away and he returned Odysseus's smile.

'The storms are as strong as ever, my friend; the reason I've left the army is to make sure Iphigenia is taken to Aulis as soon as possible. For one thing, I didn't encourage the right sense of urgency when I sent you here. For another – and more importantly – you haven't had the benefit of Calchas's insight into Clytaemnestra's thoughts.' He turned to the priest. 'Why don't you explain what you know to Odysseus?'

Calchas pulled back the hood of his black travelling cloak to reveal his bald pate and pallid, skull-like face. His eyes maintained a constant twitching and his tongue flicked over his bottom lip and teeth as he looked about at the men, considering their faces closely as if scrutinizing their very thoughts. Clytaemnestra, he informed them, had no intention of going ahead with the wedding. Her agreement was a facade, covering her real intention to find a means of escape. The ancient gods she worshipped had *suggested* to her that Agamemnon had a different purpose in sending for their daughter – a purpose that the queen had no intention of conceding to. Odysseus gave Agamemnon a questioning look at the mention of this, but the king ignored him and focused on the priest. Apollo, Calchas continued, had revealed the queen's intentions to him in a dream a few nights before, which he had shared at once with Agamemnon.

'Which is why I'm here now,' the King of Men added. 'It is imperative Iphigenia comes back to Aulis immediately – everything depends on it. I've already ordered fresh horses and provisions for the return journey; we head back tomorrow morning.'

'But why the urgency?' Odysseus asked, his eyes narrowing inquisitively.

Agamemnon raised an eyebrow. 'You'll find out in time, my friend.'

At that moment, Clytaemnestra appeared and crossed the courtyard to join them. She stood between Odysseus and Eperitus – giving the latter a strong sense of discomfort in front of Agamemnon and the knowing gaze of Calchas – and placed her fists on her hips.

'Your arrival is unexpected, husband.'

'I thought it might provide you with a pleasant surprise,' he responded, stepping towards her and placing his hand on her waist. He pulled her towards him and kissed her hard on the lips.

Clytaemnestra turned her face away and her husband released his grip on her.

'Didn't trust me to release Iphigenia into your clutches is more like it,' she hissed, not trying to hide her contempt.

'Calchas here had an inkling of your reluctance, so I thought my presence might encourage you,' Agamemnon answered.

Clytaemnestra looked at the priest, who threw his cloak back across his shoulders to reveal the white robes beneath. 'An Apollonian?' she sneered. 'I should have known one of your kind was at the heart of this.'

Calchas's eyes narrowed and his twitching stopped as he focused his disdain on the tall woman in black. 'Apollo lays bare many things. It is more profitable to follow an Olympian than one of the fallen gods you worship. The rule of Gaea and Hecate is fading from the world; you should recognize that and leave your witchcraft behind.'

'You dare to call me a witch in front of my husband?'

'It's true, isn't it?' Agamemnon said, and Calchas grinned victoriously. 'Now, I'm going to the great hall. Have food prepared for me and my men, and send Orestes to me. Odysseus, join me when you're ready. I want to talk with you.'

'And Iphigenia?' Clytaemnestra asked as her husband brushed past her, followed by Calchas and Talthybius.

'The girl can do as she pleases,' he said, turning on the steps to the great hall. 'Just make sure she is prepared to leave first thing tomorrow.'

Clytaemnestra watched him disappear through the high doors before turning to Eperitus. She looked at him with sombre, pleading eyes, then marched off into the palace to carry out her husband's orders.

'It can never come to anything, you know,' Odysseus commented as the courtyard rapidly emptied, leaving him and Eperitus alone except for a pair of guards by the great hall.

'What can't?'

'You and Clytaemnestra. No, don't act surprised. Your bed wasn't slept in last night and I'd already sent Eurylochus to look for you in the gardens before you appeared. I know there's a concealed entrance from the royal quarters, so it isn't difficult to deduce where you slept last night.'

Eperitus turned away and looked at the plain below the city, which was a lush green after the rains. He was surprised at the speed with which his friend had found him out, and did not know how to reply. Then Odysseus seized him by the shoulders and turned him around, staring fiercely into his eyes.

'You're a damned fool, Eperitus! Zeus's beard, don't you realize Agamemnon will have both of you killed if he finds out about this? Next time you want a woman for the night, find yourself a slave – not a bloody queen!'

Eperitus knocked Odysseus's hands from his shoulders and glared back at him. 'Don't forget I nearly died at Sparta because of *your* passion for a princess!'

Odysseus's eyes darkened for a moment and his giant fists were clenched tightly as he stared at the captain of his guard. Then the anger drained away as quickly as it had risen and he shook his head, breaking eye contact.

'I'm sorry,' he said, and with a sudden laugh slapped Eperitus on the arm. 'How could I forget? But *I* married that princess: I hope you're not intending to do the same with Clytaemnestra?'

'Clytaemnestra's already married, unless you hadn't noticed,' Eperitus replied lightly. 'Though she did ask me to help her escape from Mycenae. She said Iphigenia is in danger.'

'I believe she is,' Odysseus sighed. 'You and I both know Agamemnon's losing his sanity over this war, and with Calchas muttering visions and prophecies in his ear who knows what he might be persuaded to do? But Clytaemnestra has her own insight into things, too, and if she doesn't want her husband to take

Iphigenia then she must have good reason. *Are* you going to help her, Eperitus?'

'No. My place is with you.'

'I'm glad to hear it, for both our sakes. But you must remain wary. She's a desperate woman and she'll try to persuade you to help her, especially if she thinks she has an emotional hold over you. Don't let her, though – it can never work, and she might just pull you down with her.'

Eperitus lay on the straw mattress looking at the chink of silver moonlight beneath the door. The snores of the other Ithacan soldiers told him that they, unlike he, had not had difficulty sleeping. It had been a busy day after the arrival of Agamemnon, with the palace a hive of activity hurriedly finishing the wedding preparations in time for the departure early the next morning. To escape the commotion, Odysseus and Eperitus had spent the day outside the city walls, drilling the men and honing their weapons skills. But, although he felt physically tired, Eperitus's mind would not allow him the boon of sleep.

Since the evening meal he had been turning over in his mind the reasons for Agamemnon's untimely arrival. All day he had been expecting the Lion Gate to burst open and an armed guard to come out and arrest him. But none came, and he assumed Agamemnon had not guessed at his wife's infidelity. His thoughts were more concerned, though, with the fate of Iphigenia. Despite his general disregard for children, Eperitus had come to like Clytaemnestra's daughter in their few days together and he found himself pitying her. He had not seen the child or her mother all day, but from Agamemnon's talk at the evening feast it seemed she had still not been informed of the marriage to Achilles, or even that she was to leave for Aulis in the morning with her father, while Clytaemnestra remained at Mycenae.

At the thought of Clytaemnestra, Eperitus felt a sudden desire to leave the guest house and go out into the moonlight. Perhaps some time spent in the quiet gardens while the palace slept would clear his mind, he thought, so he pulled his blanket aside and put on his sandals. He unrolled the cloak he had been using as a pillow and threw it over his shoulders, then moved silently to the door and slipped out to the courtyard. A single guard stood beneath the threshold of the great hall, where Agamemnon's escort slept, but he paid scant attention to Eperitus as he crossed to the doorway that led down to the gardens. Moments later a second figure emerged from the guest house and slipped into the shadows by the wall, following Eperitus at a short distance as he descended the steps to the wide lawn below. Eperitus sensed a presence and glanced back over his shoulder, but could see nothing other than the dense bushes rippling with the night breeze. Already on edge after the unexpected arrival of Agamemnon, he assumed his sharp instincts were being further befuddled by the lack of sleep.

'I've been waiting for you,' said a female voice behind him.

Eperitus turned to see Clytaemnestra sitting on the bench by the pond. He crossed the grass and sat next to her. The features of her pale face were lost beneath the shadow of her hood, but he caught the glimmer of her damp eyes as she looked at him.

'How could you be waiting for me?' he began.

'I willed you to come,' she said, taking his rough hand in her soft fingers. 'Once I make a strong connection with someone I can put images and desires into their mind. It's a gift of the ancient gods; I can do it with Helen and Iphigenia, and I can do it with you.'

Eperitus raised his hand and tipped the hood back from her face. Her eyes were dark-rimmed and her cheeks stained with tears.

'What's wrong?' he asked.

Clytaemnestra leaned across and placed her mouth against his. Though her hands were cold, her lips were almost hot. He put his hand behind her head and held her face gently to his as they kissed.

'What is it?' he asked again, pulling away just enough to speak. 'Is it Iphigenia?'

'You know it is,' she responded, kissing him once more before lowering her gaze to the pond, where the wavering reflection of the moon looked back at her. 'Agamemnon has no intention of marrying her to Achilles. It's just a lie to get her to Aulis.'

'But why? To ensure your loyalty while he's at Troy?'

'Nothing quite so simple,' Clytaemnestra told him bitterly. 'It was the white hart, the creature you helped him to hunt through the woods at Aulis. That was no ordinary animal: it belonged to Artemis and that made it sacred. As soon as Agamemnon's arrow found its mark the expedition to Troy was doomed, and boasting that Artemis herself could not have fired a better shot only made matters worse. In her anger the goddess sent the storms to bottle up the fleet, and until Agamemnon pays the price she demands then not one ship will be able to leave the Euboean Straits for Troy.'

'Artemis wants Iphigenia's life in payment for the white hart,' Eperitus said quietly, suddenly comprehending. He looked up at the moon, the symbol of the goddess's cold nature, and felt despair creep into his heart. The thought of Iphigenia being brought to harm seemed intolerable. 'Is there no other way?'

Clytaemnestra gave a bitter laugh. 'None of the Olympians are more cruel or vengeful than Artemis. She and Apollo shot down the children of Niobe simply because the poor woman insulted their mother. When Actaeon caught her bathing, she turned him into a stag and he was torn apart by his own hounds. Even Callisto, her friend, she turned into a bear and shot dead, all because Zeus raped her. No, Eperitus, the goddess wants payment in kind, like for like: Iphigenia for the sacred hart. Only my daughter's innocent blood will satisfy Artemis, and unless Agamemnon is prepared to carry out the sacrifice then he'll not get his war.'

'But surely Agamemnon will come to his senses and give up his ambitions?'

Clytaemnestra stood and looked up at the moon, which seemed

distended to unnatural proportions as it hovered menacingly above the hilltops, its curious scars and pockmarks etched out in cold grey.

'Part of me hopes that he will look on Iphigenia and his heart of stone will melt,' she said. 'But that is just a fool's hope, because I know Agamemnon is as unyielding and pitiless as Artemis herself. And I can blame myself for that. I hated him because he murdered my first husband and our baby, tearing the infant from my breast as he suckled and butchering him before my eyes. I never forgave him for that and over the years I have denied him the love he craves, slowly turning him from a monster of passion into a monster without any feelings at all. If he has any desire now it is for power only, and his lust for war with Troy has turned his mind from its natural course. I believe he will do anything to achieve his ambitions, Eperitus,' she said, turning to stare into her lover's eyes. 'Even murder his own child.'

'Then you must leave at once,' Eperitus said, placing his hands on her shoulders. 'My heart wants this war, but I wouldn't have it at such a cost. Go and fetch Iphigenia now and leave Mycenae by one of its side gates.'

'And go where?' Clytaemnestra retorted. 'What chance would a woman and a child have out in the wilds, homeless and alone, hunted by the most powerful man in Greece? We'd be caught before the sun had set. No, Eperitus, if I'm to take Iphigenia and flee I only have one hope. You!'

Eperitus looked at the woman who only the night before had become his lover for the second time. He remembered the taste of her mouth against his and the soft and skilful touch of her hands on his body; he recalled her tenderness as they made love, and the realization that she had never given herself in such a way to Agamemnon. But if he fled with Clytaemnestra and Iphigenia, it would be to abandon his oath of service to Odysseus and lose the greatest friendship he had ever known. He would sacrifice all he had fought so hard to gain for a woman he did not love and a girl he hardly knew, to spend the rest of his life like a hunted beast, running from one hiding place to another. For all his fondness towards Iphigenia and his horror at Agamemnon's intentions, Clytaemnestra was asking too much of him.

'I can't help you,' he said, stepping away from her and looking down. 'My duty is to Odysseus. I can't break my oath to him.'

'You warriors and your damned oaths,' Clytaemnestra spat, her eyes flashing with anger. Then she placed her hands either side of his head and pulled him into a kiss. 'But you *are* going to help me, Eperitus, one way or another. If nothing else, we are lovers and I want you to make me a promise on your oath.'

'What promise?'

'I'm going to try to escape tonight, but if I fail and Agamemnon kills Iphigenia . . .' Clytaemnestra paused and took a deep breath. 'If Agamemnon murders my daughter I want your word that you will protect him until he returns from Troy.'

'*Protect* him?' Eperitus exclaimed. 'I could understand if you wanted me to kill him, but . . .'

'I intend to have that pleasure for myself,' Clytaemnestra said, her eyes as cold as ice in the moonlight.

Eperitus could see she meant what she said. 'If that's what you really want, then I give you my word I'll protect him.'

'No, Eperitus!' Clytaemnestra said firmly. 'That's not good enough. I want you to swear it before Zeus, the Sun, the Earth and the Avenging Furies. Say it.'

There was power in the queen's voice as she spoke, a power that reflected the hatred beneath. In that moment, Eperitus sensed the similarity between Clytaemnestra and Agamemnon: both were unshakeably ruthless and cold at heart, and if resolved on something would not let anything stand between them and their desires. Whether they had always been like that or had grown severe and cold over the years together, Eperitus was unable to tell, but he had no more chance of denying Clytaemnestra's will than he would an order from the King of Men himself.

'Have it your way, Clytaemnestra,' he said. 'If Agamemnon murders Iphigenia, then I promise to protect his life to the best of my ability until he returns from Troy. I call upon Zeus, the Sun, the Earth and the Avenging Furies to witness my oath. Now are you satisfied?'

'I am,' she said, reaching out and taking his hand. 'Don't think badly of me, Eperitus, for I had to extract this promise from you. Without it I could not say what I've been longing to tell you since I first set eyes on you in the great hall.'

Eperitus felt suddenly tense. He thought of Calchas's words to him in Priam's throne room and realized with a cold shiver that Clytaemnestra was the one the priest had told him to seek.

'What is it?' he asked.

Clytaemnestra stepped closer and rested her head on his chest. 'I said I would try to escape, Eperitus, and that I wanted you to help me. I expected you to refuse me at first, of course – you are bound by honour and friendship to serve Odysseus, and I knew you would not betray him for my sake. But I also knew you would never allow Iphigenia to come to harm, if you knew the truth about her.'

'The truth?' Eperitus asked. 'What truth?'

'That Iphigenia is *your* daughter, Eperitus.'

*Chapter Twenty-five*

# AT THE LION GATE

Eperitus seized Clytaemnestra's shoulders and stared at her in disbelief.

'Iphigenia's not my daughter,' he said, shaking his head and frowning. 'That's a lie to make me help you escape. Odysseus said you were desperate, but I never thought you'd stoop to this.'

'Stop being a fool, Eperitus, and use your head. We made love ten years ago and Iphigenia was born nine months later. I hadn't slept with Agamemnon for weeks when I realized I was pregnant, though I allowed him to take me as soon as I knew – I didn't want him to discover my infidelity. But even if your head is too obstinate to believe it, then search your heart and you'll know.'

He sat on the bench and stared hard at the dark surface of the pond, trying desperately to comprehend what Clytaemnestra's news meant. Despite his words of denial, he knew she was not lying to him: Iphigenia was the right age to be the product of their lovemaking in the Taygetus Mountains, and he believed Clytaemnestra when she said she had not slept with Agamemnon for weeks before becoming pregnant. More convincing, though, was the sense of familiarity he had felt about Iphigenia from the moment he had first seen the girl. He now realized that he had recognized something of himself in her features and even her character. Though her mannerisms were echoes of Clytaemnestra and Agamemnon, her determination and childish sense of honour were his.

Clytaemnestra sat next to him and laid a hand gently on his

shoulder. 'You know it to be true, don't you?' she said. 'You only have to think about how alike you are. Jenny accepted it straight away when I told her.'

'You *told* her!' Eperitus exclaimed. 'When?'

'This morning, after Agamemnon arrived.'

Eperitus's surprise quickly turned to curiosity, tinged with fear. 'So what did she say? Was she pleased – or disappointed?'

Clytaemnestra laughed. 'For a while I think she was too shocked to believe me, but when she finally listened to her instincts and accepted it was true, she was overjoyed. She's longed for a father like you all her life, Eperitus, someone to give her the love and attention that Agamemnon never did.'

She took Eperitus's hand and held it in her lap, smiling up at the night sky with more tears flowing down her cheeks. Only now they were tears of happiness. 'I've told her stories about you since she was a little girl, you know. I thought she should at least hear about you, even if she didn't realize you were her father. The funny thing is,' she said, smiling and sniffing at the same time, 'she has always thought more of you than any of the other great men of Greece.'

'Because you made more of me than you should have.'

'No – because she knew, in her heart, that you were special to her. And these past few days have proved it. Being with you has given her such joy, and learning you're her real father has brought all her hopes and dreams to life.'

Clytaemnestra looked to the east and saw that the darkness was already being suffused by the light of approaching dawn. If they were to flee Mycenae, it would have to be soon. Eperitus followed her anxious gaze and understood her concern.

'Years ago, I visited the oracle at Mount Parnassus,' he began. 'The Pythoness's words burned themselves into my memory: "Ares's sword has forged a bond that will lead to Olympus, but the hero should beware love, for if she clouds his desires he will fall into the Abyss." She was predicting a choice between fame and renown in battle, or love that will lead to obscurity. Naturally, as a soldier I want to win immortality by defeating my enemies and bringing glory to my name, so I've always been careful not to give my heart to a woman. I never realized the Pythoness could have meant my own daughter. And now it seems the choice is upon me: allow Agamemnon to have his way and then follow Odysseus to fame in Troy, or betray my own king and flee with you and Iphigenia into a life of insignificance, to have the love of a family but ultimately to die and be forgotten.'

'Then let Iphigenia be your fame and your glory,' Clytaemnestra pleaded. 'In Troy you may win renown with your spear, but who will tell of it? Will you surpass Achilles, Ajax, Diomedes or even Odysseus? Of course not. The bards won't sing of your greatness, Eperitus, or preserve your name in their poems for future generations. True fame is for kings, not soldiers. But Iphigenia will pass on your name – to her children, and they to their children. She already worships you like a god and knows everything you've done. Why not let her be your legacy?'

Eperitus thought of Iphigenia's face, recalling her different reactions and expressions during the days he had spent in her company. He remembered her sombre and respectful look – advanced for her years – as they had laid the garland of flowers over Aerope's gravestone; he grinned with pleasure at the memory of her pride as she paraded him like a captive before her friends; and then he thought of her consuming enthusiasm as she exaggerated his adventures to Tecton and his father. Suddenly he knew he could not permit Agamemnon to destroy such a beautiful and wonderful life. He would not allow his newly discovered family to be annihilated by one man's ambition.

He looked up at the thinning darkness and sniffed the air. Dawn was not far away. 'Come on,' he said, standing and pulling Clytaemnestra to her feet. He led her across the wide lawn towards the steps. 'We must head for Ithaca at once – Penelope will hide us if Agamemnon comes looking for Iphigenia. But it's more likely the expedition will break up before then, and when Odysseus returns home I'll explain to him why I had to leave.'

'And he'll thank you for preventing this cursed war and allowing him to return to the family and home he loves,' Clytaemnestra assured him, squeezing his hand and smiling. 'Now I must fetch Jenny – she's waiting for me in my room, ready to leave. Go and fetch your weapons and meet us here as soon as you can. I've arranged for a man to meet us with horses on the other side of the walls; he'll supply us with provisions for a few days, and I will bring enough gold to meet our needs in the weeks ahead.'

'I'll be quick,' Eperitus replied, releasing her hand and running towards the steps that led to the courtyard above.

Eperitus paced up and down by the pond, his grandfather's shield slung over his shoulder and his spears clutched in his sweating palm. Every few moments he threw an anxious glance towards the doorway that led to the royal quarters, but it was only when he thought of going to fetch Clytaemnestra that the door finally burst open and the queen appeared with Iphigenia at her side.

He moved towards them, but upon seeing him Iphigenia let go of her mother's hand and ran across the lawn towards him.

'Father!' she said as he bent down to meet her. She threw her arms around his neck and hugged him tightly, pressing her cheek against his.

'Daughter,' he answered softly in her ear, lifting her up and holding her close against the leather of his breastplate. She was light in his strong arms and he felt the anxiety ease from his body as she hugged him. 'What took you so long?'

'I couldn't find Eperitus,' she explained, leaning back and opening her palm to reveal the ivory warrior Tecton's father had carved. 'I didn't want to leave without him.'

'Well, now you have the real Eperitus,' he said, looking into her brown eyes and smiling. 'And I promise you won't be able to lose *me* so easily.'

'She'll lose you all too soon if Agamemnon finds us,' Clytaemnestra warned, her face strained and nervous as she joined them. 'He'll be awake soon, so we must go now if we're to get away.'

Without wasting another moment they ran across the garden to the far gate, which led to the narrow streets beyond. As they scanned the silent shadows for signs of life a cock crowed from the upper reaches of the city behind them. Seized by a sudden sense of urgency, they abandoned their caution and dashed down the sloping road towards the lower level. Soon they were at the top of the ramp that overlooked the circle of royal graves and led to the Lion Gate. The vast doors were shut, as Eperitus had expected, and three guards were seated on the ground before them, huddled in their thick cloaks and talking quietly to each other.

At the sight of the man, woman and child they sprang to their feet and reached for the long spears propped against a nearby wall.

'Who's that?' one of them called, his voice full of suspicion as he lowered his spear menacingly at the newcomers.

'Your queen,' Clytaemnestra answered, striding down the broad, paved steps towards them. 'Open the gates and let me out. I have urgent business in the town.'

The men did not move. 'I'm sorry, mistress,' said the same guard, 'but the king has given orders for no one to enter or leave – including yourself.'

At that moment, Eperitus's sharp hearing picked up the sound of many footsteps running through the palace above, accompanied by the shouts of men and the clanking of heavy armour. Somehow, the absence of Agamemnon's wife and daughter had already been discovered; the pursuit was about to begin.

'Hold this,' he ordered, slipping the shield from his shoulder and passing one of his spears to Iphigenia.

'What are you doing?' she asked, struggling to hold the tall shaft – nearly twice her own height – with both hands.

But Eperitus, knowing there was no time to waste arguing with the gate guards, had already launched himself down the ramp at the three men. Their reactions were tired and sluggish as he ran past Clytaemnestra towards them, and before they could lower their spears his shield had knocked one of them aside and sent him sprawling across the flagstones. The others staggered backwards, but as both men lowered their weapons defensively Eperitus slammed the shaft of his remaining spear into the face of one of them, catching him across his right eye and forehead and knocking him unconscious to the floor.

'Open the gate!' Eperitus shouted over his shoulder to Clytaemnestra as he faced the last guard.

Clytaemnestra and Iphigenia ran together towards the wooden portals and strained to lift the heavy bar from its brackets. Somewhere in the palace above a voice was barking orders. Weapons and armour clanked in response, and Eperitus knew that at any moment dozens of soldiers would be rushing down to prevent their escape. He looked at his opponent's frightened and confused expression, sensing the man's inexperience, and in the same instant lunged forward with the point of his spear. The thrust was unexpected and the man's attempt to parry it came far too late; the weapon punched into his shoulder and with a scream of pain he spun around and fell to the floor, clutching at his wound.

Eperitus leapt over his writhing body and helped Clytaemnestra and Iphigenia pull open the gates. They swung back with a groan to reveal the road – a dull grey in the darkness before dawn – and the colossal walls rising up to the right. Below them was the ramshackle town where their horses were waiting for them.

'Father,' Iphigenia said. 'Your spear.'

Eperitus stroked his daughter's soft hair, then took the weapon from her hands and started down the road towards the town below. Clytaemnestra was at his side and Iphigenia slightly ahead of them, half-running in her eagerness to leave Mycenae, but as they approached the furthest corner of the walls a man appeared and slid down the rocky slope to stand in the road ahead of them.

'Stop where you are!' he ordered.

It was Talthybius. Though he stood confidently before them, he was unarmed and wore no armour.

'He must have come through the sally port in the north wall,' Clytaemnestra hissed in Eperitus's ear. 'Don't let him stand in our way. Knock him down if you have to and let's be gone!'

But before Eperitus could even think to attack the herald, the chinking of metal and the soft slipping of leather sandals on stone announced the arrival of seven more men on the slope to their right. They quickly rushed down the steep incline and formed a line behind Talthybius, sealing off the only escape from the city.

Eperitus could tell by the overlapping plates of their ceremonial body armour and the boars' tusks on their helmets that they were members of Agamemnon's elite guard, and would not be knocked aside as easily as the militiamen at the gates. But as he felt his hope diminish, Eperitus knew he could not allow them to prevent Iphigenia escaping the terrible fate that Agamemnon had planned for her. He felt his old, dogged sense of determination fill the void that hope had vacated, and with a dark look in his eyes stepped forward.

'I've no fight with you,' he announced, raising the palm of his hand in sign of parley. 'Stand aside and let us pass.'

'As one of Odysseus's men you can do as you please,' Talthybius replied. 'But the queen and her daughter are forbidden to leave Mycenae.'

'Iphigenia's life is in peril, Talthybius. I'm taking her and her mother to a place of safety, and for that reason you must let us go.'

The herald shook his head dismissively. 'There's no danger to the girl as long as Agamemnon is here. Now, stand aside, Eperitus, or face the consequences.'

'Damn your stupidity, Talthybius,' Eperitus spat. 'Don't you realize it's Agamemnon she's in danger from? The king has lost his senses: he's going to take Iphigenia to Aulis and sacrifice her to the gods!'

The self-assured smile was swept from Talthybius's face and the men behind him looked at each other uncertainly. Eperitus turned to Iphigenia, standing behind him with her mother's hands on her shoulders, and saw the look of shock and dread on her face. He tried to comfort her with a smile but could hardly disguise his own fear and growing sense of panic.

'Don't be absurd, Eperitus,' Talthybius said incredulously. 'The king would *never* kill his own daughter. Even in his darkest dreams he wouldn't do such a thing.'

'But it's true,' Clytaemnestra retorted. 'And Agamemnon's dreams have become very dark of late. Calchas has told him that the only way to lift the storms at Aulis is to sacrifice his own daughter, and in his madness Agamemnon believes him. That's why I implored Eperitus to escort us from the city – and if you try to stop us, you and all your men will be committing murder.'

'Don't listen to them, Talthybius,' said a voice from the top of the slope. They looked up to see Calchas standing at the corner of the city wall. 'The king is no more mad than I am, and if you let the girl escape you'll be held accountable for preventing the war against Troy.'

Talthybius's face was filled with doubt as he looked from Calchas to Clytaemnestra and back again. 'Then is what the queen says true?' he asked the priest. 'Does Agamemnon intend to kill his own daughter?'

Calchas pointed to the heavens, where the darkness was being pushed back by the light of the new day. 'The gods must be appeased!' he cried. 'Only the girl's blood will satisfy them, and unless you want the fleet to remain at Aulis until it rots then you will do as your king demands.'

Talthybius looked across at Eperitus and shook his head apologetically. Then he stepped back and waved his men forward. Eperitus looked down at Iphigenia, his face stern and sad.

'You always wanted to see me fight, Jenny,' he said, then laid one of his spears on the paved road and turned to face the line of approaching Mycenaeans.

The soldiers spread across the road and prepared to fight. They eased the tall shields from their shoulders and slipped their left arms through the leather grips, altering their stance so that the weight was balanced evenly. Their reserve spears were cast into a pile at the side of the road and the remaining weapons turned towards Eperitus, the sharpened bronze tips gleaming coldly in the morning light.

Eperitus watched the men plant their feet firmly on the paved road and grip the shafts of their spears. The overlapping plates of their body armour guarded every natural weakness from the neck to the groin, while the layer of boars' tusks on their bronze helmets would deflect almost any blow. More concerning, though, were the eyes that stared out from beneath the ornate helmets: they were confident but cautious, and it seemed to Eperitus that every one of the men facing him was a skilled and natural fighter. If the defence provided by their armour would not prove too difficult to penetrate, then their training and experience might. Nevertheless, he positioned himself in front of them and took his spear in both hands.

'Throw down your weapons, man,' said one of the Mycenaeans, a short, stocky soldier with a long beard. There was sympathy in his hard eyes. 'Don't make us kill you.'

Eperitus took two paces forward. The three men in the middle of the line stepped back, while the two on either side edged round to form a horseshoe about him. Iphigenia stooped to pick up Eperitus's second spear, but was grabbed by her mother, who pulled her back and held her tightly. As the Mycenaeans were still moving, Eperitus lunged to the left with his shield held out before him. The four-fold leather smashed into the nearest soldier, pushing him over the edge of the road to fall crashing down the gentle slope beyond. In the same instant he swung the shaft of his spear at the face of the next soldier, who was already turning to meet the attack. It caught him above the neckguard, causing him to drop his spear and stagger backwards, dark blood oozing out between his fingers as he clutched at his injured mouth.

The remaining Mycenaeans gave a shout of anger and surged forward. The nearest struck low, stabbing with the point of his spear at Eperitus's groin. The blow was intended to kill him, and as he swept it aside with his shield Eperitus knew the battle would be to the death. He lunged at his opponent, thrusting his spear into the gap where the warrior had leaned forward to attack. The point would normally have found the soft flesh above the thigh, crippling the man if not killing him, but instead was turned aside with a dull scrape by the lowest plate of body armour.

The man stepped back, shaken by the skill and ferocity of Eperitus's attack. Two others took his place, striking simultaneously, one high from the left and the other low to the right. Eperitus sensed rather than saw the approach of both spear-points, instinctively raising his shield to deflect the first while twisting aside so that the other slipped past him. He felt the ash shaft brushing past his hip, and at the same time heard a scream of alarm from Iphigenia. Eperitus looked across to see one of the guards brushing Clytaemnestra aside and seizing hold of his daughter.

With a roar of anger, he swung the edge of his shield into the face of one of his opponents, breaking his nose and sending him stumbling backwards. The other rushed forward, only to receive the head of Eperitus's spear in his thigh. It passed through his leg and was torn from Eperitus's grip as the man fell dying to the ground, the dark blood pumping thick and fast from the pierced artery. Eperitus jumped across the screaming warrior and, casting aside his cumbersome shield, rushed to help Iphigenia.

'Stand back!' he ordered as Clytaemnestra tried to pull the tall, muscular soldier away from her daughter.

The man's shield was slung across his back and he had thrown his spear aside in the struggle with the child and her mother. He turned at the sound of Eperitus's voice, but on seeing that his enemy was unarmed stepped forward with his fists raised and a grim smile on his face. Eperitus dodged the first blow, which swept past his left ear, and reacted with an upward punch to the man's nose. The Mycenaean tottered sideways, stunned and blinking, but was quick to regain his senses. With a shake of his head, he turned and raised his fists again. Eperitus moved around him so that he was standing in front of Iphigenia.

'Father!' the girl warned, as the other guards formed a new line across the road. They were joined by the two men who had been knocked aside by Eperitus's first attack, their eyes burning with a desire for revenge.

'Clytaemnestra,' Eperitus said, not taking his eyes from the man before him. 'When I attack, take Iphigenia down the slope and into the town. Find the horses and escape – don't wait for me.'

Before she could reply, he kicked downward at his opponent's shin, scraping away the flesh with the edge of his sandal. The man shouted with pain, but was quickly silenced by a swift blow from Eperitus's fist. The next instant, Eperitus drew his sword and prepared to run at the line of men before him. That he would die on their spear-points was inevitable, but if it gave his daughter a chance to flee he knew the sacrifice would be worthwhile.

'What is this!' barked a cold voice.

Eperitus turned to see Agamemnon standing in the gateway. He was tall and fearsome in his red cloak, white tunic and gleaming breastplate, as formidable a sight as the snarling stone lions in the wall above his head. On either side of him were Odysseus and Eurylochus. Eurylochus was grinning broadly, but Odysseus's face was a mixture of concern, confusion and anger as he looked at the armed men spread across the road.

'Eperitus,' he said, sharply, 'what's happening here? Eurylochus says you were trying to run away with Agamemnon's wife and daughter. In the name of Athena, tell me he's wrong!'

'I'm not wrong, my lord,' Eurylochus announced, stepping forward and pointing an accusing finger at Eperitus. 'I followed him down to the gardens and heard him and the queen planning to run away to Ithaca. I didn't catch everything, but I know there's a man waiting with horses and provisions for a long journey.'

'You treacherous worm!' Eperitus sneered, shooting a glance at Eurylochus.

Clytaemnestra stepped forward and looked imploringly at the king of Ithaca. 'Whatever Eurylochus *thinks* he heard, Odysseus, he *is* wrong,' she answered. 'Iphigenia's life is in danger, and I asked Eperitus to help me get her away from Mycenae.'

'What sort of danger?' Odysseus demanded.

Eperitus sheathed his sword and looked at his daughter. She stared back at him with fear in her eyes, but also pride at his fierce resistance against the Mycenaean guards. He fought the urge to pull her into the safety of his arms.

'Calchas has bewitched the King of Men,' he replied, turning to Odysseus. 'He convinced Agamemnon that the storm at Aulis will not be lifted unless he sacrifices Iphigenia to Artemis, as retribution for the slaying of the white hart. When Clytaemnestra told me, I agreed to protect her.'

'A *human* sacrifice!' asked Odysseus, staring incredulously at Calchas on top of the slope. 'That sort of thing is the stuff of legend, not reality!'

'All wars require sacrifice,' Agamemnon responded. 'Didn't you tell me in the woods that hunting the white hart could cost us dear? Well, if war with Troy requires the death of my own daughter then so be it.'

He stepped out from beneath the shadow of the gate and held out his hand towards Iphigenia. His jaw was set firmly and his blue eyes were as hard as sapphires as he stared at the girl. She responded with a look of hatred and, leaving Clytaemnestra's side, ran towards Eperitus and threw her arms about him. Eperitus placed the palm of his hand on her head, but could not look at her.

With an expression of contempt on his pale face, Agamemnon signalled to his guards, who seized Eperitus by the arms and pulled him away from his daughter. Another took hold of the queen and dragged her out of the king's path as he walked down the sloping road towards Iphigenia, followed closely by Odysseus. At that moment Eperitus realized the oath he had sworn to Clytaemnestra – the oath to protect Agamemnon – was not binding until the king killed Iphigenia. But if Eperitus could kill Agamemnon now, though he would lose his own life in the aftermath, he would at least save the girl.

With a huge backward thrust of his arms, he threw off the men who were holding him and drew his sword from its scabbard. It flashed red, catching the light of the sun as it rose above the mountains in the east, but as Eperitus turned his fierce gaze on Agamemnon, Odysseus whipped out his own sword and brought the pommel down on the back of his friend's head.

## Chapter Twenty-six

# THE KING AND THE THIEF

Eperitus woke from the depths of a dark dream with his head throbbing and his body feeling as if it were made of stone. He looked up at an unfamiliar ceiling, colourfully decorated on one side with scenes of maidens dancing to the music of lyres and flutes, and on the other with naked youths boxing, wrestling and running. He briefly recalled his dream, in which he had been pursuing a silver deer through a dark forest, only to see the creature transformed into Iphigenia as he closed upon her with his spear. Then he heard the scrape of a chair nearby, followed by sandalled feet crossing a stone floor towards him.

'How's your head?' Odysseus asked, looking down at his friend with a mixture of concern and relief. 'I hit you a bit harder than I intended. You've been out cold for most of the day.'

Eperitus sat up, provoking sharp stabbing pains in the back of his head and between his eyes. He winced, but quickly brushed aside the discomfort to focus on Odysseus. 'Where's Iphigenia?' he croaked. 'What happened?'

He sat up and tried to stand, but Odysseus laid a hand on his shoulder and forced him to remain on the bed.

'Iphigenia's with Agamemnon. They're on their way to Aulis as we speak.'

Eperitus brushed his friend's hand aside and stood. 'Then we must go after them, at once!' he said, urgently looking around the room. Although he still wore his tunic and could see his sandals and cloak nearby, there was no sign of his weapons in the unfamiliar room. 'He's going to murder her, Odysseus – you heard him admit it! Surely you're not going to stand by and allow him to go ahead?'

'Agamemnon is the elected leader of all the Greeks,' Odysseus reminded him, gently but firmly. 'He can do as he pleases, whether you and I like it or not. Besides, he left Mycenae at dawn this morning, with Calchas, Talthybius and a bodyguard of twenty warriors, all on horses. It's now reaching sunset, and even if we were able to leave this moment and catch them on our little ponies, what chance would six Ithacans stand against so many? If we weren't massacred there and then, we'd be denounced as traitors for opposing Agamemnon's will.'

Eperitus slumped back down on the bed, seemingly crushed by the weight of Odysseus's information. The orange light of the westering sun shone through the small, high window on the lime-plastered walls and Eperitus knew that his daughter would already be a long way from Mycenae – far beyond any chance he would have of preventing her doom. Briefly, he wondered whether Clytaemnestra had told Odysseus the truth about Iphigenia, but there was nothing in the king's eyes to show this. Should he tell him now, he thought – surely, as a father himself, Odysseus would understand his anguish and help him? But he kept his silence and, shaking his head slowly, looked at his friend with despairing eyes.

'I can't just let her be killed in cold blood,' he said. 'It's monstrous, like something from the old legends.'

Odysseus narrowed his eyes thoughtfully, then sat down beside Eperitus.

'You did everything you could to save her, but it was hopeless from the start. Even if you'd managed to escape, what chance would you have had with every warrior in Greece hunting for you? As it is, you're only alive now because of the efforts of Talthybius, Clytaemnestra and myself. Agamemnon was enraged that you tried to help his wife and daughter to escape; he wanted you killed there and then, and it took all my powers of persuasion to stop him.

Clytaemnestra helped, saying she had told you their lives were in danger and they had to flee the city. Only when Talthybius confirmed this did Agamemnon believe you were acting in ignorance to save his family.'

'Then I owe Clytaemnestra and Talthybius my thanks,' Eperitus said. 'But if you hadn't hit me over the head I could still have helped Iphigenia to get away.'

Odysseus laughed ironically. 'If I hadn't knocked you out, you would most certainly have been dead,' he said. Then he reached across and grabbed Eperitus's arm, a fierce look in his eyes. 'Do you think I didn't see what you were about to do? Admit it, Eperitus – you wanted to kill Agamemnon, didn't you!'

'Yes!' Eperitus exclaimed, snatching his arm away and turning to face the window. 'Yes, and I'd strike him down now if he were here. Iphigenia has become . . . *precious* to me in these past few days. Agamemnon doesn't care for her or Clytaemnestra, but *I* do – and they care for me!'

Odysseus stared at his friend for a time, his expression dark and stern. Eventually, he broke the silence that had fallen in the room. 'You wanted war, Eperitus, and as Agamemnon said, war requires sacrifice. When Helen left Sparta, whether by force or of her own free will, she had to give up all but one of her children. How do you think she feels now? And what about Menelaus, who lost everything he lived for in Helen? Achilles has given up a wife and child to go to his doom against Troy, and unless the words of the oracle can be broken, then I'm condemned not to see Penelope or Telemachus for *twenty* years. It's the same story, one way or another, for every man waiting at Aulis, whether spearman or king. Even Agamemnon, the great King of Men, will be sacrificing his own humanity when he takes Iphigenia's life – a fitting price for his ambitions, perhaps. But *you* should count yourself blessed, Eperitus: at least you have no family to sacrifice to the flames of this war.'

'Blessed, am I?' Eperitus scoffed, pacing the room in his bare feet. 'By all the gods on Olympus, Odysseus, don't you realize who Iphigenia is? She's *my* daughter.'

Odysseus opened his mouth as if to speak, but nothing came out. It was the first time Eperitus had ever seen a look of anything like stupidity on the face of his astute, sharp-minded friend, and as Odysseus closed his mouth again and narrowed his eyes in thought Eperitus suddenly felt like laughing.

'But *how*?' the king asked.

'Clytaemnestra and I became lovers ten years ago, when I was hiding in the Taygetus Mountains. I never knew before we came here that I'd fathered a child – how could I? – but Clytaemnestra says Iphigenia is mine, and my every instinct tells me it's true. And now, perhaps, you can truly understand why I did what I did.'

'Of course, but . . .'

'There's no *but* about the matter,' Eperitus snapped, turning to his friend with a sudden look of intense determination on his face. 'Your message is clear, Odysseus – the gods are cruel and demanding, but no man can deny them their due. Have you given up on Penelope and Telemachus so quickly? Well, I'm not prepared to simply lie down and accept that Iphigenia is lost. I won't allow her to slip from my fingers, to be murdered by an insane king at the insistence of an unloving god; and if you will help me, then I know there's still hope.'

'Think about what you're asking, Eperitus,' Odysseus responded. 'They're a whole day's ride ahead of us, and even if we could catch up with them they outnumber us three to one.'

'No, *you* think about it!' Eperitus shouted. 'You're the most intelligent man I know, and yet you haven't seen what this means yet! If you help me save my daughter, then the words of the oracle *can* be broken. When Agamemnon can't appease Artemis with Iphigenia's life, the fleet won't be able to sail for Troy. Before long the expedition will be forced to disband, and even if you have to walk there you'll be able to return home to Ithaca – to your family. If we work together, Odysseus, we can save Iphigenia and stop the war. I know we can!'

Odysseus's eyes narrowed for a moment, then widened as he realized the insane possibility of what Eperitus was suggesting. His face broke into a grin and, grabbing Eperitus by the arms, he stared at his friend with a new intensity.

'By the gods, Eperitus, you're right! Why didn't I realize it at the Lion Gate? I could go home to my wife and son, and if Iphigenia came back with us you'd have every reason to stay on Ithaca and forget your lust for glory. Come on, man, get your sandals and cloak on – we haven't a moment to waste. I told the others to be ready to leave as soon as you were awake, so they should be waiting for us.'

'What will you do?' Eperitus asked, already crouching down and tying on his sandals.

'I don't know yet, but I'm going to take your advice and think about it. Obviously, we can't use force – it'll need subtlety and cunning – but unless all the gods are against us then we'll take whatever opportunities arise.'

They left the room – a small guest-chamber in the royal quarters – and passed through several narrow corridors to a flight of stairs, which took them down to the threshold of the palace. Here they could see the city below them, where the shadows lay long and dark, and beyond its walls a landscape of green hills in a fertile plain. As they paused to take in the view, Eurylochus passed through the pillared gateway and came running towards them.

'Odysseus!' he called. 'Everything's ready. Clytaemnestra has provided horses instead of the ponies we came on, so . . .'

Before he could say another word, Eperitus launched himself forward and seized him by the throat with both hands. Eurylochus's legs buckled beneath the attack and the two men collapsed on the flagstoned floor, punching and kicking ferociously at each other. Eperitus, his lower lip already bleeding, quickly forced Eurylochus onto his back and pushed his thumbs into his fleshy neck, throwing all his weight into the stranglehold as Eurylochus fought back with surprising strength, kicking out with his fat legs as he struggled to throw off his attacker.

'You treacherous swine,' Eperitus cursed through gritted teeth, staring into Eurylochus's beady eyes. 'If Iphigenia dies because of you . . .'

'I didn't know you were . . .' Eurylochus gagged, but the force of Eperitus's fingers crushed the words in his throat and he could only gasp for more air as his oxygen-starved brain began to fall into the unconsciousness that preceded death.

Then Odysseus locked his arms about Eperitus's chest and dragged him away with irresistible force. Eurylochus rolled over onto his knees and coughed violently, before vomiting over the flagstones. Eperitus continued to struggle against Odysseus's fierce grip for a few moments, then gave up and let the tension drain from his muscles. As soon as Eurylochus had risen groggily to his feet and taken a few steps back, carefully massaging the marks on his bulging neck, Odysseus released his hold and Eperitus stepped free.

'Eurylochus didn't know anything about Agamemnon's plans,' the king explained angrily. 'I've already questioned him on the matter, and he says he only overheard you and Clytaemnestra planning to run away with Iphigenia.'

'I did what I thought was right,' Eurylochus croaked, shooting a fierce glance at his attacker.

'Liar,' Eperitus spat, stepping towards Eurylochus. 'You've hated me ever since Odysseus made me captain of the guard. And because of your petty jealousy a young girl is going to die!'

Odysseus placed a restraining hand on Eperitus's shoulder. 'Stop this,' he commanded. 'Both of you! If we're to have any chance of catching Agamemnon, we must leave before it gets dark and ride late into the night. That means we haven't got time to waste on your differences.'

After a warning glance at both men, he strode off towards the portico that led down to the lower levels of the city. Eperitus and Eurylochus scowled briefly at each other, then followed in his wake. The sun had already gone down by the time they reached the city walls, leaving behind an azure sky streaked with avenues of thin cloud. A line of six horses were waiting on the road beyond the Lion Gate, where Arceisius, Polites and Antiphus were talking quietly. Antiphus playfully admonished the newcomers for their lateness, before pointing each man to his horse. Eperitus walked over to the tall mare that had been assigned to him and stroked her neck. She was entirely black but for a white diamond on her nose, and her coat shone with a blue gleam in the failing light. Though he had liked Melite, the pony that had brought him to Mycenae, he could feel the strength and speed in the horse before him and knew she would make a much more suitable mount for the pursuit of Agamemnon.

'We've packed your things for you,' Antiphus said, glancing briefly at the blood on Eperitus's lip and the marks about Eurylochus's bulbous neck. 'There's a few days' supply of food and a couple of skins of water for each of us. And we've brought your weapons down, too.'

Eperitus thanked him and looked across at the shield, sword and spears stacked ready at the side of the road. But as he turned, he noticed a figure standing beneath the shadows of the gateway. It was Clytaemnestra.

'Give the queen our thanks for her hospitality,' Odysseus said. 'And especially for the gift of the horses.'

He caught Eperitus's eye and smiled knowingly, before turning away and adjusting the blanket on his horse's back. Eperitus walked back to the gate, where Clytaemnestra was leaning against the smooth wall with her arms behind her back and her red hair loose over her shoulders. Her pale face seemed to have lost its harshness, and was soft and appealing in the twilight, but he could also see the redness in her eyes and the despair in her crushed expression. The promise of happiness had been cruelly snatched away from her before it could be realized, and now she was condemned to remain the queen of Mycenae – cold, beautiful and lonely. Agamemnon had not punished her rebellion, but not out of kindness: without Iphigenia he knew her life would be even more empty than before, and in time her loneliness would consume her. Soon all she would have would be her hatred for her husband, gnawing at her with a greater and more bitter intensity than it had ever done before.

Understanding all these things, Eperitus looked at her and was moved with pity. He had a sudden urge to take her in his arms and comfort her, feel her thin body close to his again – perhaps for the last time – and tell her everything would be all right. But what comfort could he offer? What hope could he give when Iphigenia was already in the hands of her murderous father?

'Thank you for the horses,' he said, resisting the urge to reach out and touch her. 'We're going to ride through the night to catch them up, if we can.'

Clytaemnestra smiled sadly, like a child without hope, and looked down at her feet. 'And what will you do if you find them in time? There are too many of them for your small band.'

'Odysseus has promised to help. If anybody can find a way to save Iphigenia, he can.'

He smiled reassuringly and took a step towards her, but she retreated before him. A quick movement of her eyes told him that the others were watching – at least, he knew, Eurylochus would be – and that they were unable to show their affection for each other.

'Goodbye, Eperitus,' she said, turning away. 'Save our daughter, if you can. But if you can't, don't forget your promise – protect my husband until he returns to me.'

They rode as swiftly as they could, long into the night until they passed the watchtowers on the northern border of Agamemnon's kingdom. Here Odysseus called a halt and they ate a cold, frugal meal before snatching a brief and fitful sleep. They were up again before dawn and galloping along the dirt road as the sun rose above the hilltops in the east. Eperitus rued the fact that they were not all experienced horsemen, for with skill they could have gone further in less time with the horses Clytaemnestra had given them, which were swift and strong; without them their pursuit of Agamemnon would not have stood a chance. As it was, Eperitus sensed his daughter, helpless and alone, was slipping beyond his reach.

They came to Megara soon after nightfall and found a room with straw mattresses – a particular blessing for Polites and Eurylochus, who were the least used to riding and seemed to ache in every muscle. The next day was again warm and sunny, and the hooves of their mounts kicked up clouds of dust behind them as they sped along the coastal road beside the Saronic Sea. Being the best rider among them, Eperitus was at the head of the file with his comrades strung out over some distance behind him. As he strained his eyes for sight of a dust cloud that might reveal Agamemnon's party ahead of them, a bent figure clad in a long brown cloak with the hood pulled over its face hobbled out into the road and waved an arm. Heaving on the reins, Eperitus brought his horse to a halt and looked down at the old woman before him.

'What is it, mother?' he asked as Odysseus and Arceisius came galloping up on either side of him, kicking up a cloud of dust as they reined their mounts in. All three riders were unrecognizable from the fine grey dirt of the road that caked their faces and clothing.

The woman did not answer immediately, but spent a long moment pondering the men, studying the shields and weapons they carried and looking in admiration at their fine mounts. Though she must have been tall in her youth, now she was crooked with age and it was with difficulty that she craned her neck to stare up at them. Finally, as Eurylochus and Antiphus joined the group, a quavery voice came out from the shadows beneath her hood.

'Forgive an old crone her curiosity. I can see you're in a hurry, and that seems to be the way of youth these days. When I was a lass they used to say that only a fool hurries, but the world no longer has the wisdom it used to. Anyway, I saw your shields and your tall spears, and I thought to myself: here are some warriors, riding to war no doubt, courageously hurling their lives into the path of danger as if they've plenty to spare, and not caring about their poor mothers sitting at home and worrying about the ones they brought into the world with such travail and pain.'

'Yes, old hag, we're warriors,' snapped Eurylochus, impatiently. 'Now, was there a point to throwing yourself into our path, or do you just want to bore us with tales of how things used to be?'

'As I said,' the old woman continued, nodding sagely, 'always in a hurry. Do I have a point, though? Yes, of course. I was just thinking to myself what magnificent, dust-covered warriors you all look, and how similar to my poor son you are, just before he rode off to his death in battle, leaving me – already a widow – destitute and poor, hardly able to feed myself but for the charity of passers-by.'

'Our hearts bleed for you,' Eurylochus interrupted, tossing a barley cake into the road at her feet. 'Now, save us the detail of your suffering and stand aside, before I'm tempted to ride over you.'

Odysseus raised his hand to silence his cousin. Despite the urgency of their pursuit, he smiled kindly at the crone and nodded. 'Go on, mother.'

The woman ignored the cake at her feet and cocked her head to look up at Odysseus. Her eyes gleamed from the shadow of her hood. 'You have the manners of a nobleman, my lord,' she croaked. 'And perhaps your patience in listening to an old hag will be rewarded, eh? I was saying you reminded me of my son, a mighty warrior with noble blood in his veins. Beloved of the gods, he was, and though I say he went to war leaving me destitute, it is not entirely true. For after he was killed – outnumbered and sur-rounded by his enemies – his friends retrieved his armaments and sent them back to me, to remind me of him in his pride and glory. And long I have kept them, *long*; not only for the sake of his memory, but also because of their great pedigree. For they aren't the weapons of mere mortals: each one was given to him by a god, in recognition of his piety and devotion to them.'

Eurylochus snorted and muttered something under his breath. Arceisius turned to him, admonishing him in a loud whisper: 'Be careful, Eurylochus. Haven't you heard the gods often disguise themselves as crones or beggars to test the quality of a man?'

'Well said, son,' the old woman cackled. 'You may be young, but you're certainly no fool. And maybe the gods are about to reward you, for though I said I have kept my son's weapons for long, I find myself forced to part with them to feed my hungry belly. My eyes fail me now and I can no longer earn my way as a seamstress, so perhaps you can spare some food and a few trinkets in exchange for a helmet, a bow or a dagger? They're all that remain of my son's proud armaments – the rest were had by wise travellers like yourselves, who knew a bargain when they saw one.'

'What would we want with a load of blunt, second-hand weapons?' Eurylochus scoffed.

'May the gods forgive your ignorance,' she replied. 'Did I not say they were the gifts of the immortals to my son? Would you insult the Olympians by turning your noses up at these fine weapons: a bow given by Apollo, which has unerring aim; a helmet from Ares himself, which can be penetrated by no weapon; and a dagger from Aphrodite, that is not only made of gold but also gives the wearer the power to woo any woman he comes across?'

'One of my men needs a new bow,' Odysseus said. He was eager to press on and, not wanting to show disrespect to an old woman, had decided the only option was to buy something and make a rapid departure.

The crone turned and hobbled towards a blanket that had been spread out on the ground at the side of the road, beneath the shade of an olive tree. Stooping a little, she took hold of one of its corners and pulled it away to reveal the armaments she had spoken of: a battered but polished helmet, a well-kept bow, and a dagger that gleamed with gold in the sunlight.

Suddenly, Antiphus leapt down from his horse and ran to look at the weapons.

'Hey!' he exclaimed. 'This is *my* bow!'

The old woman stepped back, straightening up a little as she moved. 'Impossible,' she laughed. 'I'm afraid you're gravely mistaken, lad. This is my son's bow, given to him by . . .'

'Apollo,' Odysseus said, jumping down and patting the dust from his clothes. 'Yes, we know. But Antiphus wouldn't make a mistake about a weapon he's owned since boyhood. Perhaps you'll allow us to take a closer look at these other gifts of the gods.'

At that moment, Polites arrived. The crone took one look at the giant warrior, then turned and began to hobble away at a rapid pace. 'I suppose you intend to rob me, do you?' she complained as she retreated. 'Five armed men and now a giant from the old tales! Take the damned weapons, then. A poor widow can hardly defend her possessions from determined thieves, can she, if they've a mind to have them for themselves?'

Odysseus signalled to Eperitus, who spurred his horse forward to block her escape. Meanwhile, Antiphus picked up his bow and studied it closely, checking for damage while smiling broadly at the feel of it in his hands again. Beside him, Odysseus stooped down to pick up a clay jar from beneath the shade of the tree.

'Don't touch that!' the crone ordered, hobbling back towards him. 'It's the only water I've got and the nearest stream is a good walk away on the other side of that ridge.'

Ignoring her, Odysseus poured the water over his head and wiped the dust from his face.

'Recognize me now?' he asked, after drying his face on the blanket that had covered the array of weapons.

The old woman pulled the hood further down across her face. 'Never seen you before in my life. Now, why don't you take the weapons and leave me in peace. And may the gods curse you for your wickedness, stealing from a helpless crone and all.'

'You're neither a crone nor helpless,' Odysseus replied, seizing her arm and pulling her to her full height, then throwing the hood back from her head. It was Galatea.

'This is your dagger, Eperitus,' Antiphus announced, bending down to pick up the weapon. 'And your helmet, Polites.'

'Where's my sword, woman?' Eurylochus demanded.

'And my spear?' Arceisius added.

Galatea shrugged off the heavy cloak from her shoulders and stood before them in a plain woollen dress. Her suntanned skin shone with sweat and her grey eyes gleamed with defiance.

'They went – not that I got much for the old junk. The only reason I couldn't get rid of that dagger was because nobody could afford my price, and I certainly wasn't going to *give* it away. As for that oversized helmet, I couldn't find a soldier with a head as big as a horse to take it from me.'

Polites looked hurt, but remained silent as he gazed in awe at the beautiful thief.

'Well, you can at least give Odysseus those gold bangles back,' said Eperitus.

'No,' said Odysseus, who had been watching Galatea in thoughtful silence. 'No, I'm going to let you keep them.'

The scowl fell from Galatea's face and everybody looked at Odysseus in astonishment.

'*Keep* them?' repeated Eurylochus.

'Yes – keep them,' Odysseus confirmed. 'And what's more, Eurylochus, when we reach Eleusis we'll get the girl fine clothes and jewellery fit for a goddess. What do you say, Galatea?'

Galatea could not stop her face breaking into a bright smile, but she crossed her arms and stared at the Ithacan king with her head cocked to one side. 'Keep what I took from you and get more on top? Not without something in return, no doubt. What's your price?'

'Come with us to Aulis,' Odysseus replied, patting the flank of his horse and smiling cryptically. 'I'll tell you what I've got in mind on the way.'

## Chapter Twenty-seven

# ARTEMIS

Agamemnon had ordered the leaders of the Greek factions to gather in the wood overlooking the army's camp, in the glade where the altars to the gods had been placed. The kings and princes arrived one by one, unaccompanied by their captains or advisers, to find two white tents standing on opposite sides of the clearing, their canvas heavy and sagging with the ceaseless rain. Each tent was guarded by one of Agamemnon's bodyguard, but the King of Men was nowhere to be seen.

At the centre of the clearing was a single plinth, longer and wider than the marble altars encircling it and gleaming white in the heavy gloom. A wooden pyre stood not far from it, built to the height of a man and covered by a ship's sail – stretched between four wooden posts – to keep it dry. The canvas flapped noisily in the strong north-easterly winds that whistled through the trees and tugged at the sodden cloaks of the Greek leaders. There were more than two dozen of them now, standing in silence amidst the curtains of rain that swept the clearing. A few blinked up at the skies above, where billowing clouds twisted and curled in different shades of grey, constantly blending and separating in an endless metamorphosis. It was as if Aulis had been sewn into a shroud of endless shadow, where day passed into night and night into day without a glimpse of the sun – a Hades for the living, where every moment was an intolerable drudge and there was no hope of escape. But as they gathered for the sacrifice that Calchas had promised would lift the storm, the leaders' spirits fell to their lowest ebb. Being warriors, primed for war, they longed for nothing more than to sail to Troy and reap a great victory; but when the awful nature of the sacrifice had been revealed to them there was not one who did not baulk at the horror of it. The cold looks of the men as they passed through the camp on their way to the gathering told them what the common soldiers thought about the price of Agamemnon's war, even if it was the King of Men's own daughter who had to die.

And yet they came as they had been commanded, their faces half hidden by their hoods as they formed a circle around the central altar. Menelaus hung his head and avoided the eyes of the others about him. He had known Agamemnon's intentions from the beginning, but because of his longing for Helen had not discouraged them; he was complicit in Iphigenia's death, and the girl's blood would be as much on his hands as his brother's.

Beside him, standing tall and aloof, was Diomedes. His handsome face was held high, but his stern brown eyes looked with disdain at the altar before him, openly declaring his condemnation of the act that would soon take place. Nestor, on the opposite side of the circle, shared the Argive's distaste, but, as he stood with his hands behind his back, watching the raindrops explode off the marble altar, he knew the will of the gods could not be denied. The other leaders knew it too – Palamedes, Idomeneus, Menestheus, Teucer, Little Ajax and the rest – and had come to the clearing without protest. Even Great Ajax was there, towering above them like a standing stone in the torrents of rain. When it came to battle, his faith was in his own strength rather than the whims of the Olympians, but he knew the storm could not be fought with muscle and bronze alone. It was an unnatural thing sent by the gods, and if Artemis could be appeased only with the death of a young girl then her price had to be met.

Only two of the highborn Greeks were absent. The first was Odysseus, who had still not returned from Mycenae, and the other

was Achilles. On discovering his name had been used to lure
Iphigenia to Aulis he had flown into a rage at Agamemnon,
reproaching him for his deceit and promising to have no part in
the sacrifice. Since then the Phthian prince had remained shut in
his tent with Patroclus, refusing all summons from the King of
Men. Even Nestor and Diomedes, after being welcomed with the
hospitality that befitted their rank, were politely but firmly refused
when they asked Achilles to put aside his anger and attend the
sacrifice. Agamemnon may have been elected leader of the Greeks,
they were told, but he needed to be taught that Achilles would
not tolerate the misuse of his name.

As the group of men awaited the appearance of Agamemnon, a
great peal of thunder split the clouds above them. They felt it in
the air and the ground beneath their feet, and a moment later
sensed the flicker of lightning inside the swirling belly of cloud
over their heads. Instinctively they grew uneasy, some of them
glancing upwards or across at the tents on either side of the glade.
Then, as if in response to their anxious looks, the guard on one of
the tents reached across and pulled open the heavy cotton and flax
canvas. A moment later Agamemnon stepped out, wearing his
lion's pelt and his breastplate of gold, tin and blue enamel. As he
stared at the circle of leaders from beneath the lion's upper teeth,
they could see that his face was set in a fierce grimace and there
was an almost fanatical gleam in his eyes. Then, stepping forward,
he stumbled and clawed at the guy ropes to steady himself. The
soldier reached out to help, but Agamemnon pushed him away
irritably before continuing across the clearing. His steps were
wavering and unsteady, though he tried to walk with his back
straight and his head high, and when he reached the altar he
gripped the edge of the plinth to keep himself from falling. He
looked around at the gathered kings and princes and, to their
surprise, he was smiling – a desperate grin that was halfway
between amusement and derision.

'Where's Achilles?' he demanded.

'He won't come,' Nestor answered. 'As a point of honour.'

'Honour?' Agamemnon scoffed. 'Honour! There's no honour in this for any of us; why should *he* remain aloof from it all?'

'Because he's the only sane one among us,' said Diomedes. 'This isn't right, Agamemnon. It will put a curse on all of us.'

'It's the will of the gods!' Agamemnon retorted, leaning across the altar towards him, the slurring of his words more pronounced now. 'Even Achilles in his pride won't remain untouched. He can hide away in his tent, declaring I've offended his honour, but we're all part of this. The stain of it will fall on him, too.'

There was another deep roll of thunder followed by a flash of lightning, forking down from the clouds beyond the wood and momentarily sundering the oppressive gloom. Agamemnon threw both fists up at the sky and howled with anger, then drawing a dagger from his belt struck again and again at the marble plinth, sending showers of sparks to join the spray from the rain. But the blade refused to break and, his anger expended, the king slumped across the altar and lowered his head.

At that point, the guard at the other tent lifted the canvas and Calchas walked out, pulling Iphigenia behind him. She wore a brown cloak that fell almost to her ankles, and her feet were bare as she staggered forward into the ferocious rain, looking confused and fearful. A crown of small yellow, blue and white flowers had been plaited into her hair, reminding the onlookers of the summer that had been driven away from Aulis by the storms, and which would only return when the girl's life blood had been spilled.

Iphigenia looked across at the circle of hooded men and the hunched figure of Agamemnon, and her eyes darkened with anger. Suddenly she began to struggle against the pull of Calchas's hand, digging her heels into the mud and leaning backwards as she tried to wrench herself free of his fierce grip. The priest turned and threw both hands about her wrist. The black hood slipped from his head as they fought and his bald pate gleamed white and bulbous through the sheets of rain. Eventually the combined strength of his thin arms succeeded and the girl was pulled onto her knees.

'Why are you doing this to me?' she screamed. 'I don't want to die!'

Agamemnon lifted his head from the plinth and gazed across at the girl he believed to be his daughter, kneeling in the mud with her arms stretched suppliantly towards him. For a moment the strength seemed to drain from his body, and if it were not for the altar he would have slumped to the ground. Then, though his arms were weak and numbed by the cold marble of the plinth, he pulled himself up and looked again at the weeping girl, her face now hidden in her hands. With his thoughts and senses dulled by the incessant rain, he tried to remember how Iphigenia had looked as a baby, and then as she had grown into a girl. But the memories would not come: all he could see was the face of his son, Orestes; it was as if Iphigenia was a stranger to him, a mere acquaintance flitting in and out at the edges of his life.

A clamorous boom ripped through the skies above, followed by a great flash of light. In its wake, he heard a voice in his head, telling him he did not love the girl. The voice belonged to Calchas and as Agamemnon looked across at the priest, standing now patiently at Iphigenia's side, it seemed to him the man knew his thoughts. He stared at the faces of the kings and princes around him. Their eyes were hard, disapproving, but expectant. He was their elected leader – the self-styled King of Men – and if he was to take them to Troy he must carry out the edicts of the gods, however cruel. Finally he looked again at his daughter. Her face had lifted now and there was a scornful look on her young features, a look that reminded him of her mother. Suddenly she struggled to her feet, slipping in the mud, and raising her face to the heavens began to shout: 'Eperitus! Eperitus! Help me!'

Agamemnon rose to his full height, throwing off the chains of lethargy that had bound him to the altar. With an angry frown, he thrust a finger towards Iphigenia.

'Silence her!' he commanded. 'And bring her to me.'

Calchas clapped his hand over Iphigenia's mouth, but she bit into the soft palm and he pulled away with a yelp of pain.

'I'll come freely,' she declared, glaring angrily at Agamemnon. 'I won't be dragged to my death like a dumb beast.'

With that, she took a deep breath, brushed the wet strands of hair from her eyes, and approached the altar. The circle of hooded men parted before her, and as she passed between them she saw Menelaus and Diomedes on either side of her. Diomedes could not hold her gaze and hung his head, but Menelaus held out his hands pleadingly and opened his mouth to speak.

'You are not to blame, uncle,' she said, then with a smile walked past and stood before the marble plinth, facing the man she had thought of as her father until only a few days ago. The dagger was still clutched in his hand and for a moment her eyes lingered on the beads of rain as they ran down the shining blade and dripped to the ground. Agamemnon looked at her with hard eyes and his mouth set in a firm line.

'The altar is too high, my lord,' she said, bitterly. 'You will have to help me up.'

Agamemnon looked at Calchas, who had followed the girl into the circle of men. He stepped up behind her and unfastened the cloak from around her neck. It fell to form a dark pool about her feet, revealing the white sacrificial robes beneath. For a moment it seemed to the onlookers that a pillar of light had been uncovered before their eyes, then Calchas placed her arm about his neck and, lifting her from the ground, laid her on the great stone slab. Iphigenia turned her eyes from the falling rain and shivered, though whether it was with the cold or with fear, no one knew.

Agamemnon gave another nod and Calchas stepped back, shrugging the heavy cloak from his shoulders to reveal the white priest's robes beneath. Lifting his face to the heavens, he stretched out his arms and began a low, unintelligible chant. His voice grew steadily louder and the onlookers could hear him calling on the gods to witness the sacrifice, singing their names and many titles in a wavering tone that was both hypnotic and chilling. As he sang the name of Artemis, the virgin huntress, goddess of the moon, Agamemnon took the dagger in both hands and lifted it above his head. He looked down at his daughter's chest, rising and falling rapidly, clawing at the last moments of life, and she looked back at him, wide-eyed but silent. Then there was a loud crash from above as if the sky had split asunder, followed by a keen whistling and a cry of pain from Calchas. A flash of lightning followed and for an instant the priest seemed frozen, his right arm lifted above his head and the fingers of his hand splayed wide. Through the centre of his palm was an arrow, stuck fast in the flesh and bone.

'Stop!' commanded a high, strong voice.

Agamemnon let the dagger fall to his side and looked across at the woman who had emerged from the cover of the trees, carrying an empty bow in her left hand. She was tall and beautiful, but despite the girlish ponytail of jet-black hair and the white, thigh-length chiton, her stern face was filled with authority and power. At her side was a pure white doe, which followed her on its leash as she walked towards the circle of altars.

'Stop the sacrifice at once,' she ordered. 'The girl's life is to be spared.'

As she approached, the downpour faded to a fine drizzle and the strangled half-light of the clearing brightened a little, giving the jewelled necklace about her neck and the golden bangles on her wrists a dull gleam. The nobles fell back before her, confused and stunned by her unexpected appearance. On the altar, Iphigenia sat up and wiped the rain from her eyes to stare at the elegant but commanding figure, standing like a light at the edge of the nightmare in which she was trapped. Beside her, Calchas released a sharp squeal of pain as he pulled the arrow from his palm and fell to his knees. Clutching his wounded hand under his armpit, he looked up at the woman with an angry glimmer in his eyes.

'How dare you interrupt a sacred ritual?' he hissed through gritted teeth as he felt the waves of pain bite. 'You'll pay for this with your life, woman.'

Then, to the astonishment of the gathered leaders, Agamemnon stepped around the altar and fell to his knees at the woman's sandalled feet, bowing his head in silence before her.

'You have not been chosen to lead the Greeks for nothing, Agamemnon,' she said. 'You alone among your peers have recognized that I am an immortal. While *their* stiff necks refuse to bow before me, you have shown me the respect that is my due.'

With this, she looked about at the kings and princes until one by one they knelt in the mud and lowered their heads. Her voice was clear, proud and authoritative, and even if some exchanged questioning glances with each other, they felt obliged to follow Agamemnon's lead. Eventually only Palamedes remained standing, scrutinizing the woman with disbelieving eyes.

'How do we know you're one of the immortals?' he challenged her, his fists on his hips. 'What proof can you give?'

Her face darkened with anger and she pulled an arrow from the quiver that hung at her hip. Fitting it to her bowstring, she aimed it directly at Palamedes's face.

'I am Artemis,' she snarled. 'And you can choose to kneel willingly before me, or I can bring you to the ground with an arrow through your eye. Either way, I have no intention of proving my divinity to a mere mortal.'

Reluctantly, Palamedes fell to one knee and bowed his head slightly, without removing his eyes from the female archer. Galatea breathed a mental sigh of relief and, lowering the bow, turned to Agamemnon.

'I am the one who demanded this sacrifice of you, King of Men, and now I am relieving you of the task. You have proved your willingness to obey me and that is enough – you have passed the test. I will ask Aeolus to call off the winds at dawn tomorrow, leaving only a westerly breeze to fill the sails of your galleys and take you to Troy. As for your daughter, she is to come with me to serve as a priestess in my temple at Tauris. You will sacrifice this white doe in her place.'

Galatea knelt by the animal that Antiphus and Arceisius had trapped the previous evening, noticing to her horror that the powder Odysseus had used to whiten its fur was already beginning to run in the constant drizzle. If the ruse was to work, she would have to act quickly. Patting the doe on its hindquarters and shoving it gently towards the central altar, she held her other hand out towards Iphigenia and beckoned her to come. The girl slid her legs over the marble slab and jumped to the floor, then with agonizing slowness – her eyes filled with awe – walked cautiously towards the tall white figure. All the time, Galatea could sense Palamedes's eyes upon her, watching for some chink in her facade of divine authority and making her wish she had shot him when she had the chance. As it was, she reminded herself that she was a goddess, without mortal equal, and raised her chin disdainfully as she bent her gaze forcefully upon him. After a moment he lowered his eyes to the mud.

Then the thunder returned, closely pursued by a splash of lightning that flashed off the wall of trees. Galatea looked up, sensing a sudden change in the atmosphere, and within moments the clearing was filled with driving rain mixed with sleet and hail. It blew cold against her cheeks and forehead as she beckoned urgently to Iphigenia. The girl quickened her pace and reached out to take Galatea's hand. She felt the woman's warm fingertips grasp her palm, and at the same moment there came another change in the air about them. Then there was a loud twang and a gold-tipped arrow passed through Galatea's neck. She was dead in an instant, dropping into the mud at the child's feet.

Iphigenia stepped back and screamed. Behind her the Greeks rose to their feet and looked about themselves in panic, sensing that a terrible presence was upon them. The clouds above the clearing began to move with an unnatural speed, twisting and contorting as if the skies themselves were in pain. Peals of thunder followed one upon another, forcing many of the men below to throw themselves to the ground in fear. Great columns of branched lightning struck again and again around the perimeter of the wood, and then with a great howl the wind began to rage through the glade. It plucked the sail from over the pyre and tossed it up into the clouds, where it was torn violently and carried away over the treetops; the two tents followed and their sparse contents were scattered across the long grass and into the trees while the guards fled for cover.

As Galatea fell, Polites had sprung up from his hiding place in the trees and only the quick reactions of Eurylochus and Arceisius had prevented him from running out to her body. Even then, it took all their strength and the help of Antiphus to restrain the muscle-bound giant and pull him back into the cover of the undergrowth. Eperitus, too, had risen to his feet, looking anxiously at Iphigenia as she cowered at the edge of the circle of altars, her arms thrown around the neck of the fretful doe as the storm grew in ferocity about them. Odysseus's ruse had failed at the last moment and now there was only one way to save Iphigenia.

He took a step forward, but immediately a strong hand seized his arm and pulled him back into the undergrowth. 'You can't just run out there in full view of everyone,' Odysseus hissed. 'It'll mean your own death as well as the girl's.'

'She's my daughter!' Eperitus retorted, shaking off Odysseus's hand. 'And don't forget, if she dies your hopes of returning to Penelope and Telemachus will die with her.'

'Eperitus is right,' said Antiphus. 'He can run out and fetch her in the middle of this storm and nobody will even notice.'

'Don't be foolish,' Odysseus said, catching Eperitus by the wrist as he stood again. 'Can't you see something's happening? This is no ordinary storm.'

'Look!' said Arceisius.

He released Polites's arm and pointed to the opposite side of the clearing, past the stooping Greeks and the scattered debris from the tents to where a lone figure had emerged from between the trees. He wore no helmet or armour and his blond hair was blown wildly by the wind, but he stood tall and unbent by the gale, a long sword held in his hand. It was Achilles.

His eyes roamed across the chaos before him – sneering briefly at the sight of Agamemnon and Calchas cowering behind the central altar – until he saw the terrified figure of Iphigenia.

Without hesitation, he strode through the midst of the other kings and princes towards her.

'Come, girl!' he shouted over the gale and the endless rumbling of thunder. 'This is no place for you.'

Suddenly, a shaft of lightning stabbed down into the carefully stacked pyre of logs behind him. The wood that Agamemnon had intended for Iphigenia's body burst into orange fire, the flames licking outwards in every direction. Achilles staggered backwards, throwing his arm across his face for protection. Then, to the amazement of all watching, the flames turned blood red, stretching up to a height above the treetops. In their midst, barely discernible at first but taking shape rapidly, was the figure of a woman. She was tall – twice as tall as Ajax, who alone among the gathered leaders had remained on his feet throughout the storm – and in her hand was a bow of the same height. She stepped out of the fire and even Achilles and Ajax fell to their knees before her.

'Artemis,' Antiphus whispered, his eyes wide with fear and awe. 'It was her arrow that killed Galatea.'

Eperitus stared at the goddess and despaired. Her face was young and beautiful, with pure white skin and golden hair, but her eyes were black; filled with a terrible darkness and power that were not tempered by reason or compassion. The heavy sheets of rain and the blustering wind seemed to pass over her without effect, and as her fierce gaze swept across the men many threw themselves face down on to the ground or covered their heads with their cloaks. Inevitably, her eyes fell upon Iphigenia and the doe that was still clutched in her arms.

'The girl is mine!' she declared, and even the clamour of the storm gave way to the sound of her clear, booming voice. 'Only her blood will appease the offence done to me.'

Eperitus watched his daughter look up at the goddess, but there was no fear in her eyes any more. For days she must have lived in the shadow of her impending death, hoping and praying that she would be released from her doom. Briefly, as she felt Galatea's hand slip into hers, she must have thought the Fates had spared her. But now there was no escape, and letting go of the comforting warmth of the doe, she rose to her feet. Released from the girl's arms, the animal sprang away towards the trees, but a moment later it lay dead in the thick grass, one of Artemis's gold-tipped arrows protruding from its side.

'Rise, King of Men,' Artemis commanded, 'and take up your dagger. The time to pay for your insult has come.'

Agamemnon staggered to his feet and fell back against the altar, staring up at the goddess. Behind her the clouds continued to churn in torment as the thunder and lightning growled and flickered through their grey innards. The carved ivory handle of the dagger was still clutched in his palm and he looked down at the curved blade in surprise. As Eperitus watched, he prayed to Athena that Agamemnon's mind would be filled with memories of the girl he thought was his daughter, and that any love the king still possessed for her would somehow deter him from the task that had been laid on his shoulders. Even now, the choice was still his to make: if Agamemnon desired it, he could deny the will of Artemis and let the storm continue. But as this last desperate hope of a reprieve dared to reveal itself, Eperitus knew how empty it was. Agamemnon did not love Iphigenia – she was only a girl, and unlike Orestes she would never be able to inherit his throne. What was more, Agamemnon was half-crazed with ambition. He knew the chance to unite the Greeks would not come again, and never under his own command. If he spared Iphigenia, he would no longer be the King of Men, leading a great army to renown and riches in Ilium; instead, his power would fade and he would be remembered as a gutless fool who did not have the strength to rise to his destiny. And as Eperitus guessed at Agamemnon's truest desires, the king's lip curled back in an angry sneer and he reached down to seize Calchas by his mud-stained robes.

'Calchas!' he shouted, hauling the priest to his feet. 'Fetch the girl. Now!'

Calchas stared at him for a moment, his eyes wide with fear. Then he came to his senses and lurched through the mud towards the child, who was standing expectantly in the rain, her hair swept back from her face by the wind, her eyes blank. Achilles, whose mind had been filled with debate as he knelt before the goddess, now stood and moved across the path of the Trojan priest.

'Don't provoke me, Achilles,' Artemis warned. 'Your allotted time has not yet come, otherwise I might be tempted to kill you where you stand. But this is no affair of yours; Agamemnon insulted my honour before he did yours, and I will not allow you to interfere with my revenge.'

Achilles frowned up at her for a moment, before lifting the point of his sword defiantly towards Calchas. 'Let the girl alone,' he ordered. 'Agamemnon used my name as a ruse to bring her here, so it's up to me to put that right.'

Suddenly the weight of the sword began to increase in his hand. His muscles reacted against the strain, struggling to hold the weapon up as it grew heavier and heavier, until he could no longer support it. He tried to release his grip on the handle as the sword pulled him to the ground, but his fingers could not move and he was forced to his knees, the great power of his arms helpless to free himself from the weapon.

Calchas ran past him to where Iphigenia was waiting. Though he expected to have to use force, she shrugged his hands from her shoulders and walked slowly towards the altar with her head held high. One by one, the kings and princes stood and formed a crescent around the high plinth, many of them throwing their hoods over their faces so they did not have to look at the terrible figure of the goddess. Instead, they watched in silence as Calchas lifted the girl onto the marble slab for a second time. Above the clearing the unending thunder grew in a crescendo, while the lightning that flashed around the edges of the wood now formed a curtain of flickering light, repeatedly blasting the all-consuming gloom and yet unable to defeat it. The torrents of rain cascaded from the heavens so that the Greeks stood ankle-deep in water that seethed beneath the ceaseless downpour. Iphigenia, shivering with cold under the sodden robes that stuck to her skin, looked into Agamemnon's face as he approached the side of the altar. The dagger gleamed in his hand and his icy blue eyes were hard and devoid of emotion, as if his soul had been sucked out and only the shell of his living body remained. Iphigenia closed her eyes and every muscle in her body tensed.

Then a shout erupted from the tree line and Eperitus ran out. With Galatea dead and even Achilles's unexpected attempt to save the girl stopped, he could no longer restrain himself. The leaders of the expedition, whose distaste at the sacrifice had not quenched their collective thirst for war, turned in surprise as he sprinted towards them. They saw that he was unarmed, but none came forward to stop him. They did not need to. Artemis bent her gaze upon the lone man, then thrust out her palm towards him. It was as if he had hit a wall: Eperitus fell back into the mud as Iphigenia stretched out a hand towards him and whispered 'Father'. Behind her, the gigantic figure of the goddess faded and was gone. The flames of the pyre disappeared also, leaving only a trail of white smoke as the blackened stumps of wood hissed in the rain. Then Agamemnon raised the dagger above his head in both hands and brought it down. Iphigenia screamed, and a sudden silence followed.

Eperitus lay sobbing on his side in the waterlogged grass, his body aching and his muscles heavy. His daughter lay still on the altar, and as Agamemnon buried his face in her robes, his shoulders shaking, a line of blood appeared over the edge of the slab and trickled down to the ground. The thunder and lightning had ceased and all about the wood the clouds were rolling away, taking the rain and wind with them. Soon the circle of sky above the clearing was a pale blue, and for the first time in weeks the face of the sun could be seen above Aulis. It bathed the glade in alien light, as if to welcome Iphigenia's soul, and its heat caused steam to rise from the grass and the sodden clothing of the bent figures that stood or knelt there. But Eperitus cursed it. While the storm had raged, his daughter had lived. Now that it was gone he knew she had departed with it, to become a phantom in the halls of Hades. And soon many more would follow her, Trojans and Greeks alike, to the land of mourning and forgetfulness.

book
# FOUR

## Chapter Twenty-eight

# THE CHOICES OF EPERITUS

Eperitus raised his eyes to the marble altar, a bright smudge in his tear-filled vision, and saw the white-robed body lying still and lifeless on top of it. Iphigenia, his daughter, was gone. He had failed her.

Struggling to his knees, he forced his heavy limbs to crawl towards the plinth, determined to claim the child's body and take her back to her mother in Mycenae. Then a shadow fell across him and he felt a strong hand underneath his arm, pulling him to his feet and taking the weight of his body.

'Not that way,' said Odysseus, his voice gentle and kind as he hooked Eperitus's arm over his shoulder and steered him towards the edge of the clearing.

'No, Odysseus. I've got to go to her.'

'Iphigenia is dead, Eperitus. There's nothing more we can do for her now.'

The king beckoned to Antiphus, who ran over and took Eperitus's other arm. Together they forced him against his will from the clearing, and though he struggled at first, twisting to look over his shoulder at the body on the altar, his limbs were too weary and eventually he allowed them to take him into the shadow of the wood. The last thing he saw was Polites lifting Galatea's body in his arms and, accompanied by Eurylochus and Arceisius, walking into the trees on the opposite side of the glade.

Long staves of yellow light penetrated the gloom of the wood and birds were singing in the blue skies overhead, but the three men were silent as they crunched through the debris of fallen twigs and leaves. Eperitus, now walking unsupported, was too desolated by the loss of his daughter to talk. It seemed to him that a dream of hope and joy had opened up before him, only to be snatched away again with terrible brutality; and in the wake of that brief dream the world to which he had returned now seemed more forlorn and colourless than ever. It was as if a great light had entered his life, and its snuffing out had left a darkness so deep it devoured all the purpose and beauty from living.

As they walked down the slope towards the eaves of the wood – beyond which they could see the tents of the Greek camp gleaming white in the sunshine – they heard a loud call and turned to see Achilles, sword in hand, striding through the undergrowth towards them.

'Welcome back, Odysseus,' he said, shaking the Ithacan's hand and slapping him on the arm. 'And you, Eperitus. I wasn't expecting to see either of you up there.'

'We've only just returned from Mycenae,' Odysseus explained. 'We headed to the clearing as soon as we heard the sacrifice was underway, but by the time we got there it was almost over. The first thing we saw was the goddess and in his excitement Eperitus ran straight out . . .'

'Save your imagination for the more gullible,' Achilles said, holding up a hand and smiling. 'I expect you were watching from the edge of the clearing all along. And I'll wager my armour it was *you* who sent that girl out to fool Agamemnon – it has all the marks of one of your tricks. I'd only just reached the clearing myself, determined to stop the sacrifice, when she came striding out with her arrogant swagger, just like a real goddess. Who knows, she might have even walked away with the child if Artemis hadn't appeared in person.'

Odysseus, knowing it was pointless to continue with his attempted deception, shrugged his shoulders and glanced at Eperitus for the first time since they had left the clearing. 'It was a forlorn hope at best, but I admit I hadn't accounted for the possibility of divine intervention.'

'You did the best any man could do,' Eperitus said. His eyes were pained with deep sadness, but a glimmer of his normal, resolute spirit had returned.

'Then you *were* trying to save the girl,' said Achilles. 'But why?'

'We could ask the same question of you,' Eperitus replied.

Achilles smiled. 'Then come to my tent and eat with me – we can ask each other all the questions we want there. You're welcome, too, friend,' he added, nodding to Antiphus. 'Now, by your leave, I'll run ahead and get some meat over the coals. And don't delay; I'm as hungry as a boar, so I won't wait too long.'

With that, he ran off through the trees, leaping a fallen trunk and several thickets of fern that were in his path. As he reached the edge of the wood, Odysseus called his name and the young warrior turned.

'What about your sword?' Odysseus shouted.

'Light as a feather,' Achilles replied, waving it over his head, before running out of sight beyond the brow of the hill.

The sun was bright and hot as they reached the army's encampment. The only blemish on the blue sky was a pall of black smoke from Iphigenia's funeral pyre, floating up from the woods and drifting towards the east. The tents of the main camp seemed untouched by the gales that had raged through the wood, though the amount of rain they had absorbed was shown by the steam that curled up from the sea of canvas. Achilles's own tent – wide and spacious with a high ceiling – seemed hardly to have been affected by the endless days of storm. The dirt floor was covered with long grasses that his Myrmidons had cut and dried over their cooking fires, while the early afternoon sun on the white canvas made the interior bright and warm.

The Ithacans took the chairs that were offered to them. Kraters of wine were brought shortly afterwards, followed by low tables loaded with platters of bread and freshly cooked lamb. Patroclus and Peisandros joined the small feast and the men satisfied their hunger in busy silence, but for Eperitus who sat morosely and neither ate nor drank. Odysseus watched him with concern as Achilles leaned back in his fur-draped chair, folded his hands across his stomach, and looked at his guests.

'You wanted to know why I tried to save Iphigenia,' he began. 'Well, it's a simple matter of honour. Agamemnon sent you to fetch the girl under the pretence that she was to marry me, did he not?'

'As far as we were aware, that *was* the reason we were sent to Mycenae,' Odysseus explained.

'I don't doubt it, but when I found out Agamemnon had used my name to deceive his wife and daughter I wanted to teach him a lesson. He can call himself King of Men and lord it over the Greeks as much as he likes, but I won't allow him to drag my name into his deceptions. And if it hadn't been for the intervention of Artemis, I'd have stopped this vile sacrifice and sent the girl alive and well back to her mother.'

'Even if it meant the fleet wouldn't sail to Troy?' Odysseus asked. 'I thought you wanted glory, not a quiet life at home?'

Achilles merely shrugged. 'Of course I do, but not at the price of my honour. After all, a man's name is the only thing that will outlive him, and when I'm dead I want the name of Achilles to mean something worthwhile. But I've made my point to Agamemnon and now it's time to look ahead. There's a greater will than Artemis's at work here, and you can mark my words: this war will take place and nothing we do is going to prevent it.'

'I'm beginning to agree,' Odysseus said. 'Though for a while I'd thought the storms would put a stop to Agamemnon's plans.'

'There are too many prophecies and oracles around for every-thing to stop because of an offended goddess, and you can be sure our glorious King of Men is no less a puppet than we are. This war is like a boulder rolling down a mountainside – no force on earth can stand in its way.'

He held up his krater and Mnemon, his lean and gangly servant, refilled it.

'Now,' Achilles continued, 'tell me what was so important about Agamemnon's daughter that you risked her father's wrath to save her?'

Odysseus looked at Eperitus and indicated with a nod that he should answer the question. For a moment, Eperitus was tempted to confess the truth about Iphigenia and why he had tried to stop the sacrifice. After all, Achilles was a father; he would understand. But had he not given up his own child for the promise of glory in Troy? And what of Odysseus's advice, that the secret of his relationship with Iphigenia should remain between them, for the sake of Clytaemnestra's safety and his own? He glanced down at the cut grass and the many fleeces spread across the tent floor, his mind suddenly filled with the memory of his daughter lying frightened and alone on the stone altar, then raised his head and looked at Achilles.

'Honour,' he lied. 'I promised Clytaemnestra that I would try to save her daughter. I was trying to keep my word.'

Achilles gave an approving nod, but it was Odysseus who spoke next.

'And I helped him, because Eperitus is my friend and because I didn't want the storms to end. You mentioned prophecies and oracles, Achilles, so here's another: the Pythoness told me that if I go to Troy I won't see my home or family for twenty years, so I'd hoped the storms would spare me from my doom. But they haven't, it seems, and now I have another question for you. We could have said all this up in the wood – why bring us back to your tent?'

At this, Achilles laughed out loud and leaned across to Patroclus. 'What did I tell you? There isn't a more astute man in the whole Greek army – not even Palamedes.'

'Oh, I remember Odysseus's cleverness from Sparta,' Patroclus replied in his cold, clipped voice. 'After all, it's thanks to his idea for the oath that we're all here now.'

'He could hardly have foreseen Helen being kidnapped by a Trojan, Patroclus,' Achilles continued. 'But you're right, Odysseus, there is another reason for asking you here. Your own protection.'

'Protection from what?'

'Agamemnon, of course. I'm not the only one who'll be linking the appearance of that girl with your special kind of cunning, Odysseus. Why would she have impersonated a goddess and tried to coax Agamemnon into releasing his daughter if she wasn't put up to it? Clytaemnestra could have been behind it, you might say, but with Eperitus running out into the glade like that – in front of every king and prince in the army – you'll have a hard task convincing Agamemnon you weren't trying to prevent his sacrifice. And sooner or later, when he has recovered from what he's done, he'll want you to answer for it.'

'And how will you protect us?' Eperitus asked.

'We're guilty of the same crime,' Achilles replied with a knowing grin. 'By openly inviting you to my tent I'm letting Agamemnon know that he takes his vengeance out on all of us, or none of us. But whereas he can afford to punish you, Odysseus, because your men only form a small part of his force, he won't dare to question me. He *needs* me.'

'The Myrmidons are renowned fighters and their leader's reputation as a warrior is second to none,' Eperitus responded, restraining his anger at Achilles's arrogance. 'But Agamemnon has enough ships and soldiers to conquer Troy without the contributions of either Ithaca *or* Phthia. How can you be certain he won't expel you from the expedition, too?'

'Because Troy can't fall without Achilles,' Peisandros said, leaning his huge bulk forward and taking a handful of meat and bread from the platters before him. He crammed them into his mouth before continuing. 'Weren't you there when Calchas made his prophecy before the council of Greek leaders? Either way,

Agamemnon believes everything the priest says: he killed his own daughter at Calchas's suggestion, so he's not going to risk sending Achilles and his Myrmidons home, is he?'

'I remember the prophecy,' Odysseus said, 'and what you say is right, Achilles, so we're grateful for your protection.'

Achilles gave a small nod. 'It's the best thing for the expedition, whether Agamemnon knows it or not. His insistence on this sacrifice has already lost him a lot of support, and if he starts singling out his best men for defying him with good reason then the alliance against Troy will fall apart. Besides, I like you both. Even though I prefer openness to guile, this war is going to need your intelligence, Odysseus; and as for you, Eperitus, you share my sense of honour and that's admirable in any man. And what's more, I'm going to give you some advice for the attack on Troy.' He leaned forward confidentially and lowered his voice. 'Other than Patroclus and Peisandros here, no one else knows what I'm about to tell, so you must keep it to yourselves. My mother has the power to see the future, and before we left Phthia she told me that the first Greek to land within sight of Troy would die. She knew I would want that honour for myself, so maybe she's just trying to keep me alive a little longer. But I've never known her foresight to be wrong so when the attack comes I'm going to hold back. I suggest you do the same.'

He sat back up and stretched his legs out in front of him. Odysseus drained his krater and signalled to Mnemon for more wine.

'I've never known a man so bound up by divination and augury,' he said as the servant filled his cup. 'How can you tolerate it?'

Achilles smiled broadly and held his hands up nonchalantly. 'It runs in the family. My mother was chosen by Zeus to be his bride, until the Fates prophesied that her son would become more powerful than his father. So he married her to Peleus instead. But one takes whatever precautions are practical. Take Mnemon here. My mother once had a dream that if ever I killed a son of Apollo,

Apollo would kill me out of vengeance, so she gave me Mnemon as a slave to remind me of the fact. He can't cook and he always mixes the wine too weak; and when it comes to putting on my armour, he can hardly lift my sword, let alone my spear or shield. But he knows every son of Apollo by rote, including where they live and who their sons are, just in case. If ever I face one in a fight – and Apollo has a few bastards in Ilium – it's Mnemon's duty to let me know.'

The Ithacans looked at the tall, ungainly slave and did not envy him the task of restraining Achilles in the heat of battle.

As Achilles had predicted, no mention was made of the incidents in the glade, either by Agamemnon or any of the other nobles who had been present. Instead, the King of Men remained ensconced in his tent, doling out orders for the fleet to sail the following morning. Perhaps, Eperitus thought, he was keen not to highlight the snubs to his authority and risk widening the cracks that were already appearing in his tenuous alliance of states. And perhaps it would have too much of an irony to punish the acts of men who were seemingly trying to save his daughter from death at his own hands.

By the time Odysseus, Eperitus and Antiphus returned to the Ithacan camp a messenger was already waiting for them, bringing Agamemnon's orders to prepare for an immediate departure. By the end of the day, Eperitus had worked harder than he had done in months to help get the Ithacan force ready to sail. Though he no longer had any heart for the expedition against Troy, especially under the command of the man who had murdered his daughter, he was glad of the distraction from his dark thoughts, which had been ranging between despair and vengeful anger since leaving the glade.

Men had to be organized back into their correct companies, weapons and equipment had to be stowed as efficiently as possible, and provisions for a long journey needed to be obtained. As there was no centralized supply system for the army, most of the essentials had to be squabbled over with the other factions, and items such as fruit, livestock and salt could only be extracted from the local populace at many times their normal worth. Eventually, though, everything was ready, and as the Ithacans began to settle down for the evening Eperitus slipped out of the camp and wandered into the trees.

While the sun set to leave a clear blue sky, tinged with pink in the west, he climbed the hill to the encampment of the main army. This was still in chaos, with soldiers running in all directions and captains barking orders in a dozen different accents and dialects, so he strolled under the sycamore trees and found his way to the standing stones guarding the entrance to the amphitheatre overlooking the Euboean Straits. The benches on the rocky slopes of the arena, where the Greek leaders had sat during their debates about the impending war, had been removed and the place was again a natural, three-sided bowl looking out to the east.

Eperitus moved to the eastern ledge and sat with his legs dangling over the cliff top, looking down at the vast armada of ships in the bay below. Scores of tiny black figures were still working on the galleys, some fitting spars and adjusting rigging while others knelt on the decks in teams, mending the sails that had been stowed for many weeks. Innumerable small boats crept up and down between the rows of ships, ferrying an endless traffic of crew and supplies to and from the shore. And above the hubbub of voices and the constant sound of hammering was the rushing of the westerly wind, which in the morning would drive the fleet to Troy.

But Eperitus's mind was not on the activity below, or the looming shadow of Troy. Slowly, his thoughts and emotions were learning to accept that Iphigenia – beautiful, clever, compelling Iphigenia – was gone. He had failed to protect her from Agamemnon's black ambition, and though he felt frequent surges of anger towards the King of Men, these were quickly quenched by the knowledge he could do nothing to exact his desire for revenge.

Clytaemnestra had tricked him into promising not to harm her husband, robbing him of any solace for the cold emptiness of his grief, and for the second time in his life a great evil had been carried out before his eyes that he was powerless to prevent.

And yet he was no longer compelled to follow Odysseus to Troy and serve under the overall command of Agamemnon. As the final preparations of the small Ithacan fleet were being completed, Odysseus had turned to Eperitus and released him from his oath of service.

'We've tried our hardest to stop this war, Eperitus,' he had said, 'but Achilles is right: there's a greater force at play here than we can hope to defeat. Zeus himself wants it, meaning our pathetic efforts were damned from the start. But whether that means I won't see my home for twenty years, or whether I can still cheat my doom, remains to be seen. However, that's my fate, not yours, so I've decided to grant your request.'

'Request?' Eperitus had asked, though knowing in his heart what his friend was about to say.

Odysseus turned his sombre green eyes on him, and it was as if the last shred of his hope had gone. The king seemed to have accepted, at last, that he could not escape the war; that he would not see the woman he loved, or the child he barely knew, for many long and unbearable years to come – if he ever saw them again at all. And Eperitus knew that, in his sadness, Odysseus did not want both of them to be sucked into the inescapable, all-consuming whirlpool of Troy. If his friend was free, then part of him would be free also.

'On the day Telemachus was dedicated to the gods you asked me to release you from your oath of service,' he said. 'I'm giving you the chance to go, if you still want it. I know how hard it will be for you at Troy, to see Agamemnon every day and yet be powerless to take the revenge that your honour requires. I'd rather you go back to Ithaca and protect my family and my home, until I return or Telemachus is old enough to rule in my stead. But I won't order you, Eperitus: the choice is yours to make.'

Eperitus had not responded, but the possibility of turning his back on the war and leaving Odysseus had haunted his already dark thoughts ever since. It would be a betrayal; maybe not of his honour, but at least of his friendship with the king of Ithaca. He would fade into obscurity, a failed warrior fleeing the ghosts of his past. The alternative was the torment of facing Agamemnon every day at Ilium, sworn not only to permit him to carry on existing, but also to prevent others from taking his detestable life. Odysseus, in his wisdom, had known both options were difficult, and would not insist he choose one or the other.

Eperitus lay down on the soft, springy turf – the grass lush and green from the unseasonable rain – and looked up at the azure sky, already pricked by one or two stars. Suddenly a deep exhaustion came over him and his whole body felt leaden and drained of energy. He closed his eyes and listened to the preparations going on above and below him, as if he were in a bubble protected – at least for a short while – from the clamouring of war. Then, with the sound of the west wind filling his ears, he fell asleep.

He was woken by a long, low howling from the trees nearby. He sat up and looked about himself, but everything was dark and still under a moonless night sky. The westerly breeze sighed in the topmost branches of the sycamores, but there was no sound from the camp now. Below him, the fleet bobbed gently on the oily black surface of the bay, the shapes of the galleys only faintly distinguishable in the starlight. Then another lonely, mournful cry stretched out into the night air, closer now than before, and he stood and pulled his sword from its scabbard.

As the blade scraped out to shine with a dull gleam, Eperitus saw a shadowy figure enter the amphitheatre from between the two standing stones and come towards him. It was tall and slim, cloaked from head to foot in black, but as Eperitus turned the point of his sword towards it the hood was pulled back to reveal a woman.

'Clytaemnestra!' he exclaimed, shocked to see her pale, pretty face staring back at him. 'What are you doing here? When did you arrive?'

The queen ignored his questions and, covering the small distance between them, threw her arms around his chest and laid her head against his shoulder. Even in his shock at seeing her he had felt a surge of guilt and expected her anger; so the feel of her body pressed against his and her long hands on his back brought a strange sensation of relief. He put his arms around her and stroked her hair.

'I failed,' he said softly. 'I couldn't stop him.'

'You tried,' she answered, her voice small and hoarse. 'Don't blame yourself. Our daughter is gone. I sensed her soul leaving this world as I stood in the courtyard before the great hall this morning, looking down across the plains.'

'But Mycenae is three or four days away on horseback, and even by ship you couldn't have reached Aulis this quickly.'

She nuzzled closer into his arms, so that her voice was slightly muffled by the thick cloak. 'I have powers you can't imagine, Eperitus, powers that go beyond visions and inner knowledge. I used them to come to you. To remind you of your oath.'

'How could I forget?' Eperitus replied bitterly, thinking again of Iphigenia's ordeal in the glade and the sight of her blood trickling from the altar. 'It was a cruel deception, Clytaemnestra. Cruel and hard to bear.'

'Yes, but necessary. You may be Iphigenia's father, but it was through the pain of *my* body that she was brought into the world. *My* patience taught her and *my* love cared for her, long before you even knew she existed. Would you deny my right to take vengeance on my husband?'

'Of course not – but why wait for the war to end? Can't you use these powers you boast of to destroy Agamemnon?'

'No,' she replied. 'I want to kill him with my own hands. But for that I will have to wait until he returns to Mycenae. That's why I want you to keep him alive until the war is over, if you can.'

Eperitus pulled away.

'You ask too much! If you'd seen what he did, Nestra – if you'd seen the look of relish in his eye when he brought that blade down . . .'

'Enough!' she shouted, and the echo of her voice rang off the sides of the amphitheatre. 'Enough. I understand how hard it is for you to stay your hand, and that's why I had to rely on the only force I knew could possibly restrain you – your own sense of honour. But I promise you, the time will come when you can take your revenge on Agamemnon – the gods have revealed it to me. His downfall will begin at Troy, by your hand.'

Eperitus smiled derisively.

'Then haven't your gods also told you Odysseus has given me leave to go home? He, at least, understands how difficult it will be for me to live in the shadow of Agamemnon after what he did to our daughter.'

'But you must go,' Clytaemnestra exclaimed. 'And not because I want you to protect Agamemnon.'

'Oh? Then for what? To be pulled apart by my sense of honour and my desire for revenge?'

'You're speaking like a fool, Eperitus. Don't you realize your destiny is with Odysseus? Gaea has revealed to me that Troy will not fall unless both you and he are there. I knew it long before I asked you to run away with Iphigenia and me, but I chose to ignore what the goddess was telling me, just as Odysseus has been trying to ignore his own fate.'

Eperitus turned and walked further along the ledge, looking out over the vast Greek fleet. He kicked a stone and watched it disappear into the darkness below.

'Don't worry,' he said caustically. 'Your precious Agamemnon and the doom of Troy are safe. I've decided not to accept Odysseus's offer: my place has always been at his side, so I've decided to go with him to Ilium. What else is there left for me to do? At least I can seek some form of vengeance in Trojan blood, even if you've ensured I can't look for it in the death of your husband.'

Clytaemnestra approached and took his hand. 'Don't resent me, Eperitus. I did what I had to do. But another fate awaits you at Troy, a fate that has already been hinted at by Calchas. Have you forgotten the second secret he spoke of?'

Eperitus looked at Clytaemnestra, her face beautiful but cold under the starlight.

'I'm tired of prophecies and secrets, Nestra. Let the cruel gods do as they please with me; after Iphigenia's death, I don't much care about anything any more.'

Clytaemnestra put her arms around him again and rested her head on his shoulder. 'You'll care about this, my dear,' she whispered. 'You'll care about this.'

*Chapter Twenty-nine*

# TENEDOS

Helen stood on the battlements of Pergamos, looking out across the plains and the glittering sea to where the sun was setting in the west. But for the guards at the angles of the walls, she was alone, leaning her elbows on the parapet and thinking about the events of the previous few days. Since arriving in Troy she had been treated with reverence and even love by its citizens. Paris had made a deliberate point of wandering the streets of Pergamos and the lower city with her at his side, and wherever they went they were greeted with an uproar of delighted voices. People rushed from their houses to press around the couple, their faces bright with joy for the prince's happiness, and yet awed at the sight of the mysterious woman he had brought back with him from Greece. Some of the older Trojans might have shaken their heads in disapproval as she passed, guessing that such beauty would only bring grief to Ilium, but after Priam had welcomed Helen no one would dare voice their opposition to her. And the whole city had come out to cheer the wedding procession that morning, dressed in their finest clothing and with baskets of flowers on their arms, ready to cast on the road before the feet of the newly married couple.

Helen smiled to herself at the memory. She still wore her wedding dress – a long white garment in the Trojan style – and as she ran her hands down it the light material felt smooth and rich beneath her fingertips. The delicate blooms that Andromache and

Leothoë had woven into her hair remained fresh and bright, and she almost regretted the knowledge that they would be removed before she and Paris were alone later. But she also knew that Andromache and Leothoë had prepared something special for her wedding night: a dress made from layers of gossamer that could be removed one at a time to tease out Paris's passions; and a blend of perfumes that they promised would keep her husband attentive until dawn. Trojan women, it seemed, had a gift for lovemaking. Their knowledge of how to please a man in bed stunned Helen, and her new friends were not timid when giving her their advice. All day long, even during the solemn religious ceremony that had formalized her union with Paris, her thoughts had returned repeatedly to the night ahead and the new ways in which she would stimulate Paris's passion.

Though the quietly spoken Leothoë had shown nothing but kindness and love to Helen, she also had duties within the palace and was a wife to the king, so was often away performing her various tasks. Andromache, on the other hand, was a visitor and a newcomer to Troy, and she and Helen were able to spend most of every day together, quickly becoming good friends as they explored the city or ventured out on to the plain and the surrounding countryside. Andromache helped Helen improve her use of the Trojan tongue – something that little Pleisthenes was picking up rapidly in the company of Priam's many grandchildren and their nurses – and together the two women would talk about their lives, past and present, and their hopes for the future.

Helen's hopes were already being translated into reality. She could not recall a happier time. When Paris was with her, mostly in the evenings, she felt the joy of a love she had never experienced before; and when he was busy with affairs of state in a city now preparing for siege, Helen enjoyed a freedom she had not known since childhood. She was no longer constrained by the strict palace life of Sparta, and while she missed her three other children there was much to distract her from her unresolved grief. There was the much talked about threat of war looming over Ilium, yet Helen was hopeful it would never happen. Even if Menelaus and his brother could muster a strong enough force to attack Troy, they would be too afraid to leave their own cities unprotected in a divided Greece. And, if against all her expectations they did come, Paris had given her his word on Tenedos that his fighting days were over. There were more than enough fighting men to deal with any Spartan and Mycenaean armies that dared set foot on Trojan soil, and Paris had already done more than his fair share of fighting in the service of his country.

As for Andromache, she had but one hope – to marry Hector. They had known each other for many years through Hector's close friendship with her brother, Podes, but Hector's mind was always too bent on the advancement of Troy to be concerned with matters of love. Even though Andromache had finally persuaded her brother to take her to Troy, Hector had been so busy with matters of war that she had not even set eyes on him before Paris and Helen's wedding, and then only briefly. But Helen could not tolerate the thought that her friend should not share in her happiness at being in love, so promised Andromache her help. She had already persuaded Paris that Hector needed children, and that Andromache would prove an ideal mother, and to that end Paris agreed to invite Hector to eat with him and his new wife the next night. Helen, of course, had already invited Andromache, and with a touch of her own blend of perfumes who knew what the result might be?

With such satisfying thoughts drifting through her mind, Helen had hardly noticed the sun sink below the horizon. A few fishing vessels bobbed up and down on the gentle waves in the wide bay into which the Scamander and the Simöeis flowed, but the mass of high-sided galleys that were there the first morning she had looked out from Troy's walls were gone. Hector had stopped the building of further ships to concentrate instead on bolstering the city's defences; the vessels that had already been built had been sent further up the coast to fetch the armies of some of Troy's vassal cities, bringing them back to join the force that was being amassed under Hector's command. The vast camp that had filled the northern quarter of the plain below had now moved to the eastern side of the city walls opposite the Dardanian Gate, where it was swelled every day by a constant stream of Troy's allies. When Andromache's countrymen, the Cilicians, had reached the city walls a few days before, Helen had joined her friend to cheer their arrival. The fact they were coming to fight Greeks and might die in a war brought about by her arrival concerned her a little, but she found the splendour of the military display – and the equal attention her own presence received – exhilarating.

A familiar squeal of laughter and the clacking of wood made her turn and look down into the palace gardens behind her. There was Pleisthenes, holding a wooden stick in his good hand and fighting against the combined forces of Aeneas and Deiphobus, who were similarly armed. Helen smiled, despite the fact that her son should have been with Antenor, who because of his ability to speak Greek had been asked to tutor the boy in the ways of his new homeland. Instead, Pleisthenes was driving the two young Trojans back before him, pursuing them around the rectangular pond and through several neatly pruned bushes before dispatching each of them with neatly placed thrusts of his sword.

'At least *he* won't have to worry about fighting when the war comes,' said a voice, speaking in Greek.

Helen turned and the smile fell from her face. 'Oh, it's you, Apheidas,' she said, taking a step backwards. 'What are you doing up here?'

'I'm here to inspect the guards,' he answered, glancing at the men on the walls, whose eyes were no longer snatching sly glimpses of Helen but were fixed firmly on the darkening ocean beyond the mouth of the harbour. 'I want them alert and watchful for the arrival of the Greek fleet.'

'They'll not come here,' Helen said, trying to sound assured of the fact. 'If you lived in Greece as you say, you'll know that no king would dare send an army abroad and leave his home unprotected. Not with so many old grudges and scores to settle among the different states. If he did, he'd return home to find his kingdom lost and his family murdered.'

'You shouldn't overlook the power of your own beauty, Helen,' Apheidas responded. 'With a prize like you at stake, I'm only surprised they've not arrived already.'

She gave the Trojan captain a haughty look. 'And if the war comes you'll blame me for it, no doubt.'

'*Blame* you? Not at all – I'll be *thanking* you. Nothing would give me more pleasure than to kill Greeks and send them fleeing back to their rotten little country with their noses bloodied.'

Helen's large eyes narrowed angrily. 'And what about all the Trojans who will die? What of the widows and the orphans they will leave behind? Or do you think this phantom army of Greeks will just blow away like dandelion seeds in the wind? But I suppose you don't have as much to lose as the rest of your countrymen, do you, Apheidas? You've no concept of what it means to lose your children.'

'Oh, but you're wrong there, my dear,' Apheidas said, arching his eyebrows and smiling. He turned and leaned on the wall, looking out towards the faint blue humps of Tenedos in the distance. 'I had three lads, all of them killed in battle.'

Helen took a step towards him, shocked by the revelation.

'But that's terrible!'

'Even more terrible because I drove them to it,' Apheidas added, staring into her perfect face. 'When a man reaches my age, Helen, he can look back over his life, consider his mistakes and regret them. And I wish to Zeus I hadn't encouraged their fighting spirit – especially the youngest one – but I did and now I must live with that.'

Helen looked at the tall, dark-haired warrior with his reputation for ruthlessness and aggression, and for a fleeting moment saw the remorse and sorrow that weighed heavily on his shoulders. He seemed to lean against the crenellated battlements for support, and his eyes were old and tired. Then he drew himself up to his full height again and the image was gone. He was Apheidas once more: stern and authoritative; a captain feared by his men and his superiors alike.

'The Greeks will come, Helen,' he told her. 'Don't deceive yourself about that. And don't believe Paris if he says he will not fight again. He's hinted as much to the rest of us, but when war threatens he'll be out there in the front rank alongside myself and Hector.'

'He promised me,' Helen said defiantly. 'On Tenedos.'

'When he was next to you in bed, no doubt,' Apheidas laughed as he turned to continue his inspection. 'But I know him better than you do. You've come here expecting to find love and freedom, Helen, but the reality will be war and death. Enjoy your wedding night.'

❧

The Greek fleet lifted its anchor stones before the first light of dawn crept into the sky. The sprawling camp that had dominated the landscape for weeks was gone, leaving behind a vast swathe of crushed yellow grass sprinkled with broken pottery, animal bones and other waste of no further use. The thousands of warriors who had occupied it now manned the oars that sent twelve hundred ships gliding slowly towards the freedom of the open seas. For a while the only sounds were the gentle creaking of leather and the swish of oars, punctuated by occasional shouts of command. Then, from a bank of dark cloud that lingered over the mainland like a bad memory of the storm just gone, a single fork of lightning seared down to strike the distant mountaintops. A deep rumble of thunder followed, and for an awful moment the Greeks feared the storm was returning. But when there were no more flashes of lightning, one by one the ships' crews began to cheer, until the whole strait was filled with the echo of their voices. Every man knew that lightning striking to the right was a good omen from Zeus. The king of the gods had spoken, and told them they were sailing to victory.

As each galley passed through the narrow bottleneck between

Euboea and the mainland, into the wide triangle of water beyond, the cheering fell away and was replaced by a flurry of activity as sails were unfurled and rigging adjusted to catch the strong westerly breeze. From there the ships rounded the southern tip of Euboea and headed directly east.

In debating the best route, many of the Greek leaders had advised following the southerly line of the Cyclades to the coast of Asia, then heading north to Ilium – the same way by which Odysseus's ship had returned from Troy. Though it would be slow, the many bays and coves along the way would provide shelter for the fragile galleys if the weather turned rough. Agamemnon, however, had decided they should head directly east to Chios, then turn north to Lesbos and on to Tenedos, where the fleet would reassemble before the attack. It was a more dangerous route but it was quicker by several days, and Agamemnon was desperate not to waste any more time in reaching Troy.

Another problem was the cohesion of the vast fleet. From the moment they left the Euboean Straits, passing one by one into the Aegean, they would become strung out. Rather than a broad armada, they would inevitably stretch out into a long line where the difference between the first and the last ship could be a matter of days. Anticipating the possibility that some ships, or even whole divisions, could get lost as they navigated the unfamiliar seas between Greece and Ilium, Agamemnon had made certain that the chief pilots of each nation were well versed in the correct route. But he was more concerned that a sizeable portion of the fleet should be ready to attack Troy as quickly as possible, and offered prizes to the first four kings to bring their ships to Tenedos. The winner would receive three large, newly made cauldrons with their bronze tripods, as well as a dozen talents of copper; to the second would be given a pair of unbroken five-year-old mares; the third would have a single large cauldron with its tripod and five talents of copper; the fourth-placed king would receive a small, two-handled bowl made of gold traced with skilful designs. And, of course, there would be the glory of victory.

Agamemnon's ploy worked. The natural competitiveness of the Greeks had been ignited and every morning the ships' crews would rise early, ready to sail as soon as there was light enough to see by. Then they would forge across the white-tipped waves of the Aegean in a series of individual races. Like charioteers with teams of horses, each king drove his ships to gain on the king before him and shake off the one behind, taking perilous chances as the fleets passed through each other in order to gain the edge that might lead to victory. Eventually, after several days, the forerunners passed Lesbos and picked up the line of the Asian seaboard, with the low, humped form of Tenedos on the horizon ahead of them.

Achilles's lust for glory had pushed his fifty ships into a narrow lead ahead of the nine ships of the Malians, under Philoctetes; behind them were the dozen vessels from Ithaca. No other ships were yet in sight, but as the skilled sailors under Odysseus's command began to gain on the leaders, the king gave instructions for a slackening of speed.

'But we can catch them,' Eurybates protested from the nearest bench. 'Achilles's ships are getting in each others' way, and hindering Philoctetes too. We can slip past them on their seaward side and be the first to arrive.'

'But I don't want to be the first to Tenedos,' Odysseus replied as he held on to the twin rudders and watched the fierce race between Achilles and Philoctetes. Those within earshot turned to look at him in astonishment.

'What about the prize?' asked Eperitus. 'You can't just give up on a dozen talents of copper and three cauldrons, and we'll have shown everyone we're the best sailors in Greece.'

There were murmurs of agreement from the benches, but Odysseus held up his hand for silence. 'Prizes and glory are one thing,' he said, 'but they're no good if we're not alive to enjoy them. Don't forget Tenedos is a vassal state of Troy and the first to arrive will probably be greeted with a shower of arrows – or worse. And I wouldn't want to steal Achilles's laurels, either.

Philoctetes can be the first to Tenedos if he wants, but if he incurs the wrath of Achilles then he'll only have himself to blame.'

The benches fell silent again as the sailors looked beyond the white-capped waves to the jumble of sails that marked the battle between Achilles and Philoctetes. They knew they could overhaul the mingled ships ahead of them, and despite the wisdom of Odysseus's words they could not help but feel disappointed.

'I don't see why we should hang back,' said Eurybates, crouching beside Eperitus and looking up at the wind filling the sail. 'If there's a battle waiting for us on Tenedos, we should be the first into the fight. The sooner we start the killing, the fewer of those Trojan vermin there'll be in the world.'

Eperitus grunted and turned to watch the race between Achilles and Philoctetes, in which the Malians were already beginning to squeeze through the widely spread ranks of the Myrmidons. Tenedos was soon close enough for the individual trees and buildings to be seen on its steep green sides. They were heading for the western edge of the island where the fleet was to reassemble out of sight of the mainland, but whereas on his previous journey past the eastern flanks there had been nothing more than a few farms and vineyards, now Eperitus could see a wide, natural harbour opening before them. A handful of colourful fishing boats were pulled up on the crescent-shaped beach, while part-way up the hillside was a collection of stone dwellings gathered around a single-storey palace. The small town was reached by a ramp that wound its way up the steep cliff face from the harbour.

All around him now the Ithacans were standing on the benches or leaning perilously far over the sides of the galley, cheering loudly as the race between the ships of Achilles and Philoctetes rushed to its climax beneath the cliffs of Tenedos. Clearly, the Malian archer did not have Odysseus's foresight: by a miracle of seamanship his galleys had driven through the Myrmidons to gain a clear lead. Only Achilles's own ship lay ahead of Philoctetes now, as the two men vied to be the first to reach the rapidly approaching harbour. Then they were lost from sight behind the mass of pursuing craft and it was impossible to tell who had won the race.

The cheers died away and the Ithacans returned to their places, where they debated noisily about whether Achilles or Philoctetes had gained the victory. Before long, though, they were under the shadow of the island and approaching the lines of Malian and Myrmidon ships in the mouth of the harbour. Most had already lowered their sails and dropped their anchor stones overboard, and their grinning crews met the Ithacan latecomers with a mixed chorus of cheers and heckling. Odysseus signalled to the others to throw out their anchor stones, then steered his own vessel through the mass of warships towards the harbour.

A score of galleys were already crammed into the modest bay, where their crews were being ferried in small boats to the shore. The ships of Achilles and Philoctetes, though, had ploughed straight into the pebbled beach in their headlong dash to claim victory. Their tall prows were stuck fast between great banks of shingle and the deck of Philoctetes's ship was covered in a mass of canvas and rigging, where the impact of hitting the beach had snapped the top half of the mast. The crews had spilled out on the beach and were arguing vociferously with each other, their voices a great babble as the Ithacan galley approached.

Odysseus ordered the sail to be furled and the anchor stones to be tossed overboard.

'And ready the boat,' he added as he spotted Achilles and Philoctetes at the centre of the crowd of warriors. 'Eperitus – fetch Antiphus and Polites and come with me. We'd better go and sort this argument out before they come to blows.'

As they reached the shore, Achilles was scowling fiercely and poking Philoctetes's chest with his forefinger. Patroclus stood behind his companion with his habitual sneer on his face, his hand gripping the pommel of his sheathed sword. Showing no sign of intimidation, Philoctetes stood with his legs planted firmly apart in the shingle and his fists thrust on his hips. The bow of Heracles was slung across his back and a quiver was at his side, but he made no sign of reaching for them.

'Concede!' Achilles demanded. 'My galley was the first to hit the beach. There's no doubt about it.'

'Not from where I was standing,' Philoctetes replied. 'Besides, you can't deny I was the first to jump onto the shingle. My feet touched Tenedos before yours did.'

'Nonsense!' Achilles shouted, giving the Malian prince a hard push on the shoulder. '*I* was the first out. You were still in the prow of your ship when . . .'

Mnemon, who had been standing behind Patroclus and looking nervously about at the towering cliffs, now reached across and tapped his master's arm. 'Sir,' he said, wracked with anxiety. 'Sir, I must tell you something.'

'Damn it, Mnemon!' Achilles snapped. 'Can't you see I'm talking?'

'Is there anything I can help with?' Odysseus asked, walking up the shingle towards the crowd of men.

'Yes! You can tell this fool that I won the race fairly and that the first prize goes to me and my Malians,' Philoctetes said, crossing his arms and glaring at Achilles.

On seeing Odysseus, Achilles immediately walked forward and took his hand. 'Thank the gods you're here, Odysseus. We need a man of intelligence to make this idiot understand the difference between winning and coming second.'

'My lord!' Mnemon interjected again. 'Please, I must tell you something.'

'By all the gods on Olympus,' Achilles barked. 'What is it, man?'

But Mnemon did not get the opportunity to speak. Suddenly there was a shout from the top of the cliff followed a moment later by a shower of arrows and stones. Men screamed out as bronze-tipped shafts tore into their flesh, killing several instantly while others crumpled silently into the shingle, felled by falling rocks.

Mnemon was one of these: he was struck on the forehead and slumped to the floor unconscious.

The Greeks stared around themselves in shock, then all looked up as a booming voice shouted down to them in a language none of them understood. A huge, bearded man stood on the cliff top, surrounded by a collection of archers and spearmen, many of whom wore leather helmets and carried rectangular shields made of ox-hide. His bare chest was broad and covered in black hair, and above his head – held easily by his thickly muscled arms – was a boulder the size of a young heifer. With a final challenge on his lips, he hurled the stone down towards the startled soldiers below, crushing three of them instantly.

Pandemonium ensued. Soldiers scattered in every direction, looking for cover on the empty beach from the downpour of arrows. More men fell screaming; those that did not die instantly clawed at the shingle in a desperate effort to drag themselves away; some pulled the bodies of dead comrades on top of themselves to act as shields. Only Achilles and Patroclus remained where they stood, contemptuous of the danger all about them. Then, as arrows smacked into the pebbles at their feet, the prince drew the sword from his belt and held it above his head. Turning to the men about him, he gave a deafening cry of defiance that rang back from the cliff face and echoed across the harbour.

'Come on!' he shouted, and with a look of terrifying anger and joy in his eyes he sprang across the dead and mangled bodies of his comrades and ran to the foot of the ramp.

In an instant, the fear and panic that had infected the Myrmidons disappeared. As one, they drew the swords from their scabbards and the air was filled with the sound of scraping metal. Then, with Patroclus at their head, they sprinted after their leader. An enthusiastic roar rose from their throats as they charged up the ramp that had been cut out of the cliff face, heedless of the new waves of arrows and stones that poured death on them from above.

'Zeus's beard,' said Odysseus, crouching down beside his comrades. 'What are we waiting for?'

He tugged his sword from its scabbard and dashed forward, followed by Eperitus, Antiphus and the giant figure of Polites. As they crossed the beach, quickly joined by Philoctetes and his Malians, a great shadow passed over them. They turned briefly to see a second gigantic boulder come spinning down from the cliff top to land on the prow of Philoctetes's ship with a loud crash of splintering wood.

Without further hesitation, they coursed up the steep ramp shouting loudly in a mixture of exhilaration, anger and fear. Eperitus felt his muscles come alive with a sudden rush of energy as he caught up with his king at the first bend. Together they ran to catch up with the press of Myrmidons ahead of them, passing the fallen and wounded on the way. Despite the whistle of arrows and the thump of falling rocks all around, Eperitus's spirit was filled with the joyous anticipation of battle. There was nothing like the danger of death and the thrill of facing an armed opponent to make a man feel alive and aware of his own mortality. No other experience could match the marvel of short moments of time stretched out by the sharpening of the senses, the realization of tiny details amidst a blur of movement and sound as each man fought to take the other's life. He clutched the handle of his sword tighter and grinned at the thought that this was how Iphigenia had always imagined him: charging fearlessly into battle, driven by his lust for glory.

They took the next bend in the climbing road just as a Myrmidon soldier came hurtling down from the cliff above, his bronze sword clanging as it fell from his dead hand. Eperitus stooped and snatched it up as he ran. An arrow tugged at the hem of his cloak and hung there, its barbs snagged in the densely woven wool. Beside him, Odysseus narrowly dodged the fall of a large rock, but together they ran on. Then they heard the twang of a bowstring and a moment later a man fell screaming from the cliff top. He soared over the heads of the Greeks and did not stop until his body slammed into the shingle below.

Eperitus looked back and saw that Philoctetes had drawn his

bow and was aiming a second arrow skywards. He released it and another body came crashing down to land beside the dead Myrmidon.

'Damn it, I wish I'd thought to bring my bow,' hissed Antiphus. 'Have you seen the way he's just plucking them off the top of the cliff like tethered doves?'

As he spoke there was a great shout followed by the clashing of metal, signalling that the Myrmidons had reached the top of the cliff. At the same time the relentless shower of missiles from above petered out, and with a shout of defiance Odysseus and Eperitus led the way up the last two angles of the ramp to join the battle.

Already a line of dead bodies showed where Achilles's men had pushed their enemies back. Though greatly outnumbered and armed only with swords – their shields and spears were still onboard their ships – they had smashed through the first rank of spearman and were now hacking and stabbing ferociously as the men of Tenedos fell back before them. For the first time, Eperitus spotted his friend Peisandros amongst them, fighting like a lion as he shouted encouragement to the men around him. Yells of triumph mingled with the despairing screams of dying men as black-clad Myrmidons trod on the bodies of the fallen, desperate to come to grips with their opponents. At their centre, beads of gore flicking from his blade as he scythed it repeatedly through the terrified ranks, was Achilles. And though a great press of spears and swords were aimed at him, he drove forward with unquenchable aggression, laughing aloud for the pure joy of battle as he swatted aside his enemies' attempts to resist him. At his side was Patroclus, defending his companion's left side with precise thrusts of his long sword, finding throats, hearts and stomachs with unerring accuracy.

And yet the Myrmidons were but a handful – three score at the most – against more than a hundred men led by the fearsome giant who had hurled boulders down from the cliff top. Seeing this, the Ithacans threw themselves into the midst of the melee with the Malians close on their heels, while Philoctetes leapt on top of an outcrop of rock and began sending arrows into the massed defenders.

Odysseus was the first of the Ithacans to strike, slipping inside the thrust of a spear and pushing his sword into his assailant's heart. Ripping the shield from the man's grip, he stepped across his body and hacked at the point of another spear, cutting the shaft in half and then bringing the edge of his blade back up across the face of the enemy soldier. The man stumbled backwards, his fingers clutching at the furrow that had been opened through his nose and cheekbones.

Gripping both swords, Eperitus charged into the gap created by his king and stood on a pile of bodies, slashing with determined force at the hedge of spear-points before him. He knocked them aside with ease and leapt down to run the point of one sword into the stomach of a young spearman, while with the other he chopped through the wrist of a man who had lunged at him with an axe. Without pausing to finish him off, he bore forward into the crowd of soldiers, quickly sending another to his death with a stab through the throat. Glancing to his right, he saw Polites crash into the enemy ranks and begin tossing men about like young trees caught in a hurricane. It was clear to Eperitus from the clumsy, inexperienced efforts of the islanders that they were little more than a poorly trained militia, bolstered by townsfolk armed with improvised weapons. The only thing that stopped them from breaking and running was their greater fear of the bearded giant who stood at their rear.

At that moment, he bellowed an order and with relief in their eyes the defenders pulled back to form a new line behind him. The Greeks allowed them to retreat, using the lull in battle to arm themselves with the shields and spears of the fallen. Only Achilles refrained. He could see that the enemy commander wore no armour and carried only a club of colossal proportions, so to have picked up a shield would have seemed cowardly to his proud eyes. Then the man's broad, flat face split into a mocking smile and with a slow gesture of his shovel-sized hand he beckoned Achilles forward.

With his sword hanging loosely at his side, the Phthian prince picked his way across the carpet of bodies to meet the challenge.

'Stand aside, Achilles,' Philoctetes called from the rock where he was standing. 'I can take him with one shot and the battle will be over.'

'And let you try to claim another victory you haven't earned?' Achilles scoffed without taking his eyes off his opponent. 'I give you my word, Philoctetes – if he falls to one of your arrows I'll make sure you're the next to die.'

'No, my lord,' cried another voice. 'You must let Philoctetes kill him.'

Achilles turned to see Mnemon stumbling up to the top of the ramp, clutching his wounded head, but at the same moment a warning shout from Eperitus made him leap aside. An instant later the gigantic club swept down on the spot where Achilles had been standing, splitting the sun-baked earth and sending up a haze of dust. Achilles was quick to launch himself at his opponent, knowing he would not be able to lift the heavy club in time. The enemy champion released the weapon and met Achilles's attack with his fist, punching him in the face and sending him flying backwards to land among the pile of slain warriors. With a speed that belied his size, he stooped down to pick up his club and stumped forward, intending to crush his enemy's head with a single blow.

The giant's punch would have killed many men outright, but Achilles quickly regained his senses and rolled aside as the great wooden club thumped down into the heaped bodies, breaking bones like kindling. He sprang to his feet and rushed with terrifying speed at the enemy champion. His lips were pulled back in a hate-filled sneer – his brain barely registering the shouts of Mnemon in the background – but as he lunged with the point of his sword his target moved swiftly aside and swung his club round to cleave the air above Achilles's head. Achilles ducked and edged backwards, and at the same moment he heard Mnemon shouting.

'Don't, my lord. That's King Tenes. Don't kill him!'

The giant warrior, hearing his own name called, glanced towards the injured Mnemon. Seeing his opportunity, Achilles rushed forward and kicked the club out of his hand, then with a swift jab sank the point of his sword into the huge, hair-covered chest, piercing the heart. Tenes was only able to gasp with surprise, before collapsing backwards with a thud that shook the ground and sent a cloud of dust into the air.

As the mass of defenders gasped in shock, Achilles walked over to their fallen king and placed a foot on his chest, leaning forward to study his victim in more detail. Then he turned his gaze on the men of Tenedos, who were eyeing him in terror and disbelief.

'Boo!' he shouted, and they flung down their weapons and ran back into the town.

'Sir,' said Mnemon, his voice shaking as he dragged himself toward
ss his master. 'Sir, I tried to warn you.'

Achilles looked at his servant, then around at the faces of his countrymen, mingled with the Ithacans and the unfamiliar men of Malia. Though the Malians were looking at him in amazement and awe, the Myrmidons were grim-faced and seemed somehow unhappy at their prince's victory.

'What is it, Mnemon?' he sighed, irritated by the persistence of his servant in his moment of triumph.

Mnemon wrung his hands together and hesitated for a long while before speaking. 'Sir, you've just killed King Tenes, a son of Apollo. By your mother's prophecy, you're now doomed to die at the hand of the god.'

Achilles stood and looked down at the stooping man before him. He took a deep breath, as if trying to contain his emotions, then drew back his sword.

'Then I won't be needing *you* any more, will I?' he said, and swept his servant's head from his shoulders.

## Chapter Thirty

# PHILOCTETES

Eperitus looked over the cliff edge at the massed ships of the fleet. Almost three quarters of the galleys that had left Aulis two weeks before were now gathered on the western side of Tenedos – their numbers constantly swelled by the piecemeal arrival of more stragglers – and a great traffic of small boats was weaving its way between them, ferrying men to and from the beach below the palace of King Tenes. Further out to the west, Eperitus could see the distant bulk of Lemnos, wide and blue in the bright sunshine, while slightly closer to the north-west was the island of Imbros. It was an unfamiliar seascape, but seemed pleasant enough under the blue skies of late summer.

He turned to the plateau where the battle had taken place. The town and palace beyond it were crawling with soldiers of almost every Greek state, scouring the buildings for any remaining loot or food that they could find. On the green slopes above the plateau were a large number of people – townsfolk and captured warriors – sitting and watching the pillaging of their homes as a dozen Myrmidons stood guard. Though their town had not been put to the torch, as was common in war, this was only because Nestor had ordered that its buildings be preserved for the wounded from the impending assault on Troy.

To one side of the plateau, three large mounds of rocks had been built. The largest marked the grave of the many enemies slain in the battle; a smaller one next to it covered the bodies of the Myrmidons and Malians who had died. The final mound had been built by Achilles himself in honour of King Tenes. It was a tribute to the giant warrior's ferocity in battle, but even more than that, of course, it was a testament to Achilles's own skill in defeating him.

Standing before the three mounds was a stone plinth, as high as a man's stomach and as wide as he could stretch his arms. It had been dragged from a crude temple in the town to act as an altar, where the Greeks could sacrifice to the gods in thanks for their safe arrival at Tenedos and their first victory over the forces of Asia. The air around it was full of the sounds and smells of animals. Scores of sheep and goats were held fast by slaves and soldiers, while bowls of water were placed before them. Only the animals who bowed their heads to drink could be killed, as they were deemed to have nodded their consent to the sacrifice. Else-where, knives were being sharpened on whetstones and a large fire was being lit, where the fat-wrapped thighbones of the slain beasts could be burnt for the gods. Odysseus stood beside Eperitus with a black lamb across his shoulders, its ankles tied with leather cord to keep it from struggling.

'Have you seen Agamemnon?' Achilles said, appearing before them. Patroclus was at his shoulder, a goat held fast beneath his arm.

'Come on now, Achilles,' said Odysseus, giving the prince a friendly slap on the shoulder. 'Agamemnon has made his judgement and you won't persuade him to change his mind.'

'He will as soon as I can make him listen to reason.'

'He judged Philoctetes the winner because the last Malian ship reached Tenedos before the last Myrmidon ship. If he changes his mind now the army will think he's indecisive, and with all the trouble he's had since the sacrifice . . .' Odysseus paused and looked briefly at Eperitus, who said nothing. 'With all the trouble he's had he won't want to weaken his authority any more. If you ask me, Achilles, he's trying to avoid you at the moment and will make his own sacrifices later. Right now he's with Nestor and Menelaus on his galley.'

Looking unconvinced, Achilles gave a snort of frustration and scanned the crowd for the King of Men. Eperitus, who had been supervising the removal of the altar as the Mycenaean fleet had arrived, had not been present when Agamemnon had declared Philoctetes the winner of the race. Odysseus, however, had already told him of the shocked silence with which Achilles had greeted the judgement, before turning on his heel and leading his Myrmidons back up the cliff face to continue building his monument to Tenes. Clearly, he had since reconsidered his moody silence and had returned with the intention of debating the matter in full with Agamemnon. But as his eyes scoured the crowds, they fell on Philoctetes and narrowed into a cruel squint.

'Well, there's not much I can do about Agamemnon – not for a while, at least – but I don't intend to let *that* braggart get away with cheating.'

'Leave him be, Achilles,' Eperitus cautioned. 'Agamemnon won't allow murder.'

'And you think he could stop me, if I had a mind to kill Philoctetes?' Achilles retorted. Then the dark look in his eyes was swept away with a laugh and he threw his arm about Eperitus's shoulders. 'Don't worry, my friend. I'm not so stupid as to cause a big stir. After all, I want this war to happen more than anyone, even if it means my death. No, when your mother's a goddess there are other ways of getting what you want. This goat,' he said, stroking the nose of the animal beneath Patroclus's arm, 'is for her, and in return I'm going to ask her to deal with that puffed-up Malian.'

He gave a wink, then turned and strode with Patroclus towards the altar. Patroclus threw the goat onto the stone slab and handed his friend a curved dagger from his belt. Raising the blade above his head, Achilles pointed it heavenwards and called on the name of his mother, the sea-nymph Thetis, who spent half her time on land and the other half in the depths of the sea.

'A dangerous man to have as an enemy,' Odysseus said, leaning close to Eperitus and talking in a hushed voice. 'Too proud by far. It'll be his downfall in the end.'

'Or ours,' Eperitus added sombrely.

Achilles leaned forward and grasped the horns of the goat, pulling its head back and running the dagger across its exposed throat. The animal kicked briefly against the cords that bound its ankles, then its crimson blood gushed out over Achilles's hands and its head dropped limp and lifeless at the side of the altar. The prince threw his face upwards and lifted his gore-spattered hands to the heavens, clenching them into angry fists. The men about him turned and watched as the young warrior seemed to shake with emotion. To their surprise there were tears rolling freely down his handsome face.

'Mother! Why do you allow me to be humiliated in this way? Am I not your only son, your only joy in the world of mortals? Do you wish me to be robbed of my dues by cheats and petty schemers? Then give me vengeance – if I am to be denied the glory of victory, then let the reward of him who has stolen it from me be a bitter one.'

He held his fists above his head for a moment longer, then let them fall to his sides as he bowed his head and closed his eyes. Eperitus, who had watched the sacrifice with distaste, looked across at Philoctetes, standing alone with the great bow across his back. All other eyes turned to the famous archer, who had been nothing more than a lowly shepherd before the dying Heracles had bestowed his bow and arrows on him. Many of the Greek leaders despised the presence of a man who had only joined their ranks because of a freak chance, and it seemed to Eperitus that some would have been pleased to see Achilles kill him there and then. Chief among them was Patroclus, who had not forgotten Philoctetes's accusation in the woods overlooking Aulis. Eperitus doubted he had informed Achilles of what Philoctetes had said – or the Malian would surely have been dead by now – but he wondered whether he was not quietly encouraging his animosity towards the young archer.

There was a look of disquiet on Philoctetes's face, but he said nothing. Instead he accepted a lamb from the arms of Medon, who was next in rank to Philoctetes among the Malians, and strode over to the altar. Taking a bowl of water from beside the base of the plinth, he washed away the gore where Achilles's goat had been then carried out his own sacrifice. As he slashed the lamb's throat and held up his arms in a hushed, modest prayer of thanks to Athena, there was a hiss and a sudden movement by his feet.

'Philoctetes!' Odysseus shouted, seeing a thin brown water snake appear from the long grass at the base of the altar.

The archer looked down to where he was pointing, but too late. The snake shot forward, biting him on the top of the foot. He cried out, his face suddenly contorted with terrible pain, and clutched at the bloodstained plinth for support. The serpent fled through the long grass towards Eperitus, who with a shudder of loathing unsheathed his sword and cut it in half. At the same moment, Philoctetes fell back into the grass.

'Suck out the venom!' he shouted, clutching at his foot and screaming with pain. 'In the name of the gods, suck it out!'

Palamedes, who was standing nearby, knelt down and took hold of his heel, but before he could lift it to his lips Achilles stepped forward and knocked him aside. There was a sly grin on his face as he turned and faced the crowd of shocked Greeks.

'That's not the way to deal with snake bites,' he declared. 'They need proper care. Where are Machaon and Podaleirius, the healers? They'll know what to do.'

'Their ships haven't arrived yet, and you know it,' said Menestheus, the Athenian king, frowning with anxiety at the terrible cries that were filling the air. 'Let Palamedes suck out the venom before it's too late.'

But Achilles refused to allow anyone near the suffering archer, other than a pair of his own Myrmidons who dragged him to one side so that the sacrifices could continue. As Odysseus stepped up to the altar some time later, Philoctetes's screams were still ringing out over the plateau, to be heard even by the men in the galleys below. Those leaders who had performed their sacrifices left quickly, driven away by the unbearable and undiminished noise of the archer's shrieks. Even the crowd of captured islanders on the hillside above the town had begged to be moved to the opposite side of the ridge, where they would be further away from the terrible racket.

Despite their sympathy for the wounded man, Odysseus and Eperitus were eager to carry out the sacrifice and return to their ship. A council had been arranged for that evening to discuss the strategy for the assault on Troy, but they could not bear to be near Philoctetes any longer than necessary. Not only did his cries grate on the nerves of everyone who heard them, there was now a nauseous stench coming from the wound, filling the air all around him. It was so bad that not even Philoctetes's own soldiers could remain at his side for long in the small copse where they had carried him. Indeed, following Odysseus's example, every man who had yet to make his sacrifice had torn strips of cloth, dampened them in water and tied them over his face to filter out the stench.

Because of his heightened senses, Eperitus suffered more than anyone. He could almost feel the pain of each wailing cry and the reek of the wound seemed to fill every corner of his brain. So it was with great relief that he accompanied Odysseus to the altar and helped him to sacrifice the lamb to Athena. But as they hastened away from the plateau to the ramp that led down to the beach, someone staggered from the shade of the small copse and collapsed at the side of the road. It was Philoctetes.

'Odysseus,' he pleaded, stretching out his arm towards the Ithacan king.

Odysseus removed the strip of cloth from his face and ran over to kneel at the archer's side.

'What is it, Philoctetes?'

'Odysseus, promise me you won't let Achilles kill me. He and Patroclus won't be satisfied until I'm dead, but I've a part to play in this war yet, I know it. Give me your word.'

'You have it, my friend,' Odysseus replied, his voice strained as he tried not to gag on the awful stench. 'I'll do whatever I can.'

The council of war was held on the beach below the palace. A double circle of benches had been set out in the shingle and around the perimeter was a ring of torches, flames twisting and flickering vigorously in the breeze from the sea. The foam-edged waves crashed repeatedly against the shoreline and the night air was filled with the voices of the Greek leaders and their captains as they arrived, talking at an exaggerated volume in an attempt to drown out the constant groans from the top of the cliff. There were slaves aplenty, rushing here and there with wine and food, and a large force of Agamemnon's bodyguard stood on watch all around.

Eventually only one place remained to be filled – a single, high-backed chair positioned at the western edge of the circle. This had been reserved for Agamemnon, who appeared at last, striding confidently through a gap that had been left in the benches opposite, his blood-red cloak flowing behind him. He turned as he reached the chair and looked at the torch-lit faces. On his chest was the ornate breastplate given to him by King Cinyras, and in his hand he held the staff of authority that Hephaistos had made for Zeus long ago.

'Let the council begin,' he announced as his bodyguard formed a tighter ring around the outer edge of the circle. 'Nestor, myself and others have discussed plans for the invasion of Ilium and the destruction of the city of Troy, and thereby the rescue of Helen, queen of Sparta. These plans are to be laid before the council now so that every man here will know his part in the coming attack and its aftermath. This is *not* a debate, though questions will be permitted. King Nestor?'

Nestor rose from the bench beside Agamemnon and took the staff from his hands. As he turned to address the council, Eperitus looked with hate-filled eyes towards the King of Men. It was the first time he had seen him since the day of the sacrifice, when he was bent in grief across the body of the innocent girl he had just slain. Then he had been wild-eyed and driven by evil intent, his courage bolstered by wine and his mind twisted with insanity. Now, though, the old Agamemnon seemed to have returned. His red cloak and white tunic were smooth and spotless, his long brown hair neatly combed and twisted into a tail behind his neck; his beard had been precisely clipped to the outline of his handsome, impassive face, and as he sat back in his throne-like chair he wore an air of confidence and unassailable power. Were it not for the dark circles around his eyes and the grey in his hair, he could have been the same self-assured, handsome king who had convened the council of war in Sparta a decade before.

He rested his chin between the thumb and forefinger of his left hand, the elbow of which was propped on the arm of his chair, and scanned the assembled kings with his cold blue eyes. Finally his gaze rested deliberately on Eperitus, and the two men looked at each other across the arena, Agamemnon hiding his dark thoughts behind a screen of impassivity and Eperitus barely able to conceal his distaste. Then Nestor stepped forward and raised his arms.

'Friends,' he began. 'Brothers! We have amassed the greatest fleet in the history of man. Our ranks contain the fiercest warriors ever to fight in the same army. The shores of Ilium are within sight! And yet the Trojans sleep peacefully in their beds, dreaming of their women and the wealth they have in plentiful supply. But tomorrow . . .' Nestor clenched his fist and stared with fiery eyes at them all. 'But very soon we will turn their dreams into nightmares. Soon we will drive the prows of our ships onto their beaches and teach them all about the ferocity of Greek revenge. Their high towers will burn with Greek fire, and their blood will run in the streets. Their gold and women will belong to us, and Helen will be free!'

There was a huge roar from the benches and stamping of feet on the shingle. Nestor raised his hands for silence.

'But battles and wars are not won by courage and skill alone.

There must be a strategy, and the right tactics need to be employed. The Trojan army have to be drawn out from the comfort of their city walls and destroyed, or the swift war we desire will become a long siege. Several of us have spent many days discussing how . . .'

Nestor fell quiet and looked across at Achilles, who had risen from his bench and walked out into the centre of the circle.

'Lord Achilles?' Nestor asked.

Achilles bowed his head to the old man before continuing. 'King Nestor, how can any of us be expected to listen to talk of strategy and tactics with *that* noise going on?'

He signalled with his thumb over his shoulder, and as if in answer a long, agonized wailing sailed out from the cliff top above. A murmur of agreement came from the benches.

'Something must be done about Philoctetes,' Achilles continued. 'His constant moaning and the stench of his wound are becoming a concern to the men. *We* can endure it, if that's what is required of us as leaders, but you can't ask the army to put up with it. It's already being said that this is a bad omen for the war, and you know how superstitious soldiers can be.'

'And what do you suggest, my friend?' Nestor responded. 'As soon as Machaon and Podaleirius arrived I sent them to tend Philoctetes's wound, but even they could do nothing for him. They tried every unguent and poultice known to their craft, without effect. In their opinion the snake that bit him must have been sent by a god, for the wound is unnaturally painful and resistant to healing. There's nothing we *can* do, Achilles.'

'Nothing?' Achilles asked. He strode up to the old king and held his hand out for the staff, then turned to face the council. 'Is there nothing we can do to put an end to this man's terrible pain, as well as our own suffering from the noise of it? *Nothing*? I would suggest there is. If he were a horse or a favourite dog, we'd kill him.'

'You cannot simply kill the man,' said Agamemnon calmly. He

remained sitting, but a single sweeping look from his cold eyes silenced the cacophony of competing voices that had erupted from the benches. 'For one thing, the wound isn't fatal: this would be no mercy killing, as if he had been struck down in the midst of battle and was soon to die. For another, we cannot begin this war by murdering a Greek, least of all the leader of a faction. Before long we would be at each others' throats again, just like it used to be. And unless we remain united we will never be victorious against Troy.'

'He may be a leader,' called a voice from the benches, 'but he's not one of us. He's not a noble.'

Shouts of agreement followed and Achilles, sensing he was gaining the support of a large part of the council, turned to Agamemnon.

'It's true – Philoctetes doesn't have the blood of gods or kings in his veins. He was just a shepherd boy when Heracles awarded him his magical bow and arrows, and it's only by that single chance that he has been given honour and power in his own country. By right, Medon should be leading the men of Malia, not Philoctetes. At least *he* is of noble birth.'

Achilles signalled to a short, burly warrior with leathery skin and a hardened look in his eye. Medon rose from his seat and looked about at the ring of faces.

'Achilles has already spoken to me about this,' he said in a low, hoarse voice, 'and I've agreed to end Philoctetes's misery and take command in his place.'

'How noble of you, Medon,' said Agamemnon sarcastically, this time rising from his seat and taking two steps forward. 'But isn't this more to do with your anger, Achilles, at losing the race to Tenedos? Because of your hurt pride, you would have an innocent man slaughtered like a dumb beast.'

Achilles's hand flew to the pommel of his sword. 'That's a fine accusation to make,' he retorted, his face red with anger, 'when *you* only awarded the victory to Philoctetes because I tried to prevent the sacrifice of Iphigenia. And how can you accuse me of wanting to kill Philoctetes like a dumb beast when *you* murdered your own daughter in cold blood!'

Suddenly Agamemnon's hand was on the hilt of his sword, tugging the blade free of its scabbard. Achilles's own weapon was quick to meet it and, with a loud slither of metal, the razor sharp edges grated against each other. Then a third sword swept upwards and knocked them apart, and a moment later Eperitus placed himself between the two men.

'Sheathe your weapons,' he commanded. 'Use your anger on the Trojans, my lords, not each other.'

Agamemnon was the first to step back, his cool exterior quickly reimposing itself.

'Come, Achilles,' he said. 'Eperitus is right, there's no profit in squabbling among ourselves.'

Achilles hesitated, then slid his sword back into his sheath. 'And Philoctetes?' he persisted, eyeing the King of Men with poorly disguised anger. 'What are we to do about him?'

'Send him to Lemnos,' Odysseus suggested, rising from his bench. After the bitter exchange between Agamemnon and Achilles, the King of Ithaca's deep voice seemed calm and reassuring, filled with wisdom and justice. 'There's nothing more we can do for him here, and as Achilles rightly suggests he'll only be an annoyance to the men. But there's no need to kill the poor wretch; he deserves compassion, not murder. Instead, we should leave him on Lemnos for now and return for him when the war is over. Medon can have his wish to lead the Malians, on the condition he and his men share their plunder with Philoctetes.'

There was a chorus of agreement from the benches. Odysseus looked directly at Achilles, who after a few moments nodded and handed the speaker's staff back to Nestor. Though he had seemed determined to see Philoctetes dead, he was content with the lesser victory of having the archer marooned for the duration of the war. He returned to his bench and sat down.

Agamemnon also returned to his seat, but not before he had

turned to Eperitus and given him a curt nod of thanks for his intervention. For his own part, Eperitus felt an uneasy mixture of loathing and satisfaction. He would rather have allowed Achilles's proud anger to strike Agamemnon dead – a fitting end for an abhorrent man. But he was honour-bound to defend the King of Men, and a small corner of his mind took pleasure from the knowledge that Clytaemnestra's revenge would be much more terrible than a swift thrust of Achilles's sword.

He returned to his seat next to Odysseus as Nestor stepped back into the centre of the council. The golden staff gleamed in his hand, the jewels upon its head glittering in the torchlight.

'Tomorrow, then, Odysseus will transport Philoctetes to Lemnos while we rest and gather our strength. A sizeable landing party will seize the bay a little further up the coast, as already planned, and anybody found there or on the hills about it will be killed or taken prisoner. All shipping passing the bay is to be captured and held. Every measure has to be taken to prevent news of our arrival reaching King Priam. Then, the morning after, we attack.'

'Curse you, Odysseus,' Philoctetes hissed from the prow of the ship, where he had been laid with his arms and legs bound. By now he was exhausted from the pain of his wound and a night without sleep, and his voice was hoarse and weary. 'Curse Achilles. Curse Agamemnon. Curse all Ithacans. And curse this damnable wound. Oh, in the name of all the gods, won't you please kill me?'

'It's just not right,' said Antiphus as he pulled back on his oar. His voice was muffled by the damp strip of cloth he wore to filter out the worst of the stench; all the crew had them. 'I've never seen such archery. I don't care how much he complains or how bad he smells, that man could hit Priam in the eye if he was on the loftiest tower in all Ilium. We should be taking him *to* the war, not *from* it.'

But Antiphus had few sympathizers on the galley, whose crew had been forced to endure the obnoxious Philoctetes since before dawn that morning. They had spent the night listening to his screams of pain while he was on the cliff top on Tenedos, so to be confined with him on the claustrophobic deck of a ship had driven them almost beyond the limit of their endurance. Only the knowledge that they would soon be rid of him prevented them from throwing him overboard.

Odysseus ignored Antiphus and peered out through the thick mists, looking for rocks as he steered the galley into the lee of a promontory that thrust out from the eastern edge of the island. The sail had been furled and the crew were busy at the oars. The only sound was the trickle of water running off the oar blades and the occasional cawing of gulls in the air above. The sun was in the sky, but they could only sense its presence as a concentrated point of whiteness in the dense fog that enveloped everything.

'This will do,' Odysseus announced, catching a glimpse of a rocky shoreline to his right. 'Throw out the anchor stones and make the boat ready.'

Two loud splashes followed, while on the benches an argument broke out between the oarsmen about who should fetch the boat. Clearly, no one wanted the job of rowing Philoctetes to shore.

'Stop that bickering at once,' Eperitus snapped. 'Arceisius and Eurybates, get the boat ready; Eurylochus and Polites, bring Philoctetes – and be gentle with him. And you can fetch his bow and arrows, Antiphus.'

The boat was lowered into the water and the two oarsmen took their places with a distinct lack of enthusiasm. Eurylochus shot a hateful glance at Eperitus as he moved with deliberate slowness to the prow, then stood by as the huge arms of Polites scooped Philoctetes up from the deck and carried him to the side. The rest of the crew turned away in disgust as he passed, pressing their damp face-cloths closer to their noses. Only Antiphus showed any enthusiasm, running to fetch the magnificent weapons that had once belonged to Heracles and handling them with reverence and admiration.

Once Polites had tenderly lowered the unhappy figure of

Philoctetes into the small boat and clambered out again – seemingly ignorant of the string of curses that were directed at him – Odysseus and Eperitus stepped into the small, unsteady vessel and sat down. Antiphus begged to be allowed to join them, and it was with great relief and pleasure that Eurybates surrendered his place at the oars to him. Once Antiphus was aboard, they pushed off into the mist and rowed slowly towards the shore. All about them sharp black rocks poked out of the water and more than once they felt the bottom of the boat scraping across stone. Then they reached a low, flat shelf of rock pitted with little pools of water and criss-crossed with weathered cracks.

'This will have to do,' Odysseus said, moving to the front of the boat and leaping ashore.

Arceisius threw him a rope, which the king wound several times about a finger of stone before tying a knot in it. The others carried Philoctetes ashore and set him down, where he lay on his back and looked about at the cold, lonely surroundings.

'You can't leave me here,' he protested. He winced against the attack of a fresh wave of pain, but mastered himself again and reached out to seize Odysseus's ankle. 'You'd have been better letting Achilles kill me in cold blood than leaving me to die on this inhospitable rock.'

But Odysseus stared down at the archer with impassive eyes. 'I'm sorry Philoctetes,' he said. 'I'm simply carrying out the will of the council.'

'But he's right,' Antiphus said, stepping out of the boat with the bow and quiver of arrows cradled in his arms. 'We can't just abandon him to his fate.'

'May the gods bless you, friend,' Philoctetes sighed, looking up at Antiphus.

'We'll come back for you when the war is over,' Odysseus replied coldly.

'But what about Philoctetes's bow and arrows, my lord,' Antiphus continued. 'Troy won't fall as easily as everybody seems to think, and before the end we might have need of these weapons.'

'We have our orders,' Odysseus insisted, reaching across and sliding one of the black-feathered arrows from the quiver. 'But that doesn't mean the bow of Heracles should remain idle.'

'What do you mean?' asked Antiphus.

Odysseus twirled the arrow's shaft between his fingers. 'Can you imagine your natural skill combined with the magical accuracy of these arrows? If you took the weapons, Antiphus, you could become a great warrior in your own right. What do you think?'

'No,' Philoctetes objected. 'Heracles gave them to me! You've no right to them, and I'll need them to hunt food here – even if it's just scrawny seagulls. You can't take them from me.'

But Antiphus did not seem to be listening. He had slung the quiver over his shoulder and was testing how the bow felt in his skilled hands, drawing the string back to his cheek and aiming an imaginary arrow into the billowing fog. A distant look was in his eyes, as if he was seeing himself shoot down Priam and his sons in the midst of battle, single-handedly bringing victory over Troy and being rewarded with the lion's share of the plunder. Then he sighed and lowered the bow.

'I've never handled such a fine weapon,' he said sadly. 'It's even better than the bow Iphitus gave you, my lord. But it's not mine, and Philoctetes is right – without this to hunt food, he'll starve. No, I can't take it.'

He handed the weapons down to Philoctetes, who snatched them to himself greedily. Odysseus placed a hand on Antiphus's shoulder and patted him gently.

'I knew you wouldn't take it,' he said. 'You're honourable, just like Eperitus. And I'm sorry I tempted you, but now we must go.'

The Ithacans took the supplies from the small boat and laid them down next to the Malian archer, who watched every movement with spiteful eyes. Then another wave of pain swept through his body and he threw his head back in an anguished howl before collapsing on his side. The last man settled himself in the boat and the oars were thrust against the rock shelf, pushing the little vessel out into the dark waters.

'Damn you all,' Philoctetes whimpered, straining himself to speak through gritted teeth. 'I pray to all the gods and the spirit of Heracles that you'll need me before the end. You'll be begging me to help you, and then I'll laugh in your faces. Curse you, Odysseus! Curse all you Ithacans!'

*Chapter Thirty-one*

# THE BEACHES OF ILIUM

Helen and Paris walked hand in hand along the shore, listening to the sound of the waves and the cry of the gulls overhead. A warm breeze blew in from the sea, though the morning sun was only a watery blur in the eastern sky, hidden behind the thin ceiling of cloud that stretched from horizon to horizon. To their right was the Trojan plain, ending in the high plateau from which the walls of Troy frowned towards the west. Ahead of them the shoreline was broken by the mouth of the Simöeis, while to their left a low, pale fog was seeping into the bay from the ocean, twisting its spectral fronds about the high-sided hulls of the Trojan fleet. Only yesterday the bay had been filled with activity as the sixty galleys disembarked the armies of several of Troy's allies, but now the ships were almost deserted and their sails and spars had been lowered and stowed away.

Despite the warm breath of the sea, the foamy water was cool as it washed over Helen's toes and soaked the hem of her long dress. It was a pleasant feeling, she thought; it made her feel alive and free, just as Paris's hot, rough hand in hers made her feel safe and loved. She turned her head slightly to look at him from the corner of her eye, only to find him doing the same.

He smiled. 'What is it? Having regrets about marrying such an ugly man?'

'Of course not,' she replied with a slight frown. 'Anyway, you aren't ugly.'

'Oh no? Since when have flat noses and livid pink scars been considered handsome?'

Helen raised an eyebrow and her mouth twitched sideways into a little grin.

'*I* like your face – isn't that enough?' she asked, touching the bridge of his nose where the scar crossed it. 'It has character. Those young men who gaze at me in the streets of Troy may be good-looking, but they're just boys. These lines and scars you bear show you're a man.'

'Menelaus was no mere boy,' Paris countered.

'Ah, but you forget I was awarded to Menelaus like a prize. He didn't steal me from a heavily guarded palace as you did. You risked everything for me, Paris, and no woman could want more than that.'

Paris smiled at her praise, which he knew was heartfelt, but he had not finished teasing her yet. 'And how will you feel about him when he brings an army of Greeks to Ilium, just to rescue you?'

'Don't joke about such things,' Helen said, facing her new husband with a troubled look in her eye. After a moment she looked away. 'Fortunately for us, I doubt the Greeks will bother these shores for my sake. I hope they'll have forgotten all about me in a year or two.'

'Hector *will* be disappointed,' Paris said. 'He was starting to think a Greek attack might be the answer to his prayers – expend the might of Sparta and possibly Mycenae against our impenetrable walls, then send a Trojan army across the Aegean to claim the Atreides brothers' kingdoms for himself.'

'Your brother,' Helen sighed, putting her arms about Paris's waist and pulling his firm body against hers. 'He reminds me so much of Agamemnon. Take last night, for example: a head full of your most potent wine, seated next to Andromache in that beautiful dress . . .'

'With *that* perfume,' Paris added.

Helen nodded enthusiastically. 'And all he can talk about is *the threat of Greek expansion across the Aegean, bringing their foreign gods and – don't be offended, sister – their uncouth ways to our shores.'*

Paris laughed at her impersonation of his brother's gravelly voice. Her ability to mimic others was one of the many hidden delights of his princess: her imitations of Apheidas and Aeneas were hilarious, while her talent for sounding like Hecabe and Leothoë was uncanny, so much so that Paris had nicknamed her Echo after the chattering nymph who could only repeat the words of others. Still smiling, Paris lowered his lips to hers in a soft kiss.

'I know my brother better than you do, my dear,' he said, pulling away and looking into her large eyes. 'And I can tell he likes Andromache. No, don't laugh, he does.'

'But he barely looked at her all evening, and the only thing he could talk about was Troy this and Troy that.'

'That's natural – Troy is his first love. But when Andromache spoke he listened, and on two occasions he even asked her opinion.'

'So what?' said Helen, shrugging her shoulders dismissively. 'Isn't that just being polite?'

'Not for Hector! He's rarely interested in what others think, and I can't even remember the last time he asked someone for their opinion. But we shouldn't mock him; if the Greeks do come, Hector is the best defence we have. He is worth more to Troy than all our allies put together.'

As Paris spoke a horn sounded on one of the towers behind him, followed by a second and then a third. He turned to look in consternation at the city walls, from which the deep, low notes were still reverberating. Several small figures were running along the battlements, and as he watched them more calls followed.

'What is it?' asked Helen.

'They're sounding the alarm,' he answered, his voice calm but edged with uncertainty. 'I used to hear that call every other day when I was on the northern borders, but it hasn't been sounded here since Heracles attacked – when my father was just a boy.'

He looked over his shoulder at the tall galleys in the bay. The mists were beginning to lift and the dark vessels were clearly visible now. The few men left aboard were pressed to the sides, looking across at the soaring walls of the city as if expecting to see an army drawing near, or to hear the clash of arms ringing out across the empty plains. But nothing had changed beyond the thinning of the clouds above and the appearance of a first few beams of sunlight. They gleamed golden on the parapets and towers of Troy, occasionally flashing off the bronze helmet or spear-point of a soldier.

'It's Menelaus,' Helen said, looking nervously towards the mouth of the bay. Through the haze she could just see where the headland sloped down to reveal the wide north-easterly gulf and the open sea beyond. 'He must have come for me.'

Paris stroked her cheek and smiled reassuringly. 'It's not Menelaus, I promise you. It's something else, a mistake or some kind of . . .'

'Some kind of what?' Helen asked.

But Paris's attention was focused over her shoulder, forcing her to look back and see for herself what had silenced him.

'Aphrodite save us,' she whispered.

Where only a moment before the sea had been empty, but for the mist that crept over its surface, now she could see dark shapes emerging from the wall of swirling grey. At first there were just three or four, moving with calm menace towards the mouth of the bay, but with each nervous breath that filled Helen's lungs more appeared, and then more until the whole ocean teemed with them. Their broad sails were filled with the warm breeze that a short while before she had been pleased to feel on her face and in her hair. Now she cursed it, for its gentle breath was ushering death and destruction towards her new home. Suddenly the strength left her legs and she fell forward onto her knees in the surf. More horn calls reverberated from the towers and walls of Ilium.

'Come on, Helen,' Paris said urgently. The sight of his wife collapsing released him from his shocked stupor, and he leaned forward and lifted her to her feet. 'Come on, love. We must go.'

'Why?' she retorted, trying to push him away. 'What good will it do? Menelaus has come to take me back, and the walls and armies of Troy won't stop him.' She looked in desperation at her husband and there were tears in her eyes. 'Go back, Paris. Go back to the city and leave me here. If I give myself up to the Greeks they'll depart in peace and you'll be safe.'

Before he could stop her, she ran towards the surf-edged waves as if it were her intention to swim out to the Greek fleet. Paris caught her before she was knee-deep in the water, then lifting her into his arms carried her back up the sloping beach towards his chariot. The horses stamped and snorted at his approach, pleased to be in the presence of their master again.

'You're *my* wife now, Helen,' he said, setting her down in the chariot, 'and for good or evil we have to face the consequences of what we've done. But I'm not letting you go back to him, even if it costs the blood of every man in Troy.'

Overwhelmed with fear, she threw her arms around his neck and buried her face in the rough wool of his tunic. Behind them, the crews of the Trojan galleys had abandoned their vessels and were now rowing in dozens of small boats to the shore. Further out, an endless stream of Greek warships was pouring into the mouth of the bay, the motifs on their sails now clearly visible. There were a hundred and fifty of them at least, Paris estimated – eight thousand warriors heading for his home with murderous intent.

From the walls of Troy another horn call erupted, but it was not the long, sonorous warning of the alarm. This time the sound was clear and high, repeated in short bursts, and as it rang out in defiance the gates of Troy swung open and streams of horsemen came flooding out to the attack.

※

Odysseus and Eperitus stood in the prow of the galley as a warm breeze swept the deck, bellying out the dolphin-motifed sail and pushing them relentlessly towards the shores of Ilium. The sky above was covered by a thin layer of cloud, ploughed into long channels that screened the early morning sun, while all around them the surface of the ocean was covered in a blanket of fine mist. It condensed in their hair and on their eyelashes and made their woollen clothing damp to the touch. Everywhere they looked, packs of black-hulled ships nosed forward through the white fog as if sniffing out their prey.

Eperitus looked over his shoulder at Arceisius and Polites, who sat together on the nearest bench. Arceisius's eyes stared out nervously from his pale face, making Eperitus recall the look of uncertainty he had seen on the lad's face when he had killed his first man on Samos. Did his young squire have the stomach for the coming fight, he wondered? Then, reading the look on Eperitus's face, Polites placed a long, muscular arm reassuringly about Arceisius's shoulder and began talking to him in his slow, deep voice. Eperitus smiled to himself: the Thessalian was telling him not to worry; whatever lay ahead, he would look after him.

Behind them the deck was crowded with anxious Ithacans, fully armoured in greaves, breastplates and helmets. Most wore their broad leather shields across their backs whilst they sat patiently on the benches, thinking of the battle ahead and the families and homes they had left behind. Their spears lay at their feet and their swords and daggers hung from their belts; for most it would be the first time they had used them in anger, and as they sailed towards the unknown experience of battle, fear and worry gnawed quietly away at their courage.

But many also took heart from the words of their king as the Ithacan soldiery had waited on the beach at Tenedos, ready to board their galleys in the pre-dawn light. Odysseus had stood before them in the full garb of war and spoken of their island homes – of Ithaca, Dulichium, Samos and Zacynthos – knowing full well now, after all his efforts to stop the war, that it was his spoken doom not to see them again for twenty years. He named the hills, woods, harbours and beaches that were so familiar to all of them, evoking images of faraway places that were ever near to their hearts. His voice breaking with passion, he told them they were not merely a body of soldiers – they were a band of *countrymen*! The dried chelonion flowers they wore in their belts were there to remind them that they were Ithacans. True, they might only be fishermen, farmers or herdsmen by trade, but they were also friends and neighbours: a common identity and a shared homeland bound them to one another. And though for many this day would be their last – dying in a strange country for a woman only a handful of them had ever seen – the glory they reaped that morning would be theirs forever.

Eperitus leaned forward and peered into the mist. The Ithacans were on the far left of the fleet, with the Spartans in the centre and the Myrmidons on the right; but the vanguard was made up of forty ships from Thessaly, led by the brothers Protesilaus and Podarces. Odysseus and Achilles were deliberately holding back, conscious of Thetis's prophecy that the first man to land would also be the first to die. The fact that Menelaus was not spearheading the attack, though, could only mean Achilles had also shared his mother's words of doom with the king of Sparta. Then, as Eperitus pondered these things, calls broke out from the leading ships and moments later a line of low black hills appeared through the swirling fog. The sight of land brought excitement to the Ithacan benches, but a barked order from Odysseus quickly restored silence.

The mist was dissipating before the seaborne wind to reveal a spur of land, beyond which was a broad harbour filled with warships. The sight of the high-sided galleys brought a shock of fear and tension to the approaching Greeks. Shields were pulled from backs and spears readied; archers fitted arrows to their bows and gathered in the prows of each ship, ready to fire at the Trojan crews; long lances for fighting ship-to-ship were passed forward. Then they saw the sails were furled and spars stowed. The Trojan fleet was sleeping, and with a mixture of relief and delight they realized their attack was not expected.

Suddenly the attention of every man was drawn away from the dormant enemy vessels to a new sight. Rising above the skeins of fog beyond the mouth of the bay, at last, were the battlements and towers of Troy that they had feared and dreamed of for so long. They shone white in the sunlight that was now breaking through the fine clouds, and here and there fierce flashes of bronze reflected from the weapons of the sentinels that stood on the walls. And as they looked on in awe, horns began calling from the city – deep, sad notes that rolled towards the Greeks like a dirge.

'They've seen us,' Odysseus announced.

Eperitus could see the king's knuckles whiten as they gripped the shaft of his spear, but if he felt fear or doubt as they approached the enemy harbour he showed no sign of it. Eperitus, however, felt his mouth grow dry and his stomach stir with nerves. His armour was suddenly heavy as it hung about him, as if the familiar leather and bronze had been transformed to lead. The high fortifications that he had looked up at in admiration on his first visit now seemed menacing and insurmountable. This was the city for which his daughter had been brutally slain, and for which many other terrible sacrifices would soon be required. For the sake of its walls, Odysseus was doomed to spend twenty years away from his beloved family and homeland. Even the great Achilles would perish, forfeiting the sweet joys of mortal existence to die in battle and gain eternity through the songs of bards. Many others would die also, to crowd Hades's halls with their miserable spectres.

And yet few rued the war, whatever their rank or ability. For the lowborn soldier it was a chance for plunder and riches exceeding anything he could earn with the plough or the fishing net. For the professional warrior there was the exhilaration of battle, for which he had trained most of his life. For those of noble blood, immortal renown called, while for the high-minded there was the hope of restoring the pride of Greece. Agamemnon would fulfil his desire for power over the Greeks and the subjugation of their enemies, and his brother would regain the wondrous wife without whom his life had lost its meaning.

From the first rumours of war, Eperitus had been enticed by the prospect of battle. The love of combat burned in his blood like a fire that could only be quenched by slaughter; and the fire was intensified by his desire to make a name for himself, a name that would outlive his brief time on earth. But since Mycenae, he had realized that such a desire was empty without someone to fight for, someone to cherish his memory and pass it down to others. That hope had perished with the death of Iphigenia, and he knew her loss had changed him. Once, his craving to abandon himself to danger had been driven by a nagging need to prove himself, to survive by the skill and strength that he possessed. Now his joy of battle was powered by other motives: to serve and protect Odysseus and ensure his safe return to Penelope and Telemachus; to honour the memory of Iphigenia, who had always looked on him as a fearsome warrior; and finally a snarling lust to avenge her death. And since he was sworn to protect Agamemnon, it was the soldiers of Troy who would have to bear the brunt of his vengeance.

The Thessalian ships were now pouring through the wide mouth of the harbour. Men appeared on the decks of the Trojan galleys, shocked at the sudden appearance of the Greek fleet. Within moments they were lowering boats into the water and rowing for the shore, while others jumped overboard and swam in their desperation to escape. A few of the Thessalian archers took hopeful shots at the half-naked figures, but the distance was still too great and the arrows clattered harmlessly off the decks or sank into the calm blue waters. By now the Ithacans, Spartans and Myrmidons were cramming into the entrance to the bay. There was a cacophony of noise as, in their haste to reach the undefended beach, hulls scraped against each other and men shouted warnings or angry threats. Then a series of new horn calls erupted from the towers of Ilium, high, quick notes that made men's blood race and their breath quicken. Every head turned towards the city and a moment later the gates burst open to release a deluge of cavalry. The Greeks stood and watched in excited horror as file after file of horsemen galloped out from the Scaean Gate to the south of the city, forming long lines before the western walls. Ranks of spearmen and archers exited at the same time, pouring onto the plain like an army of irritated ants whose nest had been disturbed.

On the ships, kings and captains bellowed orders to their crews and the decks burst back into life as soldiers readied their arms and sailors manoeuvred their craft into lines. But the Thessalians, who had already reformed, did not wait for their allies and surged forward to the attack. Foremost among them was the ship of Protesilaus, who had ordered his crew to lower their oars and get the galley ashore as quickly as possible. The sibling competition between Protesilaus and Podarces was well known to the Greeks, and it was no surprise to see the ship of the younger brother follow the example of the elder and make for the beach with all speed. But Protesilaus would not be caught. He wanted the honour of being first to land on Trojan soil and now he was visible to the whole fleet, standing alone at the prow of his ship as it raced towards the sand. He was a tall man whose head was covered in ringlets of black hair tinged with grey that hung down to his shoulders. Though his shield was on his arm and he wore breast-plate and greaves, his helmet had been cast aside so that all could see him and know who was leading the attack against Troy.

The rest of the forty Thessalian ships followed in the wake of their leaders, while behind them the lines of Myrmidons, Spartans and Ithacans – four deep already, with more still entering the mouth of the harbour – began to move into the attack. But the Trojans were racing out to meet them. Hundreds of horsemen, the ground thudding beneath the hooves of their mounts, poured forward across the plain, the early morning sunshine glinting on their raised spear-points. They were followed by dozens of chariots, each pulled by a pair of horses and carrying a driver and an archer or spearman in the light cars that bounced behind. Finally, row upon row of infan-try and swarms of archers came running after them, a mighty roar of defiance thundering out from their throats to fill the air above the plain.

Protesilaus narrowed his eyes at the approaching army, several thousand strong with every man viciously armed and baying for blood. With a last, hurried prayer to Ares on his lips, he gripped the high prow of his ship and waited for the impact as it hit the beach. He glanced across at his brother, who was still behind him and away to his right, then behind at his men, still heaving at the oars. A moment later the broad belly of the galley thumped into a sandy shelf below the waterline. Everyone on board lurched forward, tumbling over each other as the vessel slid to a halt. With a great shout, Protesilaus leapt overboard and landed knee-deep in the water. Clutching his long spear fiercely in both hands, he waded through the surf towards the beach.

The Trojan army was now screened from his sight by a high bank, where the beach rose up to meet the firmer soil of the plain. The ridge was crowned by a curtain of tall, dry grass that quivered in the breeze from the sea. As Protesilaus cleared the water he took another fleeting look to his right, where Podarces's galley was now juddering to a halt further along the beach, then over his shoulder to where the different-coloured bows of the Greek galleys were racing towards the shore. His own men were now crowding into the prow of his galley, but instead of leaping into the water their eyes were focused on the plain beyond the grassy ridge. Two or three archers released hurried shots, and then Protesilaus heard the drumming of hooves followed by the snort of a horse. He looked up and saw a man on a grey mare standing on the bank at the top of the beach, a long spear held at the ready in his right hand. He was tall and powerfully built. His stern, bearded face looked down at the Greek warrior with a ferocious hatred.

'When your ghost reaches the halls of Hades,' he began, speaking in Greek, 'tell the dead you are the first of many today, and that you were slain by Hector, son of Priam.'

Protesilaus felt a momentary tremor of fear, then with a rush of energy his courage returned the strength to his limbs. In a quick movement he pulled back his spear and aimed it at the horseman. But before it could leave his hand, Hector's own weapon caught him in the chest, piercing the breastplate and hurling him backwards with such force that Protesilaus was pinned against the hull of his own ship. A howl of anger erupted from the deck above him, followed by a rush of armoured bodies as the Thessalians leapt down into the surf and ran yelling past their dead leader towards the man who had killed him. In response, Hector drew his sword and spurred his horse down the slope to meet them. He was followed by a great pounding of hooves, and a moment later a wave of horsemen swept over the grassy ridge to plunge into the crowd of Greek spearmen.

From the prow of their ship, Odysseus and Eperitus looked on in silence as the Thessalians fell back before the onslaught. The Trojan horses were up to their hocks in the sea, their riders hacking and slashing at the invaders, lopping heads and limbs from bodies and filling the dark waters with corpses. More Thessalians leapt recklessly into the fray from the sides of their galley. The nearest horsemen were caught and dragged from their mounts, to be stabbed, throttled or drowned in the shallow waters. But the Trojans were winning an easy victory, enjoying the advantage of height, momentum and numbers. Hector was at the heart of the fight, a master of battle who led his men by the example of his own ferocity and courage.

The slaughter of the Thessalians was terrible to watch. The water churned all around them from the thrashing of the wounded and dying, and the breakers were scarlet with their blood. Further along the beach Podarces and his men were also hemmed in by cavalry, but a screen of archers firing from the prow of his ship forced the Trojans back and allowed him to form his spearmen into a line. Soon they were pushing along the beach towards his brother's galley, driving the enemy horsemen before them.

'Ready your shields and spears!' Eperitus ordered, looking back at the rows of soldiers. Like the Thessalians, they were mostly inexperienced and poorly armed. Fear was written clearly on many of their faces, though some seemed eager for their first battle. Others were relaxed and calm, and Polites was one of these. Towering head and shoulders above Arceisius, he chatted happily to the young squire while adjusting the fit of his armour, as if he were preparing for nothing more dangerous than a training exercise. Though the Thessalian had once been an unwelcome bandit in their homeland, the Ithacans around him drew comfort from his massive presence and confident mien.

It pleased Eperitus to see his men and he knew his faith in them was warranted. The long days of training he and Odysseus had given them at Aulis would help them to survive, and in time their experience and fighting instinct would develop. More than that, they were drawn from doughty stock, peace-loving islanders who were slow to anger, but when roused were tough, courageous and fearsome. And though not one of them had experienced warfare on such a scale before, Eperitus was sure that under Odysseus's leadership they would prove themselves more than a match for the Trojans.

Thessalian ships were thumping into the sand at every point now. Eperitus watched in tense excitement as hundreds of yelling warriors spewed onto the beach, enraged at the death of their leader and seeking vengeance in Trojan blood. But Hector was a skilled cavalry commander. Knowing his lightly armoured horsemen were wasted in a standing fight, he was already leading them back across the plain to safety. But there was another purpose to the practised disorder of their flight, and to Eperitus's dismay many of the Greeks were taking the bait.

They were led by Podarces, who by then had found his older brother's body still pinned to the hull of his ship. With tears of grief and rage in his eyes, he led his men through the screen of tall grass to the plain beyond, only to see the cavalry already streaming to safety behind a long wall of Trojan spearmen. Undeterred, the Thessalians now charged towards the disciplined line of tall, rectangular shields hedged with heavy spears. The immediate danger did not come from the infantry, though, but the densely packed archers who stood behind them. At an order from Hector, they let fly their arrows and the Thessalian ranks fell like stalks of wheat before a scythe. They wavered for a moment, then rushed forward again, only to be met by another hail of missiles. This time the survivors, Podarces among them, turned and fled back to the cover of the sloping beach. Not one man had reached the Trojan line.

By this time the first waves of Spartans, Myrmidons and Ithacans were hitting the shoreline, beaching their ships all along the great crescent of sand between the mouths of the Simöeis and the Scamander. Eperitus felt a heavy thud beneath the belly of the ship and an instant later the whole mass of wood, leather and canvas came to a halt. Within a moment he had leapt down into the surf, close behind Odysseus, and was splashing up the sloping beach. The rest of the crew followed, pouring over the sides of the galley and shouting like Furies, drunk on fear and courage. All around them masses of other Greeks were surging ashore to join the battered Thessalians, who were already reforming for a second attack.

Out in the bay, flames were blazing up from the Trojan galleys where reckless Greeks had tossed lighted torches over the sides as they passed. Now great plumes of black smoke were carried inland on the sea breeze, darkening the air over the beach and the plains beyond. Then there was a great hum of massed bowstrings released simultaneously, followed by the evil hiss of arrows as they filled the sky. Men looked up in fear, watching as the black shafts seemed to hang suspended for a long moment, before plunging down again towards the crowded shore and the galleys behind. Eperitus and Odysseus threw themselves on the sand with their shields above their heads as the deadly hail of bronze-tipped missiles fell. Many clattered on the wooden decks of the Greek ships or snagged in the sails; others hit the water or thumped into the raised leather shields of crouching soldiers. And many found their mark. Men cried out as arrows bit into flesh, toppling dead and wounded alike onto the sand or back into the waiting water. More men tumbled from the decks of the ships, clutching at the long, feathered shafts protruding from torsos and limbs.

'Keep your shields raised, damn it,' Odysseus shouted at his countrymen, as more arrows rose into the smoke-filled sky and fell again. More screams of pain rang out and more men fell.

Then one voice rose above all the others. It was a great bellowing shout of rage, a sound that filled even Eperitus with sudden fear. And then, bursting out from the Myrmidon ranks like a raging lion, he saw Achilles. He wore a black-plumed helmet with a bronze visor crafted to look like the face of the war god, its mouth open in a war cry and its eyes frowning in anger. He bore his tall shield before him and in his right hand he carried his fabled ash spear, but no weight of arms could slow the speed of his wrath or his lust for battle. Before his Myrmidons or any of the other Greeks could think to follow, he had sprinted up the beach and leapt through the screen of grass to the plain above. Startled and exhilarated by the ferocity and pace of Achilles's attack – and desperate to see him in battle – Eperitus forgot the danger of the Trojan archers and raced towards the protective bank. It seemed every other man in the Greek army had the same thought, and the roar of their voices as they charged up the beach was deafening.

Eperitus felt a new surge of energy as he dashed across the sand. Odysseus was at his side – his usually mild features now fearsome to look at – and together they plunged through the tall grass to the plain beyond. Ahead of them, looming like a great cliff in the distance, were the walls and towers of their goal – the city of Troy. In between were the lines of Hector's infantry, their spearpoints bristling as they awaited the heavily armoured Greeks. A great press of archers were behind them, preparing to release a new volley of arrows – this time directly at the front rank of the invaders – while the cavalry had split into two groups and were moving to protect the flanks. Hector sat astride his grey mare behind the rows of waiting spearmen, his burnished armour flashing in the sunlight and his sword raised high above his head. As he saw the mass of Greeks rush out from the cover of the beach, with the lone figure of Achilles sprinting ahead of them, his stern face broke into a satisfied grin. A moment later his sword fell and a thousand arrows carried death to the enemies of Troy.

Eperitus was running with his heavy shield held one-handed before him. Arrows thumped into the thick, four-fold leather; all about him soldiers screamed and crashed to the ground, to be trampled by the men behind. He glimpsed Achilles through the black smoke that rolled across the plain, swatting aside the storm of missiles with a sweep of his shield as if they were nothing more than a cloud of flies. But many more followed, and to Eperitus's amazement the black shafts broke or sprang away from the prince as if they had hit a pillar of stone. Laughing with the joy of battle and the certainty of his own invulnerability, Achilles charged straight into the Trojan line, to be lost from sight as his enemies closed about him.

The rest of the Greeks followed, hurling their spears before them and bringing many of the Trojans down into the dust. The gaps were closed quickly, though, and as the Greeks drew their swords and renewed the attack – desperate to come to grips with their enemies – Hector boomed out another order. More arrows flew into the press of Greeks, as on their flanks the Trojan horsemen couched their spears under their arms and broke into a charge. At the same time, the infantry ran forward to meet the invaders, their meticulously sharpened spears glinting like points of fire through the clouds of dust.

Many of the Greeks were skewered by the onslaught and carried back into the ranks of their comrades. More fell to the arrows that swept down on them like an unceasing rain, and at the edges of the battle the Trojan cavalry were cutting deep swathes through their disorganized enemy. But if Hector's force was disciplined, experienced and well led, their numbers were too few to drive the Greek assault back into the sea. Within moments, the shock of their attack had been absorbed by the mass of men still pouring off the ships and up the beaches. Many of the Trojan horsemen had plunged too deeply into the horde of invaders and now found themselves surrounded and cut off from their comrades, where they were killed with spears or pulled from their mounts and butchered. Elsewhere, Podarces had organized a large company of Greek archers who were returning the fire of their Trojan counterparts, killing many and breaking up the effectiveness of their volleys. And where the Trojan spearmen had at first carried their enemies before them, they were now disadvantaged by the length of their weapons against the shorter swords of the Greeks. For all the cleverness and ferocity of Hector's tactics, the momentum of his attack was being neutralized by the sheer weight of his enemy's numbers.

## Chapter Thirty-two
# THE GATES OF TROY

Eperitus and Odysseus had met the assault together, turning aside the Trojan spears with their shields and bringing their swords to bear in the confined press of sweating, heaving bodies. Side by side, they could see fear in the dark faces of their opponents as they struck them down, hacking and slashing indiscriminately with an energy born from the desperate will to survive and the heart-thumping joy of bringing death and destruction. As warrior after warrior fell to his sword, Eperitus felt as if – like Achilles and Ajax – no weapon could harm him. Though soaked in the gore of his victims, he shouted with the elation of battle, baying for more blood as he stood on a knife's edge, balanced between death and Hades on the one side and Olympian glory on the other.

At Eperitus's side, Odysseus was also a man transformed. The lust of war had consumed him and with his normally pleasant face now a red mask, he looked more like a savage beast than a man. The experienced, hard-fighting Trojans were unable to withstand the ferocity of his attacks, and many of their number lay dead around the Ithacan king. Beside him was Antiphus, who was proving himself to be as deadly with a sword as he was with a bow, while – to Eperitus's satisfaction – Arceisius was also in the thick of the fighting, using the skills his captain had taught him with the ability and temerity of a hardened veteran.

The Ithacans were killing and being killed in large numbers, littering the ground with bodies – both Trojan and their own – so that it was almost impossible to move. Those who had an instinct for fighting were realizing the power that a sword or a spear gave to them and revelling in the slaughter of their opponents; those who did not were being killed by the true warriors in the Trojan ranks. On both sides there were men who turned and tried to flee the horror of combat, though few found a passage through the solid mass of men behind them and were quickly brought down by a sword or spear through their unprotected backs. But where Odysseus and Eperitus fought, the Trojan spearmen were laid out in heaps and the line was thinning dangerously. Suddenly the last few soldiers turned and fled, leaving the two Ithacans facing the open plain with only a handful of mounted officers between them and the walls of Troy.

Seeing the danger, three horsemen urged their mounts straight at the gap in the line. At their head was a tall man with a long spear couched under one of his muscular arms. He had cruel eyes and his mouth was drawn back in a hateful sneer that revealed his broken yellow teeth. The two others were on either side of him, yelling furiously with their swords held high above their heads.

Odysseus and Eperitus raised their shields against the attack, but without their spears they knew their defence would be short-lived. Determined to save his king, Eperitus stepped forward to take the full force of the charge, but as the black stallion of the lead rider approached – the heavy fall of its hooves shaking the ground beneath his feet – a gigantic figure lumbered past him, running straight at the charging horse. The stallion panicked and tried to turn away, but Polites threw his great arms about its neck and pushed it into the flank of the horse to its right. Both fell, pinning their surprised riders beneath them and sending up a cloud of dust from the sun-baked earth.

The other horseman, who had veered aside as Polites ran out, now tugged at the reins of his white mare and spurred it back towards the huge Greek soldier who had felled his comrades. Polites heard the beat of hooves behind him and turned as the Trojan's sword swept down towards his face. With a reaction that belied his size, he threw up his arm and caught the rider's wrist, pulling him from the back of his horse as it galloped past and throwing him to the ground, where he stepped on his neck and broke it.

A moment later, Hector's booming voice called out and suddenly the surviving Trojans were pulling back.

'We owe you our lives,' Odysseus said, as he and Eperitus reached Polites's side.

'I have simply repaid you for sparing me on Samos,' Polites replied, before turning to watch the retreating Trojans.

Heedless of the archers who were covering their retreat, the three men looked on in admiration as the spearmen reformed into ordered ranks and began to withdraw across the plain. With equal discipline, the surviving cavalry were now hovering at each flank, threatening to swoop down on any pursuit. Then, as they watched their opponents marching at a steady pace back to the Scaean Gate, the Greeks let out a triumphant cheer.

'Silence!' Odysseus ordered, his deep voice clearly audible over the shouting. 'You can celebrate when the battle is over. Ithacans, form ranks on me. Badly wounded to return to the ships as best you can.'

Similar shouts were repeated up and down the Greek line as the surviving warriors formed themselves back into their units and began the pursuit. They advanced across the plain at a fast pace, the Ithacans and Thessalians on the left, the Spartans and Myrmidons on the right. Hundreds of bodies were left behind them, some of which still stirred or twitched with the last remnants of life; a dark bank of piled corpses marked where the initial struggle had taken place, with an arrowhead of dead Trojans where Achilles had cut his way through their massed ranks. And it was Achilles who now led the pursuit, striding ahead of his black-clad Myrmidons with Patroclus at his side, keen to join battle again with his enemies.

The Trojans were almost lost behind the cloud of dust that rose from their march and the black pall of smoke that blew across the plain from the burning galleys. But the Greeks were gaining on them and knew that any attempt to re-enter the city through the Scaean Gate would result in a bottleneck, allowing them to catch Hector's force and possibly carry the gate as well. It was no surprise, therefore, when the Trojans passed the south-facing entrance and continued up the slope towards the other side of the city walls. Archers on the high battlements and towers of Troy gave their countrymen some cover, but the Greeks had the taste of victory now and pressed the chase.

'This is what I feared,' said Odysseus, turning to Eperit'Come with me – we need to find Menelaus.'

The two men dropped back through the ranks and ran towards the rear of the Spartan army, where they found Menelaus striding confidently behind his well-ordered men. His breastplate and shield were spattered with dried gore and his face glowed with antici-pation of victory as he turned to greet the two Ithacans.

'What is it, my friends?' he asked with a smile, his teeth strangely white against his dirt- and blood-caked face. 'You look concerned, Odysseus.'

'I am,' Odysseus replied. 'Our orders were to keep the Trojans fighting on the plain so they can be massacred in the open, not chase them back to the city walls.'

'That can't be helped now,' Menelaus said. 'Hector's lost the will to fight, and if we let the Trojans slip back into the city it'll take months to prise them out again.'

'But Agamemnon's late,' Eperitus said, glancing across to the hills on the other side of the Scamander. 'His plan to trap the Trojans on the plain has failed.'

'And if we're not careful, it's us who will be drawn into a trap,' Odysseus added, looking up as another swarm of black-feathered arrows flew up from the city walls. They dropped among the Spartans with a dry rattle, felling a dozen men. 'Hector only wants us to believe we're winning so he can lure us closer to the city walls. Why do you think reinforcements weren't sent from the city? Because they're waiting for us to pass the Scaean Gate, and then they'll pour out behind us and block our retreat to the ships. Hector has out-thought us at every stage of the battle so far, and unless we stop the pursuit we're going to be attacked from all sides, with the Scamander at our backs!'

'Then let them come!' Menelaus retorted, angrily. 'If we can keep these Trojan scum fighting until my brother arrives, there's still a chance of a quick victory. Hector won't dare take on the whole Greek army: the Trojans will turn and run, and when they do there's a chance we can follow them through the gates. If we can do that, Troy will be ours by nightfall.'

'I wish it were that easy,' Odysseus sighed. 'But if you must go ahead with this folly, at least order the Thessalians to remain in front of the Scaean Gate. They've had the worst of things so far and there are enough of the rest of us to destroy what's left of Hector's force.'

'No, Odysseus,' Menelaus answered with a firm wave of his hand. 'As soon as we pass the walls I'm going to drive Hector eastward, away from the safety of the city, and finish him off on the plain. And if Ares has heard my prayers, I'll find his thieving rat of a brother at his side! Now, return to your men and prepare them to attack.'

Odysseus and Eperitus found the Ithacans angered by the withering fire from the archers on the city walls and keen to get at the Trojans once more. As they passed the Scaean Gate, though, and marched up the slope out of range of the arrows, it seemed they would get their wish. The dust cloud that obscured the Trojans had not moved north towards the Dardanian Gate, as Eperitus had expected, but continued east as if drawing the Greeks away from the walls. And then it stopped moving altogether and, as the haze began to settle, the lines of spearmen and cavalry could be seen as dark shapes in the brown mist, waiting silently atop the slope. In response, Menelaus's voice barked orders that were repeated all along the Greek ranks, stopping the army in its tracks.

If Odysseus was right, Eperitus thought, now would be the time for the city gates to open and pour forth the Trojan reserves.

Odysseus was obviously thinking the same and threw a nervous glance over his shoulder, but his attention was soon pulled back to the Trojans at the top of the slope. For, as the last of the dust drifted away, the true genius of Hector's plan became apparent. Before them were the remainder of Hector's spearmen, archers and cavalry – bloodstained and dirt-covered; many bearing wounds – but on either side of them a new force was emerging. Line upon line of spearmen marched into view, silhouetted black by the light of the early morning sun rising in the east; hundreds more cavalry, strengthened by scores of chariots, were massing to the left and right, ready to pour down into the now out-numbered Greeks. And as the invaders looked up at the superior force gathering before them – drawn from Troy's allies, whose vast camp was out of sight beyond the rise of the slope – horns blew on the towers behind them. In response, the Scaean and Dardanian Gates opened to disgorge a flood of infantry and horsemen, led by Paris in his battle-scarred armour and with the scarlet plume of his helmet fluttering in the breeze. Hector's trap was sprung: the Greeks were surrounded on the east, west and north, with the broad Scamander blocking their flight to the south.

'I wish you could be wrong from time to time, Odysseus,' Eperitus said, giving his friend a look of resignation.

Odysseus smiled back and gripped his spear. 'Don't worry,' he replied. 'The oracle said I would live for at least another twenty years.'

'That's fine for you, but *I* don't have that reassurance.'

'Then you'll have to fight, Eperitus,' Odysseus grinned fiercely, as the horde of warriors at the top of the slope began to march towards them, lowering their spear-points. 'And you'll have to fight hard.'

He shouted for the rear ranks to turn and face the force that was forming by the city walls, then pushed his way through to the front of the east-facing line. Most men had retrieved spears from the battlefield after the first clash, and these were now presented towards the approaching Trojans. Eperitus saw Arceisius in the first row of spearmen and forced a route through the tightly packed warriors to stand beside him.

'When will the others arrive?' the young squire asked, without averting his eyes from the enemy at the top of the slope.

'Soon, I hope,' Eperitus answered, looking beyond the River Scamander to the southern hills. 'We've drawn the Trojans out, as we were ordered, but unless they arrive soon Agamemnon's plan is going to prove a costly mistake.'

As he finished speaking, a number of things happened. The deep, sinister hum of hundreds of bowstrings came from the other side of the rise, and a moment later the sky was dark with arrows. They fell with deadly effect into the close ranks of the Greeks, and once more cries of pain and death filled the air. At the same moment, they heard the trundle of wheels and the thud of hoofs as the host of Trojan cavalry rushed down the slope towards them, bypassing the heavily armoured spearman in their eagerness to win glory. Finally, there was a great shout from the mass of warriors still forming up by the city gates, who then rushed towards the surrounded Greeks, hurling their spears before them.

Eperitus jammed the bronze-tipped butt of his spear into the ground and prepared to meet the onslaught of horsemen and chariots. He had never faced a cavalry charge before, and as the speeding mass of horses rushed towards him – the beat of their hooves thundering in his ribcage – he felt a terror he had never known before in battle. He tried to remember what his grandfather had taught him about cavalry. He knew a horse would instinctively seek a gap in a wall of spears, or would try to leap over them if they were but two or three deep. Even so, the horse would have to be well trained and sense that its rider was fully committed to the charge; then, if the leading horses attacked, those behind would follow, driven by their herd instinct.

In order to repel the charge, the Greeks only had to hold their nerve and close ranks. If they did that, the approaching horses would baulk and turn aside. But for a man to remain steady as a wave of cavalry bore down on him required bravery, discipline and trust in his comrades. If any of those qualities were lacking and men fled the charge, the terrified horses would stream into the gaps they left and their riders would bring swift death down on the defenders. In the end, it would be a contest between the courage of the rider and the courage of the spearman. And from what Eperitus could see, the Trojan cavalrymen were holding their nerve.

At the last moment, the Greek archers released a deadly volley that spilled scores of men and horses to the ground, but it was not enough to halt the attack. The cavalry came on, the riders yelling with the joy of battle and their mounts wide-eyed with fear. Eperitus watched the throng of horses galloping towards him and shouted for the Ithacans to hold fast. The order was carried down the line, and the inexperienced ranks of half-trained farmers and fishermen drew deep on their courage. With shaking hands and beating hearts they gripped the shafts of their spears and held the line.

Suddenly, the Thessalians to their right began to break up. They had lost their leader and many of their comrades, and the sight of the Trojan horsemen had proved too much. As the gaps appeared in their line the whole force of cavalry seemed to pour towards them, bypassing the unwavering line of spears presented by the Ithacans on one side, and the Myrmidons and Spartans – under the firm command of Achilles and Menelaus – on the other. As the cavalry streamed past, a hail of arrows and spears brought many of them down into the dust, but it was too late to save the unfortunate Thessalians, who were skewered from behind or hacked down as they fled.

Eperitus looked on in horror at the massacre, conscious – as was every man around him – that the Ithacans would have met a similar fate if they had not held their nerve. Then, as he sensed the lines of Trojan spearmen running down the hill towards them, he noticed a horseman chasing after a Thessalian. The Greek threw his hands over the back of his head to protect himself, but the rider's sword simply chopped through his fingers and sliced into the back of his head, killing him at once. A moment later, he turned his mount around and signalled to a troop of cavalrymen, ordering them after a knot of Thessalians who were fleeing towards the river. And as Eperitus saw the horseman's face a shock of recognition passed through him. The strength drained from his limbs, forcing him momentarily to lean his weight on his spear as he stared with disbelieving eyes at a man he had not seen for ten years. The Trojan horseman was his father.

Suddenly Calchas's words returned to him: a second secret would draw him back to Ilium, whether there was war or not. That second secret was his father, a secret that Clytaemnestra had also known but had chosen not to reveal to him. Somehow, beyond Eperitus's comprehension, the man he had despised for ten years, the man who had usurped the throne of Alybas and brought shame and dishonour on his family, was now a soldier in the army of Troy.

As he stared at the hated face of his father, a new and sudden fury began to sear through his veins like heated bronze, opening old wounds and feeding off the fresh wound of his daughter's death. It was the desire for vengeance, a rapacious, all consuming lust to lessen the shame and grief of the past – both distant and recent – by the spilling of blood. He could not kill Agamemnon, but there was no promise preventing him from taking vengeance on his father, and as his rage grew within him he saw, at last, a means to reduce his suffering.

'Where are you going?' shouted Arceisius as Eperitus broke out of the rank of spearmen and dashed towards a riderless horse.

Eperitus ignored him. Leaping on the back of the black mare, he seized the reins and spurred the animal forward. Arrows flew over his head in both directions as he rode through the broad gap in the Greek line, galloping down the slope towards the place where he had seen his father. Horsemen and chariots thundered all around, firing arrows or hurling spears at the two islands of Greek warriors – the smaller group of Ithacans on one side, some six hundred strong, and the much larger force of Spartans and

Myrmidons on the other, numbering more than five thousand. The ground in between was littered with dead and wounded Thessalians. The remainder were either being pursued towards the river or driven onto the spears of the reserves who had poured out of the Scaean Gate under Paris's command. Many, though, had formed a desperate circle of spears and were fending off repeated attacks from the Trojan cavalry. It was here that Eperitus saw his father, reforming his men for a fresh assault on the battered Thessalians.

'Father!' he called, his voice high and clear amidst the din of war. 'Father!'

Apheidas turned and stared at his son. For a moment, as they looked at each other across the field of death and destruction, it was as if they were no longer part of the battle that raged all around them. Unexpectedly, Apheidas found himself staring at his only remaining son, who in a moment of rash anger he had exiled from his kingdom ten years before. Eperitus stared back, his eyes burning with hatred. Then horn calls were blowing in the distance and reluctantly father and son turned to the hills in the south, where thousands upon thousands of warriors were streaming down towards the fords of the Scamander. At last, Agamemnon had arrived, and with him were the armies of Diomedes, Idomeneus, Ajax and the rest of Greece. They had beached their ships in the bay north of Tenedos and had marched inland, hoping to cut the Trojans off on the plain as they fought the smaller force under Menelaus – the bait, as Agamemnon had referred to them. The bait had been taken, but it was too late to cut the Trojans off on the plain. The Greeks' best hope now was that Hector would turn and fight, and that they would then defeat his army and pursue it back through the gates into the city.

But Hector was no fool. Seeing the large numbers of Greeks already crossing the Scamander and preparing to push up the slope, he ordered the attack to be broken off and for the Trojan army and its allies to return to the city. Horns called out, rising over the clash of weapons and the hoarse shouts of struggling men, and suddenly the besieged armies of Ithacans, Spartans and Greeks were left standing among the piles of dead, watching the backs of their retreating enemies through a protective screen of cavalry. Too late, Menelaus spotted Paris disappearing through the Scaean Gate, and was forced to watch in seething anger as the man who had stolen his wife slipped back behind the safety of Troy's walls.

Apheidas threw a last glance at his son, then led his horsemen away from the surviving Thessalians towards the newly arrived Greeks, intending to slow their advance while the rest of the army found shelter inside the city. As Eperitus saw him ride off, a fierce anger gripped him. He drew his sword from its scabbard, and with a roar of fury charged down the slope towards him. At the same moment, a group of three horsemen who were galloping back across the plain from the direction of the Scamander, where they had been hunting Thessalians, tucked their spears under their arms and turned towards him.

The first came dashing in from Eperitus's left, levelling the head of his weapon at his liver. Eperitus quickly changed direction, cutting across the front of his attacker's horse and switching his sword into his left hand. A moment later, the Trojan's head had been swept from his shoulders and his body fell heavily to the ground, where it landed with a puff of dust. At once, his comrades spurred their horses towards Eperitus, one on either side to prevent his escape. They were confident that they were the better horsemen, and that the reach of their spears would carry the lone Greek to his death long before he could bring his sword to bear. Then one of them jerked back, a momentary look of surprise on his face before the darkness of death took him and he fell from his horse, a feathered arrow protruding from his chest. The other ignored the demise of his comrade and leaned forward with gritted teeth, spurring his horse ever faster towards his quarry. Eperitus dug his heels into the flanks of his own horse, leaning close to her neck and extending his sword at arm's length before him. Squinting against the dust and bright sunlight, he heard the rapid tramp of approaching hooves on the dry turf and the snorting of his opponent's mount. There was a glint of armour as the Trojan cavalryman came sweeping towards him, then Eperitus's arm was torn violently aside as his sword was ripped from his hand. He heard a heavy thud behind him and, reining his horse about, he saw the body of his rival lying on the ground, surrounded by a cloud of dust. Eperitus's sword was still quivering as it stuck up from his chest.

'Eperitus!' Odysseus shouted, running towards him with Antiphus at his side, bow in hand. Polites, Arceisius and a score more Ithacans were coming up behind them. 'Give me your horse! There's still time to keep the gates from shutting before Agamemnon arrives.'

Eperitus looked urgently back towards the plain, where he had last seen his father. Horsemen were pouring back through the Scaean Gate, their task of screening the Trojan retreat complete. The only other living soldiers outside the walls of Troy now were Greek – Agamemnon's unblooded force marching up from the fords, and the battle-wearied survivors under Menelaus's command regrouping at the top of the slope, out of bowshot of the city walls. The bodies of men and horses were strewn all across the plain, from the sandy beaches where the Greeks had landed up to the slopes around the walls of Troy. Of Apheidas there was no sign.

Eperitus backed his whinnying horse away from Odysseus's outstretched hand and shook his head.

'No, my lord. You'll be shot down before you get anywhere near them. I can't let you ride to your death.'

'It's an order, Eperitus, not a request!' the king snapped angrily.

Eperitus stared down at him for a moment, then dismounted smartly. But before Odysseus could reach for the reins, he slapped his hand down hard on the mare's flank and sent her galloping towards the gates of Troy.

'The plan has failed, Odysseus,' he said. 'Penelope will have to wait a little longer.'

Odysseus watched the last of the Trojan cavalry crowding back into the city and nodded slowly, a hint of despair in his usually confident eyes.

'You're right, Eperitus,' he sighed. 'But for how much longer?'

As he spoke, the Scaean Gate slammed shut with a heavy thud. The siege of Troy had begun.

# AUTHOR'S NOTE

The events that take place in *The Gates of Troy* are based, for the most part, on original myths. There are several versions of the events that led up to the Trojan War – many of them contradictory – so I've chosen the accounts I enjoy most or feel contribute best to the story. For example, some have it that Helen was kidnapped by Paris and taken to Troy against her will, while others say she went readily, having fallen in love with the Trojan prince. I've opted for the latter, as there's nothing like love for starting a fight.

The other events in the book that I've taken direct from myth include Odysseus's failed attempt to feign madness and avoid the war, the embassy to Troy, the gathering of the Greek fleet at Aulis, and the sacrifice of Iphigenia. There was never any question in Greek mythology that Iphigenia was Agamemnon's daughter, but the tales do differ widely on her fate. Aeschylus, for example, makes it clear in the *Oresteia* that Agamemnon sacrificed his daughter to appease the wrath of Artemis. While Homer is silent on the matter, Euripides in *Iphigenia at Aulis* has Artemis replace the girl with a deer at the last moment. Unfortunately for Iphigenia, I haven't been quite so merciful in my retelling of the story.

Moving on, according to ancient tales Achilles killed King Tenes after he hurled a rock at the Greek fleet. He then murdered his manservant, Mnemon, for failing to remind him not to kill any son of Apollo! Shortly afterwards, Philoctetes was bitten on the foot by a snake and, because of his constant groaning and the stench of his wound, was then marooned on Lemnos by Odysseus. And Protesilaus was the first man to hit the beach at Troy, and consequently the first casualty of the war.

Eperitus, on the other hand, comes from my imagination. When retelling a series of popular and well-known tales, it's often useful to have an unknown element to skew events a little. I also hope the straightforward and honourable Eperitus acts as a foil to Odysseus's often unscrupulous cunning. Certainly both men will need all these qualities and the strength of their unique friendship if they are to survive the long and bloody war with Troy, of which we've seen only the opening skirmish in *The Gates of Troy*. They have another ten years of fighting ahead of them before Zeus tips his golden scales in favour of one side or the other.

But that's a different story.

extracts reading groups
competitions books new events
discounts extracts extracts discounts
competitions reading groups
books new books reading groups
events extracts events
books new titles reading groups
interviews
reading groups books events extracts events books
discounts interviews
new books events events
books reading groups
events new interviews new extracts
discounts extracts discounts
**www.panmacmillan.com** books
extracts events reading groups
competitions books extracts new